MAGE SLAVE

THE ENSLAVED CHRONICLES: BOOK 1

R. K. Thorne

IRON ANTLER BOOKS

Pittsburgh, Pennsylvania

Edited by Elizabeth Nover, www.razorsharpediting.com
Cover design by Damonza, damonza.com
Book design by Iron Antler Books, Text set in Adobe Garamond,
Adapted from design by ©2015 BookDesignTemplates.com

For Mr. Pugliano, who pushed me and believed in
me more than I believed in myself.
And for my husband, who still does.

Contents

Acknowledgements

I would like to thank my editor, Elizabeth Nover of Razor Sharp Editing, for helping me to see (and write) more clearly.

Thanks to my beta readers, Vanessa Kristoff and Jeff Hoskinson, whose valuable feedback gave me courage while also making this book far better.

And last but not least, thanks so much to my mom and dad for telling me I could do anything I put my mind to. I listened. To all my family and friends, I appreciate your unwavering stability and support.

MAGE SLAVE

I THE MISSION

"That's it. Lift it a little higher, and you'll be free," Miara whispered to the raven.

"What are you doing?" The raven lifted the latch and burst through the cage door just as the Mistress arrived.

The truth would get her beaten, but as a slave, she couldn't lie. So Miara said nothing. She watched silently as the raven circled up, heading toward a high window. If only it were that easy. Miara could change form and charm animals, summon plants and hear the thoughts of men. She could grow wings and take to the sky whenever she pleased. But at the edge of the hold's lands, she'd be thrown back, kept forever a slave. She knew; she'd tried many times before. She'd looked for a hole, any chinks in her enchantment's armor. There were none.

"I'll just get another bird." The Mistress rolled her eyes as she strode to the dais. "Don't think I don't notice your petty little rebellions. They accomplish nothing. Show her." She jutted her chin at a guard by the door, who took a bow from his back, notched an arrow, and dropped the bird with one shot.

Miara winced and turned her eyes away. She could feel it was not quite dead yet, but healing it was probably one rebellion too many for the moment.

"You are equally expendable." The older woman stopped and folded her arms across her chest, regarding Miara. Her dark hair fell in carefully styled soft curls on a blue velvet gown, the picture of a lady. Miara knew better. "I've summoned you because Dekana is dead," the Mistress said. She paused for a moment to appreciate the color draining from Miara's face. "Her tasks fall to you now."

Miara's throat tightened. Don't let it show, she thought. Don't let it. Dekana had been a spy for the Masters, just as Miara was. What had happened? And if Dekana had failed, why would they think that Miara could succeed? She was half the spy Dekana had been.

The Mistress took the mage-knots from the nearby table and approached, the rope of solid bronze catching the room's faint firelight. She and the other Masters didn't deserve such power, crafted by an air mage's own hand sometime back in the Dark Days. Each time she saw them, she wondered if the poor bastard had been willing or coerced. It was either the greatest betrayal or the greatest tragedy her people had ever known.

"What happened to Dekana?" Miara asked as evenly as she could, as the Mistress yanked the neck of her tunic aside to expose the always-raw brand on her shoulder.

"That is none of your concern." Her eyelid twitched. She did not want Miara to know, did she? "You need only think about the task at hand." And with that, she pressed the cold bronze against the brand on Miara's right shoulder.

Two decades ago, their brand had seared its pain into her shoulder for the first time, burning its curse into her flesh and leaving her with a compulsion to do their bidding. It could not heal. It festered away, changing from a fresh burn to a scab, from a gash to a welt. She could hardly remember a time without it. She had been only five when her mother had betrayed her and her father to the Devoted, whose knights had brought them here. Usually, she slept on her left side and tried not to think about it.

Each time they gave her a mission, though, her brand burned as hot as the very first time. Then pain shattered her thoughts, slicing along her collarbone, down her arm, across her back.

"Go to Akaria," the Mistress said. Her voice was a thousand demons echoing inside Miara's skull. "Find the mountain hold of Estun, where the monarchy of

Akaria hides from our might. Find their oldest son, Prince Aven Lanuken. Kidnap him, and bring him back to us. Alive. Let no one know a mage or anyone from Kavanar is involved."

The Mistress lifted the mage-knots away, and just like that, Miara's agony was over.

Stars and yellow splotches danced before Miara's eyes, and she swayed as though she might fall to the marble. No, she thought. *No.* She forced herself steady, to reach out with her mind for anything nearby to regain her strength. But with the raven gone, there was nothing alive in this hellish place, only cold marble blackness. An earth mage could have thrived here on the energy locked in the stone, but she was a creature mage. She needed living, breathing energies, and the Mistress and her guards were sadly off-limits. Another breath, and thankfully, the stars faded. Another, and she felt like herself again.

The Mistress had seated herself on her pseudo-throne behind the banquet table and was eating a grape. Miara discovered that she was on her knees. Her body ached. She could feel the Mistress's orders taking root, a new craving planted inside her, the seedling of a dark vine sprouting around her heart.

Kidnap a prince. She had never kidnapped someone before. Eavesdropping on the king or his advisers, sure, and the occasional theft from a noble. She had yet to go on a mission where the mark hadn't proved to be corrupt, if not downright evil, so she had never lost much sleep over her activities, but... could anyone really *deserve* to be kidnapped?

"Do you have any questions?" the Mistress asked.

Yes, she thought. But you can't answer that one. "If Dekana could not—"

"That does not matter." Again, the eye twitch. This is not how Dekana died, Miara thought. But she would like for me to believe it is.

"I have never kidnapped someone, or even stolen anything larger than a book—"

"And that is not a question."

"When must I begin?" she asked, trying and failing to hide the irritation in her voice. She knew to ask this from experience. If she didn't, her cursed bond would drive her mad with an irrational need to rush off, prepared or not.

"Take time to prepare and gather what you need to be effective, but no more. Master Daes has wagered you are more than capable of this task. Your precocious nature has quite caught his attention. You wouldn't want to let him down." Her eye twitched again.

The Dark Master. Daes was his real name. He was the only one bold enough to let the mage slaves know his name. Why would he wager on her? She did not want his attention. But fear of him would not help her now—she needed to focus. Was there anything else she needed to know? Anything she needed to get the Mistress to amend to the orders she'd just received?

"Do I need to bring him back by a certain day? I can be quick or quiet, but not both."

"Err on the side of stealth. No one must know that we are the ones who have him, and you must not be caught. But if you have not returned in one turning of the moon, we will send others to… assist you. Any other questions?"

Miara shook her head. She had many questions, but none for the Mistress.

"So be it," said the Mistress with a curt nod. "Go. Do not disappoint us."

Miara turned and left. Her horse Kres waited outside. They headed for the library, which would hopefully ease some of her already-mounting desire to be gone, to throw caution to the wind and ride full gallop for Akaria. She could not go unprepared, she reminded herself. The Mistress had commanded. The tension that had intensified at the sight of her horse eased.

As Kres led the way, her eye caught on a fallen branch from a large oak tree against the wall of the dormitory building. She whispered a bit of energy across the wind to it, and her eyes lingered to see the first buds. Leaves of a rosebush broke from beneath the bark, and fragile tendrils of roots reached down into the earth. Her blooms would be bloodred; they always were.

"It's high time we found a suitable wife for you, Aven."

"*Suitable*, yes. Excellent choice of words, Mother," he replied. Eyes closed, Aven took a deep breath of the crisp fall air and savored the sunlight on his face. Inside, the drafts that rattled through the stony corridors would be colder than the wind out here. This terrace was his favorite spot, a shrine of sunlight carved out of the side of the mountain.

"If you never meet this woman, how will you know if she's suitable?" He opened his eyes to see her frowning, arms folded. The sunlight shone so brightly on her golden hair, his eyes ached.

"I could meet many more if I could leave Estun." He examined the leaves on the cherry tree as if their gradual change to yellow was terribly interesting. He didn't mind going to meet this newly arrived princess, although he did dread the awkwardness that was sure to follow. But did he have to leave the sunlight? Inside, there'd be only torches and hearth fires, and not enough of them to frighten the goose bumps away. This terrace was his refuge, its wind blowing through his hair, swirling the fall leaves, tinkling the wind chimes.

"You know it's not as simple as that. Come, this one is quite beautiful. And a warrior. Wait till you see the bow she carries. Not just a puppet, or at least she doesn't play that part."

He said nothing. He knew he could not leave Estun. That didn't keep him from resenting it. What kind of bow would she have? Did it mean anything? Most of the eligible noblewomen who called on Aven had one characteristic in common—they were as docile as lambs in a herd. He couldn't marry someone like that, nor did he trust that it wasn't a ploy to gain favor. Aven had long ago resigned himself to looking for the bare minimum to meet his needs. His wants would have to be set aside. So while he might long for a warrior wife, he knew he didn't really *need* one—although someone who could also prevent him from getting killed in his sleep was certainly not a *bad* candidate. He did need someone he could trust absolutely, who would give him her true opinions, even when it was difficult. It would help if those opinions weren't morally reprehensible, if she had a conscience and an internal compass he could trust that wouldn't waver. He would like that very much. Wait, was that a need or a want?

The odds that this random princess would have even some of the qualities he needed were not in his favor.

Coming here to blindly marry him did not exactly raise his hopes.

"Are you coming?"

He nodded. "One more minute."

She eyed him.

"I swear I'll be right there."

"Try not to be excessively late this time." She shook her head, turned, and headed back inside.

The white rosebush next to his bench was in bloom again, one last display for fall. Perhaps a spray of flowers would make up for his dawdling.

The early afternoon bells had rung several minutes ago. They marked the beginning of sport in the Proving Grounds. Not only did they have a competition among the young knights and nobles beginning in three weeks, but the assembly of visiting Takaran diplomats lingered on and required endless entertainment. Another few days, and Aven would get to try out a part of diplomacy he rarely practiced—politely kicking out the rascals without damaging relations in the process.

Until then, he'd have to endure another afternoon of watching duel after duel amid the fire pits. He was beyond bored with the show—the Takarans had little skill compared to the average Akarian but insisted on taking part in every skirmish. He sighed. It wasn't like he had *real* duties to attend to or anything. It wasn't like there was a military to keep trained or a nation to tend.

Well, he might as well get on with it all.

Aven reached down and carefully plucked a spray of roses from the rosebush beside him. He reached the door before he thought better of it and returned for a second spray of the small white flowers.

What if she *were* a beautiful, intelligent warrior after all?

He headed back inside. The heavy iron doors that led to the terrace clanged shut behind him, and he was again enveloped in the darkness of Estun. He paused for a moment to let his eyes adjust, hating every second of blackness.

And, of course, he felt it start up, first a tingle inside him, then a flitter of air. Of course it would. This was the worst time for such a thing. This was the reason Aven could not leave Estun: his magic. The air began to whip around him unnaturally, threatening the torch-light with even greater darkness. It often reared its ugly head at moments like this, when he had just come in from the terrace after soaking up the sunlight. Other times, it acted up when tensions or emotions ran high. He could not control it, although he continued to try. He never left Estun and carefully controlled what he did with whom in hope of keeping this a secret. So far, he'd been fairly successful at hiding it, although his occasional strange absences did not go unnoticed. Lord Dyon was quick to point them out.

Because one day, Aven was to be king. And kings weren't supposed to have magic. In fact, most people in Akaria pretended to have no magic at all. He suspected this was not entirely the truth because, well, there could be many like him with this inconvenient gift, but successful at controlling or hiding it. Still others, he heard, chose not to and instead hid themselves in remote towns and farmsteads. For the most part, those folks were left alone.

That didn't mean anyone wanted a mage to be king, but no one had given Aven much say in the matter. The crown prince was who he was, and magic was what he'd been given, so he could only do his best to hide it. What were the gods up to, putting him in such a situation? The wind swirling around him picked up, whipping at his hair playfully. Anara mocks me, he thought.

He often tried to wait and hope it settled down, but when that didn't work, he had one other tool in his chest. He closed his eyes, took a deep breath, and focused his mind on the Great Stone of Estun. Behind the head table in the banquet hall was a magnificent rock that had been hewn in half. Its outer shell was ordinary, but the inside was encrusted with great purple crystals both large and small. The stone loomed above onlookers at the height of seven men; it had been discovered when Estun was first dug from the mountain. It filled the great hall and scattered the candlelight during many an evening meal with its quiet sparkle. The banquet hall was also one of the only rooms that had windows, and sometimes early in the morning, the light reached the Great Stone and danced across the crystals in the most peculiar way. It was something he loved to see. But enough thinking about light—he needed to think about darkness, about the stone. The stone repressed magic in general and his air magic in particular. That was part of why his parents had brought him here and chosen to live in Estun—the hope that his magic would fade away.

It hadn't worked.

Another breath, then another. He focused on the Great Stone, the heart of the mountain. Finally, the air around him was still.

He tried to shake off the sudden outbreak, but it made him nervous. What if it acted up again when he arrived to see their visitor? What if someone noticed? He'd gotten away with it this long, but how long could he continue successfully hiding his magic? Then again, what other choice did he have?

He straightened himself and headed toward the throne room to meet his potential wife.

Daes heaved open the heavy chamber doors himself, knocking the incompetent guards aside and striding into his receiving hall. Seulka jumped and straightened herself in her seat.

"Did I wake you?" he asked.

She scowled at him. Not a sign of that noble breeding to be found, some days. And yet many considered her a noble of the highest caste and he only a pretender to nobility, all because her parents had been married and his had not. Their mothers had been sisters, which made them cousins, but she made very sure never to call him that. The king, on the other hand, was *such* a close relation, even though they were both related to him through the same incompetent and powerless great-uncle.

"Did you give her the orders?" he said.

"Yes. She has begun," Seulka said. "She may be a rebellious sort, but she has the mind of a spy—willing or not."

"Her will doesn't matter. It's our will that matters." He flopped down into the armchair he'd insisted on installing behind the banquet table and kicked up his black boots on the footstool. Black cloak, black tunic, black belt—even his chair was black. A clean, strong color. It was good to be home. There was a reason they called him the Dark Master.

He had missed all of this while visiting the Devoted elders in Takar—far too much garish gold and orange for his taste. The Devoted were powerful allies of Kavanar in general and the Masters in particular, so it was good to speak with them, but also good to leave.

"Of course, Daes. Our will and the king's, of course."

He snorted. Was she being sarcastic or just poking a finger in a wound? "The king wouldn't even have gone along with my plan to start this war if we hadn't appealed to his foolish desire for revenge."

"*Our* plan, you mean."

"Fine, our plan. He's the king. *He* should be estimating the Akarian threat, as I am. He should be planning the attack of his enemies at all times. We should not need to lead him to it. He's a horse, and we're holding the carrot of vengeance for a century-old wrong."

"Perhaps he estimates the threat as greater than you think."

"He's a coward."

She glared at him, finally sick of his hyperbole if he had to guess. "Forcing the Akarians to attack us on our lands is a strategically superior plan. You agreed so yourself."

He scowled back. "It doesn't mean I have to like it."

The kidnapping attempt was part of a larger plan of intrigue that Kavanar would use to force the Akarian hand. It had been the only way Daes had been able to convince the king and the three other Masters to agree to war at all. The Fat Master had wanted to be left alone, content to supervise the running of Mage Hall and no more. The Mistress—Seulka—was still certain Daes was a paranoid lunatic to be worried about Akaria at all. And the Tall Master was so focused on enslaving mages that he barely gave a thought to anything beyond his own smithy, let alone about the wider world and their place in it. The monarch and his advisers knew of the sleeping danger that lay in their enemy to the east, but they chose to ignore it, to hope it was someone else's problem.

Daes was not one to ignore things. It could become their problem at any time. He had worked too hard to earn this position in spite of their insipid desire to focus on the nature of his birth. He would not let the lands and holds he had worked so hard to control be pissed away and left defenseless by some ivory-tower fools.

No, Akaria must be dealt with. It had taken a lot of arguing, but he'd convinced them.

And so they all assumed this mage of theirs would fail spectacularly, if they thought of it at all. Secretly, though, Daes hoped for more. Much as he resented her rebellious nature, he could not deny the skill she was proving to have, and he hated the thought that they were wasting such a talent on a suicide mission. In his hands, she was becoming a powerful weapon. One of the best in his arsenal at this point, although still a bit virginal at some of the more dangerous duties of a spy.

Perhaps she would live, although he doubted it. She had never once failed them yet, but her usual marks had all been fine artifacts, not men. Scrolls, daggers, and jewels were more easily subdued than Akarian warriors. But she had a fire in her spirit, the same fire that sparked in her eyes when he gave her orders. Perhaps it would help her achieve the impossible.

He understood her rebelliousness in a way, even admired it. No powerful creature could stand to be caged. It was still remarkably stupid of her. There was no way for a mage to ever be freed—why did she expend any energy on rebelling against something that she knew she could not change? It was like defying the sun.

Well, there was one very unlikely way a mage could be freed... but if she succeeded in this mission, they would put an end to that as well.

"It is a shame to lose a good spy in the process," he said, trying to extend a peace offering.

She sighed. "Indeed. Especially after the loss of Dekana." She eyed him sideways.

"That was an accident," he said through gritted teeth. "They *can't* kill themselves. We've forbidden it."

Her eyes bored into him. "Believe what you will. She was alone in that tower."

"There is no way to know—"

"Their minds and their actions might be ours, but don't fool yourself into thinking you're more powerful than you are. Their hearts are their own. I know you are not so thick that you can't see their hatred. If this one you've sent even survives, you'll see. The same hate grows in her that blossomed in Dekana."

"It doesn't matter."

"You might not believe it, but heart and mind are not wholly separate entities. If we push her too far, she will be of less use to us. That spy's mind will become less effective, no matter how much we bid her to do our will. We could push her. We could also break her."

"I thought you were convinced this was a suicide mission."

"It is. But on the off chance that she succeeds…"

"Then she will have gained invaluable experience, and we will have a chance to eradicate any last shred of the forbidden magic."

She raised an eyebrow. "It's been *ninety* years. Thousands of mages were killed after the Dark Days, and the rest hid and cowered in fear. The practice of magic in Akaria is nonexistent. Anyone who knew it is long dead in a lonely cave somewhere."

"If *you* were an Akarian with the knowledge to undo everything we've built here in Mage Hall, what would you do? Would you let it die? Would you just forget about it?"

She pressed her lips together but said nothing.

"Seulka, all of our power comes from one source—them." He pointed toward the courtyard. "And there's one thing—and *only* one thing—that could ever undo that power."

"The star magic." She cast her eyes to the floor, avoiding him.

"Indeed." He crossed his arms and glared. She was another fool who hoped that someone else would handle her problems, who dreamed they would just magically fade away.

Well, the world didn't work that way. Luckily for Seulka and the king, Daes would rather get a jump on his problems with a knife to the ribs.

And that was exactly what he was going to do.

Aven strolled in a side door without pomp or circumstance, and so at first, no one noticed him. His visitor was easily recognizable, though, and his mother had not oversold her or her bow. The foreign princess stood speaking with his father, and even from afar he could admire the determined set of her eyes, the confidence in her shoulders, a certain level of power in her stance. Her black cloak swept out majestically behind her. Beaded strands of the sapphire and gold of Isolte hung from a jeweled headband. Hair of clove and walnut fell straight and smooth, framing her face. The delicately carved dark wood of the bow shimmered gold in the firelight, and an aquamarine-studded leather quiver hung comfortably over her shoulder.

He must have studied her too long, for her eyes darted over and caught on his. His stomach dropped with a sudden rush of fear as she fixed a cold gaze on him for the briefest moment. He had made no special preparations today, he realized—it hadn't even occurred to him to consider what *she* would think of *him* and if he cared to influence such an opinion. Would he be able to impress her? What if she decided she didn't want *him*? How often had a single glance made his confidence crumble so? Her eyes darted back to him as she seemed to decide that he was not just another onlooker. Something in her eyes was icy as she examined him, like a hawk eyeing prey.

She was indeed different from the others. Was that a good thing or a bad thing?

Just as he began to raise his hand and step forward to meet her, a voice interjected. "Late to join us again, as usual, Prince Aven." Lord Dyon, his favorite critic. Well, if he could say nothing else for the man, he had a certain impeccable timing and a knack for observation. Dyon always seemed to notice when he was conspicuously late—almost always because Aven was trying to stuff his magic back into its stupid little box.

At the thought of it, a tendril of hair fluttered against his forehead. Oh, hell, he couldn't win. Why did he even try? Oh right—potential persecution, execution, banishment, that sort of thing.

"Pardon my delay, I was kept by pressing affairs of state," he said once a requisite amount of silence had passed. A subtle tactic his father had taught him to indicate both that the comment was not important enough to be acknowledged and was also frowned upon. Not appropriate in every situation, but certainly in this one.

"No apology is needed," she said in a confident, solid voice. "I see you keep a more benevolent and open court than my father."

"And what would make you say that?" Aven's father asked, smiling wryly.

She paused. Hesitation? No, her eyes were sure. Her own subtle technique, no doubt. With amused eyes, she flicked her gaze from the king to Aven, then looked straight at Lord Dyon when she said, "In my land, such a comment would not be tolerated."

Well, my, my! What kind of woman was this? Not another mousy puppet, that was for sure. She deftly asserted many things with the comment—that she outranked Dyon, that she herself would not tolerate such comments, that perhaps someday this would be her land, and that he should be prepared for potential future consequences. Much as he admired her deftness, he couldn't say he liked the comment. Lord Dyon, while inappropriate, frustrating, and downright maddening at times, had the interests of the kingdom at heart every time he chided Aven like a curmudgeonly, uninvited tutor. Besides, he would rather have naysayers that were looking out for what was best for Akaria than only advisors who would agree with him.

Aven broke the awkward silence that followed with his footsteps, presenting first his mother and then the new princess with roses and a quick bow for each of them.

"Prince Aven Lanuken at your service," he said, brushing his lips across the backs of her fingers as he bowed.

She blinked for a second, a tiny curve in the corner of her mouth, before she straightened her expression. "Princess Evana Paranelin," she said with a curtsy, the spray of white roses striking against her blue dress, beads swaying regally. She was striking. She was mesmerizing. Her beauty was its own diplomatic technique, and it was working on him.

Then, to his surprise, and perhaps to surprise them all, she stepped forward and looped her arm through his. "It has been such a long journey. Surely you and your attendants could show me to somewhere more comfortable?"

At this, he gave her a laughing sideways smile. He would play along. She smiled in return, and it was laughing, but not quite friendly.

"Of course, milady. If I have your leave, Father?"

His father nodded. "Yes, of course. We'll be in the Proving Grounds. You're welcome to join us, Princess."

"Thank you," she said smoothly, the picture of grace.

Aven led her from the hall. Her hand in the crook of his elbow was warm, and her body was close now, and in spite of the dress and cloak, he couldn't miss her strong, lovely shape underneath it all. She was beautiful, all right, and she scared the hell out of him.

Aven actually had no idea where his guest was to reside, and fortunately, he didn't need to. He followed an entourage of servants that sprang to life at the princess's request.

"So, tell me of yourself, Prince Lanuken."

"Call me Aven." She nodded in acknowledgement. "Ah, well, I am son of the great Samul Lanuken, whose charming personage you're already acquainted with. I am the lucky soul to be born crown prince of Akaria, and also a frequently tardy statesman."

She smiled very slightly, keeping her eyes focused ahead of them. Was she mapping the halls in her memory, perhaps? Or was she looking for something aside from a mate?

"I, uh, I've lived in Estun all my life. I am an officer in our armed force and a noted tutor of aspiring young swordsmen and shield maidens. And a noted lover of apple dumplings as well." He paused, waiting for a reaction. He got none. "What about you? Do you put that bow you carry to good use?"

"It is rare when I have a *real* occasion to use it," she said. "But I am a skilled marksman, if that's what you're asking."

"I assumed as much. Do you practice any other combat sports?"

"Only verbal sparring, I'm afraid. In Isolte, it is not common for women to fight beyond the bow. I hear Akaria is very different."

"Everyone learns to fight here," he said simply. "Have you wanted to learn?"

"Not particularly," she said, and nothing more.

"What of you, milady?" he said.

"I am the youngest of King Enin's three daughters, skilled with a bow, drawing, and the harp. I speak six languages and have traveled much of this continent and all the outer islands." She stopped as if that summed it up. A practiced speech.

"And how do you find Akaria?" he asked.

"Beautiful, if a little wild."

Wild? He had heard his nation described more than a few ways before, but wild was not one of them.

Far more of their land was settled than Takar or even Kavanar, for that matter, and the three nations took up most of the continent. What could she possibly mean by that, and how could he get at it while remaining polite?

Fortunately or unfortunately, he was out of time as they arrived at her room. Servants buzzed around delivering her belongings, stoking the low-burning fire, opening the curtains. Her room had windows. So Fayton *had* kept a few of the best rooms free, in spite of the Takaran throng invading the place. They had a wise and savvy steward.

When most of her things were settled, he gestured to a young woman waiting by the door. "Camil will be devoted to your service throughout your stay, so if you need anything, please don't hesitate to let her or myself know." Strange—something he said made the princess's eyes widen ever so slightly. What had he said that unnerved her? No matter, he continued on. "Did you want to take some time to recover from your journey or perhaps join us in the Proving Grounds to watch the duels?"

"Perhaps you would have a moment for the two of us to speak frankly together. Alone."

He could not help but raise his eyebrows. "I have as many moments as you need, my princess, as I am in no hurry to join the duels. But in Akaria, princes and knights such as myself live by a code. As part of that, to defend our honor, you and I cannot be alone." Not to mention to prevent international incidents. "But let me send all but my most trusted away—I assure you, you can speak frankly around them."

"Fine, I suppose that will have to do." Aven had the strangest sensation that he had just avoided a trap. Didn't matter. The Code was the way it was for a reason. The servants left without a specific request, and only Fayton and Camil remained. The princess motioned silently for the young woman to help her with her cloak, and Evana removed it slowly, dramatically, in spite of Camil's many attempts to be brisk and efficient. Then the princess pretended to sit casually on the bed, although it looked carefully calculated to him, and she began removing her gloves one finger at a time.

Was it hotter in the room? Certainly it was only the fire they'd stoked. Was his face turning red? Oh, gods, was that flicker of the flames just the usual drafts... or something else? The princess eyed the fire as well. The unnatural flicker did not seem beyond her notice.

"Fine," she said slowly. "Let us be frank. Would you care to have a seat? It will only be a moment, but you look... uncomfortable." She patted the bed gently beside her.

He plopped into a nearby armchair. "I am always frank with you, milady. I have been nothing but, I promise you."

"You want to know about me. You know that I am here looking for a husband of nobility."

He swallowed. That *was* particularly frank, he had to admit. "Yes. I figured as much."

"My older sisters are well married to men with no kingdoms of their own, and between the two of them, they are sure to inherit the throne. So I have turned my eyes outward for my own destiny, and that journey has led me here, to you." That explained all the travel and languages. Or perhaps that was to make her an attractive potential queen. She glanced down as if gathering her thoughts. "Do you find me the slightest bit appealing?" she demanded.

He simply stared in shock for a moment. "I can't imagine anyone would *not* find you appealing." His voice was a little more breathless than he might have liked.

She frowned. Odd. Ah, she was not sure what he meant and thought he was dodging the question. "I'm sorry, we were being frank. Something I am clearly less used to than I promised." He stopped to compose the right words. He saw the flash of a lake in the moonlight, a traditional Akarian marriage ceremony. He tried to imagine meeting her there, naked under the stars to say their vows the Akarian way. Would she insist on different customs? He tried to picture the scene, and it was indeed beautiful, but he could not imagine much beyond the icy chill in her eyes, a predator about to catch its prey. He shook off the image; he was getting ahead of himself. She hadn't proposed, she'd simply asked if he found her at all appealing. It was a simple question, really. "You are clearly lovely and strong. I do not know you, but I consider you a better potential match than others that have come before. Is that frank enough?"

She nodded briskly. "Yes," she said without the slightest hint of laughter. "Then let me be clear. I do not mean to take up an excessive amount of your time; I am sure you do have pressing affairs of state on top of your existing diplomatic visitors. I propose that we waste no time with games and set about determining if any potential arrangement could exist between us. I am not here to live off your hospitality, and if we are not a match, then so be it. I will take my leave. But I hope… that that is not the case."

It *was* refreshing to be frank about it… but it was also as impersonal as a trade agreement. They might as well be exchanging wool for iron. Her words were a more sincere compliment than he'd received from a woman in a long time, perhaps ever. Yet he was not moved by them. There was no love on the table here, only tolerance or perhaps alliance.

He smiled at her as warmly as he could. "As do I, milady."

"Evana."

"Why don't you take some time to rest and then join me in the Proving Grounds? Camil can show you the way."

The princess nodded, her jewels sparkling, catching rare bits of Estun sunlight. Aven bowed and took his leave.

The smell of the Proving Grounds hit Aven steps before he was inside. No amount of cleaning could rid the place of the dank, sweaty, wood-smoke scent. Why the Takarans liked this place so much, he had no idea. They were not warriors, but perhaps they liked feeling like ones for a little while. Aven certainly enjoyed the place at times—but to fight, not to watch. If there was no sword in his hand, it was pointless.

Except that it was his job to entertain. He surveyed those in attendance, trying to figure out where to sit. Should he sit on the usual royal benches or with one of their guests? Should he leave room for the princess to join him, or would he prefer she didn't? Seeing no useful opportunities, he headed toward his mother and his usual seats, which should leave space for Evana to join them.

"So?" his mother asked as soon as he'd sat down.

"So what?"

"So what do you think?"

"The east fire could use some more wood, I suppose. Should I send someone?"

"Quit toying with me!"

He snickered. "Your description was very accurate. You weren't wrong. She's very beautiful and no timid mouse, either. She's a little... strange, though."

She nodded, not taking her eyes from the current competition. "Cold as ice."

His turn to nod.

"Oh, before I forget to warn you, Jerrin has specifically requested to fight you today. He says he can't leave Akaria without beholding your legendary skills himself."

Aven tried not to groan. He heard her slight emphasis on leaving and understood. So perhaps Jerrin *did* know he had overstayed his welcome a bit. But why would he want to fight Aven? Jerrin was an ambassador, the highest-ranking member of the delegation now that their king had taken leave. Jerrin couldn't hope to actually kill or hurt Aven, nor did that seem terribly advantageous. They had been nothing but friendly and had hashed out six detailed trade deals, which would all be rendered useless with a war. And Takar was known even less for its armed forces than for the martial skill of its ambassadors. Takarans made a great deal of money out of trade with Akaria; they did not need to attempt to control Aven's supposedly uncultured, warlike people. Even the thought that they might be able to was ridiculous.

Perhaps it was indeed personal curiosity. What *else* could it be?

"Well, perhaps today is the day, then. What do you think, Mother?"

Her look said, if it makes them leave, by all means, do it. But there was also a streak of worry in her eyes. She, too, did not understand it. Well, he would not seek it out. If Jerrin came and renewed his request in person, Aven would accept. If he did not, Aven would let it conveniently slip his mind. These competitions were so engrossing, after all.

He watched one battle conclude and another begin between two young Akarian knights before Jerrin appeared.

"What do you say, my lord? Has your mother passed on my request?"

"I have, good sir," she said, a slight edge to her voice.

"And what say you, sir?"

Aven smiled up at him. "I cannot say I share your zest for battle, Jerrin, but what kind of host would I be to leave you unsatisfied? Certainly, if you must see me fight before you leave us, I will not deny you," he said, adding his own gentle emphasis. Aven stood. He was half a head taller than the man and twenty years younger. "Let us fight."

Jerrin clapped him on the shoulder and grinned as they turned to enter the fighting ring. Murmurs of excitement swept through the crowd. The prince and the head Takaran ambassador were going to fight.

At least he hadn't worn his favorite tunic.

The fighting area was nearly the size of the great banquet hall and could accommodate ten or more sparring pairs. At either end of the fighting area stood fireplaces that rose twelve hands high, blazing light for the fighters and warming the hall. Four more stone fire pits were placed throughout the fighting area, providing even more light to the cavernous room. The two men headed to the casual practice armory in the corner, donning mail for fairly serious protection. Aven helped the older man select his armor and appraised the various weapons at their disposal for the rapt ambassador.

"As our guest, what's your pick?" Aven asked.

Jerrin seemed sincerely excited. "Well, my people have always been more apt to fight with staves, but I hear that is not so popular in Akaria."

"Indeed," Aven said. "Most young men focus on sword and ax, or sword and shield."

"What about you? What was the focus of your training?"

"All of them." Aven grinned. "We hold princes to a higher standard."

Jerrin seemed a little flustered. "But, well, you must have a favorite."

Aven let his smile soften, a little more puppy than wolf. He'd intimidated the man enough. "A favorite? That would be the weapons of our flag—the sword and shield. A classic combination. Shall we go for those?"

Conveniently, they would also make it easier for him to avoid killing the fool by accident.

"Yes, let's!" Jerrin quickly agreed. "Akarian weapons for our Akarian prince! I will do my best, but do go easy on me."

"It would not be very good hospitality to cut your arm off," Aven laughed, "so I shall sincerely try."

Jerrin laughed, too, but a tad uneasily. What *was* he after?

As they each tried a few swords and shields, Aven noticed the princess joining his mother. Aven saluted her briefly with his shield before returning to his task. He selected a sturdy, undamaged sword and shield pair. Of course, he had his own personal weapons, but it wouldn't be fair to use those finely tuned works of art against these impersonal, public weapons. And these were much duller.

He headed for the center of the grounds and waited for Jerrin. The crowd hushed as his opponent joined him. They both bowed, solemn and respectful.

And then it began.

Jerrin mercifully began the fight with a quick lunge, easily dodged and deflected. Aven returned with a slash also conveniently easy to block with Jerrin's shield.

The Takaran staggered back. Aven pressed forward. He dare not disappoint.

He brought down a high slash. Jerrin's sword clashed with his, knocking it aside. Another swing from the side, this time blocked by the shield. The old man took a good stab toward Aven's left side, which he danced away from, sidestepping.

He backed away now. For a moment, a standstill. Then Jerrin surprised him by taking the lead with several slashes easily blocked, Aven backing away each time and being nudged gradually toward one of the fire pits. He could feel the heat on his skin behind him.

Enough defense. Aven made a new charge toward the Takaran. Jerrin blocked and sidestepped away from his advances, skirting around him oddly. It brought them even closer to the bonfire.

Perhaps the ambassador has a flare for the dramatic, he thought. Or perhaps he *is* hoping to kill me but make it look like an accident.

Either way, he seemed to be deliberately forcing them closer and closer to the fire pit.

Aven sidestepped outward so that Jerrin was between him and the fire before lunging in again. Jerrin dodged by leaping to Aven's left but this time brought up his shield and slammed it into Aven's side, sending the prince staggering.

Aven caught his balance—on the edge of the fire pit, his eyes focusing just in time to see flames raging before him. Cries and mumbles were going up from the crowd.

Aven turned back and had barely enough time to block the next swing coming at him from above. Jerrin pressed on, pushing Aven back and into the side of the stone fire pit. Aven could feel the flames licking behind him, and then suddenly—to his horror—a strange wind picked up before him, sweeping the flames back, keeping him safely clear when the blaze should certainly have caught his hair alight.

No! Gods, not now.

He had to end this, and he had to end it as soon as possible, or who knew what his magic might do.

He heaved himself forward with all his might, throwing Jerrin back and knocking the man to the ground. Enough playing nice, he thought. Jerrin's hair whipped left and right as if moved by some random, impossible gust of wind.

Before the Takaran could recover, Aven gave a swift kick, and his foe's shield went flying.

Looking scared now, Jerrin brought up his sword before him.

Aven gathered his strength and focused his mind one last time. He knew these public practice swords well, and he knew his own strength even better. If he hit the sword just right…

He gave one mighty blow with all his strength at just the right spot midway up the sword, and it shook in Jerrin's hands before clattering to the ground.

The crowd burst into applause. Jerrin was disarmed and therefore defeated. The ambassador looked a little shocked for a second, probably at the way he'd lost his sword, but he recovered quickly and grinned at him. Aven held out a hand to help him up.

"Well, you lived up to your reputation, young prince," Jerrin said. "Thanks for taking a spin with an old man like me." He clapped an arm around Aven's shoulder.

"I am honored," Aven said, steering him away from the fire and toward the armory. He could still feel the air whipping around them, but Jerrin did not seem to notice. "That was quite a blow from your shield! I think I must beg your pardon if I retire to recover."

"Of course, of course. I'm sorry to surprise you there."

"That is all the fun of sparring, is it not?"

"Thank you again, Aven. Sometimes I need to show my men I still have a bit of fight left in me," Jerrin said with a chuckle.

But the words did not ring true. Jerrin was sincerely thankful for something, but that was not the real reason he'd wanted to fight.

Aven felt the air calm as he hung up his sword, and by the time he'd removed his chain mail, it was as still as it ever was. Inside, though, he was badly shaken.

He glanced up into the crowd, searching for his mother's gaze. Before he could find it, he found Evana's eyes instead. Strangely, she had risen and was speaking urgently with Jerrin.

Aven forced a smile at her. She forced a smile back, but there was something new hidden in her eyes, a secret behind their dark glitter, a deeper frostiness that hadn't been there before.

Had she seen? Did she suspect? Could she know…? Was *she* the reason why Jerrin had wanted to fight?

Suddenly, Aven felt quite sure that he had just walked into some kind of trap. And now something was in motion. But what, he had no idea.

"Have you told Father yet?" Luha asked, her walnut-brown eyes peeking around the doorframe. Hair of the same color was tied half up and matched her cloak.

Miara jumped, then shook her head. "Shouldn't you be in the stables?"

"What about you? Shouldn't you be, too?" Her sister was persistent, as many twelve-year-olds were.

Miara glanced up, looked back at her work, and then nodded. "Don't worry about it, okay?" But she did not meet her sister's eyes as she spoke.

"If there was nothing to worry about, you would have already told Father."

"He worries about everything." Father was not really Luha's father, nor was she Miara's sister, at least biologically, but they had chosen each other and become a family when Luha had first arrived at Mage Hall, five years old and all alone.

"When do you leave?" Seeming to relax a little, Luha slunk into the room and cuddled beside Miara on the bench.

"Tomorrow or the next day. Won't be gone long. A week, perhaps two. I've got no problem handling myself out there. Don't fret for me, okay? Promise?"

"You never tell me what the Masters ask you to do. It's never good. How can I not fret?"

"*They* are not good, so how could their chores be any different? But we're still here, aren't we?" She squeezed Luha's shoulders in a one-armed hug. "You've had a full day of hard work. I've just been here studying books and maps. You should go get some dinner before the evening prayer starts."

"And you really should tell Father," Luha said, eyes twinkling. "But I won't do it for you. See you at home, then."

She was gone with a nod.

Miara hurried to finish her preparations. The itch on the back of her neck grew worse, and her shoulder panged occasionally, urging her on. She worked through dinner.

Only the dreaded clanging of the evening prayer bells roused her. She'd even forgotten to light more than a single candle, and the sun had nearly set.

She hastily got to her feet. Every night, when the prayer bells rang, all mages were forced to bow and worship. If she didn't get off the bench, she'd be in for an uncomfortable time.

She held herself poker straight even as the compulsion to kneel swept over her. Her hands tightened into fists, her nails digging in and drawing blood, as she resisted.

They wanted her daily routine to be supplication to the goddess Nefrana, who told them magic was evil. Or so they claimed.

Instead, her daily routine was resistance.

It pained her father to watch her struggle, so she was glad he wasn't here. As much as he, too, hated slavery, he feared Nefrana did not understand. He feared the Masters could be right. Miara was fairly certain she didn't need any goddess who thought she was evil when Nefrana herself had made her this way. Perhaps in Akaria she could find a temple of Anara to worship at instead of this foolishness.

With time, the pain became too great. She relented and fell to her knees, bowing her head to rest on her forearms against the dark stone floor, listening as the crystalline chimes echoed down the halls of Mage Hall.

As soon as it ended, she finished the last drawing, gathered her books and notes, and headed home. Drawing the map had taken forever, and much of Mage Hall slept. She grabbed a leftover roasted chicken leg and a pastry, eating like a roguish bard while she walked. She would miss real food that someone had actually cooked while on the road.

When she reached their rooms, she found Luha and her father were already asleep. She tiptoed to her room and collapsed onto her bed, opening *Gargoyles in the Sky*. Who needed rest, really?

Every Akarian fortress was described in agonizing, ultimately meaningless detail. Her heart sank at the descriptions. These were not fortresses for show, they were made with folks like her in mind. Well, more likely they were made with *armies* in mind. She would have to find a way to convince someone to let her in willingly—and then somehow, crazily, let her see the prince. Alone. Sure, that should work out just fine.

Maybe this was going to be even harder than she'd thought.

She thought over her past conquests, looking for inspiration. She had stolen treaties from beside the Estaven ambassador, listened to dozens of conversations that she shouldn't have been able to hear, even planted an envelope in the king's own chambers. She'd absconded with a handful of treasures. But every target had been much less rebellious than a full-grown man, and certainly much less fortified.

She skimmed and skimmed, and just as she was nodding off, her eyes caught on a passage about Estun.

> *Estun Hold is sometimes called the "Seat of the Sky Kings," as Akarian kings have from time to time chosen to take up residence there, especially in turbulent times. Estun itself was designed and built to prevent the assassination of King Irark III amid political upheavals in Akaria and beyond in Takar,*

which were ultimately settled peacefully. The hold is almost entirely underground. In exchange for this security, it gives up a great deal of natural light and air circulation. The fortress includes palatial accommodations for the king and a large family, as well as high-ranking visitors. Kings may rule for long periods of time from this hold. Estun has a full complement of servants and stockrooms that can hold several months' worth of wood, coal, grain, salted meat, and other dried foods, as well as cold chambers that keep perishable foods and provide ice. As a result, Estun can operate comfortably without opening its doors for several months at a time.

She groaned inwardly. Couldn't they have started her on a kidnapping mission a little easier than *this*? By the gods. What were they thinking? This was a suicide mission. If the hold didn't open its doors for months at a time—and had no windows—there was nothing she could possibly transform herself into that could sneak into cracks that weren't there. Would she have to become a groundhog and *dig* her way in?

Estun also has a tiny mountaintop garden terrace that is only accessible from inside the hold. Using this garden, servants can grow winter vegetables. The terrace is highly inaccessible, with steep ascents on all sides. The innovation in the addition of this terrace lifts Estun to one of the finest Akarian holds, and its independence serves the greatness of our king.

Her heart skipped a beat. Oh, now this was something. She skimmed frantically for more details, but that was the only mention of this terrace. It was enough. A servant's entrance was an excellent target for her to get inside. Highly inaccessible meant fewer guards. Or possibly no guards!

Except that it *was* accessible… if one could fly.

She breathed a deep sigh of relief. Finally, some semblance of a plan. Exhaustion hit her, and she blew out her bedside candles. Had it been her own worry driving her or the compulsion? Perhaps it didn't matter. This one clue eased her mind enough. She lay down and drifted off to sleep.

2   A Way In, A Way Out

"You wanted to speak privately again—well, here we are. This is as private as it's going to get."

Aven had strolled around idly with Evana for some twenty or thirty minutes this morning, struggling to make conversation and analyzing the tension in her jaw, before she'd finally requested they retire to somewhere less public. Privacy had obviously been her aim all along, but had she seemed to think her façade was worth it. Perhaps she'd hoped the delay would make him uncomfortable. They had finally retired to her room, Fayton the head steward in tow.

The door was barely shut before she began. "I am afraid I must take my leave of you."

Nervous tension shot through him. "Have I failed your tests already, milady? I'm sorry to hear that." He gave her his most charming smile, and it did seem to have some effect, as she opened her mouth to say something else but stopped and only stared for a moment, looking conflicted.

"No... well, yes." She seemed to wrestle with her thoughts for a moment more, then resolve herself to some decision. She set her face into a hard, deliberate glare. "Did you think I wouldn't know?"

He cocked his head quizzically, even as his hearted start to pound. "I'm afraid I don't follow."

"Would you have married me without telling me?"

"Without telling you what?" He frowned, pretending to search for what she could possibly be talking about.

She folded her arms. "Do you really think me that much a fool?"

He shook his head. "You are no fool, Princess. Of that, I am sure. But *I* am fool enough to not understand your meaning—"

"*You* are a *mage*," she spat at him. Her eyes darted to the head steward, then back to him.

Aven feigned shock, although he could feel himself failing. "Where would you get such an idea? What would possibly make you think such a thing?"

She swept toward him, skirt swirling, stabbing her finger inches from his face. "Do not mock my intelligence. I saw what you did. I *saw*. I am trained to look for such things."

Should he keep up the lie—or give in? What did she mean, "trained"? "What are you…" he whispered. His hesitation was a choice. Their eyes locked, and they both knew she had discovered his secret.

"I saw the air come alive. I saw you move the fire to protect yourself during battle. And you've been avoiding me ever since. You knew right away that I had seen what you'd done. How you've kept this secret for this long is beyond me—it is as plain to me as the surprise on your face."

Could he charm her into keeping his secret? Why did she seem so angry, as though she felt betrayed? How could she be so sure of herself? Her confidence made him wonder—how many of the servants knew and happily averted their eyes? Did more people already know than he thought?

"Evana," he whispered, "please don't feel deceived. I've known you for a single day. How could I trust you with my deepest secrets in such little time?" As he spoke softly, his face inches from hers, he took a risk and raised a hand to gently stroke her cheek.

For a moment, she watched his hand, a mixture of sadness and longing in her eyes—and then suddenly she broke herself away and stepped back. "So you do not deny it, then."

"Well, I would not call myself a mage, as I know nothing about magic."

She clenched her jaw, chin jutting upward.

"But I do have the gift, much as I might try to suppress it."

"And your family—your people—allow this? A mage to someday be *king*?"

"Yes, of course. There are no laws against being a mage in Akaria." Perhaps acting confidently would dispel the situation.

"I am well aware of this—a truly wild place, indeed."

"Why are you so aware of this? And what did you mean, you are trained?" His turn for some answers.

"I told you, I must take my leave of you. Now."

"Before even dinner?"

"Yes."

"Why? Answer me—what do you mean, you are trained?"

The intensity of the cold glare in her eyes was surprising, but the expression seemed at home on her face. He was finally seeing the real her, not the mask she wore for courts and dignitaries.

She strode closer to him again and whispered, "You live by your code? Well, I am also a knight, and we have our own code. We are sworn to rid the world of aberrations like you."

He said nothing for a moment, and there was only the sound of their breaths.

"I kill mages like you. *That* is what the bow is for."

"You're a Knight of the Devoted," said Fayton. "Is that what you are?"

She scowled at him. "Did a noble ask you to speak?"

"Answer him," Aven demanded grimly.

"Yes, I am a Devoted Knight, and my code requires me to report back to my order. I must leave at once."

"I wish you wouldn't," he said gently, his last attempt at wooing her, if only to delay her actions. "We hardly got to know each other."

"I know all I need to," she replied. "Be glad your nobility protects you. For now. Or you'd already be dead."

She turned and strode past him toward the door, cutting a regal profile as always.

"Why kill mages? Why any of this? You don't have to—"

She stopped. "Yes, I do," she whispered. "It is my life's purpose to purge the world of deviants like you. You're unnatural. An insult to the gods—one that I shall remedy. We *will* meet again." And then, without looking back, she was gone, her black gown swinging broadly as she turned into the hallway.

"What do you need me to do, sir?" He spun to Fayton. His head steward regarded him calmly, no differently than he ever had. The man could have been asking his preference for coffee or brandy.

"You already knew," Aven realized aloud.

Fayton nodded. "It is my job as your steward to know this household, my lord. All of its workings, politics, risks, and intricacies, as well as its mechanical workings."

"Who else?"

"It would be indiscreet to speak of such things, sir. I have, of course, never spoken of it to anyone." But from his tone, the man knew more than he was saying.

"Tell me."

"I believe the kitchen steward knows as well. Lord Dyon suspects but is always searching for more confirmation. The laundress Mada is very perceptive, and Master of Arms Devol has had plenty of opportunity. If he knows, he hides it well, but I can't imagine him missing some of the things I've seen you do in his presence. There are likely others. As I said, I wouldn't speak of it if at all possible."

Of course. Of course some of them knew. And yet they acted as though they didn't. Out of loyalty? Waiting for some moment to take advantage? Perhaps a little of both. Aven paused for a moment, thinking.

"Go to my mother. Come up with an excuse that she is needed privately, and tell her what's been said and that Evana is leaving. We need to figure out what the princess has told to whom. Do the Takarans know as well? Can we trust our spies to find out? Also, we must decide if we wish to… prevent the princess from leaving. I can't imagine we would, but it is a choice we must consider. Go, and make haste."

Fayton nodded and strode to the door.

"Oh, and Steward?"

"Yes, sir?"

"Thank you."

He frowned. "For what, sir?"

"You knew all these years. And never said a thing."

"What is there to say? She is a zealot, and a fool at that. I know you will make a good king. Which will make for a good kingdom and a good place for my daughter to find her own family. I don't see what magic has to do with it any more than the color of your eyes."

"Still. Thank you."

Fayton gave a quick bow in reply and hurried out.

Aven shared the news of Evana's discovery with his mother and father in the king's private chambers. The dinner chimes would ring soon, and they needed to know.

"Well, that didn't take very long," his father laughed.

"She has not taken to her carriage yet, but her things have been packed," his mother reported. "From what we've been able to surmise in the brief time that's passed, she does not seem to have told the Takarans, although it's impossible to be certain. They, for their part, are not acting any differently and continue to show no signs of leaving."

"Has she spoken to them or given any reason for leaving?" his father asked.

"An urgent duty has called her home."

His father snorted. "To think she was one of the Devoted all along. How could we have suspected?"

"We should ban them from Akaria," she said.

"That just calls attention to the matter. They are not common, nor are mages practicing openly enough to be found easily. Akaria is not a good hunting ground, so to speak. If we ban the Devoted, they will wonder why. It may even increase their numbers."

"Will they act, do you think?" Aven asked.

His father shrugged and then rubbed his short beard. "I don't know every detail of their code, especially what they advise when a mage is not a defenseless peasant. They may seek to turn diplomacy against us, or assassination. Or they may do nothing. We will have to trust our field men to go and find more about them. We just don't know."

"If we had an air mage—if we knew where they were headquartered—" his mother started.

"Now, now, Elise. The danger of the world knowing of Aven's magic is not so certain yet as to begin hiring mages into our employ. Do you know the protests I'd receive? Lord Alikar is a priest of Nefrana of his own account, and Lord Sven is born of Isolte, married into his lands here. And that's just what I know right now; the subject of magic rarely comes up for me to truly understand the politics of the matter."

"I'm sure Lord Dyon would have some protest to be made," Aven added in spite of Fayton's earlier words. Could Dyon really suspect? If so, was that the cause of his animosity?

"No, no. You know he's a reasonable man, Aven. If a mage would be the best tool, he'd be all for it."

"How can you be so sure? Will he be reasonable if he knows of my magic?"

His father smiled at him. "Lord Dyon loves you, my boy."

"He has an odd way of showing it," Aven grumbled.

"His wife feels the same way. At any rate. We can figure out how to gather more knowledge of the Devoted and their knights later, but we must act now."

They all knew what they needed to decide, but none of them wanted to say it. They *could* detain the princess and stop this matter before it started. It was possible word would still reach her order, but they would still have more information and leverage if she were in their possession. On the other hand, she had done nothing wrong. They all hesitated. The silence stretched on.

"There are no laws against knowing the truth," Aven said finally.

"Just as there are no laws against being a mage," his mother added.

"We must let her go." Aven crossed his arms across his chest. He didn't like it, but it was the right thing to do.

His father picked up his pipe and chewed on it for a moment, a nervous habit. "Indeed. Let the rule of law be upheld. We will not imprison her for our personal gain."

They all nodded.

"We will need to figure out how to deal with the effects of this incident. Even if she tells no one, we should have already realized that this could happen and had a plan in place."

"The days slip by so quickly," his mother muttered, "and suddenly your little boy is a man."

His father nodded, looking down at his desk. "A man who will be king! And possibly a mage besides."

"She may not tell anyone," Aven said. "It's possible she intends only to tell her order."

"Yes, but if she could discover this, so could someone else. Your magic isn't going away, much as we'd like it to," his mother said.

His father put down the pipe and clapped him on the shoulder. "I might have wished for an easier road for you, my son, but as you said… it is the truth. Perhaps it is time people knew it."

"And accepted it," his mother added.

"We shall all see about that, won't we?" said the king. "Dearest, why don't you send our departing princess a basket to take on her way?" She stared at him, incredulous, as his smile slowly spread to a grin. "What? Surely, she's expecting us to try and stop her. Let's send her on her way with a dollop of guilt, shall we?"

Aven couldn't hold back a bark of laughter, and even his mother grinned. "She probably won't eat it, you know. What if we've poisoned it?"

"Now there's an idea!" his father laughed.

"No, no, you're right. I will get the kitchen to put something together."

"But more seriously. Put on your sweetest, kindest demeanor. I want to give her a few things to remember later when she plans the murder of our son."

His mother shuddered.

"It's all right," Aven whispered, putting his arm around her and taking his father's hand. "Estun is extremely safe. She can plan all she wants, but I'm not waiting helplessly."

She smiled at him and nodded. "She'll be off soon, I had better go. You two continue your planning." Before her words were complete, the bell rang for the dinner banquet. "Or… not."

"And miss *another* dinner with Teron?" his father laughed. "Have you gone mad?"

"Well, it will be an excellent opportunity for you both to see if they treat Aven any differently. I'll meet you there as soon as I am done sweet-talking our dearest enemy."

"Enjoy yourself, darling!" his father joked and put his arm around Aven to head to dinner, pipe in hand.

Miara had spent most of the day checking over her maps with Sorin, and now as the sun set, she packed up her things to hopefully catch her father before he slept. She had some explaining to do.

"So they're sending you to Akaria this time, eh? Excited?" Sorin asked. She shrugged. "Have you been to Akaria?"

"No."

"You will like it, I assure you. If only because it's not here, and if you'd been born there, you'd be free. An outcast, perhaps, but free."

She shrugged again. "I haven't thought much about it. It will be a challenge."

"What do they want you to do?"

"Kidnap a prince."

He stood up in surprise. "*Kidnap* a prince?"

"That's how I reacted."

"But why would they send *you*?"

She blinked. Of course, she felt the same way. But it was hardly polite. "Thanks for the vote of confidence," she grumbled.

"Well. I didn't mean—"

She rolled her eyes. He had no experience as a spy. The lanky blond mage had only been to Akaria to fetch the herbs he could find with his farsight.

"How do you plan to contain him?" he demanded, quickly changing the subject.

She hesitated. "Well… transformation won't work. He'll go mad. I have a spell, but I've had no way to practice it."

"Sounds risky."

"Can I try it out on you?"

"Certainly, love." He sounded far from enthusiastic in spite of his words, but she could get her revenge for him doubting her. She closed her eyes. It was a difficult and draining spell, pushing the limits of what a creature mage could do. Creature mages worked with life energies, so creating entirely new things was limited to what she could bring forth from existing life forces. She could grow a plant to bind wrists, but that would be too obvious. She could grow a python if she wanted to use a massive amount of energy. But instead, she sought to make restraints from his own life energy.

"What the—"

He could feel it, though he wasn't sure what she was doing. She plucked a tendril of his power here, a wisp of it there, and wove them together deftly, like braiding a plait around each wrist, and then—snap!

"There," she said. "Did it work?"

He shook his head. "Nothing happened."

"Swing your arms around. Do something."

Doubtful, he threw his arms out, and after a few inches, his wrists hit the shackles and caught. He gazed down in horror.

"It *did* work!" she exclaimed.

He circled his arms around, looking for some way to free himself, but it was no use. "All right, that's enough. Undo it."

"I never said anything about knowing how—"

"Now," he growled, stepping menacingly toward her.

"It's done, it's done." She tried not to glare, but she could feel the iron tension in her shoulders. She had many times thought of Sorin as a friend, and he often flirted with her. Or at least, she thought he did. But there was another side to him.

"All right," he grunted. "We've all had plenty of extra enslavement for one day, love. Don't do that again."

"You *gave* me your permission."

"How is it you can do that, against the binding?" he demanded, unapologetic. "You did what the Masters do."

"No. It's a physical bond, not a mental one. And I can only do it on their behalf." She paused, hating the thought. "Convenient for them, no?"

He nodded brusquely. "Well. Good luck on your mission, then," and he was gone before she finished gathering her books.

She trotted home, heavy books and maps in tow in her bag. She was still shutting the door when she heard her father's voice.

"So, are you going to tell me about your mission before you leave, meesha?"

She turned, grinning. Meesha was her father's pet name for her, a holdover from when she was small. "My plan was to tell you now. How did you know?"

"You weren't at the stables. You should be proud of Luha, though, she didn't budge to tell me anything." He winked at her. "Have you had anything to eat?"

His casual act was a façade. She knew how much he hated her missions, but he strove valiantly to pretend he didn't. It did make it easier, so she did her best to play along. "Damn. No, I forgot to eat again. Have you?"

"Ah, the bond will do that to you. As will an intelligent mind hard at work. Do you want to tell me of your next trial as we get something to eat?"

She nodded. He donned his cloak, and she hadn't yet removed hers. They headed out in the cold to the mess hall.

"You won't like this one. I've clearly been doing too good of a job. I've drawn the notice of the Dark Master himself, it seems. They are stepping up the challenge."

"Is this because of Dekana?" he asked.

"I don't know. The Mistress wouldn't say much, but I suspect her death had to do with something else. The Mistress insisted it was not related to my task, but, well, who knows how much we can trust *that*." She would not mention it to him, but she knew the Mistress would shed no tears if she ended up as dead as Dekana. How could the Masters even hope for her to succeed on this mission? A chill ran through her as another idea occurred to her. Was it possible they had no need for her to succeed? Perhaps it was all just some kind of trap, a way to be rid of her. Simply a way to anger the Akarians. But why? She shoved those thoughts aside. It didn't matter. She would succeed and return to her life. Their motives were irrelevant.

"And what is this new task of yours?"

She couldn't meet his eyes. "A kidnapping."

His eyebrows shot up. "Well, then! You *have* been doing too good a job!"

"Not that I can choose to do anything else."

"Indeed."

"Steal too many trinkets, and they think you can steal a man."

"Or they don't think very well," his father said, grinning through a slight twist of pain in his shoulder brand.

"Well, I won't dispute that," she said, feeling a burn in hers as well. Sometimes the pain felt nearly good when you were hurting alongside a comrade in rebellion. "To make matters worse, the man they want me to kidnap is a prince."

"Of course! Why start small?"

She laughed. "I have a good plan, Father. I think I can do it, actually. I'm ready. I have everything packed to leave in the morning."

"So soon?"

"Please. Promise me you won't worry."

"Ah, meesha, you know I would never lie to you, so I can't promise that."

"Well, then promise you will pray for me and try not to think too hard about it."

"Aye, that I will. Now, let's eat, and you can tell me the details of your devious plans, or I can tell you of the evil schemes the Fat Master has me executing in the bulb gardens for the spring."

3 The Balcony of the Sky Kings

The first day's ride was more than she could have hoped for. Sorin had been right, although she hated to admit it. An entire day spent alone on the road was surprisingly uplifting, and the landscape was awe-inspiring, whether it was the rolling cornfields of Kavanar or the colorful autumn forests that awaited her in Akaria. The first night, she slept in a small, quiet inn just inside the Akarian border. She marked it on the map as a place to return to. It was the sort of town where people went about their own business and didn't want to be bothered—perfect for her purposes.

The second night she spent in a larger town with cobblestoned streets and two-story shops and inns. In the market she checked the price of horses—nearly the same as in Kavanar, thank goodness.

She and Kres rode into the third day in a driving rain, and her cloak could not keep out the bone-shivering wind and spray. By dinnertime, she was soaked through and hadn't looked at the maps the entire day. Though she risked missing something, it was so wet that she didn't want to take them out and ruin them after the days and days it had taken her to study the originals and make careful copies for herself. Then, using Sorin's farseeing, the two of them had followed the roads from the sky, checking the accuracy of the maps and updating them along the way. At this point, she knew them by heart anyway.

Where was an air mage when you needed one to quell this damn rain? Or even an inn? She hadn't seen civilization in several hours.

Go ahead and find some dinner, she told Kres, and he ambled away to find something to munch. She set about making some sort of temporary shelter. She needed to rest, eat, and examine the maps to see if she'd taken a wrong turn, and tying her oiled tarp to a tree trunk and a nearby branch would have to do. She settled another thick burlap from her pack over a pile of damp, dead leaves. Under her makeshift refuge, at least there was a break from the pattering of the rain on her head. Hell, how could summer be over so quickly?

She swigged some water from her skin and wished again she had the fiery powers that Sorin had. He could remedy this situation so easily—spark them a fire, make them a blanket of thick air above, push the rain itself away if he wished. But what could she do as a creature mage? Sometimes she loved it the most, and other times, she cursed herself for her foolish, impractical magic. What could she do against the cold—grow fur, grow a tree for shelter? If an inn didn't turn up, she might just have to try it. It was one thing to use magic to start a lovely fire, it was quite another to have to turn yourself into a bear. Actual shelter would be better.

She took some rations from her pack—soft bread and vegetables that wouldn't last the whole journey, a little smoked meat. Tired, she let her head fall back against the tree and looked out at the mountains.

On this ride, admiring the mountains had been her favorite pastime so far. As she'd ridden north, they had grown grander and grander to her left. At Mage Hall, they weren't very visible, just small peaks in the distance, but the road she followed veered closer and closer to the mountains. She couldn't help but feel her heart leap a little at their majesty. The mountains were dressed in rich reds and fiery oranges at their base, leading up to towering pines, bare stone, and snow-capped peaks. To the north she could see the mountains where Estun lay nestled—strong, snowy, and grand.

Sorin was right, it was a lovely land. Not boring and flat and a dull green-yellow, like Kavanar. Broad rivers ran with an elegant blue darkness, and the plants had a variety to them that made her feel excited and alive, with so many different and diverse energies swirling around her.

Enough resting. Her shoulder twitched at her—continue, continue, let's move on… She unbuttoned and unfolded her pack, careful to not let any water inside, and took out her maps.

Kres munched on some grass nearby. Not all the birds had flown south yet, and some sang sweetly. The light wasn't very good under the tarp, and it took some experimentation to actually see the map without endangering it.

Damn. She'd apparently made good time, and the town she'd planned to stay the night in looked like it might have been the one she had passed a few hours back. It was more run-down and poor than she'd expected, and there had been no marker with the town's name. The next town was the village nearest Estun, but it was several more hours. She could ride into the darkness and arrive dubiously in the dead of night, or she could turn back. Or she could simply camp here.

They could sleep out in the open, but the rain made a fire difficult, as everything had been soaked through for hours. She had some tricks up her sleeve, but this journey could have many more days… She didn't want to pull them out just yet.

She shook her head and folded the map back up in disgust. She didn't want to go back to the sad little town, but it was better to be more rested. She would need every ounce of energy she could muster; an inn would let her keep more.

She closed the pack up tightly and folded the tarps. Time to head back.

Darkness had fallen as she neared the town, and she stopped on the road before it, considering. Should she transform to keep any unwelcome attentions away? She didn't look rich, but she didn't look poor, either, and while she had no delusions of beauty, she wasn't repulsive. Maybe she *should* be.

Quieting her thoughts, she calmed herself, centering, concentrating. She reached out through every little hair and fingernail and inch of her skin, feeling her body pulse with life, with blood coursing energy through her veins. She pictured a woman, older but not frail, with weathered skin, a gigantic misshapen nose that had been broken a few times, heavy eyebrows, thin, judgmental lips...

She could see the change first, then feel it swell within her. Useful as air mages were, let's see them do this. When she opened her eyes again, unfamiliar eyebrows weighed her expression down. Her hands were appropriately wrinkly and callused. She couldn't see her face, but she ran a hand over her it to check her work. Two eyes, a nose, and a mouth—nothing missing. Unfamiliar. Close enough for her.

She rode into town and found the inn, the only building with a light still burning. She tied up Kres outside—not because he needed it but because people would expect it—and she strode inside.

As the door shut behind her, all eyes in the inn's main room turned toward her. Not exactly the mind-your-own-business type of place? Great.

She turned her fresh, ugly face toward the inn-keeper near the door and scowled at him. "A room," she demanded. "How much?" She had a lovely, gravelly voice to match, too, she discovered.

"Thirty silver," he said, eyeing her suspiciously. The room was awkwardly quiet, as if half the drunken townsfolk were listening, and only a few were actually having conversations of their own.

"Twenty," she shot back, cold as ice. "You'd rather your rooms stay empty?"

"Twenty-seven. You'd rather sleep in the rain?"

She turned on a heel and headed for the door, bluffing.

"Fine, fine, twenty-six silver!"

She stopped as if considering.

"Twenty-four," she replied. He glared at her, but gave a sharp nod. She produced the necessary coin, a fair price. She only haggled because she knew he'd have believed her a fool if she hadn't. He took the coin, led her to her room, lit a candle with his own, and handed her the key.

"The girl will be up to light the fire shortly, so leave the door open till then."

"Do you have a stable for my horse?" she asked.

"If you stable it yourself." She nodded. "Around the back." And he was gone. She headed back down the stairs to find Kres and get him a warm, dry place of his own to sleep.

She led him around the back of the inn, softening the sound of their steps to near silence, and listened hard for any kind of foul play. She could feel no one in the vicinity, not even a stable boy. Must be a small town if they didn't even guard their horses.

And for someone in need of a horse, this was an *excellent* opportunity.

She opened the broad door heading into the stable, and the smell of dirty horses and manure hit her like a punch in the mouth. She groaned. "This won't be the most luxurious night, but it's better than the rain," she told him.

He huffed. *We'll see about that,* he retorted. She laughed to herself. Hearing the thoughts of all creatures was one of the conveniences of her type of magic, although she tended to avoid it. She did not *want* to hear the thoughts of most people most of the time, and to dip in while a person was unaware tempted madness at the roiling layers of thought. But she was close with Kres. She knew when he might have something to say and when he wanted her to listen by the flick of his ears and the way he swung his head at her.

She led him inside to a stall on the far side of the stable. The smell was less strong here, and the stall was fresh and unused, so at least it was clean. She took some grain from her pack for him, found some stable brushes, and got to grooming.

Exhausted as she felt, soaked from the rain, she loved grooming him. She loved caring for horses, but she could always feel Kres's satisfaction and pleasure more clearly. She took off his saddle; she would take that to the room to lock it up. She took off the saddle blankets, shook them out, and laid them over the stall wall to dry, at least a little. Then she cleaned each hoof and began her brushing. Kres's ears twitched, and he shifted his weight from foot to foot, enjoying her attention.

Eventually, she left him to eat his grains while she explored the stable. There were five horses, saddles next to three of them. The other two must be the innkeeper's. She sent a tendril of her magic toward them, sensing their temperament and intelligence.

A gray one caught her eye. She was a wildish mare and lacking in grooming. Miara took the brushes and headed toward her.

The mare stomped and snorted in excitement, and Miara went to work on this new horse as well. The lovely mount desperately needed it, and as Miara worked, she listened to the horse as closely as she could. The girl was happy to have some attention, pleasant, willing.

What's your name? she whispered to her.

Cora, the horse whispered back, timid.

Would you like to come with me, Cora? Would you like to go on an adventure?

The mare shifted back and forth and stomped a foot, and Miara grinned.

After four days, Aven felt quite sure that if the Takarans knew anything about his magic, they were remarkably coordinated at hiding it. That, or they didn't know.

Several Takarans, his mother, and both his brothers had taken to playing a game of cards in the parlor. His father had retired for the evening, and so Aven remained, attending to the conversation absently.

"No, Dom—you can't play that now," Jerrin was saying after a card went down. Aven's youngest brother was still learning to play. Or so he claimed. Aven suspected Dom might just be toying with the head ambassador.

"This one? No? What about this one?"

"Dom!" Thel snapped, after his youngest brother had shown nearly all his remaining cards to the group.

"Sorry!" Dom laughed.

The game did not seem to be going terribly well.

"Prince Aven," Teron said, "your mother mentioned you are quite a fan of the stars." Teron was Jerrin's second, one of the highest ranked in the group, below only Jerrin. What exactly any of them were in charge of, Aven could never seem to get them to say. His skin was darker than Jerrin's, sporting the usual brown of Takar and then some, and he had a friendly smile.

"Well, yes. I've studied them very much. A hobby of mine," Aven said, pleased to talk about something interesting.

"Shame you see them so rarely, then!"

"Truer words have not been said." Aven chuckled.

"I have dabbled a bit as well; the sky in Takar is mostly the same as here. What are your favorite stars? Surely you have some." As it came to Teron's turn, he laid down a card, but his attention was focused on Aven.

"Well, in a sea of beauty there is a lot of competition, but I do have a few. It's hard not to appreciate the glitter of Neka, so bright and low in the sky. The clusters of the Muses and Erepha have such lovely, strange shapes."

"Arts and sciences—good stars to guide your life by. Indeed, it's hard to find fault with any of them," Teron said, grinning. "Anefin is a favorite of mine, the star of prosperity."

"Ah, yes, the stories behind them all can make some better and some worse. The story of Anefin being coaxed into the sky is one of the best! But Casel, to the south—it has a certain strange twinkle that I quite like. That might be my favorite. Yes, I think so."

"Casel! Excellent choice. Yes, I know the strange twinkle you mean, like it's winking at you. The star of deliverance, of liberation. A mighty star." Teron gave him a broad, genuine smile. "That one makes sense for you, my lord. Your guiding star, I'm sure of it."

An odd comment indeed. "What makes you say that?"

"Ah, just a gut feeling, I suppose," said Teron. Aven felt distinctly sure there was some subtext, some hidden message Teron was trying to communicate that Aven wasn't catching.

Could they know? But what did stars have to do with any of it?

"And what is your guiding star, Teron?" Jerrin asked.

"He doesn't need another—Anefin of prosperity indeed!" Aven's mother said, laughing. "He's won the whole hand without paying attention."

Teron chuckled. Aven found himself smiling at his book. Could it be their guests were growing on him? Teron's words were as good a compliment as he'd ever received. Certainly better than Evana's had been. He had never thought of a star as a guide, but if he had to choose one…

Teron stood from the game and strode to fetch two books from a table across the room, then handed them to Aven. "I thought of this subject because I have been immersing myself in your wonderful library. These are absolutely brilliant. Have you read them?"

Aven took the leather volumes and turned them over in his hands. He couldn't recall ever having seen them before, and he was no stranger in the library. "Actually, no. Where did you find these?"

"There is a high shelf by the tall eastern windows you can reach with two ladders—do you know the area?" Teron spoke quietly, subtly separating their conversation from the rest of the room.

"Yes, but I can't recall ever looking there."

"It was terribly dusty, I must say, so that makes sense. I think no one had been up there in quite some time. I find sometimes the most valuable things are hidden right there in plain sight. Wouldn't you agree?" Teron's words had an odd emphasis, as though he was trying to communicate more than he was saying. His smile spread into a grin, and he folded his arms across his chest. The other Takarans busied themselves with the cards, books, other things, as if their conversation was entirely uninteresting.

Aven's eyes locked with Teron, and he didn't look away. He didn't care what awkwardness it might create. Teron, ever the diplomat, knew how to smile and shift his weight to ease the moment more than most would have been able to, entirely comfortable under Aven's gaze. What could he be referring to? He was trying to tell him something, but what?

Could it be…?

Could he know? If he did, he had a strange way of showing it.

"This one," said Teron, pointing to one with a blue leather cover inlaid with copper designs, "is about Casel in particular."

Aven opened the book and flipped through the pages. How strange. It seemed to be partly in another language he didn't recognize. And as part of his duties, he knew enough of nearly all languages to recognize them on paper.

"Excuse me," Teron said, "but I must get a touch more brandy."

All too conveniently, Aven was alone with the books. He looked more closely at the lovely cover, the metal inlay illustrating Casel and her sisters shimmering in the dim firelight. Was it his imagination, or did they glisten brighter than the fire should let them? He propped his elbows on the arms of his chair and leafed through the pages.

A folded sheet of paper slid out of the book and fell in his lap.

He unfolded the thick, rough paper. A map of stars and constellations was scrawled in an ancient hand in blue ink. Strange notes adorned the margins in an old, old language—Serabain. He knew it, but very little.

"Prince Aven!" Lord Dyon's voice made him jump in surprise in the quiet parlor. Teron, who had been talking to Steward Fayton near the door, moved casually as though to look at an artifact, putting himself between Dyon and Aven. Was it his imagination, or was Teron blocking Dyon's view of the books?

Aven hastily folded up the paper and slipped it into his pocket as he stood.

"Yes, Lord Dyon," he said.

"Your father is going over some arrangements for the Proving, and he requests your review."

Aven nodded. "I will join you shortly."

Dyon gave him a dubious look but took his leave.

As quickly as he could, Aven flipped through the second book. It, too, was sprinkled both with the common tongue and another language. Perhaps it *was* Serabain, but some of the spellings and characters were different, twisted. He strode to Teron and held open a page.

"Do you know this language?" he asked the Takaran.

"No," Teron said. He spoke softly so only Aven could hear, and all of the usual charming lilt had faded from his words. "I hoped you did."

"No, unfortunately."

"I have seen it. It hasn't been used since the Dark Days."

What did Teron know about the Dark Days? "Perhaps one of the scholars would know," Aven said.

"If I were you," said Teron in a voice for only Aven to hear, "I might keep it to myself. Or a very trusted few. Certainly not any nosy foreign princesses." Then he gave Aven a small, polite bow with a smile.

He knows, was all Aven could think. Gods, he knows. Evana *had* told them. But—the books, the pretense, the coordinated distraction of the others—what did all this mean?

By Anara, they all know, he realized. And they're trying to help me.

Miara said goodbye to the mare Cora the next morning after she had saddled Kres and packed up her things. *Don't worry, girl,* she had told her before she left. *My horse friend Kres will be back for you.* The mare had huffed in reply. Miara had left the stall unlatched.

Then she and Kres had headed for the mountains. She had dropped the disguise just out of town to save energy. Dawn had barely broken, and she'd ridden in the direction of Estun until the sun had cracked the horizon and cast streams of light down into the forest. At least, she *thought* it was the direction of Estun. That was one location Sorin couldn't really confirm for her because the maps weren't terribly precise as to the location of the hold, probably by design. Gods, let her find it quickly because she dreaded going back to that flea-bitten inn. Perhaps the woods would do just fine tonight, whether she found Estun or not.

She picked an isolated clearing near a creek. There was good grass for Kres to munch on and a musical, clear stream as well. She stopped and splashed the frigid mountain water on her face. She tried to center her thoughts, to calm the core of her soul, but the current of her emotions twitched and trembled, half excited, half terrified.

Briefly, her fear swelled—what was she thinking, trying to break into an Akarian fortress and kidnap its prince? Her and what army?

This was insane. One lone woman couldn't do this. She was going to die. It was a fortress in a nation of great warriors, and he of all people was their damn prince. And she wasn't even sure where the hell the fortress was or what this bastard looked like.

This was impossible, and she was a fool. A sacrificial lamb on the altar. The Masters had to know they were sending her to her death. But they didn't care. Why? Why send her at all, then?

Shut up, she told herself. She forced herself to stop and breathe. One breath, another. Hear the water, the wind, the birds. Her nerves steadied.

It was not impossible. The Akarians were warriors, but they weren't mages. Magic was nearly extinct in Akaria. They were not prepared for her or anyone like her. She was a good mage, perhaps a great one. She could be as silent as the moon, as hidden as a cat in the grass, and as steady as the mountain. It was not impossible.

Another deep breath.

She put her hand in her pocket; as she moved, her hand shook a little, but she tried to ignore it. I can do this, I can do this. She fingered the eagle feather in her pocket and carefully formed the image of her eagle form in her mind. She didn't always need to have a token from the animal she sought to become, but it helped to focus her, to transform precisely into the right creature without mistake. She conjured up brown feathers, large and powerful, soaring mightily in the sky in her mind. Miara the *girl* might have difficulty with this, but she could become anything. Anything. As an eagle, what couldn't she do? Step by step. It was possible. First step: find the damned palace.

Her body morphed and changed; her fingers could no longer feel the feather. Then there were no fingers—talons crunched the leaves and dirt beneath her. She looked at her wings—perfectly formed as she'd intended. As an eagle, she could do anything. She let out a cry, testing out new lungs, foreign and familiar at the same time. Another deep breath.

Onward to Estun. She launched herself into the sky.

"Good morning, Mother!" Aven called as he passed her in the hallway, the book tucked under his arm.

"Good morning, Aven! Where are you headed to?"

"The library," he said. He had thought to check the shelf that Teron had mentioned and see if it was really dusty and freshly disturbed as he'd claimed.

"Did you hope to read or to philosophize? Jerrin has had Thel, Dom, and your father trapped there for a good hour already discussing ancient religions."

He stopped short. His poor brothers. "Well, I *was* going to read…"

"Wouldn't suggest the library, then," she said, eyes twinkling.

"Right."

The terrace would be too cold this early in the morning. He tried the parlor but caught Teron's voice before he rounded the corner and retreated quickly. How hard could it be to find a quiet place to read this book alone?

He headed back to his own bedroom, but the maidservants had turned it upside down and were scrubbing the floor at the moment. A chair at the breakfast room table was too dark, as it was beyond breakfast and most of the candles were now out. Damn this place. He *did* manage to catch an apple dumpling on his way past the kitchen, so it wasn't a total loss.

Munching as he walked, he shrugged to himself. The terrace would be cold, but at least he would be able to *see*. He collected a wool coat from his quarters and headed up the stairs to the terrace. At this rate, he was never going to get to read this thing.

The northern mountains of Akaria made for beautiful flying. Miara left the forested hills behind and soared toward the snowy peaks. The air was calm and cold, and the morning sun warmed the tops of her wings.

She swept broad circles around each mountaintop. A bright shot of green amid the snow and rock caught her eyes, and she headed for it. How could they keep things growing there, at this height, amid the snow? There must be magic at work. But she could sense none nearby, aside from the weak presence of the oppressive Great Stone.

She circled overhead, studying, but the garden was mercifully empty. She swooped down in slow circles, cautious and watchful. She perched on a wall and examined the terrace. No people in sight. A heavy, dark metal door, benches, a few high hedges, a cherry tree, many low shrubs and flowers.

She plopped down onto the dirt of the garden. Where could she hide near the door? And what form would be best to sneak inside? There were no easy hiding places, at least not for a medium-sized animal like an eagle. Should she shift to a mouse? Mice were trustily mobile and small, but also easy targets for both humans and animals. Something else? A falcon? A fly?

The door to the terrace suddenly groaned and creaked open. She stifled a gasp. Hell—her time was up. And as an *eagle,* she might as well be begging them to spot her. She had to transform, and she had to do it *now.* She focused her mind on the image of a fly and flung herself into that shape. Her body shrank abruptly down toward the earth.

When her limbs stopped twisting and her eyes focused, she could see him. The man walked toward her, face buried in a book. He did not expect anyone to be here, thank goodness. He sat down on a sun-soaked bench without looking at it, obviously familiar with the place. His dress was finer than a servant or laborer and lent him a refined elegance.

She flew on wobbly, unfamiliar new wings closer to him, crash-landing on a rosebush. Her visitor frowned over a blue leather book with gold inscriptions of stars on the cover. Shaggy blond-brown hair threatened to fall into intense eyes, their color so light and strange she almost couldn't make it out.

Should she act or wait? Others could be coming to join him. He could leave at any time. She could hope the door was left unlocked, or she could try to sneak inside along with him—a risky proposition. Or she could try to get information out of him. What was just inside the door? And how could she find this prince?

Her heart was pounding as she quickly formulated a plan. Then she went for it before she could reconsider.

She circled behind the bench. He didn't notice her. She paused for a deep breath, eyes on the door, hoping no one would interrupt what she was about to do.

Anara, protect me. Now or never.

She released her hold on the transformation, and her shape unraveled around her wildly. She could slow and control the process, but when speed was of the essence, the magic spun out of control, flinging her back into her own form like a hurricane falling to pieces.

She squeezed her eyes shut for a split second—as long as she dared—and struggled to steady herself. When she opened them, she could see no one new had arrived. He hadn't heard the thud that must have accompanied her transformation. She should have silenced the sound, but luckily, he was intent on the book. Get it together, she thought. She couldn't afford to be sloppy *now*.

She rose to a crouch, her steps hidden by the wind rustling the leaves of the cherry tree. She crept forward, one step, then another. She jumped as he moved slightly. He turned a page and continued to read.

She was just behind him now. She could hear his breath. After this, there would be no turning back. But then again, there had never been any turning back, had there?

Rising, she clamped one hand over the man's mouth while the other caught a wrist and forced it behind his back, raising him up to his feet.

A sudden gust of wind hit her from the left and knocked her off-balance, but she dragged him with her to the side and back behind the bench. Strange, it hadn't been so turbulent a second ago—but they *were* on a mountaintop. So much for luck.

They fell roughly into the dirt. She released him but only long enough to thrust him to the ground and bring her knee down on his chest. She brought the blade of her dagger just under that strong jawline.

His eyes studied her even more intensely than they had the book. He made no sound and offered no resistance. His eyes—a lovely, mysterious, grayish green—were unlike any she'd ever seen. She instinctively reached into his energies, hungrily, not expecting to find much. As a rule, she never tasted the creature energies or thoughts of other people. But at times like these, she needed to know everything as quickly as possible, so it was worth the risk of knowing or tasting too much.

Smoke. Sulfur. Air magic.

A thrill of fear shot through her.

So not a servant or a prince, but a *mage*. Oh, by the gods. An air mage could easily kill her before she could grow enough of a wing to fly away—

But she forced her thoughts to a halt, buried the fear. His unusual eyes were still staring into hers. He had cast no spells. She wasn't dead yet. And there wasn't the stark, bitter taste of corruption that hung around the Masters.

"Your name—now," she demanded.

"Aven," he said, simply.

She froze, mouth still open. Could it be? Aven was certainly a common name in Akaria. There were probably a hundred Avens hiding inside Estun. Every one named after the royal, most likely.

"Who are you? Your *full* name," she said.

"Aven Lanuken is my name. Son of Samul, King of Akaria. What of it?" His voice was soft, confident, and a little intrigued. Not the slightest bit afraid. "Who are you?" he added. A brave one, then?

She didn't answer. She could hardly believe it. Either her luck was incredible, or this was destiny. When he said his full name, she felt the brand on her shoulder throb and burn excitedly—he *was* the one her binding sought. What she had thought might be the hardest part might just be the easiest.

But she wasn't out yet.

Before she lost this chance, she began the transformations. With her non-blade hand, she pulled a scrap of white fur from her side pouch. He watched her, unmoving.

Surprising herself, she paused and said, "This might feel a little... weird." Then she ran the fur across his forehead, down his nose, across his lips—and the transformation began. The energy began to flow out of her, faster and faster, and she reached with lightning speed toward the plants around them, refilling her energy reserves as quickly as she could spend them. She tried to leave the plants alive, but there was no time for precision.

She sheathed the dagger. For a moment, he was still, and then he twisted and thrashed as the transformation took hold. His form shrank, and fur grew. His clothes did not shrink with him. She'd forgotten to spell that as part of the transformation—damn it. Eventually, there was just a small lump inside his shirt.

She quickly grabbed him. The little mouse's eyes were still a mysterious gray-green, and it was breathing rapidly. "It's all right," she whispered. "I won't hurt you."

Was that really true? she wondered. She couldn't help but think that it wasn't, that the prince *should* be afraid.

She brought out the small black cloth bag she'd brought for this purpose and dropped him gently into it. The clothes were an annoyance. She couldn't have him riding into that horrid little town naked. She gathered up the clothes and tried to tuck them in her various pockets, but the boots would go nowhere. Damn her sloppiness!

Every moment now was pushing her luck. She had to be *gone*. If she could be off with him—she'd figure something out.

She ran a finger down the edge of the eagle feather. A few dizzying seconds later, she felt her talons dig into the earth.

One talon clutched the top of the bag; the other grabbed the top of his boots. Then without another second's hesitation, she launched herself into the sky.

The wind was much calmer now, and she gained height quickly. Her ears rang, her heart pounding, but she was nearly gone, the prince literally in her clutches.

Just as she was losing sight of the terrace, she heard a woman's voice. "Aven?"

She felt a chill go through her, a pain in her wing where the brand festered even now. Had someone seen her? Hell. She should have left the boots behind. An eagle carrying a tiny bag and a pair of boots was hardly inconspicuous. If the Akarians figured out a mage had taken their prince... would that mean that she had already failed?

She felt suddenly dizzy with fear and lurched as her concentration wavered. Flying needed her whole mind. She thrust the thoughts away—whatever was done was done. She couldn't have gotten the prince any more smoothly or been any luckier. She had done her best, and that was all she could do.

Aven's head was spinning. After the woman dropped him into the little bag, which was now much larger than him, everything was still and dark for a brief moment. Then he was swinging, listing wildly left and right. His stomach dropped as he was lifted—up, up, up!

What in all the stars and moons had just happened?

Given his newly tiny size, the cloth of the bag was knit as tightly as he might have hoped. If he tried, he could see between the fibers to the snow and mountains swinging below him. This made him even more nauseous, so he shut his eyes and covered them with his strange little hands. He wasn't sure what he was, but he had white and brown fur... and a tail.

Where could she be taking him? How was she flying, and how did she transform like that? Would he ever see his mother or father or any of them again? Who was this woman who'd swept him away on freshly grown wings?

He sighed. This was just what he deserved. He had wished for something else, something beyond Estun. He had taken it all for granted. Would this be better or worse? Time would tell, but being kidnapped and transformed into a tiny animal didn't really bode well. Perhaps he would spend his eternity as some eagle-witch's pet mouse.

After a while, with his eyes shut tight, the rocking became lulling, and at some point he fell asleep. Or he passed out. It didn't matter which.

4 INTRODUCTIONS AND OBSERVATIONS

Elise stared after the eagle in shock. The blue book Aven had been carrying this morning lay on the floor on its edges, skewed open as if dropped mid-sentence. He was nowhere in the garden. She'd been *right* behind him. But he was gone, and all that was here in his place was this book.

And the eagle flying away into the distance.

She was rusty. She cursed her indulgent lack of practice; she hadn't used significant magic in years. But she desperately flung a wisp of herself after the eagle and found what she feared—the strange, musty, wild smell of creature magic, the bright lights of two beings there in the sky.

It was no ordinary eagle—it was a mage. And the mage had taken Aven.

Her pulse began to race—but she needed to *think*, not panic. Instead, she felt weak. Her thoughts swam. Someone had ripped her heart out, and it moved farther away with each second, carried off by some malevolent mage.

Could this have to do with the princess? That damned Devoted Knight? What did she need to do? What could she possibly do?

Before she realized what she was doing, she leapt into the air after them. She was no majestic eagle, but she had not forgotten how to be a sparrow, how to ride the winds like a little girl. It was not something she *could* forget.

The eagle gained distance. Her wings ached, and her little heart beat as though it might explode.

This was stupid. No one in Estun knew what had happened or where she'd gone. Even if she caught the eagle, what would she do? Fight her? She was not bad with a bow, but she had no weapons with her. She had never used magic to fight. She suspected the same was not true of her adversary. She would never catch them, and if she did, she had no idea how to prevail.

She couldn't do this alone. She needed help.

But she also couldn't just let them fly away.

She groped at the earth below her, thrashing her mind on the mountainsides, searching for any mobile creature she could find until—a hawk. *That creature!*

she commanded with all the force of two decades as a queen. *It has my son. Follow it—do not let them go!*

She could feel the hawk's understanding, her own feelings for an egg that had yet to hatch. Somewhere lower on the mountainside, the bird leapt into the air. The hawk would at least try, and that was more than generous.

Elise turned in flight and raced back to the balcony, her transformation unraveling sloppily as she continued to run from where she landed to the bench where he'd been sitting. The book was still there. She snatched it and rushed inside.

When Aven awoke, he was lying on his back in the woods. It seemed to be later in the day; the sun shone in strong, dramatic beams through the treetops. Tall, skinny pine trees, red maples, orange oaks—they all were lit up by the autumn sun against a clear blue sky.

He felt... better. More like himself. He was afraid to look and discover something different. He forced himself to raise a hand in front of his face. The lines of his palm, his fingernails, and knuckles—they'd never looked so welcome, so familiar!

But below that—on his wrist hung the bracelet of a pair of heavy shackles. The air around him stirred uncomfortably, and a wave of dread and apprehension whipped through him. Now *that* he hadn't seen before.

Glancing around from his prone position, he couldn't see much. He sat up and immediately discovered two things. First, he was completely naked. Second, a woman crouched nearby, leaning against a tree trunk. She was the one that had brought him here, and she must have been the one that had shackled him. And taken his clothes. Why in heavens would she do that?

She noticed he was awake. Her tea-brown eyes caught on his, and their gazes locked for one minute, then two. They stared at each other, like two predators stumbling into the same clearing, not yet ready to fight, but not ready to run, either. She frowned at him with eyebrows that arched elegantly over delicate skin. Her red hair was tied tightly in a bun at the nape of her neck. Her dark leather garments tailored themselves to her athletic form, both striking and threatening. She was studying him as he studied her. She seemed content with staring till the sun set and the moon rose.

Finally, he looked away. He shifted uncomfortably in the dirt and looked down at the short chain between the shackles, realizing suddenly that her study included some of his more private bits. He cleared his throat, hoping to work up his nerve.

"Well, then. This is not much of a proper introduction. You already know my name, aren't you going to tell me yours?" he said.

The wind through the trees picked up ominously. He realized abruptly that he didn't *need* to stop it, worry about it, or try to hide it. A strange, devious thrill jumped through him—so strong, it frightened him a little.

"No," she said simply. She glanced around at the leaves falling gracefully from the wind's meddling. A yellow leaf fluttered past her face. By the gods, what a striking image. She was almost as beautiful as autumn in all its sunny glory. If only he weren't naked in the dirt with his wrists shackled, perhaps he could more properly enjoy it.

"No? Well, that's not very civil." Talking might get her talking, even if it was nonsense.

She rolled her eyes and stood up from her crouch. "You don't need to know," she said as she turned her back on him and looked past the tree as if searching for something or someone approaching.

Did she have others joining her? Perhaps she would hand him off to someone else now. What was she planning? Was she going to kill him here in the woods? Really, that didn't seem likely. She could have done that already by dropping his tiny furry body hundreds of feet into the snow, or slicing his throat while he lay unconscious. So she must have some use for him first. Or she meant to kidnap him.

She must be a mage, he thought, but what kind? Damn, if only he'd gotten to read more of that book. He'd been so close to so much more knowledge. She could not be an air mage, like him.

"You're a creature mage, aren't you?" he said to her back.

She raised her eyebrows, mocking as she peered over her shoulder at him. "What powers of observation."

"Why have you brought me here?" he demanded.

Amused, she turned back to face him. She folded her arms in front of her and leaned against the side of the tree. "My, my, we are full of questions. Do princes in Akaria always get their questions answered at every beck and call?"

It was his turn to glare. "When questions are asked civilly, then usually, yes, they do."

She laughed—a beautiful, musical laugh, but with a dash of dark bitterness. "Well, this is clearly not a civil situation, is it, little prince."

She turned away from him again.

"What are you looking for?" he demanded.

She didn't answer. After a moment or two, she whistled a few low, lovely notes. Then she turned back to him.

He returned her gaze for a few moments. Her face was a little amused, unafraid. She was watching him, he realized. Not studying, just making sure he didn't try to run away. Guarding him. He glanced around. The forest seemed to stretch in all directions, at least to the tops of the hills and the bends in the paths that he could see. They were in the middle of nowhere. The mountains were to the north of them, where he was pretty sure they'd come from.

Well, it was unsurprising that she wouldn't give him a name. Clearly, she wasn't trying to make friends. And why should she tell him her plans? She might be holding him here for someone to arrive. Or she planned to do something to him or take him somewhere. None of these things were likely to be things he'd want to go along with, or he wouldn't be sitting there in shackles in the first place.

But did it really require him to be *naked*? Yes or no, digging into that might tell him something.

"What happened to my clothes?" he said finally.

"Oh," she said. She dug into a pack beside her, pulled out something gray, and tossed it at him, then something else. "There." His shirt flew toward him, and he brought up his hands to catch it but missed. To his surprise, however, the shirt flew straight through the shackle in the chain and hit him in the chest.

Forgetting the clothes for a moment, he held one hand up in the air and grabbed at the chain with the other. Nothing. He could not grasp it. But as he moved his hands apart, the chain pulled taut and would not let his hands farther apart than his shoulders.

"It's invisible, too." Her voice cut into his thoughts. "You're the only one that can see it. But that little trick you just saw will make putting your shirt on easier."

What strange magic was *this*? He sat staring at the shackles a while longer and then shrugged and started putting on his shirt. By the time he had his pants and underclothes on, his boots were thrown at his feet, and he put them on, too.

Hoof beats approached. Two horses cantered toward them, one golden and saddled, the other light gray with dramatic, dark hair. The creatures stopped just before his captor.

The whistle, he thought. She had called them with magic. There were *so* many things he didn't know. He simply stood, dumbfounded, watching her whispering to them. If he could forget the journey here and her likely vicious intentions, it was an enchanting scene. Perhaps he'd been too long under the mountain, but between the glorious sunlight, the vibrant leaves, the majestic horses, and the way the sun caught in her fiery hair, the beauty of his surroundings made him catch his breath for a moment.

She glanced sideways at him. He looked away. She focused on the horses, checking them over, no longer watching him.

No longer watching him...

No time to think it through—he took off running in the opposite direction.

Strangely, the chain on the shackles made no sound, but his feet in the leaves sure did. She made no acknowledgement that she'd seen him go, and he couldn't waste the time or energy to look back. He just went for it, fast as he could, dodging tree trunks and branches.

Then, without warning, the ground in front of him broke open and thin, wiry black vines leapt from the ground, swirling and twisting around each other until a wall of brambles rose in front of him, stopping his path.

That was just the distraction, though. Vines had twined around his ankles and were swirling up his calves and rooting him in place. By the ancients, what power! It took his breath away for a moment and would have frozen him in his tracks with or without the vines. He knew *so little*. Could his mother do things like this? He could hardly imagine it, but she must be able to. No wonder she had hesitated to give up magic to be queen.

He tried to look behind him but couldn't turn far enough. He stopped trying and just waited. Her approach was very quiet, as if there were no leaves crunching under *her* feet, but the jingling of the golden horse's bridle let him know they approached.

She came around in front of him and faced him. "Nice try," she said, a crooked smile on her face. "You're far from out of shape." Well, she had seen *that* for herself before he'd gotten his clothes back, hadn't she? She reached down and grasped the shackle's chain—the one that had fallen through his fingers and his shirt—and twisted it like she was tying a knot. And then suddenly there was another chain coming away from the center of the first. She looked up at him, eyes twinkling.

"No more of that. I hope you see that you can't get away. Now, on the horse with you." The vines curled away from his feet and back into the ground. The bramble barrier remained.

"Tell me your name, and I will," he demanded.

"We are not trading—just do it." She jerked the chain toward the horse.

He stalled, trying to think of something to convince her. "Please?"

She frowned at him but did not immediately say no. Perhaps she was weighing the potential cost of telling him her name against a reward of more cooperation—and if telling him her name would really get her that. But at this point, he just genuinely wanted to know. He felt a slight, gentle breeze that he often projected when he was desperately curious. Her eyes flicked around.

The unnaturalness of the air's movement wasn't lost on her, although its meaning was probably unclear. It was rarely clear even to him.

"If I tell you, you'll shut up, get on the horse, and do as I tell you?" It was part question, part demand.

He nodded.

"Mara," she said gruffly. "Now get on."

"Aven," he said back, holding out his hand. She eyed him suspiciously for a moment but finally shook his hand. Strong grip. His thumb felt the smooth back of her hand, but her palms told a different story—rough and callused. She worked with her hands.

"Pleasure to meet you," he said with possibly not enough sarcasm in his voice. He hoped he was maintaining an offended exterior, but the fact was that her astounding power and loveliness were making him more cooperative every minute.

He turned and willingly got on the horse. Damn, he was a fool.

This prince was not what she'd expected. This begged the question of what in fact she *had* expected, but try as she might, she couldn't put her finger on it. Just, not this.

For one, he was rather light for an Akarian—his light hair and green eyes had caught her off guard in more ways than one. For another, he was a damn *mage*. Or at least he had the power—he hadn't shown much ability so far and had made no attempt to stop her. She'd expected a showdown of some sort when he woke up, and she had *not* been looking forward to it. Air mages had spells that were far more deadly at far longer ranges than creature spells. It didn't matter what she transformed herself into or what creature she summoned from the earth if her opponent struck her with lightning from a mile away. No one said magic was fair.

And yet, he'd done none of that. Perhaps he knew nothing about combat or was saving his skills for some special moment. Or maybe for some insane reason, he'd chosen not to use them. The only magic he seemed to use came in the form of a vague swirling wind with little purpose. Did he mean to scare her? To intimidate her? Was he trying to show off his power in some feeble way? What in the *world* did he mean to accomplish by it? She had no idea, but it was more pitiful than threatening.

Add to that his playful insistence on polite and proper introductions, and well, he was a strange one to say the least. If she'd been tackled, transformed, scooped up, and ditched naked in a field, she'd be a bit more pissed off. Perhaps she just wasn't as well-bred as an Akarian royal. Although Anara knew her experiences with her own Kavanar royals had done nothing to suggest that royal breeding produced politeness.

His request for her name had caught her unprepared, and the fake name she'd given him was a little pathetic. But her real name had seemed too personal. And weren't kidnappers supposed to hide their identities? A good kidnapper would probably have clubbed him and refused to give him a name, though.

She rode Cora bareback. She'd have to get a saddle somewhere, but that was cheaper than a whole horse. Luring Cora away made her worry a lot less that she'd run out of coin. Kres followed beside her, the prince on his back. She held the reins of both horses, although she didn't need to. Neither horse was being led by its rider, but she wanted her control to be clear. She'd had enough escape attempts for one morning.

But she'd gotten him out of Estun and onto a horse. It was good start to say the least.

They certainly couldn't go back past the town she'd rescued Cora from, so they rode east through the forest at a quick walk. They probably wouldn't make it to the next town that night, and perhaps that was for the best. Handling him one-on-one was simpler than with a bunch of other folk about. She could ease into this kidnapping thing.

Occasionally, he tried to make conversation.

"Where are we headed?" he asked.

"East," she said, refusing any more than that.

"Well, I know *that.*"

"Then why did you ask?"

He groaned and tried again, but she said nothing more.

They rode for another few hours with smatterings of conversation and short breaks. She gave him some food and water once and let him relieve himself. He did not try to run again, so perhaps her show of power with the brambles had been effective. An hour before dark, she finally stopped them. It was time to make camp.

The woman—Mara—ordered him to pick up branches for a fire, and he did as he was told. On a practical level, it would be dark soon, and he didn't want to be cold, either. He wasn't above manual labor. As long as she wasn't planning to burn him along with the sticks, he didn't really mind. He felt fairly certain she hadn't gone to all this trouble just to barbeque him now. In spite of all of his failed attempts at conversation through the day, he was growing confident that she *was* taking him somewhere. The questions now were where, how far away, and why.

By the time he had returned with more branches than he could easily carry, she had quite transformed her chosen spot for a campground. Thickets of brambles three times higher and thicker than the earlier ones now surrounded the area. Inside the brambles, the needle-carpeted floor had sprung to life with soft, green grass, and the horses were happily munching. In the center, though, the dirt lay bare, surrounded by stones for a fire pit.

Here and there, a wildflower bloomed amid the grass. Interesting.

As he entered the circle of brambles, they grew up abruptly and closed the circle behind him, trapping him in. He lowered the branches to the ground.

"That's enough," she said. "Can you make a fire?"

"Can I make a fire!" he huffed. "What kind of help-less lout can't make a fire?" Did she think just because he was a prince he couldn't do anything practical? He crouched and built up a nice foundation from the larg-est branches, carefully laying some smaller ones in the middle and then a few larger ones on the top to feed it. Then he looked at her. "Do you have a flint?"

She stared at him for a second as if she were measur-ing him, refining her estimation. He stared back at her, confused. Had she expected something else?

"Am I missing something?" he asked testily. "Do I look like I can simply breathe it to life?"

Wordlessly, she took a flint from the pack and lit the fire herself. He sat down in the grass. Then she handed him a hunk of white cheese and dark bread.

"Eat. Night will be on us soon."

He obliged. Hunger strikes weren't his style, at least not yet. She took out a pot and poured from her water-skin into it. She tossed in some black leaves and put the pot over the fire.

"Well, now *that's* something civil. Is that tea?"

She stared at him, deadpan. "No, it's poison."

He eyed her narrowly, and when she didn't flinch, he involuntarily glanced at the bit of bread in his hand.

"Of *course* it's tea."

They glared at each other over the fire.

When they'd finished eating, she took some blankets from the horses and tossed some in his direction. "Make yourself a place to sleep. It's going to be cozy."

He didn't like the sound of that. He stretched out the blankets. The sun had sunk below the horizon, and the shadows grew longer. Soon the fire would be the only light.

He lay down on the blankets and looked up at the treetops reaching toward the starry sky. Neka was already shining between the branches, low and bright. He took a deep breath of the forest air. Stupid as it was, he felt pretty darn good. The air swirled with pine musk and freedom, and the open sky had been above him for *hours.* He was almost drunk on it. He should be plotting his escape, but the allure of the heavens above stole all his thoughts.

He looked over at her. Tendrils of red hair drifted down toward the papers she studied. Her orders? A map? Her black, well-made leathers fit extraordinarily well, in a style unfamiliar to him. Not Takaran. Many Takarans refused to use animal products such as leather anyway. There was Isolte, the home of his lovely princess. Could this have to do with everything that had transpired with Evana? But she had seemed more bent on killing him personally, and this woman didn't seem to desire his death. At least not yet. Evana had also described herself as having little power within Isolte, so it seemed unlikely she could orchestrate this via her countrymen. Maybe via these Devoted Knights—perhaps this Mara was one of them? But how could any mage be in the employ of an organization that sought to hunt down and kill mages? No, that didn't make any sense.

Akaria had never been on great terms with Winokin to the north, but the journey from there to Akaria over the mountains was hellish, if not impossible. The massive barrier of rock between the two countries kept a fairly solid peace, so they had no reason to kidnap him. Besides, if she were from Winokin, she should have flown the other way. They were headed toward Takar, but also out of the wilderness and toward the main roads. Their direction was likely temporary. He could think of only one other option: Kavanar, their long-time rival and enemy.

She must've felt him studying her. She shattered his gaze with a glance. He pretended to be intently studying the sky.

"Here," she said. "Tea's ready."

"Time to sleep," she told the prince. "This might be a little uncomfortable, but there's no way around it." She could hear the hint of apology in her voice. Damn. It hadn't even been a day. She couldn't go soft on him already. He'd likely stab her in the back first chance he got.

She rubbed her fingers together slightly, a small-enough gesture she was sure he didn't see. Her vines snaked from the soil and coiled around him, pulling him tight to the earth. His face was a mix of horror and fascination.

He was so utterly surprised each time. And he was an air mage who couldn't even light a fire. Did he really not know any magic? Could it be some kind of act? Could magic be that rare in Akaria?

"Well!" he said simply.

"I told you night would be cozy," she said.

He snorted. "No exaggeration. Cozy, indeed."

"Goodnight." She lay down, her back to him.

Of course, she couldn't fall asleep. She hoped to hear him fall asleep first. Thank the ancients for vine spells. She might be able to sleep just a little easier because of them. Of course, she'd woven plenty of other spells around them in case he found a way around the first spell or two. The dirt outside the brambles was ready to become a deep, thick mud that would take an hour to trudge through. Foxes in their burrows waited to rouse Miara at the sound of footsteps.

She couldn't manage this effort every night, but it made her feel just a bit safer at the start of this impossible task. Also, much of Akaria was not as forested and lonely as this stretch. A locked room in an inn would be far more defensible.

She listened to his breathing—not a slow, sleepy rhythm, but many long, deep breaths. Had he never smelled forest air before or something? She must be mistaken, but she swore there was a joy radiating from him that mystified her.

Eventually her side became uncomfortable, and she turned onto her back. He lay on his back with his eyes closed, breathing deeply. He *could* be asleep. She studied him.

The question of his magic gnawed at her. Could he really not know? Having magic had never exactly been convenient for *her*. Perhaps for an Akarian prince it was equally problematic. Or perhaps he didn't know. Either way, how sad. As a mage, he was quite pathetic.

For a moment, old fears and thoughts of her mother flitted through her mind again. Would their lives have been better if she'd been born without magic? Perhaps— no. She thrust the emotions aside. She didn't need the love of someone who would betray her own child so easily over something that Miara had no choice about. To hell with her. A shame her mother had been such an easily manipulated twit.

In Mage Hall, she had finally begun to really learn. She remembered the exhilaration she'd felt first coaxing little seeds into saplings under her father's tutelage. What would life even be like without magic? She could soar in the skies, dig into the earth, swim in the sea, capture this strong man, and control him easily. She was powerful. She had fangs, feathers, fur, fins, and everything in between. She could hear a horse's whisper and call a rose to life. She could feel this man's heart beating, his life force, deep inside her mind, the way a non-mage would hear wind outside the window—absently, constantly, without end. Imagining the world without that seemed depressingly empty.

Did he know what he was missing? Had he had a choice?

It didn't matter. He was in this situation either way, just like she was.

She hadn't been listening to him, so she stilled her thoughts and listened. Definitely asleep now. She studied the angles of his face in the dwindling firelight. His eyelids twitched a little. He was really quite handsome, as she supposed princes ought to be. She could still see his soft green eyes, the color of sage leaf or silvered elephant's ear. Who was he? Who had he been? Had other women dreamed of those eyes and remembered them fondly? Longed to be as close to him as those vines? Even... closer? Did someone even now grieve and worry for him?

What about the voice behind her on the terrace?

She forced her eyes toward the sky. It didn't matter who he was or who loved or missed him—she had no choice in this. It was best not to think about it.

She remembered Brother Sefim. He was a priest, her father's close friend, and also her teacher. Before she'd taken to the road, she'd told Sefim of her mission to kidnap the prince.

"Don't worry," she had said, trying to reassure herself more than him. "I'm sure the Akarian's a fool. All royals seem to be. Everyone they've sent me after thus far has been."

"Every single one of them a fool?" Sefim had laughed, raising an eyebrow.

"They are not the most diverse lot. I'll cling to the likelihood that this noble-born prince will be a bastard who deserves to be kidnapped." He had shaken his silvered head at her, grinning broadly. "All right, all right. No one deserves to be kidnapped. You have *no* love for my sanity, do you?"

"I have more love for your soul," he had said. "But I'm not worried about it. It is the Masters who are in the wrong here. Not you."

She smiled to herself and hoped Aven wouldn't notice. She wanted to believe Brother Sefim. But she still felt herself working magic against the Way. She still felt like *she* was very wrong. It was hard to believe she would not be punished for it, one way or another.

Was there some way to avoid such a thing? Right this wrong, short of setting him free? Although she had not chosen to kidnap him, she *could* choose whether or not she understood what she had done. Would that help? Could she punish herself with the suffering and guilt and not carry yet another debt against this man or against the Way?

And if she could understand, could she stand the pain of it?

The stars were coming out, and she could see them clearly now. She took a deep breath of the cold, smoky air, and she knew—painful or not, she had to understand. Tomorrow, she would ask her own questions.

The next morning, Aven awoke to discover that none of it had been a dream. It was all very real, and he was still tied to the ground by very real magical vines that didn't show any hope of letting go.

The sun had risen, but its rays didn't shine into the camp just yet. He looked toward the woman—Mara. She lay sleeping, or at least it seemed so. The fire burned low but still gave off enough heat to hold back the morning chill.

He lay for a while, listening. The wind through the trees, the birds excitedly singing the tidings of morning, the cracks and pops of the fire—all were lovely to his ears. When was the last time he'd left Estun? He couldn't remember. He shook his head. He had missed *so* much, locked inside that damn cave. He should be thanking this woman.

And what was it all for? He loved his parents, but they'd locked him in a dungeon of dark and earth and fire for years, and it hadn't even *accomplished* anything. His magic still lingered; it couldn't be choked out. He carried its burden but none of its benefits. This woman could easily control him with her power, and what could he do about it? Nothing but swirl the air around in annoyance!

Then, suddenly, something occurred to him. All his life, he'd hidden his magic, been afraid of the consequences of someone finding out that he was secretly a mage. But right now, there was no one to know, no one to be afraid of.

Maybe getting kidnapped was the best thing that had ever happened to him. And hell, that really said a lot about where he came from, didn't it.

On the other hand, he didn't think she knew he had any magic yet, and if she had bothered to kidnap him, chances were she didn't have his best interests at heart. Perhaps she was *exactly* the person he should be hiding his magic from. Not that that made him any more capable of doing it.

And besides. She was still asleep.

Now was the time to experiment. What to try? Clearly the air came naturally to him. But he had rarely tried to do something deliberately. Where to even start? And how would he know the difference between his magic and an incidental breeze at the exact same moment?

He probably couldn't, but what the hell. There were yellow, orange, and browning leaves scattering the ground. That'd be as good a place to start as any.

He turned his head to face the woman while he tried. Of course, blowing leaves near him meant he could blow them into the fire and perhaps then out of it again, alight. But, well, he would hope for the best. And perhaps they would blow onto his captor and this whole matter could be settled!

Eyeing her out of the corner of his eye, he focused on the leaves beside him. Now, how to begin?

First, he focused on them as intensely as he could. He tried to imagine pushing his mind and his will toward the leaves, or across the leaves from his head toward his toes. He tried to imagine the leaves doing what he wanted.

Nothing.

He was about ready to physically blow on them, but obviously that defeated the purpose. He visualized more carefully, closing his eyes, but he snapped his eyes open barely a moment later because, of course, how would he know if it had worked?

The leaves looked unmoved.

He kept trying for he didn't know how long, attempting every way he could imagine to use magic to move the leaves, but to no avail.

He felt disgusted with himself. What was he missing? What did he not know? Damn his parents for not even teaching him the tiniest bit. Was there a secret to it? Did he need a totem or token of some kind? Were there magic words you needed to know, like those listed in the star book? But then how would anyone have ever figured them out?

Suddenly he remembered the star map. He'd slipped it in his pocket in the library what seemed like a lifetime ago—it could still be there. Having survived that journey in his pocket would be remarkable, but he could hope. His hands and arms were hugged to his sides by the vines, but he squirmed his hand and felt the slight crunch of paper. By the ancients—it was still there. Perhaps that could help him figure something out if these guesses were fruitless.

But at the moment, tied up like a roast, guessing was his only option. He turned his head to face the woman and tried again to move the leaves.

After a while of trying, his mind wandered from its various visualizations of leaves moving. He thought of his mother's whispered lessons to him, the few things she'd tried to tell him in precious, stolen moments on the garden terrace. He remembered her arms around him, when he was younger, looking up at the stars with him, whispering, "The stars, the moon, the sun, the very air—they are all yours, Son. All yours to breathe your will." It had been important information, really, but it was also the moment his mother sounded most like what he imagined a mage to be. There was a hint in her voice of a lust for magic, for bending the power to your will. He sighed. It was a fine idea but sounded grand and silly when he couldn't even move a leaf.

And then suddenly it hit him—move a leaf! Of course. That night his mother had whispered that the *air* was his, the moon, and stars. Not the leaves. Those—did they belong to this woman sleeping nearby? To his mother? And the dirt—that wasn't his, either. Air, creature, earth. He could only control from the top of a leaf on up!

Feeling renewed, he focused again on the leaves. He took a deep breath. She seemed to be stirring, so he probably didn't have much time. Another deep breath—focus on the air, focus on the feeling of it moving, in and out, back and forth. He centered his thoughts and moved them up from the leaves to the air above them. He imagined tiny particles moving, a breeze blowing from his head toward his feet, struggling to visualize the invisible air.

A leaf twitched. Another.

Excited, his mind immediately brought forth the idea of a gust of wind flinging leaves into the air—and suddenly up they flew!

He gasped in surprise. The gust stopped abruptly, unnaturally, and the leaves tumbled straight down. Several of them hit him in the face. He almost laughed aloud at it.

He had *done* it! He grinned like a fool in spite of himself. What should he try next—a tree branch? The brambles? Sparks from the fire! What would be hard and what would be easy?

In his excitement, he forgot he was not alone.

"Well, looks like *you're* having a good morning." Her voice cut through his grin, and he turned to see her eyeing him strangely. "I can't imagine what you have to smile about."

He said nothing and just looked from her to the fire and back. She didn't answer his questions; he wouldn't answer hers if she didn't even phrase them as such.

She sat up, throwing off the furs and blankets she'd slept under. To his surprise, she'd slept with her boots on. Her bun had loosened, and she reached back and began to take it down. Locks of fiery red tumbled down her shoulders in a sudden rush, and he caught his breath. All thoughts of magic dwindled as he watched her brush through her hair with her fingers, toss it over her shoulder, and tie it back up. Luckily, he broke his eyes away before she noticed.

She stood up and stretched. Stiff as he was from not being able to move the entire night, he squinted his eyes and glared at her. She noticed and stared at him for a moment as if considering, and then she shrugged. She turned away and began rummaging in her pack, and he thought she was going to ignore him, but slowly the vines began to loosen.

They had somewhat untangled, but not completely. He was studying them when he realized she was coming toward him with a dagger. He jumped, but she gave him a look of disdain.

"You think I'd keep you alive all night just to kill you now?" she said, gripping the vines and taking the blade to them vigorously. She cut them from top to bottom in a gesture or two; he was glad it was the vines and not his stomach.

"Well, pardon me for not thinking clearly first thing in the morning," he replied. He sat up as she headed back toward her pack. His stomach gurgled. Ah, to be in the kitchen at home—eggs, bacon, oats and milk and sugar. He doubted she had any of that in her pack. And the wondrous head cook's sugar-dusted apple dumplings—that was definitely not in her pack. Would he ever taste them again?

He swallowed and watched carefully where she slid the dagger back into her pack. Perhaps that would come in handy later. But killing her was out of the question. Beyond the Code and the matter of honor, there was something about her. Instincts told him he would pay the gods if he wronged her. He had no desire to. No, he would have to focus on some kind of escape.

Miara tried to focus on choosing which of the two main roads the maps showed could take them most of the way to the Kavanar border. But something that morning flared the animal instincts in her, and she couldn't help but feel the sense that she was being watched. Each time she checked for anyone who could be studying them, she found nothing, however. And if someone was indeed watching them, why hadn't they acted after she made camp for the night?

According to the map, it looked like they could make it to a town if they rode a little farther east and then started heading south when they hit the main road. The towns would be larger than some she had passed on the way here, which would help her to fade into the background, but she hadn't seen these towns before to know anything about them. It was hard to know which road would be easier. She hoped she was choosing well.

She turned her eyes to the forest around them, but she could find no sign of any creature. The treetops seemed empty. Could it be under the ground? There was only one way to know, although she dreaded meeting mind-to-mind with anything that watched her.

She cast out a tendril of thought, feeling for life in the earth beneath them, around them. It teemed with life—insects, rodents, spiders—but nothing that cared about their presence. She worked her way up slowly— nothing, nothing—*there.*

Cleverly hiding itself in the autumn leaves, a hawk perched in a high treetop. Its mind regarded her without thought or word, aside from its mission to indeed watch her. She stood so she could partially see it through the leaves. It did not seem particularly keen on what they were doing—just knowing their general location.

The woman's voice on the balcony. Perhaps this prince wasn't the only mage they had. Although that gave her a small thrill of fear, this "spy" wasn't much of a reaction. A simple bird tracking their location? An Akarian mage knew she had their prince, and this was *it*? Or were they working toward something more?

She glanced at her captive. He was sitting cross-legged on the bedding, munching on the hardening bread and cheese she'd given him. He didn't seem worried, frightened, happy, or unhappy; he just sat, munching and staring into the fire. He was beginning to show slight stubble around his chin, which she had to admit had a handsome effect on his already-striking jaw. His skin was quite pale—probably from living in that underground fortress. How long had he lived there? And the brightness of his eyes! It made her long for him to look into hers again. But really nothing good could come of longing for that.

He was definitely an odd one. She could still see the grin she'd woken up to on his face, which disturbed her most because she couldn't explain it. Handsome as he might be, he might also be a little batty. Wouldn't be the first member of a royal family to turn out that way.

She folded up her maps and took her last bite of bread. She thought of her resolution the night before to learn who he really was. In the daylight she dreaded it more. They had a long journey, more than a four-day ride at this more careful and burdened rate—at least six, she guessed. Wouldn't there be plenty of time later to figure him out?

She shook her head at herself. Kidnapping a foreign prince—no problem. Talking to him? Now *that* was scary. Still, she did not want to know. What if he had a wife—children! By the gods, she couldn't do it. At least not this early in the morning.

She readied her things. They needed to make good time today, and she needed to find a town where she could buy a saddle from someone, preferably without too much suspicion. And all the while she'd need to keep him seeming anonymous, uninteresting, docile— and, of course, keep him from escaping at the same time.

She glanced again in the hawk's direction, then cast her mind after it. She found nothing. It was gone.

"So are you going to tell me any of your plans? I'm guessing no?" he asked suddenly, making her jump.

She stared at him, saying nothing and letting the silence stretch as a response. Perhaps she'd have her conversation whether she liked it or not.

"Clever answer. I suppose I can't blame you. But I'm at least wondering about a time frame here. I mean, how long do I have left? Hours, days? Minutes?" He was laughing as he said it, but she suspected he meant it.

She hesitated. The binding would keep her from telling him anything the Masters didn't want him to know, right? "You'll receive no harm from me unless you force my hand. I am only to transfer you to another."

That seemed vague enough.

"And then?"

"I don't know." It was true. He seemed to believe her.

"Then how far till we get to wherever you're taking me?"

"Not minutes or hours."

"Days, then. Or weeks?"

"Depends." She shrugged. He was staring at her hard, and she could see his brain churning, trying to figure out how to get her to tell him more. What did he want? Peace of mind? He wouldn't get that by actually getting answers to his questions. He looked down at his lap, still thinking but saying nothing for now.

"C'mon," she said. "Pack that up and make ready to ride. You can ask me your questions while we travel."

"I suppose you can avoid them just as well on horse-back as on foot."

She snorted, smiling. "Yes, exactly."

5 THREATS

Aven didn't ask her many more questions that day. She didn't ask him any back. They rode mostly in silence, stopping occasionally for the horses to drink and rest. From time to time, she felt sure the eyes of some creature were on her back, hawk or something else, but she couldn't catch one. They reached the next town as the sun was three fingers above the hills.

She reined their horses in and turned to him. "We'll sleep more comfortably tonight if we can make it into this town without event. I can't have you causing any disruptions or drawing attention to us, so this may be slightly uncomfortable—"

"More uncomfortable than being tied to the ground all night?" he said. By the gods, he didn't want to be a mouse in a pouch again—or whatever he'd been.

"No, but I can't have you being recognized—"

He laughed aloud at that. "There's really no danger of *that*."

"Well, I'm hardly in a position to believe *you*, am I?"

"But I've hardly ever—" He was about to fire off another snide remark, but a strange tingling, twisting sensation in his face caught him off guard. He put his hands to his face and felt—to his sudden shock and disgust—his cheeks and jaw and neck suddenly *move*. It only lasted for a moment, but his hands felt and felt. His face was no longer his own. For one thing, he had a beard.

"I told you it would be uncomfortable."

"What in the name of—"

"That won't do either."

He heard a small snapping noise, perhaps the noise of her snapping her fingers, and suddenly he could not finish his exclamation. By the gods! He tried to speak but not even a croak came out or a whisper. Just air.

She had taken his voice!

Was such a thing even possible? Had he gone mad? Shocked, he watched her cork a small jar and put it back into a purse that hung from her belt.

Damn him and his incompetence! Just what had she done?

"Now, don't make a scene, and maybe I'll give you that back at some point."

As if he hadn't been quiet enough all day! Now he regretted it and wished he had prattled on incessantly. And what was he going to do now? Even if he found a way to get free of her, what would he do without his voice?

If he could get his hands on the purse, maybe he'd find a way to get it back. Perhaps the key to these magical chains was in there, too. She would have to sleep sometime. Maybe with more people nearby he could figure something out.

She led their horses toward the small village. A few low buildings clustered together with gardens and fields around them. The town was likely little more than a gathering point for folks from surrounding farms and cabins to trade and socialize. Of course, he knew about the larger cities of Akaria and had briefly visited those a few times, but towns like these he'd never seen. A shame, really, if he was to be their king someday. Perhaps that was one silver lining to this gray cloud.

The horses walked calmly down the road into the center of town. The buildings were run-down and old, but colorful fall leaves decorated windowsills and flower boxes. Some residents had gathered the leaves into lovely wreaths hung on doors. The streets were mostly empty of all but the brisk autumn wind, but the chimneys puffed welcoming black smoke that said there were people and warmth and hot food inside.

His stomach gurgled. He hadn't realized he was so hungry. But the smell of the fire and food cooking tantalized him.

She was leading them toward a building where other horses were tied. A painted sign hung from some ironwork that read: Twisted Oak Inn.

She dismounted and tied their horses, giving him a hard look as she did. To his shock, her own face was transformed, but at the same time he could still recognize her. Her hair was streaked with white, and her skin was creased and wrinkled with age. Her eyes were green. But he could still see the face he'd discovered in the garden.

Was it really her face? Or just another disguise? It hadn't occurred to him until now that perhaps her beauty was designed to distract or hide her true identity or even attract him. For all he knew, she was far uglier. Or far more beautiful. Really, there was nothing about her he could know for sure, even the name she'd given him.

She was glaring at him now, but in his surprise, he just stared at her, realizing how little he knew and trying to adjust to her new face.

Get off the horse.

He gasped and shakily dismounted without consciously choosing to. She had spoken into his thoughts—how? By now, just how little he knew was starting to terrify him.

Follow me, she said now. *And like I said, don't make a scene. It should be obvious what we need to do. We just need a room. Which will be far better than vines on the ground, but we can do that if you prefer.*

He shook his head. She nodded. He was learning more about magic every minute, but he hadn't imagined it to be such a shocking process. He followed her into the inn.

The air was thick with smoke and loud conversation, and light was dim inside the inn. He followed her to the innkeeper's desk near the entrance. The tavern was packed with people and smelled like it; he was tempted to hold his breath.

"A room, please," she said. Her voice, too, was older, gravelly. "My son and I need refuge for the night."

"Of course, ma'am," the innkeeper said with a smile. He had friendly, twinkling eyes and a thick brown mustache that reminded Aven of Tepolt, the cellar master, and gave him a pang of longing to be back at home.

A stray bit of wind whipped leaves around the floor beneath them. Strange, since the door was shut tight and the place was far too warm to have drafts all about. What could it be?

Oh no, he'd been thinking of home. Was that him? As he felt a shot of fear mixed with embarrassment at the idea, the leaves whipped around again. It was definitely him. Him and his cursed, stupid magic with a will of its own. Hopefully she wouldn't notice.

"Stable your horses? Would you like supper, too?"

"Yes to the horses." Mara glanced at the packed tavern room with clear hesitation. But he hoped she would want a hot meal as much as he did. She looked back at the innkeeper. "All right. We've got to eat. Two meals and two ales. What's cheap?"

She paid him her coin in exchange for two rabbit stews. Then she moved toward the most private table in an emptier corner. Although there were still several drunks nearby, they looked to be the type that kept to themselves.

Mara and Aven sat and drank their ale, obviously not saying much. He toyed with things he might have said. So, should we rob them all now or later? My, that fellow next to us looks very ugly, don't you think? This town isn't good enough for you, Mother! Where did you stash our treasure again? Do you think the bounty hunters will catch us?

He hoped that last one was at least a little bit true.

Hmm, yes, she was probably right to silence him. He smiled wryly to himself. The things he could have said! My, you're a crazy mage, kidnapping a prince—any of you subjects want to help me out here? I'm going to be your king, you know. What, you wouldn't recognize your prince from a mute fool? What kinds of subjects are you! And what kind of a prince do you have that you wouldn't even recognize him if he weren't transformed by a witch?

Well, now he just felt like shit. He hadn't gotten himself into this situation, but it was entirely his and his parents' fault that he had such little ability to get out of it.

"Hey—you, lady," said the drunk next to them. "That yer man there?"

She shook her head, her eyes hard as steel.

"Who are you then, man?" said the drunk to him.

Aven, of course, could not respond. He only stared at the man, hoping his gaze was as steely and cold as hers was.

"He's my son," she said.

"And you answer all his questions still? You're old to be treated like an infant, don't ya think, man?"

Aven looked into his ale, hoping the man would shut up. Mara, too, looked toward the fireplace, trying to disengage.

"Not much of a man, are ya?" the drunk leered. Aven's eyes flicked to him without intending to, and the man grinned, waiting for a retort. Aven studied his ale. "My, not even a word outta ya. You must be quite the whip, lady, to keep him in line like that."

You have *no* idea, Aven thought. If all mothers had shackles and magic, children in general might be better behaved. Aven caught himself smirking at his own joke and straightened his expression. He was finding far too much entertainment in his captivity.

"Look at the fool smirk—see he knows it! Well, if you got no man, then you oughta spend the night with me, then!" He slid toward her from his seat, then circled his hand around her neck and pulled her face toward his, perhaps trying to kiss her.

A gust of wind knocked over the drunk's ale, spilling it down onto his leg. Another blew out the candles on the wall above them. Confused, the man tried to right his ale, missing entirely the dagger Mara had drawn. Aven watched her slip it back into her bodice, unnoticed by anyone but him. The others were too busy looking around for the source of the wind. The door was shut tight, and no one had recently entered.

Smaller tendrils of wind whipped in tiny vicious bursts around the room, nipping at the candles, the fireplace, grizzled beards. The drunk frowned at his wet pant leg, and Aven again found himself smirking. He straightened his expression as soon as he realized it. Served him right, though. Mara might be his captor, but Aven was still a knight, and such behavior he would not abide.

The man locked his eyes with Aven's, his glare growing more angry and suspicious by the minute. Aven stared back. The light in the room flickered as a blast of air threatened the fire.

"You're too drunk for your own good if you can't keep your ale upright," Mara said suddenly. "Do I need to call the innkeep?" The drunk grudgingly turned his eyes from Aven to Mara, still suspicious.

Thankfully, the stew arrived. The barmaid came between the two tables, breaking the tension slightly, and Aven hunkered over the stew and shoveled. Damn, he'd been hungry.

The air in the room continued to misbehave. Usually, at home, he would try to still his thoughts and calm himself until whatever was motivating his magic to misbehave was cleared from his mind. But not this time. Why should he? For once, he didn't have to. For once, there was no one to stop him from letting his magic do as it pleased. And... it was strangely exhilarating.

He stifled a laugh. But it was damn funny. Now that he was in shackles, he felt freer than ever. Perhaps magic was more a part of him than he'd realized. It felt good to let it run wild, even if it was making this drunk suspicious of them. He couldn't prove anything. What could he do? Leer? He glanced at Mara's older face as she took a sip of ale. She was staring at him, a complex and unreadable expression in her eyes.

No number of years she could add would hide the beauty of her face. But he did miss her dark, brooding eyes. The white streaks in her hair gave her a wild, exotic look, and he had a feeling that the world-weariness in those wrinkles might be true to her soul, if not her face.

They finished their stew and retired to their room without a word.

The room held two low beds next to a warm, roaring fire. Aven headed straight for one of the beds and sat down in hope of somehow claiming it rather than the floor. The innkeeper brought them a pitcher of hot water for the basin. He ran his fingers over the rough but reassuring blankets folded at the foot of the bed, amused to watch the shackles slide over them, jarring against the brown linens. Nothing like the blankets at home.

When the innkeeper had left them and Mara had thoroughly locked and barred the door, she turned and glared hard at him. "I *told* you not to make a scene!"

He opened his mouth to try to answer but then looked at her flatly and shrugged. Of course nothing could come out.

"That was stupid. Moronic! What did you think that was going to accomplish?"

He shrugged again and looked at her, puzzled. What was she talking about?

"Damn drunks. Damn ale. Shouldn't have had any myself. Maybe that was it—was it the ale talking?"

He stared at her blankly, unsure what she was even saying at this point.

Even more irritated, she grabbed the bottle from the pouch, hastily yanked off the cap, and tossed its invisible contents in his direction, as though she were throwing water in his face. With a strange sort of thud, his throat felt suddenly heavier. He coughed, testing it.

"I can't wait to be done with you," she said. "You're going to get me killed."

"What are you *talking* about?" he finally choked out.

She shook her head at him in disgust, hands on her hips. "You are a fool."

"A fool!"

"A damned fool." She sat down on the other bed with her back toward him and jerked her boots off roughly, kicking them against the wall. "Going to get me killed."

"Well, then let me go."

She glowered at him. "Nice try. Not going to happen."

"Why not? If I'm such an idiot, you'd be better off rid of me, don't you think?"

"Don't waste your breath." Her stare was even icier at him than at the drunk.

"Why are you doing this?" he demanded.

She said nothing.

"Isn't there something I can do—something I can get you? Something I can trade for my freedom?" She sat still, watching the fire. She didn't reply or turn to meet his gaze. "Look, I don't know what I've done to be a fool, so I'm not likely to stop unless you tell me."

That got her attention. She twisted and stared wide-eyed, incredulous. Then she snorted and rose, heading to the window and surveying the street.

"C'mon, be sensible. You'll never get away with this," he said, trying to sound practical.

"Really? Is that a threat or your attempt at an observation?" She shook her head at him again. "You know nothing about me. How can you even dare to say that? Would you care to make a bet on it?"

"No. Gambling is against the Code." She looked away from him and back out the window. "You've kidnapped a prince, you realize. It's not like no one will notice I've disappeared."

"Oh, damn, what a mistake this has all been! I was trying to find the court jester and mistook *you* for him—imagine that." She rolled her eyes.

Finally, *some* confirmation of something. It was *because* he was a prince that she'd captured him. "I'm just trying to say, they are going to look for me."

"Hadn't occurred to me," she laughed.

"What can I give you?" he demanded. The question was on the table now, he might as well push it to its furthest conclusion. "If you're looking for something, Akaria will find it for you. Whatever someone is paying you, we can make it more. There has to be *something* that motivates you. If there's some wrong I've committed, I'll right it. What is it that you are after?"

She stared him dead in the eye for a long time, face filled with the strangest sadness and almost... was that despair? She shook her head. "My enemy is not you, Prince. It is within me, and there is nothing you can do to free me from it. There is no money that will buy it off or jewels that will sway it. There is nothing you can do. Give up on it."

Her voice was dark and emotional and told him so little while suggesting so much. What could she mean?

"We have mages in Akaria, too, you know. They will be coming for you." Now his voice was half threat, half warning.

She barked a laugh. "I'm *shaking* in my boots."

His every dart glinted off her armor easily, and it was starting to piss him off. "You don't have *on* any boots. And my mother is a mage—she *will* find you—" He stopped, horrified.

She turned, smiling with pleasant surprise at his mistake. "Is that so! Well, that explains why *you're* a mage but not why you're such a terribly bad one."

He gasped. She knew—she knew! How could she know? Did *everyone* so easily figure this out? It didn't even feel like much of a secret anymore! The air must have given him away. Of course. How could he not have remembered to hide himself? She was right, he *was* a fool, but she didn't know the half of it.

"Oh, don't look so shocked. The whole damn village probably knows after your little stunt down there! We'll be lucky if they only try to shun and ignore us. More likely they'll try to kill us. Of all the stupid ways to try to draw attention—"

"I wasn't trying to draw attention."

"Then what were you *trying* to do? I inclined to just leave now and ride all night. Stupid! You're lucky they have our coin already." She strode angrily toward the hearth, hands in fists on her hips. She folded her arms and leaned against the wall, facing away from him, staring into the fire. The firelight gave the outline of her body a golden halo of light, silhouetting her curves. He became strangely aware that they were alone in the room together, of how far away she was, of the sound of her breath above the crackling of the fire. Damn, she'd kick him if she realized how he was staring at her, but he couldn't help himself.

"The man was out of line. It's against my Code to tolerate such behavior. But it... it wasn't intentional," he said.

She turned and eyed him over her shoulder. She didn't believe him.

"I can't control it." He hesitated, trying to figure out how to convince her and sound sincere, though there was really no way to force someone to believe you, especially if they couldn't trust a word you said. He groped for words. "Really, I can't. Whether it would have been a good idea to get me free of you or not, that wasn't an idea of mine. I can't stop it." He paused, trying to gauge her reaction, but she revealed nothing. "It's been like that all my life. It's not an easy secret to keep."

She made a disgusted noise in the back of her throat. "You can't even *stop* a spell? Unbelievable! Well, I'm sure these Akarian mages of yours will be quite formidable. They're going to kill me with a blink if their training is at the high level of yours!"

"Training! I don't *have* any training," he snapped, trying to keep his voice plain but failing. "There is no training for mages in Akaria." Oh, by the gods was he stupid. Another thing he should not have said. Few people made him this agitated. He was getting sloppy. It also upset him to realize she was right—they would have little defense against her. How could they be so ill prepared to not have some way to defend against this scenario? Once he was back in Estun, he would have to start forming such a force immediately.

"How can there be no training?"

"I'm supposed to be *king*. Kings aren't supposed to be mages." He took a deep breath and was irritated to hear it come out ragged.

She glared at him, furious for some reason. "Oh, how *inconvenient* for you."

"You have *no* idea," he spat back at her, for the first time a real edge of anger in his voice.

"Yes, I damn well do."

What could that possibly mean? He met her glare with his own furrowed brow. Her eyes softened as the moments passed. They were both mages. Why was being born a mage always such a curse, it seemed? Were the zealots right that magic was against the Way of Things? No, they couldn't be.

"Do you think I asked for this? I didn't ask to be born a mage, or a king, and certainly not both."

She turned to look back at the fire, saying nothing for a while. Then, eventually, she said, "None of us have ever asked for this. And yet it is what we are."

The silence stretched on, but the air was charged with intense emotion—was it grief? Despair? Something worse?

"Listen," he said. "I don't know if you can believe me. But I didn't realize I was putting us in any danger. I wasn't plotting anything to get free. I just didn't like the way he was looking at you."

That was the truth. It wasn't the Code or the intoxicating freedom of being able to let his magic run wild. At a deeper level, seeing the drunk leer at her made him want to break the man's legs. Or neck.

She said nothing. How could she just stand there? He was laying himself out on the table, and she just stared coldly, analyzing, never letting her guard down.

Then something insane leapt into his mind. "Look, you want to keep that from happening again?"

"Yes."

"Then teach me."

"Excuse me?"

"You don't want me calling attention? Then you're going to have to teach me enough to stop my own spells."

Her mouth hung open in surprise; she said nothing, eyes searching his face.

He shrugged. "Otherwise, this is just going to continue."

She met his eyes, frowning now, stare icy and hard, cutting into him as if she wished to see into his soul. Perhaps she could see into it, for all he knew.

"You're an obstinate fool," she said. Then, after a while, "I will think about it."

Miara decided to let him sleep more freely that night, binding him to the bed with the saddle chain. It wouldn't be as comfortable as sleeping normally, but it had to be a great improvement. She had to balance security and her own rest with keeping him from getting any more belligerent.

She had readied herself for sleep and directed him to do the same, and now she sat in the bed, listening, thinking. He appeared to be trying to go to sleep, but from his breathing, he was awake. Intentionally or unintentionally, she wasn't sure.

She'd been furious after the encounter with the drunken villager, but really, she had been angry at herself. She'd just taken it out on him. She had known that there could be a problem, and sure enough, there had been. Her instincts had told her not to go into the room, but she'd done it anyway. Out of hunger or a longing for mere comfort, she'd endangered her mission.

And, of course, it was safer to take his voice, but there was no finesse to it at all. So heavy-handed on her part. Of course, the day she tried it, that would be the day someone would talk to him and make a scene. She could have gone with a more complex spell, restricting the things he could say. Perhaps to only yes, no, or maybe. That could work for tomorrow. There were so many other ways; she just hadn't thought about it very hard. She could have given one of them some kind of

grotesque disguise that scared people away. Or transformed him into her pet dog, perhaps, although that
would take more energy, and he probably wouldn't
be too happy. And she wouldn't be able to sustain it
overnight or indefinitely, and then folks would wonder
where the mysterious man in dirty silk robes had come
from. If she were a stronger mage or had a shorter road
ahead of her, she could easily dominate his thoughts
with a barrage of commands, especially with his lack
of training. But beyond the fact that that would be
exhausting, she had no desire to use such horrible tactics. It was the kind of thing the mages in the Dark Days
had done, the kind of unbalanced use of magic that had
gotten them all into this mess.

How could she even try to keep any semblance of
honor when she was kidnapping a man and probably
dragging him to his death? But there were so many
things she had no choice about. When she *did* have a
choice, she was going to make the right one.

And now she sat, waiting. She was sure the drunk,
or someone like him, would make some kind of move
tonight. The question was when. She was ready for
them now. Let it be soon, she thought, exhausted. She
would pass the time by thinking of a way not to kill any
attackers—and how to get some sleep if they waited till
the wee hours of the morning to make the attempt.

Aven was still awake. She listened to his breathing again, then returned to her planning. Her options for sprouting defenses were pretty limited by the cleanliness of the inn and the room's position on the second floor. Many animals and plants would draw far too much attention. The most peaceful option would be to transform the two of them into something tiny when the villagers came so that they'd be too confused to even realize what had happened. Still, there was risk in that, too. Vanishing from the room would be a confirmation that they were mages, and the villagers might spot their tiny transformed selves and kill them more easily with the squash of a boot, especially Aven, who would likely be too inexperienced as another type of being to successfully run and hide. As a creature mage, she had few weapons in her arsenal now that the villagers had seen their faces and knew where they were.

Footsteps out in the hallway. She tensed and tightened her grip on the handle of her dagger, but the footsteps kept going. A door up the hall opened and shut.

That left smaller, more common animals as her only allies. Hearing no one nearby, she swept the house with her senses. A few mice and rats—as most inns had—many people with no magical talent whatsoever, and then finally in the kitchen, she found a cat.

Perfect.

She whispered to it, musical bits of thought, greeting, warming it to her presence. It was curious. It liked the attention. Ah, cats could always be counted on for both of those traits. She reached out to it more and discovered it was a big orange tomcat, relatively neglected but very proud of his dominion over the tavern. Then, ever so politely, she asked him to check if the drunk was still drinking in the tavern room.

Sharing his eyes for a few moments, the tom strode proudly into the tavern room. He dodged a few feet as he skirted the room, scouting. When he found their corner, the drunk was still there.

Will you watch this man for me? she whispered to the cat. She used images and thoughts more than words because they were what the cat himself used. *Follow him to see if he goes anywhere? Warn me if he moves? Do this, and I'll tell you where the mice are hiding.*

The cat curled up in the corner of the tavern room, standing guard. She was sure he would have done it without the offer of mice, as he was quite the curious and bored little beast. But that just didn't feel right. It was not the Way to simply bend him to her will without offering something in exchange.

Settling back into her own eyes, she opened them and turned toward the prince.

He appeared to be sleeping now. He lay on his back, arms over his head where she had chained them. He didn't look much like most of the mages she had always known. His muscled body was stocky and hardened from effort. A warrior more than a mage. What was this Code he spoke of? Did he really know anything about fighting, if he knew nothing about magic? He sure *looked* like he could fight. The only mages she knew that looked like that were the ones who worked on farms or in the smithy.

His bargaining and threats were only logical; she should have expected them. What was far more surprising was how unafraid he appeared and how comfortable around her. He was always at ease. That made him seem more royal and princely than anything else, even that kingly face of his. He knew his strength, and he owned the air around him, perhaps too much so. It was refreshing. Of course, he was impetuous and had the magical skills of a three-year-old, but her annoyance at that was wearing off and fading back into pity.

He offered her an interesting proposition. Teaching him some ability to control his magic did seem useful. Of course, it was probably the opposite of what the Masters would *want* her to do, but that made it all the more enticing. Especially because her brand did not burn and her thoughts did not tremble at the idea. It seemed to know that he was right, and teaching him truly would help her on the mission. His wild magic was a danger and made stealth in any populated area much more difficult.

If the brand would let her, and if they made it through the night, she'd teach him something in the morning. What was the first magic her father had taught her, before the Devoted Knights had come, before they'd become slaves? Where should she start?

She reached back to the tomcat. The drunk was still there, getting drunker. But he was talking to two friends now. The tom could not hear what they were saying.

Well, she knew where he was, but that didn't help her do anything beyond killing the bastard if he attacked. There *had* to be some other way, but nothing was coming to mind. She so often relied on evasion and hiding that she feeling underprepared for a direct confrontation. She sighed. This *was* her first kidnapping; she shouldn't be so hard on herself.

She spread her thoughts again, this time out of the house, up into the sky and fields around the inn. Not many people out in the town. A few more cats, plenty of rodents and insects and the like, squirrels, their horses in the stable.

And then—a bat! Just what she was looking for.

Rising, she opened the tiny window and whispered to the bat to come. After a few moments, a terrifying flutter of wings caused her to duck in spite of herself as the bat swooped inside. Bats had always struck her as intelligent, and this one proved no different. He landed and hung by the door as if he understood what she wanted without a verbal request. She shut the window most of the way but left a large crack open in case the bat needed to get out without her. The cold autumn air smelled fresher than the room anyway.

Well, it wouldn't be a defense, but at least it would be a warning. And perhaps the bat would scare the hell out of anyone opening the door long enough to stall them until she'd gotten her eyes open. And then she'd kill them, unless a better idea came to her in a dream. Because for now, she had to get some rest. There was no point sitting there staring at the door, wishing for a peaceful way to end someone.

Dagger in its sheath under her pillow, she got into the bed. The linens were quite soft compared to the rough outer blanket, to her surprise. She reached back to the tomcat briefly; the drunk was still leering at his two companions. Perhaps he'd get so drunk he'd forget their encounter. Or perhaps not. She closed her eyes and quickly fell asleep.

Aven woke to—of all things—the sound of a bat screeching and the drunk man from earlier that evening shouting and pounding on the door. He sat up quickly, caught himself on the chain, and twisting awkwardly to sitting.

He glanced at Mara, hoping to the gods that she was awake. She was already on her feet, blade in hand.

This could not be good.

"Unchain me," he demanded. She ignored him.

Instead, Mara launched herself at the door just as the drunk flung the bat against the wall, where it fell lifelessly to the ground. She'd probably aimed to just push him out of the room, but instead, she smashed him between the door and its frame. He screamed, clawing at her with one hand.

Aven yanked the chain; it held hard to the bed. But the frame was wood. He was probably strong enough to break it. He heaved harder, holding his hands closer first and then lunging to build momentum.

The intruder got her by the hair and swung her around, freeing himself and throwing her to the ground. She was on her feet quickly.

"Get out," she said. "The Balance will come upon you if you hurt us." The traditional phrase, a measure of warning and a measure of curse rolled into one.

He slammed the door shut with one hand and scoffed at her. "The Balance! Religious horse shit." His words were slurred, but not much. "The Balance will come upon *you* for harboring a mage! Or has he already turned you into his puppet?" He pointed at Aven.

Try as he could, the bedpost held strong as an oak. Maybe she'd fortified it, too, or something. Maybe he could kick it apart?

"He's not a mage; you're just intoxicated," she insisted. She was not a good liar, but either way he doubted the drunk would've bought it.

"Shut up," the drunk said, slurring again. "What's he doin'—stuck to the bed over there? Don't ya wanna help your woman?"

"Don't make me kill you," Mara said, voice suddenly sharp.

The bastard chuckled and lunged at her. She struck him with the blunt of the dagger and grappled, but she clearly did not want to stab him. She landed a good kick to his groin, which stunned him for a moment but only made him more determined.

Aven heaved again against the bedpost, but it was no use. His wrist was going to break first.

A lucky blow knocked the blade from her hand, and Aven gasped as the drunk slammed her against the wall. Her head hit the plaster with a cracking sound, and her eyes were unfocused, wide, glassy. The drunk made the best of it and groped around her hips, and now Aven could see his intentions were not just to kill them.

And what could Aven do? Sit there like a damn fool. He felt a lump of fury mixed with panic rising in his throat. What he would give for just the tiniest bit of magic he could *control*! He gave another kick to the bedpost, but without boots, he was just about breaking his foot. By the gods, what kind of wood *was* this! Damn whatever tree this bed was made from!

The trees… Suddenly, he thought of the leaves that morning and the gust of wind flinging them into the air.

Could he do that to the drunk?

Mara had regained her wits and was doing her best to fight him off. They were locked in a wrestling match at this point, and considering her smaller size, she was doing surprisingly well. But blood ran down the wall behind her head, and she did not equal the drunk in strength, even if she surpassed him in fighting skill. Aven wasn't sure how much longer she would last.

To his surprise, he realized her face and body had started to change. Her canine teeth lengthened into fangs, and her nails grew longer until they were talons suddenly digging into the flesh of his shoulder. The drunk screamed, then heaved her out from the wall and slammed her back against it. She barely grunted, digging the talons deeper into his shoulder.

He closed his eyes, trying to block out their sights and sounds. He focused on the air, felt it immediately start to move, swirling, whipping erratically this way and that. *Not* randomly, he commanded. The *man*, hit the damn *man*! But still it whipped and twisted. He couldn't focus as he heard the drunk grunt and Mara hiss. No, block it out, *focus*, he commanded himself, clutching his hands around his skull, over his ears. *Block them out.*

And for one brief second, he found the picture in his mind of the brilliant gust, saw leaves flying through powerful particles rushing from his left to his right, from one side of the room to the other.

Behind him, there was a heavy thud. He turned, hoping he wouldn't see her on the ground and bleeding.

She was still up, leaning against the wall, panting, staring at Aven. Only, her face was part human, part something else—cat-like, mouth extended and full of fang-like teeth, eyes large and almost black. The hand without talons had been completely replaced by a large, heavy paw like a panther's. Fiery red hair had sprung up as fur on her arms, shoulders, face, neck covering much of the skin he could see. Disconcerting as the combination was, it didn't scare him. It was fitting and oddly beautiful. Beneath all the disguises and secrets, there was some unavoidable truth in what he saw now—her true self when death was on the line.

The warrior in her. And she was a fine warrior, there was no doubting it. Perhaps that was why he liked her so much.

Well, well. Her fighting skills were not *exactly* what he'd estimated. He doubted he would have ever attacked her, but if he had… a creature like this, he had not been prepared for. And now he saw she could partially transform into many different animals. Could his mother do this as well? And he could barely manage a single gust of wind.

And yet, it had done the trick. The man lay unconscious on the floor.

Glancing back at her, her face had become her own again and the talons had receded, but the fur and paw remained. She was staring at him, panting, seemingly shocked. Her eyes held much emotion that he couldn't quite decode.

"Did I…?" he asked her, hope hanging on what she said next in spite of himself.

She nodded, seemingly speechless. The fur was half gone now.

"I wasn't lying to you today, I *swear*," he said, realizing she might think his earlier claims were a lie. "That's only the second time I've done that in my life. I swear to you!" He probably shouldn't admit his weakness to her; she could just exploit it. But wasn't he thoroughly under her control already? What difference did it make? It was freeing to be able to admit his lack and even talk about magic openly in the first place. "I just couldn't bear it, since it was my fault he showed up here in the first place—"

"You saved me," she said, a little incredulous.

"Yes." Of course he had saved her. How could he not?

"You didn't have to," she said.

"Yes, I did," he replied flatly. "The Code, remember?" But it was obvious that was not the reason. Clearly, he needed to work on his skill at deception.

She came around to his front and sank down on one knee, placing her hand over his. All animal traces had faded now.

"Thank you, Aven," she said. "I believe you." Then she rose and strode to the opposite wall, kneeling down where the bat had fallen.

Aven found he was breathing strangely hard, and his hand felt cold where her fingers had left his. As far as he could remember, it was the first time she'd ever said his name. His mind seized on it, savored the sound of her voice, tucked it away for later.

Oh, damn, he was a fool. Of all the stupid, moronic things he could do. His heart was pounding, blood racing as an idea both horrible and wonderful slowly dawned on him. He glanced over his shoulder and felt the thrill in his veins at the sight of her.

Oh, no. Oh, by the gods. What an idiot he was.

Of all the women he could fall for, he had picked the one that was probably going to kill him.

A high-pitched squeak broke through his thoughts— and he ducked instinctively as the bat lurched into the air and out of the slightly open window. Mara rose and stepped back to the drunk.

"The bat—did you bring it back to life?"

"I only healed him. He was unconscious, not dead. He did us a great service."

Aven nodded as she bound and gagged the drunk. Then she took the heavy blanket from her bed and threw it over the shallowly breathing body.

She stood, put her hands on her hips, and regarded her efforts. "Think that'll hold him?" she asked, looking at Aven over her shoulder.

He grinned in reply, beaming like a stupid schoolboy.

She strode to the window and looked out. "That'll muffle him for a time when he wakes up, but I think you knocked him out pretty good. It's still dark. Hopefully, with the alcohol, he'll be out for a while. Let's try to get a bit more rest, but we gotta get out of here first thing in the morning. Might as well get our money's worth."

They both lay back down, but neither fell asleep. Images kept flashing through his mind—of the drunk attacking her, of her strange animal form, of her hand over his.

"Oh, also—are you still awake?" she said suddenly.

"Yes," he said, opening his eyes. He turned his face toward her. They were side by side, face to face, almost as if lying together.

But she was all business. "In the morning, I'll teach you," she said. "At least a little. We can't have *that* happening again."

She wasn't a particularly good liar, either, it seemed. That was obviously not her real reason. Did that mean this was the first time he'd heard her lie? She was trying to pass it off as a practicality, but her tone revealed it was also a reward—for saving her, for even trying to save her. Or at least, he thought he could hear that in her voice.

He rolled away from her, smiling, and closed his eyes.

6   THE PURSUIT OF MAGIC

Of course, Miara didn't sleep any more after all that. But she needed the time to just breathe, meditate, recover from the chaos. She needed to recharge her powers to face the day. She listened to the fire crackle, Aven's breathing. The drunk in the corner didn't make a sound, and she refused to worry over him. He shouldn't have mocked the Balance. That was the Way; it was fitting that he should end up tied up on the floor. Where were the Devoted and priests now to convince her that it was right for this man to attack them? If one believed that magic was inherently against the Way, then yes, perhaps it followed that any act to control or end magic would not unbalance the world.

But how could Miara—or anyone—believe that? As if killing could sometimes be right. As if the end justified the means. Magic was more like the wind, the ocean, the seasons, her breath—it was just a part of the world. Her brand burned lightly at the idea. But no one ever declared that the wind or the sun or the mountains were evil. And since the king had enslaved the mages and handed them over to the Masters, had the world gotten any better? No. If anything, it had gotten worse. She shook her head, thinking of Brother Sefim again. He was the only priest who spoke any sense. What she wouldn't give to talk with him again right now. Sefim had always been the one to reassure her, to insist that she wouldn't be forever in debt to the Balance for these wrongs on behalf of the Masters. She wasn't entirely convinced, but she would have welcomed the sound of his voice now. He was the only priest she could respect, though, as the rest were nothing but fountains of hatred and self-loathing.

Finally the brand burned a little too much, and she let the thoughts slip away. She glanced at the window. The light of dawn was turning the sky to a deep indigo. They might as well get started; she was rested enough.

She rose and got some food for them from her pack. Aven, of course, was also awake. She ate briefly, washed her face and neck in the washbasin, and began packing her things. She gave him a few moments with the basin and fire as well, finally unchaining him from the bed. He stretched—as well as he could with the shackles—and then, fairly quickly, they were on their way. Well, her way. But she felt quite sure he didn't want to stay in that inn any longer than she did. They left the drunk behind on the floor, untied, unconscious, but breathing.

They took to the road as the sky was brightening to an overcast white. They saw no one. Few townspeople seemed to have stirred; it'd be a while before anyone found the drunken lout in their room.

"It just occurred to me," he said in the quiet morning air, "that there must have been others in the inn. The innkeeper, other guests. They must have heard him, right?" He stopped, letting the silence speak for him.

She nodded. "Yes. They let him come."

"The question is, do they suspect he succeeded or failed?"

She shrugged. "Maybe they're not sure. Maybe they don't care. Maybe they think he succeeded. Best to get out of here, whichever way, and be more careful next time."

He nodded.

As they rounded a bend and were out of sight of the town, a question finally struck her that she wasn't afraid to ask him. They'd skirted the subject, but they might as well face it head-on.

"Why weren't you trained?"

He said nothing for a moment.

"If I'm to teach you anything, I must know at least that."

He shrugged awkwardly, looking nervous now. Self-conscious or secretive? "Like I said, I'm to be king. Kings need to know battle, economics, military history, diplomacy. Not magic."

"So, just out of neglect? No one ever bothered? Or were you just too busy to get around to it?"

He glared at her. "No. People don't know. I certainly wouldn't have told you about it, but turns out you already knew. No one knows there's anything to neglect."

She frowned. "Mages would know. You said your mother was a mage. Surely she knew."

He nodded, saying nothing.

"And still you learned nothing?"

"She feared for me more, and for the kingdom. She gave up most of the practice of magic when she married my father. It was a hard decision for her, but they were—and still are—very much in love. She has tried to sneak me a few tidbits from time to time, in secret, when we were alone." He paused, measuring his next words carefully. "I... I've heard it is a very bad thing to have magic in Kavanar, though never in much detail. That's the way Kavanar prefers it, I'm sure. So I don't know what it's been like for you, but it's not popular to have magic in Akaria. It is mostly kept secret. There are no open teachers of magic."

She paused, frowning. "I would think a king or queen could do whatever they wished."

"Perhaps we could. We didn't try to find out. We're caretakers, not plowmen or slave drivers. Our service is not about me or my needs, but about what the people need. If it had seemed like they needed my magic, well, perhaps we would have tried. That has not seemed to be the case."

He puffed up his chest a little with pride. He deserved to be proud of such a stance. To have power but know its purpose… that was a rare thing. But there was even more to what he said that she couldn't quite articulate. Her life was dominated by plowmen, and she was cattle, as her brand attested. He was more different than she could have ever guessed.

"To tell you the truth, they hoped my magic would not emerge or that it would fade away," he said into her long silence. "But it did not cooperate."

She could not help but scowl at that. "Fade away? You are an air mage—have you been told at least that much?" she asked.

"Yes."

"Do you know what an air mage can do?"

He sighed, then fidgeted. Of course, he was thinking through his answer. Admitting any lack here was weakness that she as his captor could exploit. But how could he not admit it if he wanted teaching from her? And she could see he wanted it very much. Who wouldn't? This was working out quite well for her, really. She could find out quite a bit of useful information. But in return, she would make him not quite as weak as before. And while that might be a bad idea from some angles, she did not care.

"No," he said. "Not really. Definitely blowing drunk men into walls. Swishing at leaves and candle flames seem to be my specialty. That's about the end of my knowledge."

She nodded, thinking. Now came the part where he was the one that benefited. Should she tell him what they could do? She doubted he could attempt most spells without training; air magic was notoriously hard to learn because magic required seeing things so clearly in your head, and things like light and air were themselves invisible. How does one picture something that's invisible? But he had developed some magic on his own in spite of this. If any mage could learn these spells on their own, chances were in his favor.

"I won't tell you everything, at first," she said, deciding as she spoke. "The first spells are the best place to start. You already know about calling the wind. Air mages are also prized for their ability to ignite fire. Calling fog can be a useful tool for hiding, which may come in handy for us."

He looked deep in thought. "Oh! Oh. That was the bit about the fire, then. I… see. You knew even then."

She nodded. "I knew the first moment I saw you."

He cursed under his breath. "How many others…" he whispered, perhaps to himself.

They rode in silence for a while.

"So what causes this vigilante magic of yours?" she asked sometime later. "If you're not causing it to happen, is it random, or is there some logic to it?"

"It seems related to intense emotion of any kind—joy, anger, irritation, fear—but once in a while, it seems unrelated to anything."

Of course! He was like a child. Magic running wild like wolves in the hills. How could she have not seen that sooner? There were few children at Mage Hall, and nearly all of them arrived after their magic had surfaced on its own. She'd seen a woman pregnant three times in all her years there. Children were not something most mages wanted, her father being one notable exception. Why bring another into the service of the Masters? Why create another mage just to do their will? The greatest act of rebellion would be to let themselves die out—then who would the Masters have to order around and exploit? She sighed. So much darkness in her heart that even a child was just a symbol of suffering or rebellion.

When the occasional child was enslaved beyond the age of seven or eight, their unchecked powers could wreak havoc until they learned to control them. The havoc was likely what had brought them to Mage Hall in the first place. Luha had not been like that. She'd always had a masterful command of her powers but had simply gotten caught using them. Miara wondered suddenly how Luha was doing in her absence. How were her horses? Her father? Sefim? Depressing as Mage Hall was, she missed their faces.

"I'm making more sense of this now. Sometimes young mages do this. I've never known any as old as you are without training, so it didn't occur to me. You're also stronger now than if you were a little one, so it's not the same."

He nodded. Was he blushing? "So what you're saying is I'm a child. Magically, at least."

"Well… I wasn't going to put it that way."

He shook his head and laughed.

"Now, I'm not sure about this, but… chances are that you *are* calling the wind, but you're just not very conscious of doing so. Maybe if you become more familiar with how to call, you will be able to sense when you are doing it and stop or avoid doing it at all. There are also the ebbs and flows of energy. You are expending energy each time. Do you feel any sensation like that?"

"No," he said. "I don't think so."

"Well, maybe we can start there. We've got a ways to ride before a break and some food, but when we do stop, we'll try something."

He only nodded, a small smile touching his lips that lasted up and down the next several hills. For a man who'd been kidnapped, he seemed very content.

She must just be an excellent captor. The Masters could learn a thing or two from her.

He was downright antsy by the time they stopped the horses for a small break and a bite to eat.

Thank the gods for that stupid drunken man. He wouldn't have convinced Mara of this need otherwise. To think, of all the years he'd spent in safety with his parents, now that he was being dragged across Akaria against his will, he would finally be free to learn some magic.

He could not deny how thrilled he felt. What was the prospect of ruling a kingdom compared to blowing a twig twenty feet in the air! Damn, he was stupid. But ruling Akaria was never something he'd been asked if he wanted to do, just as he'd never been asked if he wanted to learn about his own magic. Really, nothing about his life had been up to him. His parents were kind, and Akarians were deserving, so he had gone along. What else would he do anyway? And he had a responsibility, just as his father before him. So he'd never put much thought into not doing what was expected of him.

But now he faced the very real possibility that he would not become king. Current kidnapping predicament aside, his magic was not going anywhere, and they couldn't keep it a secret forever. Beyond that, he was indeed in quite a predicament. Add to that fact that he certainly hadn't seen the slightest opportunity to escape from Mara yet, his chances of returning and taking the throne grew weaker with each horse's hoof beat.

He knew somewhere in his mind that this could not end well. The despair in her eyes the night before when he'd tried to bargain with her—there was something cold and dark at the end of this road. But some part of him insisted on being irrational. In this moment, the sun warmed his skin, broken by streaked shadows of tree branches overhead, and the forest air smelled amazing in his lungs. A clearly smart, fierce woman rode by his side, and soon he would be learning magic from her. What did he have to complain about?

As the sun approached its zenith, they reached a small bridge shaded by tall oaks, and she decided it was time to stop. She took some bread and cheese from the saddlebags and handed it to him, and then she led the horses down to the river to drink. She didn't watch him; he didn't try to run. Why should he? Certainly, she could stop him easily, and beyond that, he had less reason to than ever. She offered him something he'd been searching for in Estun but could not find there. Should he run back to be a bad potential king instead? He felt a moment of guilt. Perhaps this was just an excuse to shirk his duty. But no. With no control of his magic, he was basically unfit for everything. Long overdue to change that.

Also, if he escaped, that would mean never seeing her again. And… he wasn't ready for that just yet.

The horses were drinking. She strode uphill from the riverbank to where he sat, back against a tree trunk. Her strong, lithe frame tempted his eyes; he tried to keep them fixed on her face or the horses.

"Ready?" she said, arriving at the tree with a boyish, mischievous grin.

"For what, exactly?" Saying yes would be too easy.

"For your first lesson. I will drain some energy from you—a great deal, quickly—to give you the feeling of it, make it obvious. So. Ready?" She sat down beside him as she spoke.

He nodded.

"Close your eyes," she said, stern but smiling. He did.

Then it was quiet. He could feel the bark against his back, the roots and dirt under him, pressing into him. A breeze floated in off the river, and the sunlight danced warmly on his skin, making some small part of him vibrate with joy.

And then, abruptly, that part of him fell out from under him, like a cave collapsing in his chest. At his center, growing outward, cold spread like snow tumbling down the mountain, growing in speed and devastation. Out from his chest to his shoulders, his arms, his toes. Like waking up in Estun in the dead of winter when the fire had burned down and only darkness wrapped around you. The top of his head tingled, and fatigue crashed over him. His whole self, every finger, was a dead weight, turned to stone like Estun itself.

He thought of the Great Stone, shining in the hall. On a smaller scale, this was the way it made him feel. That was no coincidence, was it?

"Open your eyes," she murmured.

He struggled to. Her eyes were twinkling and locked on his.

"How does it feel?"

He grunted, barely able to keep his eyes open.

"As a mage, you want to keep yourself from getting to this point unless it's an emergency, because as you can see, you are nearly incapacitated. Only rest or more energy from another source can restore you. Try it—try to feel the energy around you and pull it in."

"How?"

"Well, you've got to pick something and send your mind toward it. Hear its song, know its whisper, understand its being, its very essence. Honor it deep in your soul. Feel its energy. Like this!" She pointed at a small mushroom growing beside him.

He tried to grope for it but felt like he was just pretending. There was nothing there, at least not to him. Maybe as a mage he wasn't quite formed right. Maybe he couldn't do things normal mages could do. Or maybe he was just too sleepy…

"Aven! Can you feel it?"

"No," he said sleepily. "There's nothing there." Resigning himself to sleep that was soon coming, he took a deep breath of the fresh air, scented by the river, and felt the warm sun on his face. So restful. The soft, dappled light felt sweet on his skin. He could sit in this sunlight by this river forever.

"Oh! Oh! You're doing it!" she cried.

"I am?"

"Don't stop! Oh, of course. The mushroom isn't there to you like it is to me. You need light. You need air."

That made sense in his mind, but how to put it into practice? He took another deep breath, this time imagining the cold and fatigue fading away. They didn't.

"Reach out to it," she whispered.

As he took another breath, he felt outward from his mind. He felt nothing different. This was never going to work. Except… was that what she spoke of? A light and thin energy, ephemeral, fleeting, bright. He focused on it, and it grew and grew, ready to blind him.

Energy, he realized. Pure, raw energy. The light—the sun. It was *his*.

He lurched toward it mentally, dying of thirst, starving, full of greed for more.

The cold was gone, the fatigue was gone. Then after a moment there was warmth, a fire—a blaze. His body trembled with energy. He had to get up, to move. He had to do something, he had to jump, he had to run!

His eyes snapped open and locked with hers. Excitement twinkled in her dark eyes as she smiled at him. Her face in that moment was the most beautiful sight he would ever see, he was sure of it. The sun—the sky—he had never felt so alive! By the ancients! His thoughts flew by in a torrent, an engorged river rushing toward the sea. Everything of the last few days and more flew by him in an inebriated swirl. He saw Evana's glare as she pronounced him a dead man, the drunk hitting the wall with a thud, his mother and father worrying for him, the clouds churning, the sky darkening and brightening. He saw Mara standing by the horses, the first time he spotted her. He saw himself lean toward her to kiss her, desperate to touch her, to feel as alive as he could possibly be—

When had the images changed from what had happened to what he wished to happen? And what did that mean? But he was too full of energy to make sense of it, thoughts rushing around in a whirlwind.

"Is… is this what it always feels like?" he whispered, staring into her eyes.

"Sometimes it's even better."

He let out a low breath. "Praise Anara!"

She chuckled. "You're too full! You took too much. You're drunk on it. Do something!"

"Like what?"

"Shake us down some leaves, clean the bridge off, tease the horses, something! Anything! And listen— *feel*—as you do it."

He glanced around. He looked up at the sky; orange leaves still clung to the oaks. He couldn't hesitate. He tried not to think. He just imagined the air racing through the treetops, like he would feel riding on horseback, but he was the air, powerful and fast—

A gust swayed the trees mightily, like a storm was approaching. By the gods, that was *him*. This was power like thunder rolling, like wind off the ocean—and he barely knew anything. Leaves swirled down from the treetops, and she smiled up at them, blinking in the flickering sunlight.

The heat in his chest had dissipated. He felt normal again. He hadn't quite felt it fade because his thoughts had been on the wind. Perhaps that was his problem. He'd focused on the drunk, the Devoted Knight, his own annoyance at his lack of control, and he'd failed to notice the slight coldness, the fatigue.

She nodded. "Well, then, good start. For a prince, I suppose." She winked. "You seem *well* rejuvenated now. Let's go. Try to keep listening to that energy inside you. I may be tempted to steal a bit here and there to see if you notice. So you better be paying attention." She narrowed her eyes at him playfully and shook a finger.

"And if I'm not?"

"Rocks and pebbles for dinner again."

"I'm doomed to starvation from your horrid mistreatment."

"You princes are soft! A mage must be hard. Rocks make warriors." She snickered, punching him lightly on the shoulder as he rose. "Now shut up and get on the horse."

"Missed it again."

He smacked a palm to his forehead, tugging on the opposite wrist with his chains in the process. This was the third time now she'd stolen some energy and he hadn't noticed.

"Two out of five isn't bad."

"It isn't very good, either," she laughed. "That was a lot of it, too. Were you nodding off over there?"

"After the night we had, how can you blame me?"

She only shrugged. Her eyes darted around them every once in a while, and seriousness would temporarily cloud her face. Did she hear something, see something? He couldn't hear anything out of the ordinary. She squinted hard at the road up ahead of them. In that spot, rosebushes sprang from the ground and straight into bloom, flowers red as blood.

"What's that for?" he asked.

"What makes you think I did that?"

"You were just eyeing that spot."

"I don't know what you're talking about."

He snorted.

"Well, I have all your excess energy. I must do *something* with it."

She really wasn't much for lying, was she? "You could give it back."

"How will you learn to fend for yourself then?"

"Excellent point." He pondered for a moment. "Can anyone pull energy from anyone? Is there a way to stop it from happening?"

"You want to stop me?"

"Well, no, but it seems like it could be—"

She grinned. "It's okay. You *should* want to stop me. You've got to be able to recognize it's happening, first, however."

He dismissed that with a wave of his hand. "Assuming I figure that out."

"Mages can extract energy from many things, but you will pull more effectively from your element. So, since you're a creature, I can pull energy from you more easily than, for example, you could from me. Magic is often not balanced in each small instance, but overall, it seems to even out. As you discovered, you have sources like the *sun*. If that isn't abundant, I don't know what is."

"Unless you're underground," he grumbled. This explained why he always enjoyed the terrace—it *hadn't* been just the monotony and the coldness in his bones. Or perhaps it *was* the coldness, but that had come from using his magic, not the damn stones. Fascinating. So much he didn't know.

She shrugged. "Different mages have the advantage in different situations. It's something to keep in mind— don't go into situations where you will have the disadvantage. But how often is one underground?"

"I've lived nearly my whole life underground." He glared.

"Oh." She said nothing for a moment. "As an air mage, that must have... Did you like it there?"

"No."

She watched him, seemingly unsure of what to say.

"I love my people. But I hate the mountain. It's making more sense now, how miserable it felt. That's why I would go out onto the terrace—where you found me. Only place there was much sunlight."

She frowned, lost in thoughts he knew she wouldn't share. She said nothing for a long while, and neither did he. His magic had led him to frequent the terrace, and being on the terrace had led him to her, and being with her had led him to his magic. Strange, indeed. It could be a coincidence. Or perhaps it was something more.

"You asked if it could be stopped," she said eventually. "It can, but even if you're sensitive to tiny fluctuations in your own energy levels, it can be tricky to notice at the start, which is when you need to stop it. And noticing it is like seeing the wind blow. Seeing the wind blowing and making the wind *stop* blowing are really not in the same realm at all, are they?"

He nodded. They were nearing a stream up ahead on the road.

"Let's stop for a moment. The horses could use a short rest and a drink." She led the horses off the road through a clearing in the trees and down to the water's edge. She dismounted, and he took that as his cue as well. He stretched, then groaned. Hell. He wasn't used to this much riding. How was she managing without a saddle?

She lumbered back up the hill to look up and down the road. Checking if anyone was following them? Her stride was awkward, so perhaps she wasn't managing as well as he thought.

She turned back, heading for the water. Light from the creek cast lovely dappled light on her face and the trees around them. He wondered what she looked like with her hair down. He wondered what she looked like in a dress like his mother wore, of flowing gray silk. Or would she pick something different? He imagined her on the terrace at home, wearing such a dress with him. She would probably choose something more practical. Dark blue tunics, leathers like the royal guard? If she had lived in Estun, how might she have looked? He imagined her not as his kidnapper, but as something… else. As a woman. As a queen? That *was* what he was picturing, wasn't it? Her riding leathers fit her in their own way, but what did she look like outside of this armored shell?

She must've felt him staring because she glanced at him. He would normally glance away immediately, but just this once, he held her brown eyes in his gaze for a split second longer. Then he turned toward the water. He lay down on the grass, stretched out his legs, and closed his eyes. The image of her in a gray silk gown hung in his mind—powerful and surprisingly detailed. She strode confidently among nobles, in between shafts of sunlight in the great hall. She sat at the tables among the lords and seemed no different than the others. Most were refined, but all were warriors nonetheless. He thought she would like it there.

It was probably a stupid fantasy. It *was* a stupid fantasy, he told himself. But of all the suitors that had come before, he'd never met one he could quite see as an Akarian. None he could really see as a queen. He'd never met anyone he could imagine... by his side.

He certainly wouldn't have expected *this* to be the place to find such a woman.

As if sensing his thoughts, she came and sat beside him. She'd washed her face and drunk from the stream, and now they waited while the horses grazed. He couldn't help but smile, though he hoped she wouldn't notice.

She also looked out over the river, her keen eyes sharp. A sparrow fluttered down and hopped around on the grass before them. She glared at it. The sparrow flitted away.

"Someone is watching us," she said flatly. Her eyes lost focus. She cocked her head slightly, listening. He could only hear the babbling of the water.

"Someone is coming," she hissed, staggering to her feet. She grabbed the front of his shirt and hauled him up as well. Not letting go, she dragged him away from the water and across the road, heading up the hill and into the forest.

She slipped her dagger from her boot. Had the villagers pursued them? Took them long enough. She made for a large fallen tree just up ahead. She threw him down in its shadow, crouching beside him.

A gust of wind blew leaves furiously over their heads. Mara peered over the top of the tree from her crouch. Aven twisted so he could see a little.

Only swirling leaves and debris. Some kind of bizarre windstorm? But as the moments passed, an image began to form, figures made from blue-white light.

It was his mother—or, at least, her image traced in light. Two others flanked her. The broad-faced man with long, braided hair to her left he did not recognize, but Lord Beneral of Panar stood to her right, as regal and poised as always although minus his usual ebony staff. By the gods—was Beneral a mage too?

"Hold," his mother's voice rang out, strong and clear, the voice of a queen. But it was a silvery, echoing version of her voice—was he hearing it with his mind or his ears? Her golden hair was pure white light, her gown the faintest blue. The image swam strangely, as though she were underwater.

Mara's blade was still drawn. She did not move, nor make any sign that she would run, either. She said nothing.

"Who are you?" his mother demanded.

Mara said nothing, dark eyes darting, measuring, calculating.

"I am Queen Elise of Akaria. You have my son as your captive. By all five mountains, I demand you tell me your name and release him immediately."

Mara was breathing quickly. He saw her jaw tighten, then release, then tighten again, as she considered how to respond.

She called back simply, "I cannot."

His mother's lips pressed together as she frowned. "Don't be stupid. This *can* be settled peacefully."

"No," Mara said, her voice a mixture of strange emotions. "It cannot."

His mother shook her head. "I will give you one last chance. Do not force my hand. I have come to you to negotiate. Are you turning me away? We will have no choice but to pursue and destroy you if you will not cooperate."

He saw Mara's form tense as if poised for immediate attack. But nothing else changed.

"I wish there were some deal that could be reached," Mara replied. Odd thing for a kidnapper to say. "But there is nothing I can ask you for. You have nothing I need. It cannot be. My—" She tried to say something else but winced and cut herself short. Her hand moved briefly to rub her shoulder, then back to steady herself against the log.

"So be it, then," his mother said. "You choose to bring the wrath of Akaria upon you. A fool's choice— you will die before I let you hurt him." With another blast of the wind, the figures in light were gone.

Aven blinked at the ferocity of her words. In a hall full of warriors, his mother often seemed to be a beacon of refinement. It was easy to lose sight of the powerful warrior queen she really was.

Mara stayed frozen for a moment, listening, the vanishing image putting her by no means at ease.

"Come." She grabbed him by the shirt and rushing back toward the horses. "There are some ruins on the crest of the hill—let's go. This isn't over."

Kres was happy to break into a gallop for once, and Miara was happy to oblige him. They dismounted when they reached what appeared to be the remains of a temple—elegant, tall, and tragically indefensible. She had dared to hope for some kind of fortification, but no such luck. They ventured inside on foot, bringing the horses with them. Ancient stone columns rose up, holding high stone halls and roofs intact, leaving a darkened shell with shafts of sunlight streaming in. Writing she didn't recognize was etched into a white stone wall to their left.

"Tell me what it says," she said.

"This is a temple of ancestors," Aven replied, voice echoing. "A place to commune with generations before."

Just her luck—she did not think past generations were cheering her on, certainly not on her mother's side. Ah, well, it was better than an open plain. Perhaps there would be quarters for the priests and priestesses that would be more defensible than this shooting gallery.

A pebble tumbled across a rock somewhere behind them.

Someone, or some thing, was following them.

She held a finger to her lips to indicate silence. Of course, she couldn't trust him, but she also needed every bit of energy for a potential fight. He seemed to want to learn magic more than he wanted to escape. Perhaps it was a ploy, but it was a chance she was willing to take.

She dropped the horses' reins to leave them in place. She muffled the sound of her and Aven's footsteps against the stone and drew him against the wall. She paused and scanned for any motion. Nothing. They slid along the wall toward the main altar of the temple.

Another sound of stone crumbling, tumbling against the rock.

She felt her heart start to pound now in spite of herself. Would it be mages? Warriors? How many? Something else? The queen herself was unlikely—or she wouldn't have visited them via the light. She could have visited in person and attacked immediately. No, the queen was not that close. But she would not have approached if she hadn't planned to make a move.

Visiting via the light meant the queen could be an air mage. But if she were, she would have also have attacked right away. Perhaps she was untrained or waiting for a certain moment, but most likely she wasn't an air mage. Another air mage probably cast the light visit spell. That meant the queen was either a creature or an earth mage, and since the ground wasn't shaking, Mara had a fairly good guess as to which.

What if it wasn't anything, just a stray cat, and she was wasting energy on nothing? She could reach out and find out, but using her magic to search the area would reveal their presence to any pursuers. Was the sparrow nearby? Kres knew how to keep out of a creature mage's view, but what about Cora? With the sparrow following them and their altercation with the queen so close behind, Akarian eyes had almost certainly followed them and knew their general location, if not their exact one. So perhaps location wasn't much of a secret to be kept.

If she could simply get close or edge up alongside them, maybe she could sense their presence without alerting them to her own. If she found nothing there, knowing for sure would save her a lot of energy. If she discovered a mage, well, their pursuers were likely close enough to find her and Aven anyway.

She reached out slowly, cautiously, to feel for any sign of life.

The plan of attempting to remain hidden failed miserably. Her mind became aware of them at the exact instant they became aware of her. Wolves. And they were hunting *her*.

She didn't need to hear their feet on the stone to know they were coming. She abandoned Aven and sprinted in the opposite direction, trying to buy herself at least a little time to call for help. To continue her mission, she'd have to survive this first.

She reached out around her for any creature to help her—but there was nothing. She found nothing. How could there be *nothing* alive anywhere close? Unless... there were creature mages behind this who had also called possible help away. How could it be?

She was nearly to the altar when the first wolf reached her, leaping on her from behind. She felt its claws dig into her shoulders as her body thudded into the stone floor. One claw in particular dug into the brand on her shoulder as the wolf closed his mouth over her neck, then yanked its paw away as if burned.

Please, wait— she started, unsure of how to stop the attack.

Release your prisoner, it insisted, tightening its bite.

I can't!

Its teeth dug in deeper, breaking the skin slightly.

I can't! I swear! I, too, am a prisoner.

Now the wolf seemed to hesitate. *You are poisoned. You are sick. What is wrong with your shoulder?*

Magic. I must do what others say. I am their prisoner. I am a slave. They made me capture him. She didn't know if the wolf would understand the concept of a slave, but what else could she do but beg?

The man you hold is good. He does not deserve to be harmed. It is not the Balance. The wolf's voice was stern.

I know, she answered back weakly. I know, she thought. *Go ahead and kill me. It is the only way to set him free. Perhaps it would be for the best.* She squeezed her eyes shut and braced herself.

Instead, her neck was suddenly cold. The wolf gingerly released her and backed off.

She opened her eyes to see it looking at her. Two others stood behind it, watching, as did another out of the corner of her eye—Aven. *No— No, don't—*

The man you hold is good. His mother is justified in protecting her cub. But we cannot kill you. That would be against the Balance, too. We will not bear either debt.

There is no other way to free him.

There is always another way if it is against the Balance. The wolf's eyes narrowed and glittered yellow as it regarded her for a moment. Then it turned with a huff and a nod and trotted out.

Aven rushed toward her now and crouched down. "What the hell was that? You're bleeding. Are you okay?"

The fool hadn't run. He was more concerned about her injuries. Damn it all to hell. The wolves and his mother were right. For the first time in her life, she wished she were dead. Bastard wolves and their moral standards. Damn it all.

She pulled energy from him again, this time to heal her wounds, as she found a rag in her belt pouch.

"Hey! I felt that," he said, glaring mockingly at her.

"Very good. Getting better. You're not hopeless, I guess."

She shut her eyes for a moment, feeding the energy to her neck, her shoulders, her throbbing head, where her wrists had slammed against the stone. She felt him take the rag from her hands and dab at the blood on her neck. He caught his breath as he saw the wounds close.

"You're not afraid of blood, I see," she whispered as she opened her eyes.

"You're not afraid of anything, it seems."

"That's not at all true."

"Akarians are warriors. Warriors bleed. What kind of Akarian would I be if I were afraid of a little blood?"

Still quite a good one, she suspected. She reached up and covered his hand with hers, stopping him from wiping blood from healed skin for a moment. His skin felt rough, strange, electric. "Enough. I'm fine. Don't be kind to me. I don't deserve it."

He gave her the rag but shook his head. "That's where you're wrong." He turned and knelt before the altar to pray.

"What are you doing?"

"Praying to my ancestors. For guidance. The Code decrees I must pay homage if I'm near a temple like this. But also—I could use some. If I'm going to survive your training." He gave her a sideways smile.

She knelt beside him. She didn't know if any of her ancestors would even be on her side. But guidance didn't sound like a bad idea.

"How will we know when she's dead?" Seulka asked him. They'd been simply eating their lunch, and then out of the blue, this. How long had she been thinking of asking? "She's probably lying dead in a ditch somewhere, and we're just sitting here waiting like a patient dog for its master to return."

Daes snorted at that analogy. "How can you be so sure? Perhaps she has him or at least has reached her objective."

She made a disgusted noise. "Please. We should check. Are we just going to wait for them to declare war? What if she was somehow extra subtle about it? What if we have to do something more to provoke them?"

"When did you get such a thirst for battle? I thought that was my job." He grinned at her, and she scowled back.

"It's only been a few days. Give it time. Even if she's captured him, Akaria will have to determine how to respond. She's just one mage." He hadn't spoken much about it to Seulka, but he'd begun training units of them together. He had big hopes for what he could accomplish with four times the power and a complementary variety of skills assembled. But she worried too much. He would tell her of his units when he had an imminent, easy victory for them.

She was eating angrily, cutting her fowl into viciously tiny pieces.

"Well, there's no need to be in a huff," he said. "We can look in on her, if it would make you feel better." He had been planning to check the mage's progress today or tomorrow anyway—might as well let Seulka think it was her idea.

She stopped, then gave a curt, but relieved nod. "Summon a farseer, we are in need of their services," she called to the guards.

He and Seulka ate in silence while they waited, he relieved, she far less vicious.

A guard announced the air mage's arrival. A slender, blond man approached the dais and bowed.

"You are one of Brother Lithan's pupils, if I recall," Daes said.

The air mage nodded with another somber bow. So this one was not the rebellious type. Brother Lithan was in line to be the head priest of Nefrana in the region, and only his never-ending quarrels with Brother Sefim had held him back so far. Lithan was also one of the most dogmatic, self-hating zealots Daes had ever met, and his students tended to admire these qualities. While Daes knew he ought to prefer the logic of obedience, he found himself disliking the air mage a little. Perhaps the creature mage was stupid to resist her fate—but she was strong. By contrast, she made this air mage look a little pathetic to bow so willingly, to embrace the dogma of hating the self so readily.

Was he going mad? How had she gotten into his head so? All resistance was foolish, and no one was going to convince him otherwise.

"Your name," Daes demanded.

"Sorin, sir," the mage replied.

"Sorin, I am glad you take Lithan's words to heart. Many do not want to believe that evil can come from within their own heart, but wishing does not make it untrue." Daes used his name this time as a compliment. It was not the typical way they addressed mage slaves. He said the usual spiel, but the words felt hollow. Truthfully, deep down, Daes did not care if magic was evil or not, only that this power was his to wield.

"Well said, sir," he replied.

"Mage, we wish to see another mage," said Seulka.

"Who, Mistress?"

"The creature mage Miara. She is in Akaria, or should be, on our command."

There was a subtle change in his expression, but Daes could not quite decipher it. This mage knew Miara and had some sort of connection to her. But what? Did he disapprove of her? Or was it in fact the opposite? Men sought to hide many things, but infatuation was among the most difficult conceal.

"I reviewed her maps before she left, Mistress, so it should be quick if she's on the routes she planned to take."

The mage spread his arms and bent at the elbows, palms up, as though circling some invisible tree trunk. He closed his eyes. The empty air between his arms shifted into to a shimmering, pale light. A river solidified into view, then a bridge. They were following a road. They traced it all the way to some high mountains and then into the woods. Leaves flew by for quite some time until, suddenly, the mage appeared.

Seulka gasped. "She's done it!"

His rebellious mage, his best spy. It frightened him a little, the excitement that he felt when he saw her. She'd done it, just as he had thought she could. But of course he would be rooting for her. The nobles had doubted her as much as they had him, but he and the mage slave were showing the fools that talent mattered far more than lineage.

The mage rode on a horse, the prince on another by her side. Her captive didn't appear to be restrained in any way, but he also wasn't fleeing. She must have something holding him, if only trickery. Daes didn't care how she got the job done as long as she succeeded. They appeared to be two unremarkable travelers, riding along through the forest in silence.

It was a work of mastery.

"That was quick," Daes said, smirking at Seulka. "I told you she could do it."

She rolled her eyes at him. "Listen to your bad manners. I told you so, I told you so." She glared, but then softened. "Remarkable. A lone woman holding a man captive. It seems hardly possible. How?" she breathed. Was that a hint of jealousy in her voice?

"One piece of iron holds hundreds of mages captive," said Daes. "Clearly, neither is impossible."

Seulka simply frowned down at the circle of light, still marveling at what she saw.

Then something occurred to him, a way to test this mage and see what exactly that glimmer in his eyes had meant. "But now that she's captured him, you have me thinking. One lone woman—why not stack the cards in our favor? Perhaps we should send this mage to help her."

Seulka's eyes brightened, as did the mage's. So he was excited to accompany her? Infatuation, indeed. Daes immediately regretted the suggestion—this air mage was far too excited for this task. If he had his own agenda, he could endanger the real purpose. Although, if that had been to send the mage to her death and cause a diplomatic incident, everything was already going well awry—to the minds of his colleagues, at least.

"No, it's unnecessary," he said hastily. "She is already farther along than we thought she'd be. We should let it be."

"Don't be silly, that's a brilliant idea. What's the harm in it? I told her I'd give her a turning of the moon, but more assistance can't hurt, can it?"

"I suppose not, but—"

"Nonsense, Daes. You should really learn to follow your intuition. Mage, come over here." For once, she was quick to act. The air mage dropped the circle and stepped forward, and the image of Miara and the Akarian faded.

Without hesitation or warning, she seized his shoulder over the brand. Sorin gasped and scowled in pain but did not shrink from her. Perhaps not as weak as Daes had first assumed, or he was deeply passionate about his commitment to their service. He hoped for the former.

"Go, mage," she whispered. "Go to Akaria, and find this mage and Prince Aven Lanuken of Akaria. Aid her in his kidnapping and bring him back to your Masters as quietly and speedily as you can. Let no one know a mage was involved."

When she let go, he wilted, recovering from the pain. Then after a few moments, he straightened and met Seulka's gaze.

"I request my leave, then, so that I may begin your task," he said. "They are already a long way away."

Seulka smiled, pleased. "Go, then. Prepare, pack, and be on your way."

The mage nodded and left the room at a trot. Daes scowled after him into the empty hallway.

7 CONFESSIONS

Miara and Aven reached the next town well after night-fall. "Ready?" she asked.

He nodded, jaw clenched. He looked regal in the dim light from the moon and windows from the village. She delayed for just a moment at the stateliness of his expression, the line of his jaw. She transformed him, but the image stuck in her mind.

"I'll leave your voice, especially after what happened last night," she said as she herself was transforming. "But one false word, and it will be in my pocket, and you will have a sudden case of excruciatingly intense nausea." Yes, now *that* had some finesse.

"You can *do* that?"

"There's only one way for you to find out." She winked, now an older woman twice his age. "I can make you blind and deaf, too. Don't make me try it."

"You're quite the battle ax, Mother," he said. "I assume that's our story again?"

She nodded. "Stick to it."

"But when I don't, I learn so much!" She shot him a cold look. He grinned back boyishly. "I'm teasing. I don't want a repeat of last night, either."

"Good."

The new face she'd created was less handsome, but his smile was still very much his own and undeniably alluring. She could transform someone into an entirely different person, but there were always essential elements that fought their way through—the certain angle in a squinted eye, a wry smile, the kind of features their mother would still recognize.

When they reached the inn, they tied off the horses and headed inside.

"Good evening! Travelers! Fancy that!" the innkeeper exclaimed almost before they were fully in the door. The man looked delighted. Slow business these days, perhaps? "Pray tell, are you in need of a room?"

She nodded. "My son and I—your price?"

"We've only got one bed—can you share?"

Her stomach dropped, and she hesitated. Not slow business, then, but just unusual to see total strangers, especially after nightfall.

"That one bed is available at the fine price of seventeen silver, with a meal and as much ale as you like."

She nodded crisply at that. One bed would have to do; she couldn't justify leaving and sleeping in the woods for that price. Her mouth had already started to water at the thought of a hot meal, and who knew what tomorrow or the next town would hold? "Better than sleeping in the dirt. Stable?"

"My son will clean those horses right up for you. Sul—get on it, boy." A young man not yet old enough to be married jumped with surprising energy and headed toward the door.

"The golden and the gray tied outside," she called after him, tossing him a silver. He nodded dutifully and headed out.

"Can we get our meal in the room?" she asked, dreading the answer.

"Room's tiny, ma'am, nowhere to eat. But the tavern isn't too crowded. I'll sit you with my daughter, if you're worried about being bothered?"

She smiled. "How did you know?"

"Drunks will be drunks, ma'am. And we got more than a few of 'em, locals that keep this place running."

"Indeed. We would appreciate your daughter's company, thank you, if you think it would help." This man, unlike the last few, seemed to have a decent head on his shoulders. "Here's twenty for your trouble, sir, if you can give us breakfast in the morning. I'm also in the market for a saddle, if you have one for sale."

He raised a slight eyebrow at that but took the money gratefully. "After breakfast in the morning, I'll walk you out to our stable and you can have a look. We've got a few."

With that he led them into the tavern room and sat them at a table with a young girl of maybe five years.

"Emie," he said, "these are some out-of-town guests. Would you mind if they sat with you? And you come and get me or your mama if anybody needs anything."

Emie nodded solemnly. By the way he said it, he'd said that line to her before, and it had more meaning than its face value. She knew the routine. He brought them some ale and left them. For a moment there was an awkward silence.

"So you know my name," the little girl said with a happy little smile. "What are *your* names?"

"Aven," Aven said, smiling at the little girl and clearly not thinking. She kicked him under the table.

"Lenara," she said, trying to sound pleasant and pretend nothing was going on.

The little girl was having none of it, however. She laughed at them. "My mum does that to me sometimes as well," she whispered at Aven, giggling. "Aven! That's a nice name. That's the prince's name! Did you know my brother's named after the king? Samul is kind of long to say, though, so we call him Sul."

Aven nodded, smiling. "Samul is a good name." Miara sighed with relief when he said nothing more.

"Is Emie short for anything?" she asked into the growing silence.

"Oh, yes, it's short for Emilira. Kind of hard to say, too. Not like Lenara! That's pretty, flows right off the tongue. Lenara!" She clicked her tongue for the fun of it.

"Thank you," Miara said, smiling. The girl had a sweetness and energy that lifted the dark feeling that hung over Miara. Emie reminded her of a younger Luha. An ache panged in her chest. How was her little sister and her laughing brown eyes? What would she be up to at this moment?

"It's almost time for snow, you know!" Emie said.

"Do you like snow?" Aven asked.

She nodded vigorously, her whole torso bobbing in excitement. "I do. It's pretty, especially this time of year, when it's light and lovely and doesn't get too deep."

Miara relaxed a little, leaning back into the bench. Aven seemed enchanted by the girl.

"It's nice when it's deep, though, too. You can go out and dig tunnels and roll up big balls of snow and throw them—but they don't hurt! Well, as long as you don't hit someone in the eye or try to make ice balls or something. Sul got hit in the forehead once. There was a lump the size of an egg. It was red as a coal for two whole days."

"No! The size of an egg?" Aven was good at playing along.

She nodded her violently enthusiastic nod once again. "Sometimes this time of year, we don't get snow, though. Sometimes it's not for a few months. It's still warm for snow. I wish I could make snow and have it whenever I wanted. Wouldn't that be lovely?"

Aven grinned. "It would." She studied his eyes, but he didn't seem to realize that he could do precisely such a thing. Should she tell him later? It took cooling the air and calling the rain and then combining them together. If wind came naturally to him, perhaps the weather would be the logical next step. But if he wanted to stop her from taking him back to the Masters—well, there was nothing like a gigantic snowstorm to lock people in one place. It was doubtful he could pull that off. He would be lucky if he could summon a single flake. And even if he did, she could easily drain away all his energy until he gave up or passed out. She wouldn't tell him about the snow, but he almost certainly couldn't do anything with the knowledge even if he wanted to.

Aven prattled on with the little girl in a variety of harmless ways. They discussed all manner of weather conditions and then life around the village. He seemed very interested in that.

"What kinds of problems do people have?" he asked. "We're from far away, near the sea."

"Well, this year, a lot of people keep getting sick, but Old Man Jones can't cure them all. He tries, though. This summer was pretty dry, so the harvest isn't so good for some of the farms. It may be a hard winter. Pa tries to hide it from me, but I can tell he's worried. Remol, the blacksmith, likes to fight with my Pa, but Old Man Jones gave him a talking-to, so I think he might be done with that."

They continued. She listened, checking for the wrong words, but he only seemed interested in chitchat, and the little girl would probably think he was joking at this point if he tried to explain he would someday be her king. Miara just sat and listened to their idle prattle, as she sometimes liked to listen to Luha talk to the other girls, and just let her thoughts be quiet—let herself not think for a while, especially not about *her* life. The meat pie the innkeeper's wife brought them was blissful and steaming. The words of the queen and the wolves still echoed in her ears, but she tried to focus on Emie's instead.

When they'd finished eating, Emie led them to their rented room, taking the stairs two at a time. Aven followed behind Mara up around a corner to a small back room. Warm and with a belly full of meat and ale and a mind full of Emie's sweetness, he was feeling better than he had in a while. The other rooms looked to be either rented or the innkeeper's. Emie opened the door, showed them around, and bowed.

"Can I get Ma to get you some hot water?" she asked. Mara nodded, handing the girl the pitcher from the washstand. Then Emie was gone.

The room was, indeed, awkwardly small. There was barely room for the washstand, chamber pot, and double bed. A small stove heated the room, which was a good thing, as the bed would've been practically inside the hearth of a fireplace. Still, one of them would likely be too hot or too cold. He looked at Mara, who was staring at the bed in dismay. There wasn't even another chair in the room.

"If I can make a request…"

She narrowed her eyes.

"Which surely I can't. But if I could… can we skip the vines again, please? I'm not claustrophobic, but I think I'd rather sit on the stove and try to sleep." He ventured a wink.

A sly smile crept onto her face. "You prefer the stove. Got it."

He let out a laugh, turned his back on her, and plopped down on the side of the bed nearest him. He reached down to rub his sore knees and kicked off his boots. How could he ease this tension?

Just then, his eyes caught on the shackle on his left wrist. He probably could have run today, but it hadn't even occurred to him. All he had done was stare, heart in his throat, as the wolf seemed to consider killing her… and then change its mind. Mysteries upon mysteries.

"Those wolves. Did my mother send them?" Now was as good a time as any to ask.

There was a knock at the door. She glared at him in warning. "Come in," she called.

The innkeeper's wife entered and brought in the steaming pitcher. Then she left with a modest nod and a bow. Aven smiled at her as she shut the door. The woman did not show any signs of having heard anything suspicious.

"Yes." She started to wash the dried blood from her neck.

"I thought they were going to kill you."

"So did I."

He hesitated for a moment, hoping she would say more. Nothing came.

"Why didn't they?" he asked. Did his voice give away more than it should?

She stopped washing and stared at her own reflection in the mirror behind the washbasin. "I wish I could explain. Honestly. But I can't."

He glared at her. This again? He had held nothing back from her, and she had complete control over him. Why would she possibly not tell him something as simple as this? "Can't or won't?"

"Can't," she said, an edge in her voice.

He gritted his teeth, not wanting to believe her. "Did my mother call them off? Did you overpower them? I want to know what happened. I think I deserve that much. Why did they stop?"

"Oh, you'd rather they have kept going?" she spat.

"No!" he said, very certain now the falter in his voice gave away far too much. "But I know you know why. Why can't you tell me?"

She strode toward him abruptly and fell down on one knee, not two feet away. He watched the fiery strands that had escaped from her bun fall around her face; she pushed them out of her eyes absently. She reached up to the collar of her tunic and pulled it out to the right, twisting until he could see her naked neck and shoulder.

He caught his breath.

"This. This is why. This is why they didn't kill me and why I can't explain."

"But that— Did the wolves— I thought you healed yourself. Are you okay?" The wound on her shoulder was the size of his palm, scabby with bits of dried blood. It could not be more than a few days old. He had seen a few wounds in his day, but this was unlike any created by any normal weapon.

"No," she said. "I'm not okay. Does it look okay?" She slowly covered it again.

"But that wound is fresh. Did the drunk do that and I didn't notice?

"No."

"When did it happen?"

"Fifteen years ago."

He blinked now, simply not comprehending. "Why hasn't it healed?"

"It never heals."

They sat for a moment in silence.

"But what does it mean?"

"I told you I can't explain. Please believe me. I truly wish I could."

She stood, covering it again. Fifteen years? She had had a wound for fifteen years that somehow stopped her from—well, many things. He stared into her dark eyes for a long time, struggling to process what she'd said. He wanted to shake her and insist on the truth. But he was beginning to realize that this *was* the truth. Now, he wanted even more to find whoever had put that wound on her shoulder and give them a wound or two. How could a wound not heal for fifteen years? Unless...

It must be magic. Dark magic. Like the kind that had led to mages being feared and loathed in the first place, the kind that had brought on the Dark Days. He had thought it had all been lost in the sands of time.

Finally, he simply nodded. "I believe you. I may be a fool, but I do."

She nodded curtly, but there was relief behind her eyes. "Go ahead and wash up."

She moved to take off her boots. Still stunned, he obediently headed to the washbasin. He was filthy. Did he dare take off his shirt? He glanced at her. She sat with her back to him, eyes fixed on the furnace, not moving. She seemed exhausted, worn down.

Hell, she'd seen him naked the day they'd met. What did he have to hide at this point? He stripped off his shirt and began washing as best he could.

"So, no vines, then?" he asked, hoping to change the tone. He examined his grimy shirt and wondered if he should put it back on.

She turned to glance at him with a crooked smile, her eyes widening ever so slightly at the sight of him. "No vines," she said. "I'm more in a stomach flu sort of mood today. Did you forget? The door, however, will not be so lucky."

He glanced at the door and jumped in surprise—spiders had clustered around the locks and hinges, weaving elaborate webs across the door. So she hadn't just been sitting still. Good thing he didn't really *want* to escape from her. He didn't want to figure a way around those buggers.

The image of the wound on her shoulder flashed through his mind again, and for the first time, fear shot through him with a cold, nervous energy. Everything else had been speculation, and at a certain point it was a waste to worry. But this was something real. Surely the same people who'd sent her were the ones who'd given her that gash. Would they give him one of his own?

Again, speculation. It would get him nowhere. Moving on.

"This shirt is filthy. Is it all right with you if I leave it off?" he asked. She hesitated, then nodded. "These folks do seem friendly. Perhaps a second set of clothes wouldn't be a bad idea?"

She nodded, a twist of a smile in the corner of her mouth. "You *are* beginning to look more and more like a recently rich beggar," she said. "We'll see to it in the morning."

Since he wasn't going to wear it, he washed it thoroughly and then hung it nearby to dry. He might be a prince, but warriors needed some basic self-care skills when on a campaign. He was glad for them now. He wasn't used to all this magic and gallivanting around on horseback under the *sun*, of all things.

He sat down on the bed behind her, feeling her back warm and only inches from his own. Should he offer to sleep on the floor? He probably should if he wanted to really be a gentleman. The Code did not cover kidnapper-captor etiquette, but in general, it was not princely to sleep beside a woman he wasn't married to. But this mattress was springy beneath his fingers—better than the usual straw. Some amount of moss, perhaps? Not his bed at home, but not the rocky ground either. He longed for the feel of it beneath him. He'd just stretch out for a moment, and then he'd offer to leave the bed to her…

Almost as soon as his head hit the pillow, he fell asleep.

Aven.

A voice cut through his dreams and roused him. For a moment, he thought it was his mother, reaching out to him—but no. He was still asleep.

He stood on the balcony in Estun. Stars shone in a majestic night sky above. It was not quite the balcony he remembered. Rows of neat vegetables grew instead of ornamental shrubs and flowers. The cherry tree was there, but it was only a tiny sapling.

He was not alone. A tall, black-haired woman stood, gazing at him with familiar eyes.

"Who are you?" Aven whispered, feeling as though he should already know.

"Tena Idal Lanuken."

Tena had been the name of his father's father's mother. His prayers that afternoon for guidance—someone had been listening! Could it truly be a spirit dream?

He fell to one knee hastily and bowed deeply. Tena had been a legendary queen and a powerful warrior. She had triumphed in several major battles with Takar and finally achieved the lasting peace Aven knew today. Whatever she had to say, he must listen carefully.

"I am honored, Great-Grandmother," he whispered.

"You remember me. I'm glad. I knew Samul would not forget us."

Aven nodded, head bowed.

"Tell me the purpose of an Akarian king," Tena demanded.

"To serve Akaria," he replied, following tradition. "To serve our people. To protect them from harm, to bring law where there is chaos, to keep the peace. To bring prosperity, if possible."

"And what does it mean to be a Lanuken?" she asked.

"A Lanuken defends those who cannot defend themselves. A Lanuken stands up for honor, for the Code, for the Way of Things. A Lanuken as king preserves the Balance and helps his people." The first parts were more of what he had heard his father say before, although he believed and breathed every word of it. He added the last bit himself.

She considered his answer. Aven took a deep breath, waiting. Starlight glittered off a circlet of diamonds in her dark hair and tiny jewels on her navy gown.

"You love this place, don't you?" she said.

Had he passed her test? The queen smiled down, a twinkle in her eye. "This balcony?"

"Yes."

"I do," he said.

"Why do you think we built this terrace?"

"Everyone says it was for the extra food source, the vegetable garden. Plus it is beautiful."

She smiled. "You know the official story, but your heart knows that there's more. You don't even grow vegetables there anymore. Why is it that *you* love it, Sky King?"

He hesitated. "The sunlight."

She grinned. "Yes. The sunlight." She paused, strolling toward the cherry sapling. "I ordered this terrace built. You know, our line has always included men of the earth. Mages of stone. Of diamonds. But every once in a while, there are others. Others who are strange and different and powerful. Once in many generations, we are foretold of greatness."

Aven shook his head. "I don't understand."

"We were foretold of you."

Aven frowned. "But what— Why—"

"I built this terrace for you."

"Thank you," he said. It might have been the truest thanks he'd ever given. "But why?"

Queen Tena just smiled. "Knowing the future is not good for mages. Knowing the future has only driven men mad. So I will tell you a little, just as I was told only a little, for the sake of our sanity. Instead, look up."

Aven obeyed. The moon faded to darkness as he looked up, and the stars shone brighter. For a moment his heart ached at the familiarity of it, and he longed to be back home.

Tena approached, took his hand, and pulled him to his feet. She pointed into the sky. There, in the south, one familiar star seemed to twinkle especially brightly.

"Do you see that star?" she whispered. "That is the star of your rule."

He shivered. Her words echoed the Takaran's.

"Casel."

She nodded. "The freedom star."

"So… I will rule someday?" Aven said, looking from the star to his great-grandmother's eyes. They were the same gray as his own.

"We are a line of kings. We serve our people, whether on the throne or not. We help our people, and all those who suffer oppression, on the throne or not. I do not know your future any more than you do. I only know that the star Casel calls out to you. And that there is war on your horizon."

War. The word rang true in his heart. Some part of him had known it was coming.

"My brothers?"

"They have their own beacons, in the earth, that can only be told to them."

Aven looked back into the sky. Casel twinkled.

"Go now, Aven, and rest. Let the history and power of your ancestors bolster you."

Aven smiled and bowed to the queen even as she and the terrace faded into darkness.

He opened his eyes. He didn't even remember falling asleep, but he lay on his back in the inn, the fire dwindling. Mara slept beside him, breathing slowly. She lay on her side, the shoulder with the brand on it facing up. Did it hurt? Did she lie on her side so as not to aggravate it?

She had not used the saddle chain to fix him to the bed. He glanced at the windows, hoping for a real glimpse of the stars. They, too, were webbed shut. He wouldn't see Casel again tonight, aside from more dreams.

The star map. Could it possibly have survived all this? His hands were free to find out. He slipped his hand down and into his pocket, and—it was there! It was crumpled and a little sweaty, but it was there. He unfolded it gingerly and studied it in the dim firelight, careful not to make a sound. Was Casel on the map?

She *was* there, toward the bottom. He could not make out the notes nearby, though. One particularly clear inscription was at the top of the map near Anefin. He squinted and studied it for a while in the dimness, trying to make out the ancient, twisted Serabain. The odd little hooks, the sharp, angular glyphs. He studied it for a long while. Mages were rumored to have used Serabain in the olden days. They'd seen the same language in the temple earlier, and it was still used in some nations across the southern sea. He knew a little, but few of these words looked familiar. Many looked incomplete, as if only part of the word was there. Some letters, too, looked broken and not fully formed.

He puzzled through it for a while until his eyes began to ache and his vision blur. He could hardly decipher it if he wasn't alert enough to read it—and the dimness didn't help. He'd have to keep looking for chances to study it.

He wouldn't show it to Mara just yet.

He folded it back up neatly, slipped it into his pocket, and listened to her breathe. He thought of the dream. Tena's words stuck with him—a king is a king even if he doesn't sit on a throne. A Lanuken was always a Lanuken. He could help people and serve Akaria even if he was in shackles. He'd felt all along that he could probably do more good in these shackles than he had been able to in Estun. But the question remained—how could he best help anyone?

His thoughts became less solid and less serious as sleep approached. He listened to the crackle of the fire and felt its warmth. Soon winter would be here; Emie would be happy about that. By the time winter came, he would likely know what lay in store for him. Questions would be answered, good or bad. The darkness of the room and the warmth of the fire reminded him of home. He missed the snowy peaks of Estun now. But even if he never returned, soon the whole world would have its coating of snow, just for Emie. He sighed and drifted off to sleep, thinking of the drifting flakes falling on the windy road that led home.

Miara awoke with a start, the sharp and sudden knowledge that they had traveled two days from Estun at the front of her mind. That meant they were a two-day ride from home.

Halfway. Already.

She glanced over at Aven, closer to her than she'd expected. He was still asleep, his head resting against her shoulder softly, his body warm and close. Two day's ride from servitude—or likely worse. The Masters couldn't mean the same thing for him that they meant for just any other mage.

Did they know he was a mage? She wouldn't be the one to tell them unless they forced it out of her. Still, she had to wonder. Was she really on some kind of mission to save the world from itself, helping them hunt down all these mages in the world—no matter how powerful they were—and keep them from getting out of control? If magic really were evil, wasn't someone like Aven exactly the last person you'd want to have a good command of it?

She sighed, shaking her head. She couldn't believe that even if she tried. Those bastards had no right, and that was that.

Her eye caught on the window; the light coming in was strangely bright. She got up and brushed aside the cobwebs delicately woven over the glass. The white glare stung her eyes... snow!

Snow? In the middle of autumn? Not unthinkable, but after all of Emie's talk of it last night, it would be quite a coincidence. Or was it actually something else? Her eyes shot to Aven again. He was sleeping soundly. Could he have...? Was he capable in his sleep? Of course he was capable.

She should probably stop teaching him. She could be underestimating how quickly an adult mage could come into his powers.

She reached over and shook him awake. His gray-green eyes grimaced, squinted, and then finally looked at her, revealing that lovely, heavenly green. She said nothing for a moment, just staring into them. Then she remembered herself abruptly.

"Get up."

Ignoring her gruffness, he stretched and yawned, like it was any other morning. "I was having the strangest dream!" he said. "Several, actually. I was trudging through a snowstorm."

"I don't think you know the half of it," she said, standing up and striding over to the window for a better look. A little bit of shifting energy about, and he's manipulating the weather in his sleep? Gods. He was either lying or very powerful.

Frowning, he got up and came to her side. His mouth fell open in shock.

Emie was already outside, shaping a mound of heavy, wet snow into a heap. Three other children had joined her and were lobbing snowballs at each other's heads. So much for caution. It might have been the loveliest snow Miara had ever seen with fat, heavy flakes swirling whimsically in a gentle wind.

"I—I feel *cold*," he stammered. "In fact, I feel *freezing*. Did I...?"

She shrugged, not completely sure.

"Could I have? Can an air mage...?"

"Oh, yes."

He stood staring, mouth open, a twist of a smile creeping into the corner of his mouth and breaking into a grin. Looking farther, she could see that the snow hadn't fallen everywhere; it ended a little way up the road. The coverage centered around the inn. Around Emie.

She didn't know whether to be frightened or awed at the sweetness of the gesture. "You better hope they don't suspect us for this," she muttered, halfheartedly threatening.

He just gave her a sideways glance and an even bigger grin. He wasn't falling for her tough act in the slightest, at least not in this moment.

What on earth had she started? Did it really matter? Did she care? They'd be back to the Masters in a day or two, and it would all be over. How much trouble could they get into before then?

Wouldn't it be delightful to find out?

Miara sat and studied her maps as they ate some porridge near the inn's roaring hearth. The road back was disgustingly straightforward—a little to the west and a lot more to the south, and they'd be back. She hated the thought; no part of her wanted this trip to end.

Her shoulder stabbed at her angrily. She tried to brush it off.

Deep breath. In and out, in and out. She surveyed the room, memorizing every detail of the moment. This mission was different. This was more of an illusion of freedom than she'd had in a long time. And then there was Aven. When they arrived at Mage Hall, she'd know exactly the magnitude of what she had been forced to do. There was no point in dwelling on that now, but she was still filled with dread.

For now, she sipped some steaming tea and watched him eat his porridge, trying not to be too obvious about it. She felt a strange, quiet peace and contentment. It couldn't last forever, but for now she'd try to bottle it up in her mind to open up on another day, a rainier day, just to take a sniff of a memory and remember that there was at least this much good and peace in the world, that she had gotten a tiny slice of it in the midst of her pain.

Before breakfast, she had sorted out the details of a new saddle and some items for Aven with the innkeeper. All that was left to do was ready the horses and leave. She hoped the temperature hadn't dropped too much with Aven's snow because she wasn't prepared well for deep winter travel. But perhaps she should hope for the opposite, or the snow would be that much more suspicious—and melted before they were even out of town, perhaps. They finished eating and headed out to get on the road.

As soon as she turned the corner and got a whiff of Kres, she knew something was wrong—or more specifically, *Kres* knew something was wrong that she didn't. Cora, too, was shifting, antsy, nervous. In alarm, she sent her mind out in all directions just in time to feel a man running up behind her.

But not in enough time for her to turn around before the cloth was over her mouth, his arm circling her neck, her sight fading from the white of the cloud-covered sky to darkness.

8   DEVOTION

When Aven came to, for a few minutes, all he could really perceive was a splitting pain in his head, a sickening rocking motion, and an awful, dry, vinegar-tasting fabric in his mouth. He wanted to groan but felt too terrible to bother. He lay on his side. His hands were bound behind him. His body was pressed between something hard behind him and something soft and warm in front of him. After a while, the pain lessened, and he felt less dizzy, so he opened his eyes.

A few inches from his face was Mara's. Her mouth was also bound, but her dark eyes were already open. She met his gaze. She nodded calmly to him as if to say, good, you're awake, we can start figuring out how to get out of this mess.

He glanced around at their surroundings, trying to distract himself from the beauty of her eyes and what he now realized was the continuous pressing of her body against his. They appeared to be in the bed of a narrow wagon meant for seating men on each side. The sides were wood, and some canvas hung over the top for shelter—or secrecy, perhaps.

He listened as he studied their bumping, swaying prison. Mostly he could only hear horse's hooves, but there were two men talking. At first he couldn't make them out, then he realized—they were Takaran.

Why would a group of Takarans kidnap two strange travelers? What could they want? Or could it have been two *mages* they'd been kidnapping?

Perhaps they hadn't heard the last of that stupid drunk yet.

He turned his eyes back to Mara. She had shut hers. Perhaps she was resting. Her red hair was tousled. He could feel her breath hit him evenly. Was it his imagination, or could he smell the faintest jasmine or lavender on her skin? Curves pressed against him drew his thoughts… but that was *not* helpful. He needed to focus on something that would get them out of this, not embarrass him for all time.

What were they *saying*?

He could only catch snippets of words, and none of them were particularly useful: horse, north, grain, fifty coins, river. He glanced down toward their feet but couldn't see much. He closed his eyes again and just listened for a while.

Minutes or hours could have passed, or he could have fallen asleep. He wasn't really sure. His head hurt less after a while. Little else changed.

Do you understand anything they're saying? she spoke into his thoughts after a while.

He sat still, confused for a moment at how to respond.

Air mages can't speak like this. Only creature mages can. Just think and I'll hear you.

Can you always hear any of my thoughts? he tried to, well, think back at her.

Yes. If I'm listening. But it's not that simple. Especially if you aren't trying to tell me something, it's hard to sort out the thought from the noise. It can drive a mage to madness. We don't do it without need.

Well, no matter. He had nothing to hide.

Everyone has something to hide.

Oh. He hadn't realized she would hear that. A smile crept to his lips in spite of himself. This could get interesting. *I can understand some of what they're saying, but not much. Nothing useful. Any idea who they are?* he thought, perhaps to himself.

But she was indeed listening. *No. I could get us out of these bindings by shifting us, but we'd be jumping out of the wagon into who knows what. Not sure how prepared they are or if they know we're mages or not. Could be folks from the last village told them to pursue us. But if they don't know we're mages, we don't want to reveal it.*

He gritted his teeth into the gag at the thought. How could things like this go on in a civilized land? If he ever made it to the throne, he would find a way to crush these kinds of criminals.

You are an interesting fellow.

That thought wasn't for you.

It wasn't hidden from me, either. I thought you had nothing to hide.

He shook his head. *What are we going to do? I wish I could see into your head like this. Talk about someone with something to hide.*

I never claimed to be telling you everything. What kind of kidnapper would that make me?

Well, he thought it might make her an honest one. The thought jumped into his mind before he could stop it, and he immediately regretted it.

Honest, perhaps. Not a very good one, though, I think.

Thank goodness she didn't seem offended. *I'll give you that. Kidnapping is not a talent I ever contemplated deeply.* Perhaps he should have, though. He'd have to give more thought to the training of spies and assassins in his employ, given the latest events. Ack, military forces and their training were *not* the wisest things to be thinking about, that was for sure.

I'm always the very best at whatever I do. You can be sure of it.

There was an oddness to the words, a silly, jiggling, shaking feeling, like a thought in his own head that he thought was funny. Not laughter, not like the tone of voice she would have spoken with, but more purely that the thought shook with her amusement.

Yes, speaking this way can be very strange. Sorry to introduce you to it now. I don't think we should do anything yet. Let's see where they take us. In the night, we'll have a better chance of escape.

He opened his eyes, and she opened hers in return. He nodded to her. She nodded gravely back.

For now, let's rest as best we can in this stupid contraption.

He shut his eyes again and tried to resign himself to sleep. It was hard, with her body pressing so close to his. He didn't want to sleep—he wanted to think about something far more interesting. He had seen the scar on her shoulder, but he'd also seen the smooth skin of her neck, her back... He longed to know its touch against his lips, to feel her hair on his face, her hands against his hands, her skin against his skin.

But getting all amorous for her was a truly terrible idea, given their close proximity and utter lack of privacy at this point. The Code had no rules for this particular situation, but if it did, he figured the guidance would be to think about something *else*. And who knew when she might choose to dip into his thoughts for some idle conversation? No, it was best to keep from thinking about her neck at all costs.

Easier said than done.

Resting did not work. They'd gotten a decent amount of sleep, but even if they'd been exhausted, Miara wasn't sure the damn wagon would let someone sleep in the bottom of it. It bumped and rocked her bones against the wood, and just when she thought she'd found a rhythm she could sleep to, it would lurch nauseatingly just to keep her on her toes. The arm she was lying on had long since fallen asleep and was now numb.

She couldn't take it anymore. She had to have something to think about. And it couldn't be their current situation or where they were going. She needed to think about another place, another time.

Cautiously, she reached toward his mind again. His thoughts were wild and unguarded, of course, which made it harder to communicate. His mind felt more like that of an animal than most mages she'd brushed thoughts with. Mages were trained to keep things orderly and efficient when speaking with other mages.

It was better for everyone's sanity that way, as one never knew who was stark-raving mad under that shell.

He might have been asleep. Images were whirling through his mind in odd, fractured sequences. The snow on the ground, Emie sitting by the fire, laughing. A clash of swords, a shield in his face, and the lick of flames at his back. A dark pool of water in the moonlight, a woman wading out into the water, naked. Lips against the soft skin of a woman's neck, red hair smooth against his fingers, brushed softly to one side…

She felt her face flush with heat and reeled her mind away from him suddenly—what had *that* been! Had he been thinking about… her? Or had that been an errant daydream of her own? Were the close quarters twisting her mind to even deeper depths of foolishness? Of course, he did feel good against her, warm and strong and solid. But that didn't mean— She hadn't been thinking of—

Or had she? It did sound like a terribly good idea.

Now firmly back in her own mind, she remembered that moment in the inn, pulling aside the neck of her tunic to show him the scar. Could he possibly see her as attractive in spite of the horrifying parasite in her shoulder? Would any man run his lips across her shoulders like that, with that burned hole in her soul so close by? Could he really imagine himself kissing her neck, nipping at her earlobe?

She blushed even harder at the thought. She hoped his eyes weren't open.

He was a prince. She was probably an idiot.

Back in Mage Hall, she had never allowed herself to entertain such ideas. She wasn't entirely sure why. Everything seemed so dark and low. She tried to find joy, but joy like *that*—love or affection—it was too much. It was too powerful. It was just one more thing the Masters would use as leverage. Just one more thing to twist an arm farther behind her back. And they would do it, too. Nothing was beneath them. But did that mean she should really deny herself such pleasures? The Masters had ruined enough things in the world for her, she shouldn't give them control of anything she didn't have to.

She opened her eyes for a moment, breath quickening. Thankfully, his eyes remained closed. He did seem to be sleeping. She studied him carefully. Somewhere in the attack, the charms on their disguises had weakened, but not completely faded. His transformation had loosened but wasn't gone. He looked like a very tired, very worn version of himself. His strong jaw had returned. She could still see that kingliness that she'd noticed the other day. He was terribly handsome even with her best attempts to make him not look quite so much that way.

Could he really long to do what she'd caught in that glimpse of a thought? Had it been her daydream or his?

Would a prince ever lower himself enough to brush his lips against the skin of a slave?

For a moment her mind went on a wild flight of fancy. Perhaps they really only did mean to enslave him as a mage as well, to keep the world safe from all unchecked magical powers. With his lack of control, he could've gotten their attention that way. Even if it had been at the king's bidding, perhaps really nothing would come of that—as did plenty of missions the king demanded she be sent on and then promptly forgot about. She'd even heard the Mistress rant at his fickleness. Perhaps Aven would end up just like her, another slave imprisoned within Mage Hall but, within its confines, free to do as he pleased. Perhaps she was not really taking him to his doom. Certainly, it was a lesser existence, but perhaps, if they could be together there, would it be a wholly undesirable one?

If he really desired her, if it wasn't all a figment of her imagination, if someone outside this wagon didn't kill them first...

But her optimism didn't last long. Even if *all* that were true, the Akarians still knew a mage had captured him, and there was yet time for these new captors to figure that out.

But to hell with reality. For a moment, she let herself fall into the last remnant of the thought, and she could almost feel warm hands on her back, soft breath against her neck, tender lips grazing her shoulders.

She wasn't blushing anymore.

Aven felt Mara rouse him from a light doze with a question placed gently in his mind like a smooth pebble onto a satin pillow.

What was Estun like?

Groggy, it took him a moment to formulate an answer, and it wasn't so much words as memories and images at first. He thought of the library at night, the huge fire raging in the massive hearth casting ominous shadows across the leather spines. He thought of his father presiding at the head of the banquet for the harvest feast last year—so strong and handsome and proud. The stone halls of Estun had been filled with laughter and the smell of beer and wine and roasts cooking. He thought of the darkness of his room, the darkness of the kitchens, the dark, heavy stone pressing in around him. He thought of the way his magic would whip little currents of air through the dank, black hallways, torture the blazes and the flames in the candle sticks, tease at women's hair and men's beards—searching, restless, looking for more. He thought of how small it all felt, and yet how vast and empty.

He thought of the glorious sun of the balcony, the many days he'd spent reading there or helping to tend the plants when he was younger. He thought of picking cherries and eating them right off the tree in the summer with his mother. He thought of the first time he'd seen Mara there and the striking beauty of her face that day.

He stopped abruptly, scared. How much had he revealed?

His eyes snapped open, and hers did a second later.

You think my face is beautiful?

Her voice was not in its usual slow pace, with carefully timed words. It was just—plain, surprised. He swallowed hard, horrified at his own impoliteness and indiscretion. *Well, certainly, you must know how beautiful you are*, he tried to tell her. *Why else do you disguise yourself?* He closed his eyes, embarrassed, unable to stand simply staring any longer.

Only so I am not recognized later. I... No, I have never... No one's told me that before. Perhaps in Estun there are not many women to compare me to.

Her voice had the same jingling, shaking laughter to it that told him she was teasing. But he couldn't help but respond seriously. *Well, I haven't traveled the world like you, but I don't think the number of faces I've seen has anything to do with judging a good one from the rest. I don't need to have seen all the gems in the world to know the ones in my father's staff sparkle with a certain zest. Just because no one's told you that doesn't make it untrue.*

She said nothing back to him for a long while. Then, eventually, she could only say, *I haven't traveled the world, either. The darkness was killing you, wasn't it? I know you said as much, but I didn't imagine it could feel like that.*

He might be a Lanuken, but he didn't think he was much of a mountain king. He didn't know how to respond.

I'm sorry I keep disturbing you. It's just that this rocking and waiting is maddening. I can't sleep, and I don't want to think about… what's to come.

He sensed her dread, deeper and more real now than before, even though he still didn't understand it. It sent a chill down his spine. *What are you afraid of?*

She either didn't hear him or refused to answer. *Let's try to rest more. The sun seems to have passed overhead now and be lowering again. They have to stop eventually.*

He hoped so. His stomach gurgled angrily, and damn did he have to pee.

By the time they finally stopped, the sun had begun to set. The inside of the wagon had grown dark, and only dim shafts of light drifted in from outside. When the damn thing finally rolled to a slow stop, Aven thought his arm and leg might never wake up from the sleep they'd sunk into.

He listened intently in the growing silence, hoping for a clue of some kind, but he heard nothing but the sounds of men making camp. They barely spoke. Someone was making a fire.

Gods, do they plan to leave us in here all night? Bastards! Miara must be as uncomfortable as he was.

How long do we wait before we do something? he tried to ask.

She paused to consider. *At least till the sun is fully set. If they've still left us lying here, we can try to make a break for it. Feel like mouse or rat tonight?*

Not again! He groaned inwardly. *Well, as long as I'm not being dangled thousands of feet above a mountain, I guess either will do.*

No promises. We might get away faster as birds. Think you can fly? Or perhaps—

But before he could exclaim how unlikely that was, a figure cast a shadow over them, blocking what little light fell into the wagon. It reached in for them, starting with Mara first and yanking her to her feet. He was surprised at the sudden surge of rage that shot through him at their hands on her.

He was next. They dragged and bounced him harshly off the bottom ledge of the wagon as they hauled him unceremoniously out and gave him a push. His numb leg nearly gave out; Mara had fallen to her knees and was struggling to stand up. If he'd thought riding a horse all day made him tired and achy, it was nothing compared to *this* form of transportation.

Someone behind him was roughly removing the gag while another untied his hands. He tried to swing his head around to see better but regretted the pain imme-diately. At least five dark hoods circled them. Large faceted stones hung on chains around their necks. His hands were retied in front of him. Then they grabbed him by one arm—the numb one, of course—and led him toward a tent.

He couldn't see Mara. He didn't hear her following behind him.

He turned to one side to try to see her, but they pushed him harder toward the fire. He jerked his whole body and twisted then instead, turning at least part way toward where she'd fallen. To his relief, she was on her feet and being led behind him.

"Eh, she's right behind you, mage—now quit your trouble and get on with it before I break your arm," the one who'd lost control of him grunted.

Devoted Knights, she whispered. *They hunt mages.*

God, how many Devoted Knights *were* there in Akaria? Not this again.

The stones around their necks resist magic. Spells will be much more costly in their presence, if not impossible. Wait—again?

But before he could even try to figure out how to answer, they had arrived at the large tent. The door swung open, and they were pushed inside, the knights entering behind them.

It took his eyes a moment to adjust to the darkness and the few candles. He blinked. The tent was sparsely furnished with a cot to one side, several chests that acted as both tables and seats, a regal chair facing the entryway, and a brazier of warm coals in the center for heat.

As his eyes adjusted, he gradually saw the figure in the chair more clearly. A woman, also in dark robes. No, a black dress. A bow crusted with jewels leaned against the chair's back.

Evana.

"Well, well," she said. "We meet again."

Miara tried to hide her gasp as she realized the woman in the tent knew Aven. It was not just her greeting but also his face. The look there was strange indeed.

You know her? You know a Devoted Knight?

It's… complicated. That was the clearest response she could pull from the swirling vortex of his thoughts.

"I trust my mother's provisions helped on your unplanned journey, Princess," he said in a voice smooth as silk. A prince's voice—a king's. Not the one he typically used with her. It gave her a strange thrill.

"Yes, the horses dined well, thank you. I'm no fool."

"But the horses are still in good health, I'll wager. So perhaps you are." Again, Miara caught her breath. That was quick to insults.

"And to think I didn't kill you the moment I learned of your magic," she said. "And disrespect is how you repay me?"

"You would have done it, if not for your code. You said so yourself. Does it also permit deceit? I'd wager it does."

She glared at him.

"What does your code say now? Your elders?"

Her chin jutted out, indignant. "I travel to Kavanar on a different mission. But I eagerly await their reply."

He grinned, looking amused. What in the world was going on? "Is that so?"

She glowered at him. "I may just have to make an exception this time. In your case, any repercussions may be worth it." She turned now to Miara. "Now let's see. What is this pretty thing traveling with you? Did your parents think it best you take a turn out of the public eye for a bit after all the turmoil? My only regret is that

I didn't stay long enough to see what the Takarans had to say to you after I told them."

"They didn't say much, so it was good you didn't put yourself out by waiting for it. And what are you doing in these parts? I thought you'd be headed to your order to write my death warrant yourself."

"I have other allies to the west I had hoped might assist me in your demise. But perhaps I may not need them now."

What had happened? The knight stood and strode to Miara, inspecting her. Then she turned to face Aven. He said nothing, his face sober now. Miara could see the knight's hand moving slowly toward the belt of her dress—did Aven see it? Miara wasn't likely to be able to dodge well at this range in the tiny tent, with half her body still tingling back to life and all of it aching. The resistance from the stones around their necks pressed at her from all sides. How much harder would it be to work magic in their presence? Was it even worth attempting?

"I *said* who is she?" the knight said more insistently.

"Just a friend I met on the road," Aven replied. He was a bad liar. She regretted not giving him a story that would work in this situation. What could he say, even if he wanted to say the truth?

"You may be a diplomat, but clearly deceit is not one of *your* fortes. You should really avoid it. Did you save all your skill for hiding your magic? Or perhaps if you were truly a talented liar, you wouldn't be in this situation right now. But no matter. Once my order sends me their decision, you won't have much more time to lie to people anyway. Now. Back to the nature of your companion."

The nature of the situation hit Miara. The knight had discovered he was a mage but also knew he was a prince. Their code must make exceptions in that case, for royalty or important political figures, but it still put Aven in a very bad situation.

"She's a cousin," he said, "that I decided to visit for a few days."

The woman let out a bark of laughter. "Which would conveniently protect her from me slicing her throat. Please. Try again, with the truth this time. I thought you promised to be nothing but frank with me."

"It is a promise I strive to keep to this day, Princess."

"Well, then? Quit stalling."

"She kidnapped me, and I don't know where she's taking me."

Now, the knight laughed outright, but the laughter faded to pure irritation. "A girl like *this* kidnapped a warrior like you? You're just trying to make me angry now."

Aven hesitated. Miara struggled to hide the laughter in her eyes, and she thought she could see him doing it, too. What could he possibly tell this woman that would appease her when the truth was so outrageous? He paused for a long time. Was he thinking, or was it just for dramatic effect?

"My mistress," he said, voice so soft it was almost lost in the wind.

Miara gasped involuntarily but didn't regret it. It gave a ring of truth to his words.

"Your *mistress*?" The anger in the knight's words made Miara wonder if the choice had been a mistake. What right did she have to be angry? "You had a *mistress*—"

Had they been involved? It seemed in line with Aven's luck that he might have fallen for one such as this, but the knight's anger only seemed to grow as he struggled to figure out what to say.

"Perhaps you are better at deceit than I'm giving you credit for because it doesn't seem there's an area you *haven't* lied about." She turned to the Devoted who'd escorted them in. "Go. She's a mage. That's all we need. Concubines are not protected. Are you ready?"

One of the dark hoods nodded.

"Burn her."

"Evana—" Aven started.

"My lady, there is no need, we can simply—" started the hooded knight.

Evana turned and slapped Aven across the face. Then she turned to the man who had questioned her.

"Do it, or I shall burn you with her."

And just like that, they were dragging her out of the tent and toward the fire.

Aven struggled to get a count of them, desperate for some plan of action to leap into his mind. The black robes and hoods made them all blend together. There could have been twenty—or thirty, he wasn't sure. Either way, it was too many. He scrambled for some kind of plan, anything. He drew a blank.

"It needs to be built up more, milady. The fire is too small as of yet," said the hooded knight who'd taken Mara by the arm. It was a large cooking fire, four or five feet across. Did they really know just how large a fire they needed to burn someone? Had they done this before? How many times? By the gods. He *had* to stop them, but how?

Evana strode forward from the back of the group. Knights parted to make way for her. She wrenched Mara out of the lesser knight's grip and, without even the slightest pause, shoved her into the fire.

Aven's heart leapt into his throat, and he lunged forward without thinking, breaking free of the knights that held him and landing on his hands and knees before the fire. Evana stopped him with a boot to the shoulder that sent him reeling to the side as he looked up at her in horror.

Mara screamed. Her body writhed against the flames, rolling to the right. Evana forgot him and lunged for Mara's boots, grabbing them. It took him a moment to realize her goal: to keep her from rolling or crawling her way out of the fire. Mara twisted and kicked, fighting to get free of both Evana's grasp and the heat. He could see her body itself morphing, twisting, animal forms mutating from one to the next—but what could possibly help her?

Aven lunged shoulder-first at Evana, knocking her to the side. But to his surprise, the boots came with them. He hauled himself off of her and scrambled toward where Mara had rolled out of the fire.

The charred, strange form—part woman, part animal—had no feet and large portions of black, lizard-like, scaly skin. He hoped to the gods that she had transformed herself that way, that the fire couldn't work that quickly.

He knelt over her, trying to shield her with his body, as he felt the knights rush toward them.

"Mara," he whispered desperately, "can you transform *me*?"

He had no weapons, no way to fight for her. At least not against so many. But he would have to try. He hauled himself to his feet and turned to face them, ready to fight. If she could transform him into something, anything more powerful than a human, maybe they had a chance? But with the resistance stones and her injuries…

The knights came at him, but haphazardly. Some hesitated. They did not really want to fight one on one. Most were clearly not warriors, unsure of how to begin in spite of their knightly titles. Pathetic. The first one reached him. Aven managed a solid blow across his jaw, sending him spinning.

His chest felt cold. A now familiar nausea twisted in his gut. He glanced down and saw the grass beneath his feet had gone straw-like and dry. She was doing it!

He tried not to think about what was happening or what he was becoming. It was too sickening, too much to process. He simply closed his eyes and opened them to furred paws the size of his head, with long, black claws at the ready.

A bear.

He batted at one, then another, knocking them flying, claws piercing and slicing along the way.

The others stopped. Hesitated. Now this, they *really* didn't want to risk. The scene stilled long enough for him to catch a glimpse of the flap of Evana's tent closing behind her. It was not like her to flee—what was she up to?

Aven turned to check on Mara. She was nowhere to be found.

He turned back to the crowd just in time to see Evana knocking an arrow to her bow, pointing squarely at him.

He dropped to all fours, turned, and ran. Indeed, Mara was no longer behind him. He didn't know where she was. He plunged into the forest, running at a diagonal.

A whistle, then a thud into a tree to his left. Moments later, another whistle-thud landed in a tree to his right. He was getting the hang of running as a bear, and he changed from a zig to a zag. Running at diagonals threw off archers. He picked up speed.

He felt the twist of transformation again but focused on running. His paws shrank smaller and smaller as he ran, but he tried to keep going anyway. Soon, the bear was gone, and in its place scurried some kind of rodent.

He wasn't sure how long he ran or how far. After a while, he realized there had been no noise nearby for quite some time. He stopped.

Where was Mara? Was she nearby? Was she injured? Had she… survived?

He gathered himself into a ball, but he was too cold. Too cold. He looked up at the treetops—yes, yes, he could see the stars. Not Casel, but he could spot Anefin. He took a deep breath and reached for the whispery energy of the light from the star. It warmed him slowly. The forest around him was quiet. He basked in the starlight and listened for any sign of pursuit.

Minutes passed. Perhaps longer. Then he heard one crunch, another. He uncurled himself, trying to figure out if he needed to run.

It's me.

He sighed with relief, feeling her voice in his mind. She did not sound well but not terribly weak either. And she was alive.

Are you okay?

Yes. Not fully recovered—but better. In the morning, I should be able to heal the rest of the way. The form of a small chipmunk neared him, approaching slowly and steadily. It had to be her. Chipmunks never moved that slowly.

How did you get away?

As you got bigger, I got smaller. You were a good distraction.

He laughed—or made some strange animal noise that he hoped she would take as one.

There's a log over here. Think you can tolerate a few hours as a chipmunk? she asked him. *It's dangerous to remain out of our own forms for too long, but it will be the best way to hide.*

I'll manage. She led him a short way toward a hollowed-out log. The darkness of the forest floor was dense and amazingly uneven. Things he would have normally not even noticed as he stepped over them became huge obstacles he now needed to circle around once they were discovered. Moss carpeted their tiny haven, and he crawled inside behind her.

She settled herself on the soft moss. He curled in beside her. His stomach gurgled, and he was hiding inside a hollow log as owl-bait.

But he was alive. So was Mara. They'd escaped Evana, at least for now. And for once, he'd had something to do with the situation. Things could be worse.

9   HEALING

When Miara woke up the next morning, it took more than a few moments for her groggy mind to process the strange bedding, her strange fur, and her adorable bedfellow. Right. Chipmunks. There was one nearby—right. Hell.

She had planned to wake up in a few hours and change them back, but apparently they'd both been exhausted. Hopefully it hadn't been too long for Aven.

Her mouth was parched, and her head spun with hunger. But there were no noises of men nearby, so perhaps—just perhaps—they had gotten away from that she-devil and her bastards.

She rolled onto her paws and crawled out of the log. Aven shifted but didn't wake. As cautiously as she could, she let the transformation unravel back into her current self. Or an injured version of it.

She had regained energy slowly in the night. The vibrant life of the forest around her helped, but keeping up their disguises was still a drain, so she had yet to heal completely. Burns were subtle, expensive injuries, with so many layers of skin to individually rebuild.

She looked down at her hands, the skin still covered with burns. She felt a little vain, but she didn't want him to see her like this. She would use what energy she could gather. She reached out into the pines, the roots, the fungi, a family of robins, a stand of birch—gathering what she could without injuring them. Gradually, she eased the skin and muscle back into the way it was supposed to be.

She twisted herself back into a chipmunk. She had to find some food. It felt a little safer until she could be sure there was really no one nearby.

What did chipmunks eat? She took a deep breath, and a wave of scents washed over her, suddenly appealing. Instincts twitched. Time to scavenge some breakfast.

When Aven awoke, he was still a chipmunk. He didn't mind being a chipmunk quite as much as he'd minded being a mouse, and Mara—or at least a chipmunk he assumed was Mara—was piling dark green needles and small nuts nearby.

Eat! she said. *Are you all right? You've been a chipmunk too long. Eat, and then we can go back to being ourselves again.*

He felt surprisingly well as he plodded over to the pile she was making. *What if we didn't?* he thought, only partly joking.

Didn't what?

Didn't go back to being ourselves. Just stayed here in the forest, as chipmunks.

She stilled, an acorn between her little paws. The wound on her shoulder she had shown him was still there, even in this brown-furred form. *Just stayed? You would stay here? With me?*

He nodded as best he knew how as a chipmunk. *What if we did? I would. We could.*

I wish that were true. She dropped the acorn and scurried away.

Was it something he'd said? He made his way slowly to the little pile, sniffing. Once he caught their fresh scent, they smelled surprisingly delicious. He chomped away.

A few minutes later, she returned with more nuts and ate. Watching her cheeks bulge made him snicker to himself, and for a moment he was amazed at all that he'd experienced since she'd plucked him from his balcony on the mountaintop. So much that he'd been missing, so much to discover.

All right. Ready to be a man again?

If I ever was one. Sure. He laughed, half to himself.

Boy, man, hardly a difference in most that I've met. Okay, brace yourself.

He shut his eyes, sat as still as possible, and after a few moments, the dizzy whirling began. It seemed to last not quite so long this time nor be quite so horrifying, and he opened his eyes to find the two of them on hands and knees above a tiny mound of pine needles.

He burst out laughing, and so did she. He immediately regretted it, though, with all the aches and pains that came back with the gesture. They both lurched stiffly to their feet.

"That seems to get easier every time," he said.

"You get used to it," she grunted as she tried to stretch out her shoulders. She glanced up at the sun and around them. "Well, I have no idea where we are now or where my bag is. I can call the horses, or they may be able to find us on their own or get free if someone hasn't locked them up too well." She looked upset at the thought. "I'll call them, and then we'll head out."

"Which way?" He listened for pursuers as she seemed to pick a direction. "They'll still be looking for us."

She nodded. "We'll go in the opposite direction and hope for the best. That way." Then she crouched down to the earth. He wasn't sure how she could manage it if she was anywhere near as sore as he was. Placing her palm flat on the dirt, she let out a long, low whistle. Her eyes were closed, her mind clearly moving somewhere else, the sound of the whistled note beautiful. He had a sudden longing to fall to his knees and kiss her. Before he could do anything crazy, it was over.

She stood, dusted off her hands, and smiled. "They heard, I think. They're free, or at least so it seemed. Let's head out. They'll catch up."

They had been traveling an hour, maybe two. Aven's ears caught the sound of horse hooves clomping slowly on dull earth. Mara grabbed his arm and pulled him with her into a crouch. They scrambled behind a nearby pile of brush.

He caught her eyes. "Our horses?" he whispered.

"No, they'd be at a gallop."

They waited. Could it be the Devoted? Around a large pine tree, horses finally came into clear view. Several wagons shuffled along, with women, men, and children shuffling along beside them.

Nomads, Aven thought.

"Regin, he's getting weaker," someone called out. "We need to stop."

"They could still be nearby." A woman's voice.

A long moment of silence. Aven spotted a wiry older man with tawny brown skin and peppered hair who moved forward and peered into one of the wagons. Then he spoke, his voice grim. "We have no choice. Make camp. Huz, Muj, do a search of the area for signs of them. The rest of you, hunker down."

He could feel Mara tense without looking at her. They were not hidden at all. Should they try to get out of here? Who were these people? They certainly didn't seem like Devoted. The nomads started their search on the opposite side of the road, giving them a moment to consider. They clearly weren't soldiers—there was nothing systematic or experienced to their searching. He glanced at Mara. Her eyes darted around. He braced himself for another transformation.

Instead, she stood up and motioned for him to follow her. She walked boldly toward the people moving just off the road to make camp. Still surprised, he staggered up and followed her.

The old man noticed them almost immediately. He made no sound, only watching them levelly, still, hands clasped in front of him. Waiting. Another man noticed, then another, as their footsteps crunched needles and branches with their approach.

"Hold," a man's deep voice rang out. "Announce yourselves."

The nomads all fell silent now, turning toward them. They might not be soldiers, but their faces were grave and serious, like the war-torn.

"We cannot announce ourselves," Mara called, "but we mean you no harm."

"I demand—" the man started.

"Demand all you want, we cannot," she said.

"Of course they cannot say who they are, Temul. Not with all these Devoted roaming around, wreaking havoc, killing children, looking for *them*." The old man spoke now.

Mara's face was blank as a mask, but he thought he heard her breath catch.

"You are the mages these Devoted are looking for," he said.

Mara said nothing. As in the confrontation with his mother, perhaps she was unable to say anything. It certainly wouldn't help to own up to it.

"Be gone. You have already done us enough harm."

"No," Mara insisted.

"*Yes*," the old man hissed. The camp fell silent. Two men were coming out of the wagon the old man had peered into before, carrying someone on a palette made from fabric and two branches.

It was a child. A boy.

Aven took two steps toward him without thinking. Mara put her hand on his arm to still him.

"They haven't stopped looking for you, but they headed south again. You're lucky you missed them. We were not so lucky," the old man said gravely. "Now if you cannot help us, go."

There it was. Aven had felt sure something was coming, that the nomad hadn't been planning to just turn them away. He'd just wanted to make a show of it. This old man *knew* they could help, or was betting they could. He must know something of magic. He was hoping to pressure them into offering their help.

He turned to Mara and whispered, "Could you heal the boy?"

She clenched her jaw. "Well, yes, but—"

"No. If you can heal him, we must do it." He could see the old man, who was pretending not to listen, perk up.

"I'm exhausted, Aven," she hissed through gritted teeth as quietly as she could. "Even on a good day, when I didn't need to heal, when we hadn't slept on the damn floor as *chipmunks* all night and eaten needles and pinecones—"

"What about the trees? Or take the energy from me, then."

"*No.* It's still not enough." She glared at him.

He glared right back. In that moment, he suddenly felt the heat of the sun on his skin. He pointed up at it. "You said I can pull it from the sun. I've done it before."

"Only *once*. Are you mad?"

"I did it last night, too. I can do it."

"No. Aven, you—" Her voice was getting louder.

"What has more energy than the sun?"

"I could *kill* you. If you don't pull at just the right rate, you'll go mad—or go dead. I won't. I could kill you."

"You won't," he said firmly, looking at her, face hard.

"We can't risk—"

"That boy's going to die because of *us*," he hissed, lowering his voice so the man couldn't hear him, preparing to beg her. "We must do it, Mara."

"But—"

"They're my people," Aven said more gently now. "Take me wherever you must, Mara, but can't you at least let me help them once? While I still can?"

Aven's voice was a mixture of command and vulnerability, both demanding and pleading. Much as she hated to admit it, he was right. Her bond would almost certainly keep her from killing either of them. The ordeal could probably make them both terribly weak, though.

But he was even more right that it was the right thing to do. The last thing she wanted to do with her newfound freedom from the Devoted Knights was risk it to these nomads she'd never met. If she was incapacitated, which was likely, who knew what they would do? And healing a life-threatening injury was usually the work of a team of skilled healers, sometimes as many as ten. She was talented but not necessarily *that* talented. She would likely be unconscious by the end of it.

She glanced from Aven's stern glare to the old man's and back again.

She sighed. At least she and Aven had lost everything these nomads could potentially steal.

"Fine. Damn you. I *told* you you'd get us both killed," she grunted at him.

"What if we could help you, old man?" Aven called.

The nomad turned, smiling, one eyebrow raised.

"The Devoted took our packs and horses. We need food, water, rest. If we try to help the boy, will you give us that in exchange?"

The old man nodded. "Come. The boy is dying. He lives, and you can have all of those." He motioned them forward.

"And if we can't save him?" Mara asked.

"We shall see."

Aven trotted ahead of her toward the boy, and she launched into a jog to keep up with him. The nomads had lowered his cot to the ground outside the wagon. The middle of the road was hardly a discreet place to do magic—let alone such intense magic—especially when there were Devoted Knights hunting them. It was stupid.

But they needed light, and time was precious. The middle of the road was as good as they were going to get. She said a quick prayer to Anara that they might actually be able to do this. Let the boy be younger and smaller than she guessed. Let pine needles be more nutritious than they tasted. Let Aven be an even more talented mage than she suspected he was. He was definitely more persuasive than she'd bargained for.

Or perhaps she was just falling in love with him. Almost certainly, that was what turned her into a confident wet noodle that would assuredly do whatever he wanted. No time to ponder that now, though. At least he, unlike others, was determined to turn her power toward good.

"What happened to him?" Aven asked.

"Arrow to the chest," a young blond woman answered, speaking only to Aven as he took to one knee. "We removed it, but he's having trouble breathing and has lost a lot of blood. Knights said they didn't like how he looked. Said they smelled magic on him." The woman took a ragged breath. "Can you actually help him?" Aven turned and looked up at Mara.

"Yes," she said. "We can." On another day she might have wavered, but something about the look in his eyes… She didn't want to fuss or hedge. She just knew.

They would because they had to. She knelt down beside Aven and looked at him solemnly. "Are you ready?" He nodded. "All right, let's do this. I'll start with the trees and critters around here, but I can only go so far without leaving a blackened crater of death. Then I'll rely on you. Put this hand on my neck. Yes, that's right." She moved his fingers to cover the back of her neck fully. She put her hands on the boy's arm, his skin cold and clammy under her fingers. "I suggest you close your eyes, but look toward the sun. See it behind your eyelids. Do what feels right, whatever you must to keep focused on the energy and pulling it. You can't stop." He nodded somberly. "When it is done, I will pull away from you—or more likely fall away. That's when you know you can stop."

He nodded just once, crisply.

"Ready?" she whispered, her eyes locked with his gray-green.

"Thank you, Mara." His fingers grazed the back of her neck softly.

She did not respond. Words would have stumbled out of her mouth if she'd let them as she felt a flush of warmth.

She tightened her grip on the boy's arm and began. She pulled slowly at first, feeling herself fill up, trying to give him a chance to catch on. Damn his insensitivity—it would only make this harder. He wasn't made for this.

But to her surprise, she felt his energies replenish immediately, then a little more. She pulled more. "Faster now," she whispered to him. "Ready? Going faster."

Now there was enough to feed a little into the boy. Tiny streaks of energy went zipping from her through his veins, seeking the tears, the blood, the holes.

"More," she demanded. She pulled more. He found more, somehow.

Now she could feel the boy's bones, feel the blood coursing through him, the brokenness, the sick blackness that was not the Way. Healing required little thought, just great energy. The body already knew what it should do, how it should be. She simply helped it do what it was already attempting. The boy coughed, then sputtered out the blood from his lungs.

His veins pulsed with magic, his bones shook with energy. The magic coursing through them both was intoxicating. Euphoric. The body longed to heal itself— but it needed *more*. She was possessed by the magic now, the spell, the process. Her body and the boy's were one system, magic flowing between them in a vortex. She lost all restraint. She lost all control. It needed more.

She drained energy as quickly as she could. The magic was in control of her now. She was a conduit, Aven was the source—and the boy *would* be healed.

The bones snapped and crackled in his chest. The blood fizzled. The boy screamed as his body violently and gracelessly rearranged itself. Nerves crackled with snaps and sizzles, alive again, desperately sucking every ounce of energy she had to once again—feel—alive—

She heard herself choke for breath. She saw herself, as if from just above and behind her, fall away from the boy. His eyes were wide and blue, looking around frantically, charged with the energy they'd stolen from the sun. She saw her body fall away from Aven, too, and crumple to the ground.

10   OLD SECRETS

A dull, piercing pain. Darkness. Heat.

Aven's consciousness returned slowly, orbiting around a dull knife of pain in his temple. Then he could feel his whole head ache, then the dryness of his mouth.

He lay for some time without thinking. Every part of him ached.

Slowly, thought returned. His current situation flooded back to him. He was not in his room in Estun. He was not a naïve prince holed up in a mountain anymore. He was— Mara. Where was Mara?

Nearby, he could hear children laughing, pots clanging, women talking quietly. It *sounded* like the kitchen in Estun. The smell of morning apple dumplings would be just wafting into the halls. He would have liked to curl up on a library window seat with his mother nearby and had a dumpling with tea. His heart twisted a little, aching at the thought.

Would he ever see her again? Did she know where he was now? Did she know about the Devoted? He had to assume she had been the sparrow watching.

Could the Devoted still be on their trail? At those thoughts, the air around him twitched unnaturally, and to his delight, he could feel that slight cold in his chest easily, right away, without trying. But with that cold feeling, the throbbing pain in his skull also intensified to the point that he had to cradle his head. Yellow splotches like stars flashed against his eyelids and faded again.

The pain stilled his thoughts and, therefore, his magic. Then the pain eased slightly.

He wiggled his toes and feet tentatively; he only felt stiffness. He clenched his fingers into fists and then stretched them back out again; they, too, seemed perfectly normal. He didn't seem to be bound at all, except by Mara's invisible chains. The pain in his extremities lessened as he began to move and stretch. Only the pain in his head stayed constant.

He opened his eyes just a crack. He was in some kind of small, dark tent. The only light came from the tent flap that led to the outside.

Wind ruffled the tent flap, sending his head splitting but also his stomach roiling. Apparently, he was hungry. *Starving*, actually.

Of course. The memory of harnessing the energy so Mara could heal the boy came back to him now. The feeling of the energy coursing through him, the vibrating bliss of the hot sun's light, the violent cold as the energy left him again. He had been standing between a blazing fire and an open window on a snowy day—but only within his mind.

But where was Mara?

Now he snapped his eyes fully open. The tent was small and barely had room for one person to sleep; no one else was inside. There was no sign of her.

Impulsively, he pushed himself up to sitting and regretted it immediately. His head spun, and the stars in front of his eyes returned. But he wouldn't let himself fall back down. He was determined to make sure Mara was okay.

"Ho, he wakens!" a woman's voice called. "Get Regin." The sound of little feet scurried and pitter-pattered away out of earshot. They must have heard me cursing, he thought.

A figure suddenly filled the slit in the tent where the light came in. He struggled to turn his head and focus, and a bowl was extended toward him. Hoping his strength would not give out, he took it. The visitor was gone.

The smell was heavenly. His stomach demanded he eat.

Could this be poisoned? He had no idea who had even handed him this. What if they'd turned him and Mara over to the Devoted? What if they were the very ones handing him this bowl?

Still, if they really wanted to hurt him, wouldn't it have been far easier to do so while he was incapacitated and unconscious? Hadn't they already had their best chance?

His stomach roiled again. There was no guarantee the food was safe. There was only one thing he could do. Eat. And perhaps pray.

Ancestors, he whispered in his mind. He lifted up the bowl on a whim, thinking of his great-grandmother Tena. *Let this food be safe, and let us be safe with these people, at least for a short while, and I will do what I must to put an end to these Devoted that roam our lands. If I'm ever free again, I'll do what I can to end all this injustice.*

Then he ate it quickly and licked the bowl dry. He was alone; no one but Mara knew he was a prince here, if she was even alive. He would do what he pleased.

When he had finished eating, he slowly laid himself back down and stared up at the top of the tent. Where was she? What if something had happened? What if she was—

The wind whipped savagely, disturbing the sides of the tent and threatening collapse. A savage pain stabbed behind his eyes.

He couldn't think of it. He couldn't think of her until he knew exactly what was going on.

Footsteps approached. Perhaps this Regin had arrived.

Sure enough, a figure leaned in. "Mind if I join you?" came the old man's voice.

Aven grunted, then croaked out with a dry, unused voice, "Please do."

Regin crawled in and sat, legs crossed, near Aven's feet, closing the tent flap carefully behind him. He held a skin and two round-bottom mugs, and he seemed completely at home in the tiny tent, as if it were just the right size for him and several more people.

"I brought you some water," Regin said.

Aven struggled to sit up again, albeit with somewhat less difficulty and fewer spinning stars this time. By the time he'd righted himself, Regin had poured some water and handed it to him carefully. Then the old man poured some for himself.

"That was a good thing you did back there," Regin said, voice soft.

Aven slurped up the whole cup and held it out for more. "The least we could do," he grunted.

"You may have felt that responsibility, but it was not you who put the arrow to his chest." The cup was refilled and in Aven's hand again. Regin's voice sounded like it spoke for the ages, having pondered every subject deeply. "I said you would have water, rest, food, and safety, and I swear to you that you have it, at least until you are recovered. We can't afford a run-in with the Devoted any more than you can, but we are glad to give you asylum. It is also the least we could do in return. A life is worth far more than that." Regin smiled, a twinkle in his eye.

"Thank you," Aven replied, bowing his head with the sincerity and formality of an ambassador accepting a very generous treaty. "The boy lives?"

"He is the very one who came to fetch me."

"Good," Aven said. "We will not overstay our welcome, I assure you. How long have I been out? And where is—my—" He stumbled. She wouldn't want him to reveal her name, and he wasn't at all prepared with a fake one or how to dance around the subject delicately. And what could he possibly call her? Please, sir, I'm concerned about the health of my kidnapper, is she safe just next door? I do hope so!

"About two days. She's in the next tent. Not awake yet, though. I expect she might have another day or so before she wakes up."

A cold chill ran through him. This was it, he realized. He should leave. He should run. She'd kidnapped him from his home and was taking him to gods-only-knew where. This was the best chance he was likely to get to run away.

But then again, he could hardly sit up. And beyond all that, he knew it was ridiculous to think he would go. He didn't *want* to escape her. He was far more concerned that she be all right. He was an idiot, clearly.

"More stew?" Regin asked.

Aven nodded, a little dazed at the feelings swirling through him, how intensely he wanted to stay with his captor. He needed to see that fiery hair at least one more time. He needed to tell her how amazing she'd been to watch, how a boy was alive now because of her, how much he loved her for that.

How much he loved her, period.

Ah, hell. He might as well admit it to himself. He was hopelessly and stupidly in love with her, and it wasn't going away. What would his parents think if they knew? What an impossible match. What an unlikely queen. But even as he knew how much some might hate the idea of a foreigner or an obvious mage—and there were probably other reasons, for she was probably a commoner, too—he could also see what a queen she *could* be…

They'd probably never have to overcome those obstacles because they were already up to their necks in worse ones. He should just shut up and keep the dreaming in check until it was at least the slightest bit within reach.

Suddenly, he realized Regin was quietly watching him eat his stew, occasionally glancing at the way the swirling air around Aven disturbed the tent. He wondered what Regin might think of his little quirk. Did he recognize it as magic as well? Not that they really needed to hide that from him at *this* point. He thought back. When Regin had run into them in the forest, he'd immediately called them out as mages. How had he known? A good guess, or was it more?

"Are you a mage?" Aven asked abruptly.

Regin hardly reacted or moved, just a slight smile curving his wizened old mouth. "Of a sort, yes. But not of your sorts."

"What do you mean?"

"Oh, I do have the gift. I know a trick here and there. Keep the fruit fresher longer, make the buds bloom a little sooner, make the leaves open in the sunshine. But they're only tricks. Not your sorts."

"What do you mean by our sorts?"

Regin smiled broadly. "Oh, you know, the talented sort. Well, and she's a mage slave. I'm a rare freemage, like you."

Aven stopped mid-spoonful. Could this man tell him what he needed to know? "A mage slave?"

Regin frowned. "You travel with one, and you don't know?"

"Why do you say it like that?"

"Like what?"

"Like *that*. Like there's more involved than riding horses or something."

"Isn't there?"

"No!"

"Well, *that's* more unusual than encountering a mage slave riding around in Akaria to begin with!" Regin let out a deep chuckle. Aven glared at him. "Oh, calm yourself, son. I mean nothing personal. But really, you don't know what a mage slave is?"

"Well… no. I've gathered she's from Kavanar. She doesn't look the slightest bit enslaved, if you ask me."

"She won't tell you more?"

"She doesn't seem to be able to. She says she can't. Perhaps she just doesn't want to. I can't blame her—you saw what happens when people know… more than you might like."

"Point taken. Well, you know what the Old Ones did, of course, that led to the Dark Days. The king of Kavanar was not forgiving. In line with their sins, all mages would pay. Since those days, all their kin have been enslaved. Many Devoted Knights, the really pious ones, do not kill. They capture mages and take them there to be slaves."

Aven gulped down the bite of stew in his mouth. Was *that* the fate awaiting him? "But how can a slave roam Akaria freely like she does?"

Regin gave a dark, bitter smile. "Ah, yes, she looks so normal, does she not? I wouldn't have known it if I hadn't met another mage slave, years ago. Those Old Ones—they didn't lock the king up and feed him only bread and water, did they? There were no shackles. No, it wasn't a *physical* enslavement. It was an enslavement of the mind. They took over his thoughts. It was his very being they enslaved, and they could make him do their will."

Aven felt himself go cold.

"And so when the king was finally freed, he turned their magic back on them. As they enslaved his mind, so he ordered to be done to all the other mages," Regin said in his gravelly old voice, shaking his head and looking down at his hands. "The last Old One, the last conspirator, before they killed him... they set him to the coals in the smithy and then forced him to use his magic one last time. Not to enslave anyone but to make a tool—a brand—that would allow its wielder to enslave, even if they had no magic. The king himself could do it. And probably did."

Aven found he was holding his breath. He let it out and forced another deep breath in. "Her wound, the wound on her shoulder, that's how you knew she was a mage slave."

"Yes."

"That brand made it?"

"Yes."

"It never heals."

Regin shook his head. "Sometimes it's almost a scar, sometimes it's bloody, never makes up its mind. The mage slave I knew was a good man; he told me what I know of this." He sighed and was quiet for a long moment. "So you see, they do not need chains or locks; they are enslaved from inside their heads out."

Maybe the stew was bad; maybe the idea was sickening. His stomach turned either way. It all made sense now. Was that why the wolves had attacked and turned away? Had his mother figured this out? "And all mages in Kavanar must submit to this?" he grunted through his anger.

"Yes. Their king made it law, not long after the Dark Days. He supposedly didn't want them getting out of control again. But some say it was more than that. Some say he wanted their power to be his alone, and mages were too powerful to tolerate as rebels. And so instead, he found a way to harness their power for his own ends. An excuse."

"Bastard," Aven whispered. The thought that a king could conceive of enslaving his people, let alone desire to—that wasn't just disgusting, it made his blood start to boil. Only a weak king or an evil one would be so afraid of rebellion. A good king wouldn't need to worry, or at least he hoped that was true. No freemages had ever shown up trying to enslave his father, at least not that he knew of. "How corrupt."

"Well, don't say that around the church. Or the Devoted. Or in pretty much any part of Kavanar or half of Akaria. The church has grown into an ally of the slavers. They preach righteousness, they celebrate their slavery. Thank King Demikin for keeping them safe. A right crock of shit, if you ask me. No one is asking, though, of course."

"I am," Aven said boldly, without thinking. "I am asking."

There was a little too much meaning in his voice. Regin could hear the arrogance behind those words, the kind of arrogance that came from someone with power. He raised an eyebrow but was wise enough not to press. Their eyes merely met for a moment, acknowledging the trust Aven showed in revealing the tiniest hint at a very large secret.

"Well, if you're asking, then I'll tell you. In the Dark Days, mages using magic to enslave others. That was against the Way. How can they possibly argue that someone else using magic to enslave mages is *not* against the Way? It's the same damn thing. It's as simple as that."

Aven nodded.

"How can a church claim it's not evil to enslave hundreds of children before they even know they've got magic? Seems like the same thing to me, only instead of being done to one stupid, greedy man, it's being done to hundreds of innocents. Thousands, for all I know."

Hundreds, Aven thought. Thousands. If Demikin and his fathers before him sought to harness mage power, Kavanar could be building a military force of thousands of mages like Mara, perhaps some even more powerful. By the gods.

Regin continued. "How does that make sense? How does that add up? No preacher or Devoted is going to feed me that nonsense. It's *not* the Way of Things, that's for sure, and no one will ever talk me out of that. That king is building up a mighty debt against him, and someday I tell you the Balance will set things right."

Regin regarded Aven for a long moment. Aven hoped he would go on, but he seemed to be waiting for a response. Aven shrugged a little and spread his hands before him. "The Way says that it is natural for people to be free. Of course, if they go against the Way, everything goes out the window. I guess that's how these slavers justify their actions, not that I agree."

"Who gets to say what is against the Way, or what is a just punishment once you've gone against it? Who gets to judge?" Regin spat. "Let me ask you something— did your magic *feel* against the Way? Did it feel wrong? Could you hear that little voice in your heart telling you not to use it?"

Aven snorted. "No. It feels... so far from wrong. I've never felt so right in my life." He paused. "How can they justify punishing hundreds or thousands of mages for the sins of a few?" He shook his head, feeling a dark mixture of despair and fury.

"Don't know," Regin said. "I suppose they no longer need to justify because no one's questioning them. Except us in this little tent." Regin grinned. "Kavanar's pretty much gotten away with it for this long. Those poor mages must follow their orders; from within their minds they are compelled."

So, it was just as it sounded, really. She was a mage, therefore she was a slave. She belonged to another and had to follow the whims of another—like kidnapping the prince of a foreign land. This is what she meant about not having a choice. This was why they couldn't just stay in the forest as chipmunks forever. This was why she could not settle things peacefully. She was compelled, as fully and completely as anyone could be compelled, by magic. Her choices were not her own.

No, it couldn't *be*. Just as Regin said, it was *so* wrong, so against the Way of Things. How had the Balance not righted itself already? How many decades had this gone on? There *had* to be some way to right the situation—to fix things—to make her whole again.

"Can they be freed?" he said quickly.

Regin's face brightened with laughter in the corners of his eyes, his mouth. "There's *something* more than riding horses going on, I swear it! Maybe not as much as I thought at first, but…"

Aven glared at him again but did not deny it this time. No point in lying when it was already obvious to the old man.

"Not that I know of, son. I've heard rumors, but they're probably just hopes and dreams rather than shadows of the truth. However, if you ask me, magic is magic, even if it's used to enslave. And any magic that can be worked can be un-worked or worked in reverse. The question is how and with what."

Aven stared into the now-empty bowl. How? Where could he find the answer to that question? Would his mother know? Someone more trained? But how could one find someone like that in Akaria? Certainly, to keep the king's power safe, anyone that had known was probably killed at the start. Anyone that knew how to free the mage slaves would hold a huge amount of power against Kavanar and its king.

He smiled at that thought. Exactly why he was going to figure this out.

Then a new revelation occurred to him: if she was kidnapping him to become a mage slave as well, then he could soon be in the same predicament. He had more than one stake in this game, and the sooner he could find a way out, the better. If such a way existed.

Regin refilled his mug and took the stew bowl. "This has been more than enough excitement for now. You should get some more rest."

Aven bowed his head deeply in thanks and lowered himself back down to the bed as Regin crawled from the tent. For a while, he lay racking his brain for a way to free her, wringing the few facts he knew about magic for anything that could help him. But mostly he just cursed himself for knowing so goddamn little.

He was going to be extremely lucky if it didn't get him killed.

The next time Aven awoke, the ache in his head was gone. He was hungry, but not so hungry as the last time, and in dire need of a bath.

He got to his hands and knees and lifted the tent flap, squinting at the bright fall sunlight. His eyes watered. When they finally adjusted, he could see a fire pit before him with a young boy tending it.

"Hello there," he called.

The boy looked at him but said nothing.

"Is there a stream or something to wash in?"

The boy nodded. "Over that hill and down by the boulder. About a hundred paces."

"Thank you," he said, nodding. He proceeded to crawl the rest of the way out of the tent and carefully try righting himself. After a few dizzy moments and muscle spasms, he was able to stand well enough. He lurched unevenly down to the creek.

The shackles on his forearms remained. Given how little they actually did, they seemed almost silly. It was not the shackles on his wrists that held him here.

In spite of them, he felt oddly free. No one was watching him or directing him in a certain direction. No one was waiting for his arrival at a specified time or requiring his presence. He could stumble on forever if he wanted to, or nowhere. Perhaps he should think about running more seriously. The threat of slavery was all too real if what Regin said was true. Freedom was something Aven had always had; how could he know how much he would miss it? Not every captor would be like Mara.

He crested the hill, only a little dizzy and out of breath, and headed down the other side. He spotted a large boulder among the trees, and sure enough, water flowed beyond the brush. The area around the camp was lightly wooded, occasionally opening up into fields of tall grass and flowers. Was this the same camp, or had they moved? He wasn't sure anymore; he knew little of the terrain from their nighttime escape. The skies were bright and clear, and most of the leaves were yellow and ready to fall. A strong, brisk wind hit him from the top of the hill down, and he couldn't help but feel exhilarated by all that energy, the power rushing by. Power that he could now harness.

He reached the boulder. Near it, the brush had been cleared to make an easy path down to the water. He called out, but no one answered. He looked around the other side of the rock, upstream, downstream, but saw no one. He surveyed his clothes. They were beyond filthy now. They needed to go in with him to be washed thoroughly. He might as well just wade in with his clothes on.

He kicked his boots off and pulled off his socks. He dipped his toe into the stream and gasped. Just as he feared—ice cold. Well, at least it would wake him all the way up. He waded in a little and then a little more, starting to shiver.

As the water was lapping against his calves, he suddenly remembered—the star map!

As if a wave were rushing at him, he darted back out of the water and onto the bank and pulled the map from his pocket. Seeing it made him want to stop and study it, but he needed to focus on the task at hand. He wandered around behind the boulder and searched till he found two dry, flat rocks that were well back from the stream's bank. The earth near the stream was moist, so he used the dry tops of the rocks on either side of the map to pin it down safely from the wind and protect it from the damp soil.

Now his ankles were freezing. He needed to get this over with, so he rushed back around the boulder and stepped into the water again.

For a moment—fueled by either his imagination or his exhaustion, he wasn't sure—he thought he saw Mara before him, laughing in the sunlight, bare shoulders just breaking the stream's surface. And then the illusion, or whatever it was, was gone. He stepped in again, but this time he pretended he was joining her in the water.

Was there a way…?

There was no time to contemplate such things. It was too damn cold. He needed to wash his clothes. He started with his shirt, removing it and beginning to scrub.

As he worked, he went back through everything Regin had said. He racked his brain for clues, ideas, loopholes, anything that might break the spell enslaving her. No ideas came.

When the shirt was clean, he pulled it back over his head and made for his pants and undergarments. He was going to have to let these clothes dry somehow; he wondered if the nomads would loan him some, if they even had any to spare. Mara had said he could make fire, tease the sun—wasn't there some way he could warm himself while his clothes dried on this cold autumn day? He was just finishing with his pants when he sensed a presence, like someone was watching him.

He turned toward the bank just as his mother's glowing apparition formed, Lord Beneral and the third companion behind her.

"Aven!" she called.

He stared at her, blinking. Oh, gods. This was going to be hard to explain.

"Mother!" he called back. "And Lord Beneral! I hadn't expected to see *you* here."

"Hail, my lord," said Beneral, bowing with a grin.

"Apparently you are not the only one who's been hiding some magic," his mother said wryly.

"Your steward Fayton is quite the observant one," Beneral replied. "This is my apprentice Vonen, who assists us by casting this spell."

"I am pleased to have you as allies." With as regal of a nod as he could muster, Aven grabbed his pants and made his way toward the bank. He stopped as close as he could while remaining in the water. "Water's cold, but the air's even colder. Can we talk from here?"

"Of course," his mother replied. "Are you all right? We've been following you—well, watching. Via the birds."

"I figured you would be."

"Clever work getting out of those fools' clutches back there," she said.

"The nomads? They're not fools."

"No, the Devoted. Evana. I knew you were a great warrior. But I hadn't imagined you with your own set of claws." Her eyes twinkled with laughter, even more now as a being made of light.

"Ah. Well. Thank you."

She was silent for a moment. So was he.

"You're not leaving," she said flatly. A slight smile remained in her eyes.

He said nothing.

"You're free. She isn't here holding you. And yet you sit like this is where you belong."

He looked at her as solemnly as he ever had.

"Maybe it is where I belong. I can't leave, at least not yet," he said, unsure how to broach the subject.

"I assumed you had a reason. What is it?"

"I just…" How could he explain?

"Is it magic? A spell? Does she have something? Know something?" She watched his face at each question for a sign or reaction, but found nothing. "She's going to kill you or enslave you at best. But—you already figured that out, didn't you."

He nodded.

"Then what is it?"

He wasn't sure if it was the words or the frigid air on his shoulders, but he did find himself shaking. "*She's* not the one trying to hurt me, Mother. She's a slave."

She paused, frowning. "Does that make a difference?"

He shrugged, searching for words. "To me, it does. I'm not a fool, I know I'm in danger." He searched her eyes, hoping to find the words to explain that Mara was more than a kidnapper, more than some mercenary from Kavanar. If he was inexperienced in love, he was even more inexperienced in telling his *mother* he was in love. With an audience, no less.

"I don't understand. What could be worth giving everything up—" Then she stopped, as if the only reason why he might be so crazy and irrational had just occurred to her. "Ah, but there is that one thing you *don't* have. And have struggled to find."

He glanced up to meet her eyes, hopeful.

"By the gods. You're in love with her, aren't you."

"Indeed." He looked away, then down at his feet. Anything to dodge her stare. She said nothing. He swallowed hard. Maybe now he could explain the situation if he didn't have to relay the craziest part of the story. "She might have been born a mage, and so in Kavanar that might mean that she's a slave. But she didn't ask for this. She didn't ask to kidnap me. Just like *I* didn't ask for this. But fate brought us together. I can't leave her. I have to help her. Somehow. I have to."

Her eyes bored into his, a mixture of sadness and love that he didn't know how to interpret. "How, Aven? She can't be helped."

"Yes, she can. I have to free her."

The apprentice Vonen gasped, then tried to hide it. Beneral raised his eyebrows. His mother only smiled. "Stubborn as your father," she whispered.

"I have to find a way," he insisted, his voice hard.

"I tried to argue with a Lanuken in love once, and I wound up married to him. I won't fight you, crazy as you are."

He sighed with relief. Thank the ancients, she understood.

"Well, he's said he wants to free her. Seeing that he can't be argued with, what shall we do next, mages? Any suggestions?"

"We could at least check the libraries for spells or histories to give us any clues," said Vonen.

"We can contact some of the elders. Perhaps there is one who at least knows if it's possible," Lord Beneral added.

"All right, you heard that, Aven. We will go back now. It's midday. Be back here at sundown if you are still able, and I will try to return and see if we can find anything to help you."

He nodded earnestly. "Thank you, Mother."

She nodded with a smile as their forms dissolved into the air.

He was alone by the water. He listened to the stream gurgling, the birds, the wind in the leaves. The air across his chest made him shiver, and he dunked back into the water. He hoped they would find something because otherwise, he was purely on his own.

There *had* to be a way to free her. He was committed now; he would find a way to free Mara or die trying.

Aven fetched his star map from the riverside and retreated to the warmth of his tent to wait for his clothes to dry out. He took them off, laid them out beside him, and hid himself under the furs. Regin brought him a generous helping of some sort of soup this time, as well as some kind of herbal tisane. For the first time since their journey began, Aven felt warm, clean, well-fed, healthy, and safe all at the same time.

"How is she doing?" he asked Regin before the man could leave.

"She's fine, just needs more rest, that's all. She did the heavy lifting." Regin ducked out of the tent with a wink.

As his clothes dried, he studied the star map. Two large circles graced the top half, each overlapping with the other. Dozens of characters circled the outside of each ring. Several characters indicated the months of the ancient lunar calendar. The bottom half of the map was divided into thirteen tall, narrow sections. Now that he had some time to study it, he felt sure he could make out several familiar stars at the top. The names still seemed wrong, for what little he could recognize of the angular, hooked Serabain script. Why would characters be missing, broken? And beyond seeing them labeled, what good was this map? What did it have to do with magic? What did the sections at the bottom mean? Could it just be a very old, very ordinary star chart? Was he ridiculous to think there must be something special about it? Perhaps Teron had just been enthusiastic about the stars. Or trying to indicate something else entirely.

He sighed, folded the map back up, and laid his head down to take a nap.

He awoke with a start, realizing that he had no idea what time it was. Dusk could be long gone. He yanked his still-damp clothes on, shoved the star map in his pocket, and lifted the tent flap. The light sliced through the trees in long, dramatic, beautiful rays. It was not dark yet, but it was coming. He headed for the stream again as quickly as he could while still trying to look casual; he hoped Mara had not woken to see him sneaking off into the forest as fast as he could.

No one stopped him or seemed to notice him. He was back at the stream, sitting on top of the large boulder, with plenty of time to wait till the sun set. A few women were washing clothes in the water, talking softly, laughing. They nodded to him, then ignored him. It was a lovely, if cold, fall sunset, and they were all simply going about their business.

In the better light, he examined the star map again. He found Casel, and he studied the characters around it, struggling to translate the old Serabain. The paper was faintly translucent, and the sunlight made it glow a little. Between the sound of laughter and rushing water and the time alone to himself to study the map, he felt a strange contentment. Even with all the other problems in the world, there was still this moment.

As the sun faded, he stopped trying to read the map. The only parts he could decode were names of stars he already knew. The bottom portion completely eluded him. Indeed, the words seemed wrong, nonsensical. If only he knew more of ancient languages, but such scholarly study typically had little practical use. Thel would probably have known better what it said as he'd taken to the more esoteric subjects. Aven sat back and watched the water swishing by. The young women finished their work and strolled back to camp, smiling as they passed. He smiled back, nodded, and pretended to be enthralled by the beauty of nature at the moment. Which wasn't far from the truth.

As soon as the women crested the hill, his mother and her companions appeared near the water's edge. His mother's face looked tired. He hated hurting her. He really hoped they'd found something.

Their glowing forms glided toward him in an odd blend of walking and sliding until his mother could sit near him on the rock. How that worked, he had no idea.

"What did you find?" he asked.

"Not much concrete, but a few things," she said. "First, Beneral was able to reach Wunik, one of the elders and his teacher."

"He believes freeing Kavanar mages is possible, based on the oldest tales," said the lord. "Although he does not know how, he believes that if the tool they use to bind the mages was made by a mage, then it must be possible. We have no examples of magic that cannot be undone with other magic. Aside from, perhaps, this one."

His mother nodded. "Anything that can be bound should be able to be unbound. The question is which kind of magic, what technique. But that we could find nothing on. Since the Dark Days, Kavanar and the Devoted appear to have been working to hide that knowledge. And it was rare enough to begin with."

"Wunik also advised that he felt you'd have the Way of Things on your side, which can't hurt," said Beneral, "although I'm sure there are a few Devoted who would disagree."

"The old tales also say air magic is used to bind the slaves," his mother added. "Which is good news."

Aven nodded solemnly. That was a positive, but not much help. To even believe he had a chance of success, he had already assumed all these things were true. It was nice to know it was indeed *possible*, but that didn't tell him what to do. "Anything else?"

"Unfortunately, no," she said. "We tried to reach several other elders. Three of them knew nothing of the subject, but two of them that should've known… could not hear our calls. We could not find them with squirrel or hawk, either. We've sent riders to check on them. I have a bad feeling about them."

"Wunik wishes you all the luck of the gods," said Vonen. "He said he hopes to speak with you when you return."

Aven smiled. "That's good of him to say. I'm going to need all the luck I can get."

"I found the book you left on the balcony," his mother said. "I just noticed today—it's a book of magic, isn't it?"

He nodded. "I never got to read it. Teron gave two books to me. Wait—"

"Teron!" she cried.

"I never had a chance to tell you! That's why we were headed to the balcony to talk. I had the strangest conversation with Teron, where he gave me those two books. Inside one was a map of the stars that I managed to bring with me. Otherwise, I didn't get to look at the books. But what was so strange—it seemed like he knew about my magic, that Evana *had* told him. But for some reason, giving me those two books was his only response."

She said nothing, dumbfounded. Beneral and Vonen frowned and glanced at each other.

"Surely they are gone by now. He never mentioned anything of it?"

She shook her head. "It's only been three days, Aven. They are not gone. A drop in the bucket of their extended stay. But we felt sure they didn't know. They've carried on just the same. Accepted our excuses at your absence readily. Why?"

"They're mages," Aven asserted. "That must be it."

"What! No. How could that be?"

"Teron, at least. I'm telling you. Confront them."

"And if they are not?"

"You have been nothing but polite to them. I'm sure they can take a good-natured accusation. But think about it. Why would they want to stay in Akaria so long? How can they have nothing else to do? Maybe they have some ulterior motive."

She nodded slowly. Beneral spoke up. "Takar does not have mage slaves—or at least not that we know of—but the Devoted are based there. My merchants say it is not a good place for mages."

"Evana seemed to have a kill-on-sight policy."

"Perhaps it is worse than we thought, and they don't want to return."

"Ask them. Ask him why he picked those books, how he found them. He said they were in our library—why did he go looking?"

"I will," she nodded. "Vonen's power is waning, Aven. This star map, can we see it?"

He turned and picked up the map to show her—and gasped in surprise.

The light had faded, only glimmers of twilight left. But the map was not dim. It glowed with a silvery, shimmering light.

"It's like... starlight," his mother whispered. "Moonlight."

"By the gods," whispered Vonen.

Looking closer now, he saw the most fascinating thing of all. There *had* been parts of characters missing. The bottom half of the map was now littered with new and transformed characters that glowed only in starlight, with no ink beneath. He had read the map in the darkness before, and it had never glistened like this.

But he'd never tried outside. Under the night sky.

"A map made with star magic. Very rare indeed," Beneral muttered.

"Star magic? You're sure?" Aven asked. The lord nodded. Star magic was a type of air magic—specific, rare, and, in some places, forbidden.

"What does it say?" his mother asked.

"Well, this top part is mostly a standard map of the sky. But you see here—much of this section is written only in the starlight. I couldn't read it till now! I don't know what any of it says. Yet."

New characters lit up with each moment that passed. They sat in silence for a while, watching the letters glimmer and fade into view. Aven looked up. Only a few of the brightest stars were shining. There were many more yet to come out. It had not taken much starlight to activate the map.

He eyed Casel as they watched. At first, there were no marks next to her. Every other star seemed to fill in first. Then one appeared. Moments later, another.

"These," he said, jabbing his finger at the ones near Casel. "Can any of you make out what those mean?"

They all shook their heads. He gritted his teeth. Another character appeared.

"We can't stay much longer, Aven," his mother said. "I will talk to Teron. And we'll look in the book for answers about this map. And we can try to find what this means, or a translation. Is it Serabain?"

"I think so," he replied. "Try this word. And these." He pointed at those near Casel, and another word in the bottom portion of the map directly below Casel.

"Got it," said Beneral. "We must go, my lady. I'm aiding Vonen, but his energy is fading."

She nodded. "Be safe, my son." And for a moment, she placed her hand over his. He felt nothing physically, but the gesture made his heart ache. For a moment, he longed to hug her, kiss her cheek, assure her somehow.

He couldn't. He swallowed. This was the path he had chosen.

She stood as if preparing to physically leave.

"I will be safe, Mother. Don't worry. It will be okay." Ridiculous words, but it was all he could say.

"If we find something, we'll watch for a chance to tell you." He nodded. "If we don't, well, gods be with you, Aven."

And then she was gone.

He sat there for quite some time in the darkness, feeling the loss of her presence beside him, wondering if he'd ever be in the same room with her again. He watched as more characters faded into view. The earliest ones shone brighter as time passed.

Soon, the whole map was filled. Its maker had tried to cram tomes' worth of knowledge onto a single sheet. He stared at the words near Casel. More characters had appeared by each, and whole words had solidified since his mother and her escorts had left him. Had they seen enough to go on? He hoped so because all the new characters were foreign to him.

There was one word near Casel that he could have added himself—freedom. But what was the word *beside* it? He tried to shrug off the crick forming in his shoulders and stared harder at the cryptic glyphs, as if glaring would tell him what he needed to know.

11 NEW SECRETS

Miara awoke. The pain in her head competed with the pain in her shoulder. But the pain was secondary to the binding haunting her dreams—tugging at her—demanding. She had just enough strength to finally let it move her.

She did not know where Aven was. He had to be gone.

For a while she simply lay still, partway awake but too weak to even open her eyes.

She had to find him. Her shoulder ached, burned, urged her on. She struggled to sit up.

The tent flap opened. A woman peered in, disappeared, then reappeared with a bowl and a cup filled to the brim. Miara accepted them gratefully.

Then the woman was gone before she could ask about her captive. Eating the savory stew consumed nearly all her strength, and she lay back down again. Sleep took her in spite of the nagging at the edges of her mind.

She did not know how long she slept. The next time she woke, she was determined to find Aven. The pain in her head had lessened, but her brand's insistence had only increased. She had to ease it, or it would drive her mad. And she wanted to see his face, make sure he was okay.

She emerged from her tent into darkness. There was nothing nearby but other tents. A hundred paces away, people swirled around three boisterous fire circles, two small and one large. She studied the dramatic silhouettes, looking for his dullish blond-brown hair and sharp jaw amid the sea of dark beards and flowing curls. There was no one like the Akarian. He was not there.

Her shoulder stabbed at her suddenly, so intensely that she stumbled, then fell to one knee.

She was not alone. Someone close by gasped and came to help her. With their hands on her, the pain in her shoulder eased. She looked up through her tangled, sweaty hair to see the brown, old man who had welcomed them.

"Are you all right?" he said. "Some food?"

She nodded. She needed to ask him about Aven—but did he know Aven's name? What should she call him? Her thoughts whirled, and she was far too dizzy to formulate an answer.

The old man sat her by one of the smaller fire circles and put a bowl in her hand. She ate mechanically. He said nothing of Aven, and Miara didn't ask. Certainly, it was obvious. He must be gone.

She stared into the stew bowl, shoveling food into her mouth more out of habit than desire. Gone. He was gone. That would mean she had failed. How would the Masters react? What would they do? She did not think the Dark Master would like being proven wrong.

But that was a distant worry. Her future had already been bought and sold long before she was born. Until now, she'd had the *present* at least. Now that, too, was gone.

And she had failed. She *could* fail; she couldn't do just anything she put her mind to. Her confidence in herself had been misplaced. And much worse—until now—she'd had him.

Her heart suddenly ached in her chest. The pang was more sincere and more painful than any in her shoulder could be. The pain was her own. A wave of longing for him flooded her, irrational and stupid, but honest. She had tried not to admit the way he made her feel. How could she, when she was taking him to them? How could she admit the way she felt when he looked at her, or the thrill she'd felt at the wispy tendril of his thoughts, as though she could already feel him kissing her neck? She had already felt it, in her soul. How could she stand those feelings in her mind right beside the knowledge that she was most likely the instrument of his death?

Or... perhaps not. She caught her breath, then hoped no one would notice. She might be defeated, but *he* had defeated *them*. She had never had a chance of beating them—but he had. Wasn't it far better for him to have his freedom, to exact some justice in the world? That was a worthy failure indeed. If he had escaped her, she should rejoice in her own defeat. Through it, he had defeated her Masters. What more could she want?

Darkly, selfishly, she knew of one thing more she wanted. To have him as her own, to get to really feel those lips on her neck. But she hated herself for wanting him, because she couldn't have him without his own enslavement. She didn't want anyone to have to endure that, let alone a man who longed to do so much good for the world, who had the power to do it—if he were free. If he were not with her. She knew his freedom was worth her failure.

The pain in her shoulder intensified to a dull, insistent cramp, but with a touch of burning at the edges. Her bond was displeased. And yet, it did not insist she ride for Mage Hall. Either it knew that was impossible without more rest, or perhaps it was weaker this far from Mage Hall. She doubted that.

In spite of the nagging pain, she felt her heart growing lighter. A weight had been lifted. She ought to be filled with dread. Certainly, the Dark Master would do his worst. Perhaps she would find out what happened to Dekana firsthand. But… Aven was free.

She asked the old man for more food. He told her his name was Regin and brought her a hearty soup, a crust of hard bread, and even some ale. She ate it with relish now and listened as one nomad, then another told stories. She finished eating and sipped the ale as a pair of sisters brought out some drums and a flute and began to sing. The ale was probably a bad idea. She didn't care. What was a small celebration without ale? But the taste was bittersweet.

As she listened and sipped, she began to feel that someone was watching her. At first, she ignored it. She was surrounded by strangers who had a right to stare. A new person among them was an object of curiosity, especially one that had saved someone's life. But as the feeling persisted, her eyes darted to the other fire circles. None of the nomads were watching her, all caught up in the entrancing song. Still, the feeling did not pass.

And then—the next time that she glanced around—there he was.

It was as if time had slowed and stopped. Her heart leapt, and she heaved in a ragged breath. Aven stood just outside of the firelight. He leaned against a tree, watching her. Their eyes locked. His twinkled with laughter and the flickering firelight. Was he a ghost? Was she dreaming? Was she delirious and needed more rest? She stood and strode toward him, leaving the circle. None of them seemed to notice. She stopped just short of him.

They simply met each other's gaze for a long moment. It was as if they were meeting for the first time, as if they were two free creatures coming together in the night. Everything about him seemed strangely clearer and more vivid. A halo of firelight danced across the stubble on his chin, the pale green glitter of his eyes, the cut of his shoulders, and his arms folded across his chest. She could feel his breath, his gaze on her skin.

How would things have been different if they'd met in other lives? Could she have been just another lowly peasant in the crowd around a handsome soon-to-be-king? Would he have noticed her? Could he have been just another farmer in her village? Would they have found each other if either of them had been born free? There was no point to this flight of fancy. They were not free. They never had been. Neither of them had any choice in their fates, whatever they may be.

"What are you doing here?" she said, blurting out the only thing she could think to say.

"What kind of question is that?" he said, laughing. "Where else would I be?"

"Don't be ridiculous. You could've run. You're still here."

His face grew serious, although he still smiled. He said nothing.

"You didn't run. Why? You could've run."

He shrugged and looked into the fire. He was silent for a long moment. "You're right," he said eventually, now meeting her eyes. "I could've."

"You *should've* run." She gritted her teeth angrily through the flash of pain.

He shrugged again and turned his eyes back to the fire. "Maybe."

"But you didn't. Why?" she whispered, heart aching.

"You really don't know?" He met her eyes with a small smile.

All of her lightness had evaporated, and the weight that returned felt twice as heavy. The drums of the nomads pounded darkly in time with her heart. The Masters were not defeated. Aven was still here. They would still enslave him or kill him. She would still have to watch. She felt tears forming in her eyes and frantically tried to blink them away. How could he not leave? She rushed toward him then and pounded her fists against his shoulders, feeling the hot tears in her eyes and struggling to hide them. "Damn it, Aven! Why! You should have run—damn it! Damn you!"

He caught a fist mid-thrust, then grabbed her other arm and held her tight against him, trying to calm her. She fought, then collapsed against his chest in defeat, trying to swallow the emotion and exhaustion that overtook her.

Her ear against his chest, she could hear him breathing now. She could hear his heart beating. The beats of hearts and drums steadied her somewhat. She straightened and stared at him. His face was fraught with emotion that she couldn't read. He had such a noble face— indeed, the kind a king should have. Nothing like their sniveling king in Kavanar. Aven seemed filled with wisdom beyond his years, the weight of heavy decisions on his brow. He was staring hard into her eyes, his jaw tight.

"Everyone would probably be happier if I'd run," he said. "But I don't care. I'm not going to."

She caught her breath at the determination in his voice. It was a voice people would follow to their deaths, a voice that could command thousands. But gods, why? Why was he so determined about *this* of all things— gods, please, make him run away from me. Ice stabbed into her shoulder, pain shooting along her collarbone and toward her heart at the openly rebellious prayer, sending needles down her leg, up her neck, making her cry out.

"What's wrong? Are you all right?" he demanded.

"Yes, ignore it, ignore me," she whispered, wishing he would listen.

"That's just it. I can't."

She forced her eyes open, catching his. What could he mean? His voice was heavy with significance. Could he possibly…

"You should get as far from me as you can," she said, grunting each word through clenched teeth, steeling herself to the now-savage pain of outright defiance.

"I can't. And I won't," he said boldly. To her surprise, he leaned in and stopped, his lips close but just barely not touching hers. Did he really mean to kiss her? She gasped and then found herself leaning closer too without even thinking. And in response, his lips met hers, and he kissed her on the mouth.

In the same instant, both her greatest wish and deepest fear became real. At first she stood frozen, shocked. Her pain had vanished—her bond approved. The Masters would approve. The thought sickened her.

But there were more immediate things to think about—namely, his mouth. Before she could stop herself, she found herself returning his kiss hungrily. His lips caressed hers, and she felt it all with a sharp intensity—the wetness of his mouth, his hands circling around her body, pulling her close. He pulled her out of the firelight, into the shadow of the tree trunk, and pressed her body against it with his own. She kissed him as though she might never kiss anyone again. Perhaps it was true. Perhaps she wouldn't. She could not think of how another kiss could possibly be better than this one in this moment.

The flutes from the campfire wove fine melodies around each other, and the drums pounded a driving beat, urging them on. Still, something nagged at her—something was wrong with this, something was wrong, terribly, terribly wrong… And it wasn't her brand for once.

You fool, you're helping them.

She broke away from him abruptly and staggered a few steps away. If he thought she loved him, he would *never* run. He would never get away. He would be bound to the Masters even more surely than she was. This was the problem, the cause of her grief. She could need his kiss like a seedling needs the sun. She could want him like a drowning woman wants breath. But if he knew she needed him so desperately—how could he ever leave? He never would.

And he had to. He *had to* get away from the Masters if there was ever another chance. Her shoulder sliced into her with agony, and she lurched to one side.

She had to find some way to drive him away. As much as it would hurt, as much as she would hate it, she hated helping them much more. She would not see him destroyed if she could prevent it. Her shoulder seemed to have sprouted thorns that now ground and twisted and ripped through her flesh. She could not defy the brand, but perhaps she could at least not help them willingly. She would not show him how much this hurt.

"What's wrong?" he said softly, a note of fear in his voice.

She said nothing for a long while, unsure of what to say. Should she pretend? Could she? Should she lie? Would her bond even let her? Could she stand to break his heart?

"We can't do this, Aven," she whispered, her voice rough and breaking. Her voice was made of gravel, it seemed.

"Why not?" he said simply.

She wanted to tell him—well, everything. But there was no way. "I wish I could explain. But I can't. I am not worthy of this," she whispered.

"Don't be ridiculous. Yes, you are." There it was again, that king's conviction aimed right at her. She couldn't help but instantly believe him. And yet, it changed nothing.

"You don't know what they'll do to you. *You* are worth more than this. Nothing is worth what they'll do."

"You're wrong, Mara." She wished for a moment she had told him her real name.

"I know what they'll do, and you don't. How can you be so sure?"

"Tell me, then."

"I told you, I can't. There is darkness there. You can't imagine."

He circled in front of her and grabbed her shoulders with both hands. His eyes bored into hers. "Don't you see, I don't *care*. Please, please, listen to me. I will go into that darkness with you. I will go into *any* darkness with you. I swear it to you."

She bit back a gasp at the beauty of his words. They were almost a vow. She tried to pull away, but he wouldn't let her go. "No! Don't follow me. You don't have to go there. I *hate* myself for dragging you there." She clutched at her shoulder at the pain her words inflicted. His eyes followed the gesture. She wondered if he understood.

"You're not dragging me. Not anymore. I'm going willingly now."

She cried out even as the physical pain lessened. "Don't you see that that's the *last* thing I want?"

"Why? I felt the way you kissed me. We belong together. You and me. We'll go wherever you've got to take me, and we'll find a way out."

"There *is* no way out," she whispered. "You don't understand what you're promising."

"Well, it wouldn't be very courageous of me if I did, now would it. Don't you know that this is a prince's specialty? Making fine, foolhardy promises and then having to live up to them? Many such promises have been made over much less worthy causes and people." He smiled a little, and the attempt at humor did seem remarkably brave.

She tried to smile back, but she couldn't do it. She ached too much, inside and out. Perhaps he *was* a fool— but he was a fool because of her.

He started to pull her close to him again, but she resisted. He stopped immediately. The sudden sadness in his eyes almost broke her; it drove a spike of ice straight into her chest. But what was this small sadness compared to a lifetime of enslavement? Compared to the whole world losing him forever? She wouldn't be a part of doing this to him if she could at all resist it.

"We cannot do this," she whispered again.

"Are you promised to someone else?" he asked suddenly. Her mind went blank as she blinked at him, shocked. "Please, I would rather just know." She shook her head. "Are you… in love, then?" he asked, swallowing hard. She could only stare in surprise. She was convincing him, wasn't she? It was working. What should she say—a truth that would damn him or a lie that might save him?

Those eyes, that face… She couldn't lie, even though she should. She shook her head.

"Then what's wrong?"

She stared, thinking, searching for a way to drive him away that she could actually force out of her own lips. She twisted away from him and took a few steps toward the fires.

"Regin told me what it means," he said to her back.

"What what means?" She looked at him sidelong over her shoulder.

"The mark on your shoulder."

A chill sliced through her. What had Regin told him? What would he think? What did he think he now knew? "Is that so?"

"Yes. I know this isn't your idea. That you didn't choose this."

She turned a little more, her side facing him, and they stared at each other for a long moment. "Then maybe you'll understand why I want to control this one thing," she whispered. "Why I can't just kiss you and forget about the world we live in and the shackles on your wrists of my own making. Why I *hoped* you were gone, in spite of how much it hurt to think that."

He hadn't understood, but now she could see that he did. His mouth fell open as his eyes widened ever so slightly. She had to get away, think this through, figure out what to say to him.

"I'm sorry," she whispered. "You should've run." And with that, she fled from him, back to the firelight, back to her tent. He did not follow.

He watched her flee, darting through the shadows and vanishing into her tent. He stood there, confused, wondering. How had he expected that to go? Perhaps he hadn't expected anything. His body felt cold where she'd been against him.

He seemed to have hurt everyone except himself by not running. He hadn't counted on that. It hadn't felt particularly selfish. But perhaps it had been. He didn't care if Mara didn't want his help; she was going to get it. She didn't have to love him back, but she couldn't stop him from helping her.

It figured that once he finally found someone worth loving, she did not return the sentiment.

There was only one thing for him to do, besides mope—continue struggling with the puzzle that was the star map. Or was it a distraction? Was there some other loophole, some other way to save her? Regin had agreed, this enslavement was not the Way of Things. It was a safe bet that the forces that ran the world were in his favor… but the combination of foolhardy love and wishful thinking could be skewing his judgment a little.

He slunk back to a low-burning fire circle, where only a few children remained on the other side. He pulled out the star map and opened it. Would it still glisten in the dimming firelight? It shone faintly in response.

He studied it for a while but noticed nothing more.

"What's that?" a young voice said beside him.

He jumped, not having heard anyone approach. The little boy they had saved smiled up at him.

Aven faltered when he tried to speak, then cleared his throat. "It's a map."

"Of what?" the boy asked. "I've seen maps of Akaria before. They don't look like that."

He smiled. "You're right. It's a map of the stars."

"Oh!" the boy said, leaning closer. "Why would you need a map of the stars?"

Aven shrugged. "That's what I'm trying to figure out. I found it one day and have been trying to figure out how to use it. Or what it means."

"Have you discovered anything?"

"No." If the boy hadn't noticed the magic of the starlight, he wasn't going to call attention to it. And that was really the only thing he'd discovered.

The boy sat down beside him, losing interest in the map. The flames danced as they both watched.

"How are you feeling?" Aven asked the boy. "Better now?"

"Yes!" he replied, smacking his palms against his chest. "Good as new! How did you and the lady help me?"

Aven smiled. "Didn't they tell you it was magic?"

"Well, yes, but what kind? What does that mean?"

"I don't know all the details, my friend did most of the work."

"The lady?"

"Uh-huh. I just helped her. What did it feel like?"

The boy's face went pale, thinking of it. "It hurt worse than when that man hit me. But not for very long. And then *all* the pain was gone, so it was worth it. Can you do that to heal *anything*?"

He laughed at the enthusiasm in the boy's voice. "I can't do it, but she can. I am not sure if she can heal just anything, but that seemed pretty bad. So maybe."

"But what about other things? Dogs, horses?"

He thought of the way she treated the horses, the bat, the way she'd looked when she'd called after them all. He wondered if their horses could have returned when he and Miara were unconscious—he should try to find them. "I think she can. I think that's maybe even easier for her." It didn't matter if he was wrong, did it?

The boy was sweetly curious, and he probably wouldn't meet another mage for a long time, if ever.

"And what about other things? My uncle Lem was born a little you-know," the boy said, making a wild, twisted face. "Can she fix that, too?"

"Not sure," Aven said. "But I'll ask her in the morning for you."

The boy smiled and bounced his legs up and down over the log, watching the dancing flames again. She was a creature mage, no? Were humans creatures, or was that something different? He groaned inwardly. So much he didn't know. His eyes scanned the star map idly as he thought. He would bet she could heal plants.

But what about people's minds? What about their souls? What about Lem?

What about— He caught his breath as his eyes caught on Casel.

What if he could pull down the energy of Casel herself? What if that word freedom actually alluded to more than just a spiritual meaning arbitrarily assigned to the star by some philosopher, a name, a label? Rather, what if it had been charted thusly as instruction by a mage like him—an air mage?

A star mage.

What if the same process she'd used to heal the boy with his light from the sun could be used to heal that horrendous wound in her shoulder?

He almost flew to her tent to demand the details of how she had done it. Were there risks? Specific techniques one needed to know? But then her face turning away from him, twisted with emotion, came flooding back to him. No, he couldn't go to her. Not now. Not yet.

Maybe by morning things would feel differently. He wasn't sure exactly how he wanted them to feel. But different would definitely be better than this.

He glanced over at the boy, who gave him a grin. Aven smiled back. Indeed, he and Mara had been indebted to these people, but perhaps their deed had not gone unrewarded.

Ah, the Way of Things. Perhaps he wasn't a total fool after all.

He gathered a few twigs from the kindling pile nearby and held them for a moment in the air as the tiniest offering. The boy watched him quizzically, but Aven did not explain.

He held them up and closed his eyes, and in his heart he whispered a prayer, *Great Gods, Honored Ancestors, guide me along the path of Balance, take me toward the Way of Things, let me be the sword of righteousness. If what I long to do is truly the Way, then guide my hand, sharpen my blade, and put the wind at my back. I seek to serve you and my people.*

And Mara, he thought, as he let the twigs fall into the glowing embers.

Miara awoke but didn't open her eyes for some time. As dreams and grogginess fell away, the events of the night before slid back into focus.

By the gods. Aven was in love with her.

Suddenly, her cheeks flushed. She was a fool. It wasn't every night that a handsome man kissed you. And she had to go and ruin it with all her qualms about helping to enslave him. And then it turned out he knew she was a mage slave anyway. Certainly, he must have guessed that was his probable fate, too.

He'd stayed anyway. He'd kissed her anyway. She'd run away. Like a coward.

Today was a new day. Today, she could walk out of the tent and kiss him on the mouth and never look back. If they got out of Mage Hall somehow, then gods be praised! And if they didn't... she was still better off. Wasn't she? What did she really have to lose in this situation?

Her lightness of feeling couldn't last. She couldn't do it. The more she knew him, the more she admired him. No, she loved him. It was beyond time to admit that. The stronger she felt, the more she didn't want him to end up like her. Even if that meant she couldn't be with him. Was it possible to be happy even without your freedom? She shook her head at her wishful thinking. If it were, it certainly wasn't when the life you left behind was that of a *king*.

No. She had to keep her distance. She had to treat him such that if he got a second chance to run, the fool would take it.

She cracked open the flap of the tent. No one was in sight. The air was still crisp with the early morning. A few tended fires, prepared breakfasts, but mostly the camp was still hushed with sleep.

She slipped from the tent and headed toward the stream. A glance at Aven's tent told her nothing of his whereabouts; her shoulder panged in annoyance at the thought. Stupid thing, not even smart enough to know that Aven wouldn't run away from her if she shoved him on a boat and shipped him downriver. As if to confirm her evaluation of its stupidity, her shoulder twisted again in pain at that thought.

She headed over the hill toward the river. Maybe the cold water would clear her thoughts.

Cresting the hill, she discovered she was not alone. Dozens of tiny waves caught bits of the sunlight, creating a blinding reflection. In spite of them, she could see a figure was in the water. As she got closer, she could make out a masculine, muscled back, broad shoulders, and now-familiar light hair.

Aven.

She slowed, then clung to a tree nearby, hiding behind it. Should she turn back? She peered out, melding her visage with the tree's to keep hidden.

Certain he couldn't see her, she watched. He was surrounded by that nearly blinding halo of morning sunlight, splashing the water, jumping up and down to keep warm, scratching at his hair. The water sparkled like stars as it fell back to the river. She could not ignore the clear strength that ripped through his shoulders, the grace with which he moved through the water. A wave of heat shot through her. Was that embarrassment? Excitement?

This was the man that had kissed her only hours before. *This* was the man that had promised to follow her into darkness and back.

This was the man she'd rejected.

She remembered the day she had kidnapped him and transported him to the forest, inadvertently without his clothes. She remembered waiting for him to rouse, noticing almost against her will what fine shape he'd been in. At the time, she'd felt more intimidation and fear than admiration, but now...

He had claimed to command troops and fight with swords, and it must have been true. How else could he have gotten so strong in a tiny mountain hold? He still felt like so much of a stranger, like there was so much she didn't know about him.

But maybe she knew plenty about him. And maybe he knew plenty about *her*. Maybe their lives were horrid situations that had nothing to do with who they really were.

Maybe that was how he knew he loved her in spite of not knowing what lay ahead of them, or behind.

What must he be thinking about falling in love with her? He was a prince—wasn't he promised to someone? He was an eldest son, an heir. Certainly, he couldn't throw his love around lightly. What was he really saying with that kiss? Just that he wanted to bed her for sport, as was the style of so many nobles? Did he want a mistress? Or was he actually saying more? That was almost unthinkable. She did not dare to even articulate that potential future, its likelihood was so distant. But he also did not seem like the kind of man to casually take a lover. Some men might have sought to distract her with the promise of love and fortune, only to escape when her trust was earned. But not Aven.

And that was not the kind of proclamation he'd made. Men didn't tell women they just wanted to sleep with that they would follow them into any darkness and out the other side. Did they? She really was not experienced enough to know. A shiver went through her at the intensity of his words—caused by delight or fear, she wasn't sure.

A prince could not bestow his love casually, and indeed, he hadn't. Did he know he could be leaving his kingdom behind? Had he really thought it through? She had assumed he hadn't, but what if he had?

He'd finished bathing and was climbing out onto the riverbank. The heat she felt rose even higher, her face flushed. Her breath was quicker than normal. His body was wet, and the sunlight shone brightly, exaggerating every curve, every droplet of water that slid down his skin toward the earth. A fine piece of breeding, that one—not at all like herself.

Should she continue to hide? She could keep herself hidden. He would go back to camp and be none the wiser of her scrutiny. It was too early for awkward conversation, and her cheeks were red, she was sure of it.

But much as she did not want to lead him on, part of her wanted him to know that she'd seen him, that she'd admired him, or at least wanted him to wonder if she had. Just as she'd waited for him to rouse and ask for his clothes on that first day before giving them to him, she wanted to be near him and just once more feel the tension between them, like electricity in the air.

She dropped all attempts at hiding while cursing her foolishness. He had put his pants on now and seemed to be planning to let the rest of him dry as he walked. He started up the path.

She stepped out from behind the tree and started down the path as if she'd never been hiding. He jumped, and then so did she as if she'd just seen him.

"Mara!" he called brightly, as if nothing had happened between them. "Good morning!"

She smiled back. When they reached each other, they stopped. There *was* a tension in the air, strange and different, that she didn't understand.

She had to prolong the moment, study it.

"How was the water? Cold?" she asked him.

He nodded, grinning. "But it will wake you up, all right."

A long, almost comfortable silence ensued that neither seemed to want to break. Odd. Shouldn't it be more awkward between them?

Finally, she said, "Did you sleep well?"

He nodded. "Feeling fully recovered?"

"Yes, thank you," she said. "At least as much as I can this early in the morning."

He smiled, shifting his weight. "I saw the boy we healed at the fire after you... retired," he said, faltering for the first time. "He was just fine. Thankful. He wondered if you can heal other things. Dogs, horses..."

"Anything," she replied, with a slight smile.

He laughed. "Anything? Is that so? I mean, really. It's against my Code to lie to little boys, you know."

"It's true. At least theoretically, with enough energy. A lone creature mage would not usually have enough energy—we'd kill everything in the vicinity trying to suck up enough. So I couldn't have healed him without you."

Now *he* seemed to blush. How silly this was! After the things they'd said last night? Now they were all niceties and compliments? Why were they acting like this?

"What about maladies of the mind? You know, like a madman?"

She raised her eyebrows. He thinks *he's* crazy for loving me, she thought with a smirk.

"His question, not mine." He shrugged, grinning.

"I don't know," she said. "I have never tried. At home, I was a healer of animals."

"Ah," he said. Silence stretched on. "So there were two types of healers, then?" He seemed to speak more to end the awkwardness than to really find out anything.

"Three—human, animal, and plant. But the plant healers consider themselves gardeners."

"Do they all use the same techniques?"

"Mostly, yes. Some systems want to heal themselves but can't. Those you can brute force and pour energy in, and the system will do what it has been trying to do all along. Other systems, you have to coax into behaving."

He looked thoughtful at her words. His chest was still bare. Her eyes darted from his pensive frown, across the skin of his chest, his stomach, downward, and then back again. She hoped he hadn't noticed. Again, the silence stretched on, although slightly less awkward this time.

"Well," she said, "the water calls. Wouldn't want it to warm up too much, now would I?"

He smiled. "No, of course not. I'll see you back at the camp. Do you think we will head out today?"

"Most likely. If we can find the horses."

He nodded and turned back up the path, wheels still whirring.

She headed straight for the water. It was going to be freezing and if she thought about it too much, she'd lose her nerve. She stripped her clothes off without waiting to be sure he was gone and plunged into the water without looking back. She did not want to know if he hadn't thought to catch a glimpse of her, and she didn't want to meet his eyes if he had.

Back in the camp, Miara set to trying to find the horses. Last time, they had seemed relatively close and running free, so why were they still gone? They should've arrived by now.

She sat cross-legged outside her tent near the fire and put her hands to the earth, fingers spread wide. She could not move her mind through the earth, but she could run from tree to tree, through the roots entwined beneath her. She reached in deeper until she felt the tendrils of life beneath the soil, the tangling systems silently drawing nourishment. She whispered into the trees, sang the softest of songs to their roots, and glided her mind among them, looking for one that had word of Kres and Cora.

Not far off, an elm led her to a maple, and there they were. The horses were not far away, but they *were* under someone's control. Someone was with them, riding a third horse and headed her way. She moved up the roots and into the maple's branches and leaves. And she could sense the rider, a familiar creature—

Sorin.

They'll wait a turning of the moon, my ass, she thought. Sorin had been sent to hurry her, and he'd probably followed the roads they'd charted together. Only, this detour the Devoted had taken them on had likely slowed him down. Well, at least he had the horses, as little help as that was. But why *him*? How had he manipulated his way to follow her on this mission?

She released her hold on the trees and let her mind return to her body. Too quickly, too, for the speed of the movement left her reeling for a moment. She scrambled to her feet anyway. She had to find Aven—she had to warn him—but of what? What could she tell him? Sorin was a friend—or at least not an enemy. Wasn't he? But she just knew, somewhere in her heart, that this would not go well.

She found Aven in his tent. Not thinking, she burst in without a word, causing him to jump. She shut the flap, tied it, and turned back to him. His chest was still bare, sprinkled with water droplets from the river. The tent's heat pressed around them, and she was suddenly keenly aware they were alone and very close to each other.

"What is it?" he said when she didn't speak.

"Another mage is coming. To supposedly help me. To hurry me on my mission."

Aven nodded. "What does that mean? Do you know them?"

"Yes, he checked my maps for this mission," she said. "I'm not sure what it means. I have never worked with him like this. I'm always alone."

"You're afraid of his arrival," he said matter-of-factly.

She nodded, then frowned. The implied question was why. "I can't think of any specific reason. Perhaps it's that this mission is almost complete. Or perhaps it's that I don't *want* to complete it. I just don't know." She winced and rubbed the throbbing in her shoulder absently. The pain faded quickly as she let her resistance slip from her mind. She let her thoughts go blank. This could be the last time she could talk to him without Sorin around, she realized. Was there anything she could tell him, any way to prepare him for Sorin or what was to come? "You know, I did not know you would be a mage," she said as quickly as she could. "You must try to hide it if you can. He doesn't need to know. No one needs to know."

His face fell. "Mara, you know that's not *exactly* my specialty."

"You can do it," she urged him. "I know you can. You've learned so much, so quickly."

"What type of mage is he?"

"An air mage."

"Great! He'll know it the minute he sees me."

"No, he won't. He won't be looking for it. He's not a spy. He doesn't remember being untrained; he has no idea what it's like not to have control of his power. It won't be as obvious as you think." She wondered if what she was saying had any relation to the truth. She didn't care; she just hoped he believed. Perhaps if he believed he could, he might stumble on a way to actually hide it.

"And—" she started but then faltered, unsure of how to say what she needed to. Well, imperfect was better than nothing. "We must not let on that we are anything but… kidnapper and captive. They will use it against us, I'm sure of it."

"Are we anything other than that?" he said gently.

Her mouth fell open slightly, and she wished for a moment she could just melt into the earth. "Aven, I…"

He shook his head. "Of course. It's fine. That is one thing I can hide, although I wish I didn't have to."

She struggled to regain her composure. "We—we must prepare to leave, as if we were already planning to. He has our horses. That's how I found him, looking for them. I'm not sure how much time we have, but I would rather we looked busy."

He nodded and reached for his shirt, pulling it over his head. She got to her knees to leave the tent, but a crazy thought occurred to her, and she hesitated.

In a week, he might be dead. Or in a day. Or she might never see him again. Sorin could sweep him away and send her back with orders to fly the rest of the way.

What if this was the last time she saw him at all?

She stopped, frozen in indecision. Should she let him continue to believe her lie? She could lean over right now, kiss him hard on the mouth, run her fingers through his hair, feel his hands reach for her, and end the lie in a moment. This was likely the last moment of unguarded freedom she would ever have, and part of her soul was dying for him to know the truth—that she really did love him. That if they'd been born in different lives, she would have kissed him with abandon, become his partner, and never looked back.

But she didn't move. More of her wanted him to take any opportunity to run. More of her did not want him to know her torment—or any of the past, present, or future forms of it.

It took all her strength to move, to pass this opportunity by, to plunge out of this brief respite from her life and back into reality. She shifted her weight and crawled out from the tent, and—

Sorin's boots greeted her standing just before her, an amused smile on his face.

"My, my, Miara," he said, his voice dark. "What *have* you been up to?"

I2   STAR MAGE

Aven heard the voice outside the tent and knew the other mage had already arrived. Had he heard what she'd said? Well, it was too late, but he hoped not. He straightened himself so that it didn't look like they'd been up to anything. When he felt at least reasonably presentable, he got to his knees and crawled out of the tent.

The mage stood before the tent, as did Mara, and they were talking in hushed tones. The man was shorter than Aven, with nearly white hair, a thin face, and frowning eyes that seemed more than a little bitter. He did not seem physically fit, more of a scholar's figure—how did he ride those horses at all with that bony frame?—but he still cut a striking image in dark, almost black Kavanar leather. The two mages were engaged in hushed conversation.

"They couldn't wait, eh? Told me she'd wait a turning of the moon," Mara said, voice rough.

The man shrugged. "Since when have they had any sense? Or manners? Or kept a promise? I'm just following orders like you, love."

Aven tried not to bristle at those words, but his shoulders tightened. Could he find an excuse to punch this scrawny bastard in the mouth? Or perhaps a well-time and well-placed elbow in the kidney as an "accident" would be more appropriate. The new mage's eyes flicked to him for a moment for the first time. Maybe it would be harder to hide Aven's feelings than he'd thought.

Thankfully, Mara did not react to the mage's affectionate turn of phrase. "Yes, well, I'm glad you brought the horses, at least." She sounded more irritated than pleased to see him. Small wins.

"How were you parted from them, might I ask?" Did the mage's voice sound suspicious, or was Aven only imagining it?

"We were attacked by Devoted Knights, days ago. Barely made it out alive."

The mage gave a crisp nod. His demeanor was strangely similar to Mara in some ways—confident, self-assured, down to business fast—but for some reason he seemed completely unlike her at the same time. Aven instantly did not like the man. He was hiding something, Aven was sure of it. Aven knew the way a man acted when he wanted to hide something; too many men acted that way around kings. Recognizing it was a survival trait.

Now the mage turned back to him. "Well, well, so this is *him*, huh? I can't believe you pulled this off." He looked Aven up and down from head to toe and back again. Aven returned his appraisal with a scowl, crossing his arms across his chest. He didn't have to be in love with Mara to be annoyed with the disrespect in that comment. "I really didn't think you could do it until I saw it with my own eyes."

Mara glanced around uneasily. There were many ears around, and many things the wrong words could give away. Aven was sure could feel Regin somewhere watching. The old man did not miss a thing. Aven would have to make sure that Regin didn't get too alarmed; he wasn't sure what havoc this mage could cause, but they would probably all be gone quickly enough. And so be it. The sooner they were away from these kind folks, the better.

"Don't attract attention," Mara snapped. "Which direction did the Devoted take us?"

"A bit farther south than you had intended if I recall correctly, but we are about a day and a half's ride from home. The horses are well rested. We can ride the whole way, no need to make camp."

She frowned at him. "This is my mission, I'll decide how long we ride."

"If we ride the whole way, you can rub it in their faces that you didn't even need me. Plus we'll be home that much sooner." His voice had a friendly and affectionate turn, but it was manipulative underneath. There was more, always more, something hidden. Perhaps there was coin in it for him? "Besides, she grows anxious. And I do not relish camping on our own in our land; too many things can happen."

And now he knew for sure that that was where they were headed. He'd assumed so all along... but now he finally knew.

"We'll see. I will not change my mission or jeopardize it because you have a distaste for camping." Mara tuned to Aven. "Make ready to leave," she said. "Pack your things." The softness in her voice had faded. She was the same commanding woman he'd met among the falling yellow leaves, sitting naked in the forests beneath Estun. He liked that woman just as much. And it was good if that's what this mage expected. She is better at hiding what is between us than I am, he thought.

Or perhaps there was less for her to hide?

He brushed the thought aside. "The Devoted took everything," he replied. "There's very little to make ready. But we must thank and say farewell to our hosts."

Mara nodded. "Come with me. Sorin, go wait by the horses." And now Aven had a name for the other mage as well. Sorin bowed the slightest bit and headed obediently toward the horses.

Mara's eyes met his for a moment, vaguely apologetic.

He smiled the tiniest bit, his only way to convey forgiveness. "He's over there," he said, gesturing toward the fire where Regin sat, his back to them.

Regin stood as he heard them approaching and smiled his broad, old smile. Aven noticed the little boy was across the other side of the fire ring; perhaps he could say goodbye to him as well.

"It's time for us to take our leave," Mara said, her tone again different, regal, gracious. "Thank you so much for your hospitality. It has been a pleasure."

"It was the least we could do. Thank you for healing Galen; it was truly a feat that cannot ever be repaid."

The boy—Galen, apparently—perked up at his name. Aven inclined his head with a quick jerk, motioning to him to join them. Galen smiled and scampered to their sides. Aven squatted down to look him in the eye.

"I didn't know your name was Galen."

"Now you do," he said wryly.

Aven grinned. "My name is Aven. It's been an honor to meet you." He held his hand out and shook the boy's hand, and while he did, he whispered, "I asked her, and she said she can heal just about anything."

"Really?" the boy whispered back.

"Anything," Aven replied, "although not right now because we have to leave."

Aven stood. Galen turned to Mara and said, "Thank you, lady."

She smiled and put a hand on his shoulder for a moment. Was there sadness in her eyes? She hated to leave this place, he thought. But he could be imagining it.

"Regin, do you need help with our tents? Can we pack them up or clean them for you?" he asked, hoping Sorin could not hear and Mara would not mind.

"No, no worries, friends. We will stay a few days longer, someone will find a night in them. No need to pack them up yet."

They all stood for a moment, wistful, wishing it could go on a little longer. Now he fully understood the sadness Mara felt when he'd quipped that perhaps they could just hide away as chipmunks forever. Indeed, they could not.

Their fates awaited them.

Mara reached out her hand and shook Regin's. Aven followed.

"If you ever run into us again," Regin added, "you are always welcome in our ranks."

"And if you are ever near Estun, stop by and say hello," Aven added, a bit spitefully as they strode away, back to the horses. Mara glared at him a little but only mildly. Surely, she did not know if Aven was a common name in Akaria or if many people or few worked in Estun.

Of course, many did. But Aven was not a common name. He felt he owed that much to Regin, that he know some of the truth after all he'd done for them. The comment did not look lost on the old man, either; he gazed after the two mages with a new intensity, as if now he knew there was a puzzle before him and he struggled to solve it before the pieces rode away.

How could a mage slave from Kavanar and perhaps the prince of Akaria come to be traveling together at all, let alone through Regin's neck of the woods? It was quite a mystery.

But, of course, Regin had all the information he was going to have. Aven mounted his gray mare and stroked her charcoal mane in greeting.

And they were off again.

"Keep to the Way," Regin called after them. "And may Anara watch over you."

Was that a formal blessing or merely a wish from an old man to a young one? Well, he was pretty sure he would need both, wherever they were going. Whatever was waiting for him, it wouldn't be long now before he was staring at his destiny, face to face.

They rode straight till nearly nightfall, with only the slightest breaks. Sorin had bread and cheese in his bags, which he shared when they first got on the road and later, around midday. They passed a wine flagon from time to time.

They talked very little.

The air mage seemed to be enjoying the scenery. Mara looked dark and withdrawn. Aven tried to look bored and not look at Mara. But at times he caught himself studying her, and he thought the other mage might have noticed. How long could you look at trees and a mare's neck without glancing around, though?

As the sun started to sink below the mountains, Mara pointed to a nearby clearing. "There. This is a good place to stop. We're stopping."

"But we're nearly there!"

"This is far too long of a ride, they can't take any—"

"Oh, certainly they can—"

"I didn't *ask* for your opinion. We're making camp."

They rode into a clearing that was near the road but secluded by brambles and towering pines, so they were not easy to spot from the road.

Aven had barely dismounted before Sorin grabbed him by the arm.

"I'll take him to relieve himself, meet you back here in a few," Sorin said, voice gruff.

"You think I made it this far without enchantments to keep him in check?"

Sorin said nothing and continued to make for the brush with Aven in tow.

Mara rolled her eyes. "Fine, whatever. Have it your way. But he *is* chained, you know. He can't run far."

Sorin shrugged as if he did not care. What did he have up his sleeve? "Can't be too careful with the Masters' precious goods, Miara," he said.

Miara! Aven almost stumbled at the word. Was that her real name? He glanced quickly back at her, finding a new color of fear mixed with sadness in her eyes. Her mouth hung open as if she wasn't sure what to say, but to him it was a confirmation—that was her real name.

But he didn't have much time to think of that. The mage was dragging him roughly toward the woods' edge, around and behind some large pine trees. Aven's shoulders tensed—clearly Sorin was up to more than being helpful. But what?

He did need to go, so he did at the mage's first direction. Sorin also did, and Aven was very tempted to look and make a comparison, but he didn't need any more problems than he already had.

"She's mine, you know," the air mage said in a whisper.

Aven raised his eyebrows but didn't meet the mage's gaze. So this was what the fuss was all about. Perhaps

Sorin had heard their words in the tent, but more likely he could simply tell. A man could sense these things, sometimes, if he was looking for them.

Deny it, he told himself. To hell with your pride, deny it. Act like you don't care in the slightest. It's none of his business. He knew he should, but he couldn't form the right words.

"If she's yours, then why are you whispering?" he replied, buttoning up his trousers.

"I see you looking at her. Stop it. She's mine."

Aven felt quite sure Mara—Miara?—did not want to be Sorin's. Although, could this have something to do with what she'd said? No, she'd said there was no one. Deep breath. He needed to be diplomatic. He should shrug and walk back to the campsite as if he didn't care in the slightest.

"Like hell, she is."

Sorin lunged at him, and Aven dodged the first blow, but he was stiff from riding so long. The mage's elbow struck his chin from the side, sending him spinning.

Aven tried to stagger away, but walls of air solidified around him, keeping him from dodging. Well, that'd be a neat trick to learn someday, when he wasn't getting pummeled. The wind kept thrusting him back toward Sorin, but it never sent the bastard off-balance. Air magic in combat, indeed. He should be taking notes.

The air didn't just solidify. It thickened and roiled and felt wet with... was that rain? Aven stole a glance up, and even in the growing darkness, he could see the cloud forming above them, tiny bolts of lightning flashing.

Aven didn't put up much of a fight, mostly dodging and ducking and spinning as much as the air would allow. He got in a good staggering blow or two to Sorin's jaw, but with each contact, Aven felt a light sting along his skin—as though he was being shocked. Strange magic, indeed.

Aven knew he could lay his foe out quickly if he wanted to. But killing the man would only complicate things. One particularly off-kilter dodge and a blow to his temple sent Aven tripping to the ground as a loud clap of thunder rumbled above them.

Either Aven's thud or the very unnatural thunderclap must have caught Mara—*Miara's* attention, because she came running around the corner of the pine trees and cursed as Sorin kicked him hard in the ribs.

She threw herself on Sorin, heaving him away from Aven and into the trunk of a tree. Small flashes of light sizzled from him as he collided—the storm's energy in him. She was stronger than the bastard, Aven thought with some amusement.

"What the hell are you doing?" she hissed.

"Whatever I damn well please," he spat at her. He balled his hands into fists, and Aven could see spasms of lightning gathering in the trained mage's hands.

"This is *my* mission. How *dare* you endanger it."

Sorin finally seemed to realize Miara was not going to capitulate. "He tried to run."

She snorted at him in disgust. "So you were going to lightning bolt him as he ran away?"

"Just a reminder of why not to leave, no?"

She glared at him. "No."

Sorin was panting. His face grew colder, voice icy. "These non-mages. These so-called normal people. They hold *every* freedom and never appreciate it. And we have to grovel at their feet? Why should we have to risk our lives for just another sack of flesh—" He stopped, shaking his head, and started toward Aven again. Convincing cover story, or perhaps both motives were true.

"Don't make me fight you, too." Miara's voice was stony with warning. "My orders are specifically to return him alive. Stop now, or I'll be taking you both back captive."

"Fine, love," he said. He looked pointedly at Aven with the words.

"Get back to making camp," she ordered. "And don't call me 'love.' "

Sorin huffed and stalked back to the horses.

Her face was creased with concern and anger in the dim twilight. But not surprise. This was only the beginning, wasn't it? This is why she wanted me to run, he thought.

But he could never have done that. He could not leave her. Especially not now, when the stars were just about to come out.

Suddenly, he remembered how weak they'd gotten after they'd healed the boy. Maybe there was a way he could use Sorin's foolishness to his advantage.

As she took his hand and heaved him up, he did in fact see stars, and dizziness swam through him. It did not take much pretending to allow himself to fall back to the ground like a sack of potatoes and pretend to pass out.

"Damn it," she swore. "By all that is good and holy. Sorin, look what you've done." He returned from the clearing as she groaned in disgust. "Fine, no camp. We'll keep riding. He may need one of the healers. And how can I stop you from killing him if I'm asleep?" She cursed again.

"I knew the horses could do it" was all Sorin said. Was that an attempt at humor, or was he just that much of a jerk?

"Shut up. Help me get him on his horse."

Many curses from Miara later, she and Sorin had managed to get a comatose Aven onto the horse and tied such that he wouldn't fall off. Pretending he was unconscious throughout the process might have been one of the hardest things he'd ever done, requiring him to ignore both the awkward, painful positioning and nearly being dropped a time or two. The position they left him in was not terribly comfortable, with the pommel jutting into his stomach, but he hoped it would be worth it. If he did indeed pass out after what he was about to do, they would be none the wiser. He had never successfully tricked Miara before, but if she had any clue that his unconsciousness was a ploy, she didn't show it.

The night had only just fallen by the time they were back on the road. The sun had set, but the stars were not yet bright. He caught glimpses of a sliver of moon when he felt sure they weren't looking in his direction.

He could not see Sorin. His horse was between theirs, and his head had fallen facing to the left. Sorin was on his right side. From the sound of it, though, Sorin appeared to be dozing upright from the slight snores and snorts coming from his general direction. Miara stared straight ahead, cold, leaden, her eyes and face dead of emotion.

The gods were with him, it seemed. They were traveling west, and so not only was his face turned toward

Miara, but it was also turned toward the southern sky. It was hard to catch sight of Casel amid the tall trees, but if there was a chance for him to do it, he would find it.

His eyes closed, he fought sleep and waited until the group neared a clearing. He watched for the faint light on his eyelids to brighten. The forest was dense around them, but if he could just get a brief expanse of open sky, he could get a clear view of Casel.

He listened to the horse's hooves, Sorin's snores, Miara's quiet breathing, the sounds of the forest at night. The slight amount of light from the sky flickered on his eyelids, but he waited for it to brighten just a little more, just enough to be worth the risk—

A moment later the light was even greater. He opened his eyes the tiniest sliver. The hillside they passed had fallen away, and there were no trees on that side of the road. There, just to the right of Miara's shoulder, he saw the familiar sparkle of Casel.

Don't second-guess yourself, he thought, hearing her words again.

As he had with the boy, he reached out, but this time more desperately, more determinedly. His fists clenched, sweat broke out on his forehead. A cold, silver, fragile energy twisted into his soul, like white smoke coming from the sky. It came from far away, and it was weaker than the sun, but... it was still there. He drank it up like he had never been so thirsty, feeling his chest grow warm, then hot. He drank it up till he felt crazy with energy, full of this peculiar, whispering, twisting magic—

And now—to try to use it.

He knew where the wound was. Of course, he could not touch it without revealing his unconsciousness was a ruse, but he knew. Would it be enough? He trained his mind on her shoulder, like he had focused on the movement of the wind, and pushed.

For a moment, nothing felt different. Then something caught, like a key suddenly turning in a lock. The swirling white energy flew faster now, faster, no longer swirling but streaming toward her at breakneck speed, until he found himself suddenly empty and starting to shiver. He turned his eyes to the sky again, found Casel, and pulled. There came the whispery tendrils of power, and then there they went, funneled toward Miara with all his might. He could not do both at once. He could hardly control the rate that the energy flew through him, so much so that he worried he would pass out before he'd done the job.

How much would be enough to cure her? Would any amount be enough, or was he throwing energy at her for nothing? His gut told him that it was working. But Miara didn't flinch or move; she only stared ahead with that hard, dead face.

The look on her face spurred him on even as he felt himself tiring. Pull, push, repeat.

He wondered if this were a brute-force system or a coaxing system. He did not know how to coax anything, or sing to it. If that was what was needed, he was just too undertrained… but perhaps he could try? Making something up couldn't really hurt anything, could it?

He fixed his eyes on Casel, hoping Miara would not notice his more open stare. As he began this new pull, in his mind, he whispered, *Casel, star of freedom, liberator, my guide. I seek the freedom of this woman that I love.*

Immediately, the energy did not seem so fragile, nor so whispery—the cold smoke turned to a trickle of icy water flowing into him, faster and faster. Was it working?

Freedom star, guide me. It is not the Way of Things that this woman be a slave. I seek to restore the Balance. Aid me!

Energy surged, making him glad he was tied to the horse. He didn't need any training to know that this much would drive him mad in only a moment or two. He stopped pulling and just pushed as quickly as he could, shoving down a growing panic and forcing his thoughts to focus on her and only her.

More and more energy poured into him. He felt his body twitch involuntarily. He poured energy back out as fast as he could, but it was barely fast enough. He was filling up. The star's magic was too much, more than he could handle. It was going to drive him insane. In fact, he was pretty sure if he tripped up in the slightest, the sheer energy would addle his brain and kill him.

He wanted Miara to be free, but he did not particularly want to die trying. Surviving would be nice. The only way out was to keep going.

He pushed aside the panic and concentrated on pushing. As he drew his mind nearer to her, he could sense the burning in her skin. The antithesis of the cold, hard, watery energy of the star, it was hot and festering and writhed like so many maggots. *There.* He pinned it down with his attention, trying to drown it in the cold deluge of the star and hoping he didn't drown himself in the process.

And then suddenly—the outpour stopped. Stopped so fast that he had emptied nearly all the energy in him at that horrible little spot in her shoulder—he felt his chest grow cold, then suddenly icy.

The world whirled and went dark.

I3   RESCUE

Out of nowhere, Miara felt an unusual pang in her shoulder. It was not the typical twisting or burning, and she couldn't remember such a feeling ever before. It was almost like ice or mint—like menthol on a cut, a burning, stinging, icy sensation, but not altogether unpleasant. She did not know what to make of it. She had never felt anything but pain or a lack thereof from it, and suddenly this.

But it was only for a moment and then gone.

She felt colder now. This forest was a strange one. At first, when night had fallen, she'd felt sure that the days and nights were growing colder, toward winter. But then she had started to feel warmer and warmer till she'd had to shed her cloak because she'd started sweating. Now the air felt icy again. Was she going mad?

Perhaps she was sick. This had certainly been a far more demanding mission than most, and riding all night wasn't helping anything.

She couldn't believe they were almost back. Shouldn't she just get this over with? How much longer could she draw out this pain without going mad? Might as well get back to her horrible life knowing that she had given the Masters one of the best men she had ever known. Might as well start accepting that all her magic was only good for punishing innocent, honorable men.

Could this *really* be the Way of Things? Was there really any justice, any Balance in the world? If there were, then Aven would have run away from her. If there were, the gods would have given her an ugly face to make him *want* to run away. If there were, mages wouldn't be slaves in the first place.

Predictably, her shoulder ached at the thought, but weakly. Perhaps it was as tired as she was, or sick along with her. She would have to get checked out as soon as they arrived back and the Masters were through with her. Assuming they were ever through with her. She snorted quietly at the thought. It didn't matter; she was alone anyway.

Or was she?

Sorin dozed on his horse, and Aven had been well incapacitated by the idiot. She felt her rage bubble up again at the thought; she could have killed Sorin. But there was something else. She had the sudden sense of someone watching her, somewhere in the shadows. Was someone there?

Noises in the woods always spooked people in the middle of the night. But that was partially because sometimes there *was* something there.

To her left, there had been a few too many cracked branches, whooshes, leaves falling. Like there was someone—or something—following them alongside the road.

She swept her mind out toward the noises, targeted at first and then sweeping more broadly. If there was a bear or a wolf, she could dissuade them.

She felt nothing at all.

But promptly, another twig snapped. Whatever it was, it was still there.

"Damn it, Sorin," she snapped. "Wake the hell up. You were the one that wanted to ride all night. You're going to be up with me while we do it."

He jumped—surprised at his own slumber—blinked, and rubbed his eyes. He glanced around, trying to rouse himself.

"How long was I out?"

"Do you hear that?"

He, too, bent his ear to listen now, and there was only the sound of the horses and Aven's light breathing to interfere.

There was nothing now. Perhaps whatever was following them had heard her. Or perhaps it was all in her head.

"No," he said. "I don't hear anything. You woke me up for that?"

He shook his head and looked away from her, gazing around as if they were on a scenic pleasure ride through the hills.

She heard another branch crack to the left of her a little too late. Before she could even turn her head to investigate, a dark, heavy form collided with her shoulder. Claws aimed at her eyes missed but dug into her cheek instead, and she fell from the horse.

It was not *possible*—nothing had been there. Unless—

She didn't have time to really think, for whatever was on top of her was royally shredding her left forearm as she tried to block it from getting to her face and throat.

A blast of icy air sent the creature toppling off her, and Miara rolled to her hands and knees, scrambling away from her attacker. A ball of flame the size of her head flew past her left.

Damn, Sorin was deadly serious. But perhaps still not enough—suddenly her back leg was caught by something, then her wrists. Vines coiled around them as she heard a snarl from behind.

Mages. Of course.

It was indeed *not* possible for her to have missed animals following them in the woods. She had not been mistaken; it had been creature mages instead.

"Akarians!" she cried. Sorin's confused look melted away, and he quickly cast another strong gust at the animal, knocking it off the road. Then he made a broad gesture, laying down a wall of fire that licked fiercely and frighteningly up at the edge of the trees. Two more growling creatures lunged from the forest's edge, then another. Wolves, or mages in that form.

"How?" he demanded as he continued to beat them back with thrusts of air. The flame wall grew. She could smell the storm he called in the air. With every gust that knocked one back, another wolf charged forward. She fought to uproot or unspell the vines entangling her. She could see they were going for Sorin's ankles as well.

"I don't know!" she called back. She'd thought after losing the Devoted, no one could have tracked them this far. Although Sorin had found them, he'd had the help of the horses.

Sorin twisted the air around them to form some makeshift barrier. He thrust his arms straight out at shoulder height and spun once, twice, coating the air wall in a fiery, sparking blaze. She gave up on ripping the roots and simply began transforming her feet and hands to slip through the vine's grasp. Freed, she ran to Aven's horse, Cora. *It's all right, girl.* Unlike Kres, she had not seen much magic before, and Miara could feel her panic rising.

"Why now?" he yelled over the din of the wind he was raising.

"We're nearing the Akarian border?"

Sorin nodded sharply. "I'd say we're across it. We are almost certainly in Kavanar now! Can you sense it? The bond grows stronger."

She actually could not sense it but didn't feel a need to point it out. She hadn't noticed much of a decrease when she'd traveled into Akaria, either, so perhaps she just wasn't as sensitive as he. She stroked Cora's nose and mane and stole a stroke of Aven's hair and cheek out of Sorin's sight. He was still out cold.

Suddenly, Cora's fear surged, and Miara looked around frantically for the source. Fresh vines encircled Cora's legs, and the other horses, too, to keep them from bolting. *It's okay, girl. It's okay. I'll free you.*

"Sorin, your dagger!" she demanded. "The horses!" Her own blades were somewhere in some Devoted Knight's pack, stolen and long gone. He handed Miara his.

She slashed away at the vines as quickly as she could and tried to glance around them. What could they use to get out of this situation?

Up ahead, one side of the road seemed to drop off, no trees in sight. A cliff?

"Sorin—up ahead. Does the road drop off there?"

He looked, and then his eyes blanked for a moment as he saw far ahead of them and then returned. "Yes. A bluff that now falls down to the valley's river."

"Can we—" she started, but then she hesitated, hating what she was about to say. "Can we use it somehow?"

His eyes lit up. "Ah, I like the way you think. If we can get them near it, we can... make use of it, shall we say?"

The vines continued their pursuit of the horses, but they were also putting up a struggle, prancing and jittering out of the vines' grasp as best they could.

"Let's go." She gave one last savage slash at Cora's vines and then whispered, *Make for the road up there, I'll be right behind you.*

She leapt to Kres's back after a quick hack at one persistent vine. She quickly tossed the blade back to Sorin and charged forward. At the same time, she gave a half-hearted attempt at pulling energy from the vines, not enough to really stop them—at least not yet—but perhaps to take some of her adversary's energy for her own.

To his credit, Sorin was quickly on her heels, as were the wolves. She rode all the way to the very edge of the road at full speed and watched in horror as Sorin executed her plan. A blast of perfectly targeted wind sent the nearest wolf over the edge, tumbling down toward the rocks below.

Her heart in her chest ached. She gripped Kres's reins tighter in her hands.

She maneuvered Kres away from the edge itself, dodging each of five wolves in turn. And each Sorin dispatched with astonishing speed. When the third started to dart away, seeing what was coming, he changed tactics. A lightning bolt touched the ground just in front of the wolf sending rocks sliding, and the creature lurched until it, too, fell to the cliff.

Silence fell, aside from their panting. She looked at Sorin, who smiled triumphantly, but she couldn't return the expression. She could only hurt at the loss of these mages who'd fought valiantly for something she, too, believed in.

As her tension eased slightly, the pain in her forearm and cheek throbbed suddenly with full force, and she gasped for a moment at the intensity of it.

"Did you bring any bandages in that pack?"

"What would you have done without me, love?" He reached into his saddlebags.

"And some water," she said gruffly, and nothing else. As if he'd have even survived the encounter they'd had with the Devoted, let alone still had his bandages with him. To hell with him.

What would she have done without him? Perhaps she would have died at the hands of honorable mages trying to save their future king, rather than having been

the instrument of his destruction. She might have pre-
ferred that end to the one that waited for her. Instead,
the Akarians had made a last-ditch effort to save him.
And they had failed. Because of her.

But she had no choice in the matter. Sefim had told
her time and time again that it made a difference. She
could only hope he was right. She cleaned her wounds
and bandaged her arm but left her cheek open to the air.

Let the Masters have no illusions. This journey had
scarred her for good.

As the sun rose, they were surrounded by the thinner
forests of Kavanar. The mountains in the distance were
the same ones that sat beyond Mage Hall.

They were nearly back.

She and Sorin ate as they rode, trudging on even
though they needed to stop. Aven, strangely, did not stir.
She hadn't thought Sorin had hit him *that* hard. Perhaps
it was also just the fatigue of the journey. Hopefully,
they could rouse him before they arrived—she didn't
want to explain an unconscious Akarian to the Masters.
Damn Sorin.

The forests thinned even more, and soon they
reached the farmers' fields that lay to the west of Mage
Hall.

Eventually, Aven roused. He didn't sit up at first—
she just noticed that after a while, his eyes were open,
watching her. She risked a small, sad smile for him, and
he smiled back. She let him have his peace. When he
finally moved to sit up, he discovered how they'd tied
him down, and she stopped the horse to untie him.

"What happened to your face?" Aven said, voice
barely above a groggy whisper as she untied him.

"Wolves," she said. "Wolves attacked us while you
were down." *Akarian wolves*, she added, straight to his
mind so Sorin couldn't hear. *Mages, I think, transformed.
I think they were trying to save you.*

Aven said nothing in response, in his face or even in
his mind. His thoughts were a sad, blank expanse, not
that different from her own. There was a vague pain in
his eyes, possibly from his own impending doom or riding a horse like that for so long. He had his choice of
pains to pick from.

His eyes studied her as they rode, as if he were looking for something. Did he hope in these last hours that
she would let him see some slight indication of her love?
Would it really hurt anything now if she did show him?
But she wasn't about to show him anything with Sorin
around to notice. It was too late. She'd lost her chance.

They rounded a bend, and the last of the trees
stopped. Mage Hall squatted in the distance now, a

black, disgusting lump between the flat green fields and the grayish mountains.

Sorin kicked his horse into a canter when he saw it. "Almost there!" he cried as if excited. Maybe he was.

At any rate, she was not excited, but she did want to get this over with.

She grunted. Kres knew her meaning, and Cora followed, and they sped past the farmers at a faster rate now. Occasionally, a man would stop and eye them suspiciously, whether for the right or wrong reasons, she didn't know.

At the next field, several men stopped working, turning to look at them at once, on both sides of the road. Now, the farmers might hate the mages, but was it really worth such…

Seconds later, she discovered what they were *really* staring at as a shadow crossed Kres's mane.

"What the—" Sorin started. He turned to look up just as talons sank into her shoulders.

She couldn't withhold a cry. Animal impulse took over now, and she felt herself change. Clawed paws reached toward the feathery beast above her, scratching, writhing, but also twisting the talons deeper into her shoulders.

The creature shrieked, releasing her as huge wings flapped into the air. She glanced back over her shoulder at it—an eagle! She had injured it, and it was struggling to gain altitude. Two others behind it were headed right for her.

Perhaps some of those creature mages had survived after all.

She dug in her heels and hugged herself to Kres's neck. He did not really need the encouragement. She groped for Cora's reins as the two horses hit a gallop. The east gate to Mage Hall was now easily in sight.

She risked a glance over her shoulder. Sorin had not been as lucky as she in fending off the eagle. His horse had stopped because he was on the ground, the eagle diving at him from above, dodging his wind blasts, riding them as if they were a normal part of the hunt. A second eagle joined. Served him right. Thick storm clouds gathered quick and low above him, preparing for his use in an attack.

She had no time for this. She had no time to analyze the situation. Sorin would have to fend for himself, and she knew he could. If not, she could send more help from inside.

Protecting Sorin was not her mission. Aven was. Much as she might like an excuse to fail.

She pressed herself down harder against Kres's mane as a shadow swept overhead again. The eagle circled around and headed for Cora instead. Miara jerked both horses' reins abruptly to the right as close to the last second as she dared, and the eagle missed. Cora was spooked, but it only made her run faster.

They were close now. Miara reached her mind toward the gate—were there mages there? Indeed there were.

We're under attack—get ready! she cried to them. She could feel from their confusion that they had yet to spot her racing toward them or the eagles circling above.

She glanced back at Sorin. The air was whirling now, clouds thickening above him in the otherwise blue sky. She couldn't see him, but she could see several eagles circling and diving.

More shadows dotted the ground between them. Four? Six? More than she'd be able to fight off on her own.

She glanced at Aven and found him watching her, also bent down on the horse, eyes wild but with what, she wasn't sure.

She trained her eyes ahead on the gate. There wasn't much more she could do now. Her abilities only went so far. There were no animals to call from the surrounding fields, no time to transform, and nowhere near enough energy. She didn't want to kill them anyway—escape was the priority. Hers was not the best magic for defending oneself in this sort of situation, even against other creature mages.

The first shadow enveloped her. She winced and held tight to Kres's reins in anticipation. Even if they attacked, if she could just stay on the horse until they were inside, endure the pain and hang on—

But instead of the pierce of talons, she heard a shriek from above. Her eyes darted around frantically—what was happening? To her left, an eagle careened off-balance into the fields.

She whipped her head around. Her eyes caught on Aven's. They said everything she needed to know—the sadness, the love, it was all there.

He was defending her. Saving her, when he should be saving himself.

"What are you doing?" she shouted.

Another eagle was blown away from her. A third got through. Talons scratched through the leather on her back, and she felt a hot, sticky wetness on her right side. Before it could sink its talons in again, it, too, was batted out of the way by a powerful gust.

The horses reached the gate. The eagles did not follow, instead circling back toward Sorin.

Several mages came running. "We heard your call!" "Are you all right?" "Get a healer!"

She shook her head, dismounting quickly. "No, no, the danger's over for me. Sorin is still out there—under attack from those eagles. Get a warrior, not a healer. Get someone to help him. But don't go out of the gate if you can't fight."

"You need a healer, I insist!"

"Fine," she relented. "Fetch a healer, but only after you fetch help for Sorin. I must see the Masters first before I can be helped." They looked from one to another and seemed to believe her. None of them wanted to interfere with a mage on a Master's orders.

Turning away from them, she found Aven had dismounted as well. He waited next to Cora, watching her.

She strode to him and stopped, running a hand through Cora's mane as she spoke. "Well," she said. "Here we are. This is where I've been taking you. At least you'll get some answers now."

He nodded grimly.

She turned back to one of the gate mages, a young boy. "Take these horses to the stable, and see that they get fed and brushed down." The boy nodded and started off.

She took Aven's arm, partly to keep up the pretense that he was in her charge and partly to be closer to him. She led him down the path and into the compound.

"This is where I live," she whispered, as if only the two of them were listening and not her bond as well, eavesdropping and choosing what she could say and what she couldn't. All constraints of the mission should be released at this point, given that she'd basically achieved it. She should be able to say more about herself. "In that building there, I sleep. And in that one there, I work—the stables."

He followed her gestures with keen eyes. Was he sincerely interested? Plotting the landmarks for a potential escape? She could only hope.

"I mean, when I'm not out kidnapping innocent people and the like."

He snorted. They were passing between two buildings and were about to head into the main open courtyard. She stopped abruptly and glanced around. No one was nearby. She pulled him off the side of the path, hoping that her bond did not torture her for delaying a few moments longer.

She felt nothing at all. Perhaps since she had succeeded, it did not mind a few stolen moments. Perhaps this served its purpose somehow? There was no reply from her shoulder.

"Well, Aven Lanuken. This is where we will reach our end. In a few moments more, I will take you to those that bind me. I do not know what they will do, but know this: if I could have my way, I would do nothing but take you back to Akaria." Her bond was strangely silent at her words.

"I know that, Miara," he whispered, using her real name for the first time. His rough voice and the sound of her name on his lips sent an unexpected thrill through her. "And if I could have my way, I would have you come with me."

She felt herself blush. "Ah, but what use are these idle wishes? They cannot be. What can we say about a world like this, a world where people like the Masters can control people like us? How can there be a Balance or a Way when there are moments like this? If I had died on this journey, or if you had run away, then I could have died knowing that the world was just. But as it is, my heart breaks to see them win."

"Don't lose faith," he whispered.

She nodded. She was not about to argue. And she wanted desperately to believe him.

"I have something to give you," he said now. He reached into his pocket and withdrew a folded piece of paper. "I think I would rather have it in your hands than theirs."

"What is it?" She wanted to open it, but it might not be safe. She slipped it into her pocket without a glance. The Masters hadn't said anything about possessions or owning folded pieces of paper, so it should be safe with her for now. She would hide the paper as long as she was able.

"I'm not sure," he replied. "A map of the stars, I think. Just promise me you'll look at it and remember all this."

She nodded solemnly. "Of course." They said nothing for a moment, just looking into each other's eyes.

Should she tell him? Should she confess how much she really loved him—the honor she felt when his eyes rested on her with that look in them, the desire she felt when she saw him move or laugh, the way she looked at him when she knew he wasn't looking? Would it make it easier for him—or harder?

Certainly, he had a right to know, but—

A shout rang out from behind her. "Miara! Don't hog all the glory for yourself! Wait for me!"

Sorin. He was scratched and scraped but largely fine. He strode toward them.

No time to tell him now. She sighed.

She turned back to Aven. "Just one more thing. I am so sorry," she said.

"I'm not," he replied. "For any of it."

Daes's ears perked up at the first sound of bells clanging during their midday lunch. None of the others seemed to notice, all too intent on the hearty potatoes and roast rabbit. All four Masters were convened for one of the elaborate midday banquets Seulka insisted on orchestrating. It gave her some joy to have a household to preside over, but he was also quite sure that she simply enjoyed having something to order the slaves to do.

Sounds of shouting by the east gate reached them on the wind, finally stirring his companions. Daes rose and strode to the window, unwilling to hope just yet. Could it be? Could she have actually succeeded?

Indeed. Three horses stood at the south gate, and mages were swarming around them as if something very out of the ordinary had occurred. To underscore this, unnaturally low clouds dotted around them, fog-like, but flashing with snaps of lightning swirling around their length.

He sat back down. It wouldn't be long now if it were the mage slave and the prince. The compulsion in her must be strong by now, so close to her goal. She would not dally.

"What is it?" the Fat Master asked into the expectant silence.

Daes smiled wryly—the others were all eyeing him. "Three horses have arrived at the east gate," he said casually.

Seulka glared at him. "Why must you always be so opaque?" She paused, but he would offer no more explanation.

"Is it *her*?" the Tall Master demanded.

He shrugged, smiling. "I'm sure we shall see any moment now."

Just as a roast boar was being added to the feast, the hall doors thundered open.

And there they were. His fiery, rebellious creature mage, the air mage, and another, presumably the prince. He met the description—light haired, green eyed, the muscular build of a seasoned soldier.

"I see you have returned," Seulka said smoothly, probably delighted to have this to preside over on top of her unnecessary dining affair. "And not without gifts. Tell me what has transpired." Her voice was smooth and authoritative when it came to commands, one of the few things he enjoyed about her.

The air mage spoke first. "I found Miara not far into Akaria and was able to be of service on the perilous journey back."

Daes wanted to roll his eyes, and he heard the Tall Master cover a laugh with a cough. Yes, he had a few scuffs, but he was far too proud of them. Not as a true warrior would be, one who'd seen a thousand scratches in his day, as Daes once had.

As his eyes turned to the woman, the rebellious one, he missed those days a little. Or perhaps envied her just the slightest for the power, the experience she had gained. Bragging rights she would not use. Her eyes were bright with a fire he recognized, dormant too long in himself—the fire of battle. Not long now, though, and he would get to stretch his legs again. Wounds on each of her shoulders oozed blood that had begun to drip strikingly down the front of her black tunic and leathers. Bandages on her arm were beginning to bleed through. Fresh claw marks on her cheek gave her a raw, savage beauty soaring beyond what she'd already possessed. He had to admit that it appealed to the fighter in him.

When she spoke, her voice was strange. Different than before. "I present to you, milady, Aven Lanuken, Prince of Akaria. As you asked, and before the turning of the moon, I might add."

He smiled. She hadn't missed that they had sent help before they'd said they would.

Daes eyed her as Seulka left her seat and marched around the banquet tables to get a closer look at the prince. She turned to Daes. "How can we be sure this is him? He looks like I've seen in portraits, but—"

"Well, aren't we fortunate to have a friend to identify him?" Daes turned to one of the guards. "Fetch the knight."

Seulka turned to the creature mage again. "How did you identify him?"

"He gave me his name before he knew my purpose," she said. "And he was dressed more finely then."

Interesting. A foolish mistake, but beauty did have a way of getting men to talk.

The Mistress nodded and looked at the young man once more up close. He eyed her back with a level, searching stare, fiery, but biding his time. He had the assurance and confidence of royalty, that was for sure—a distinct air of aloofness and superiority that was hard to fake. Daes had no doubt it was the prince, but it couldn't hurt to be sure.

The side door opened, and the lovely knight entered and stopped in her tracks.

"Well, well." She grinned and folded her arms across her chest. "We just cannot seem to quit each other."

"Knight, you said you were in Estun not a fortnight ago. Will you hold those words as truth, to your oath?" Daes demanded formally.

She turned to him, solemn. "Yes. Of course. On my noble parentage."

"Can you identify this man?"

She looked hard for a moment at the prince. The young man returned her gaze, a mixture of rage and sadness in his eyes. From just that look, Daes knew they were acquainted. Something had transpired between them, something more than dry diplomatic exchanges.

"I know him to be Aven Lanuken, Crown Prince of Akaria."

"How can you be sure?" Seulka prodded.

"I had hoped to be his wife."

"Now that's—" the prince suddenly started. The creature mage's head snapped to look at him. Ah, now what was that? An interesting reaction. Could there be something between them? The prince was quite handsome, so it was not hard to imagine.

"On my knight's oath, I swear to it." The Devoted cut him off and smirked at him, looking pleased. "I was looking forward to doing my duty and ending you. But if my allies must do it, my goals are also achieved. Such are the mysteries of the Balance."

The prince glared at her. The creature mage's jaw tightened. Very interesting. Was he seeing the result of the wiles and seductions she had used to keep her captive so effectively? Perhaps they had backfired on her as well.

"Thank you, that will be—" Daes started.

"I have another piece of information. But it's not for free. Half a bounty," she said.

He raised his eyebrows. "I'll be the judge of its worth. But I'm listening."

"I also ran into these two on the journey here. You should keep your slaves on a shorter leash."

"I was achieving my purpose," the creature mage snapped. "Which you would have prevented, I might add." Daes frowned and looked expectantly at the knight.

"He is a mage," she said with a self-satisfied smile. The creature mage's jaw clenched, and she looked as if she might have killed the woman had she been free to. Ah, so she knew? Had she hoped to hide it from them?

"I agreed to no bounty," the Fat Master interjected, irritated his funds were being spent so speedily, with so little negotiation. Daes had no time for nitpicking, but that *was* the Fat Master's job.

"An air mage, to be specific," she said. "I witnessed him work magic in Estun. I had to leave immediately to get permission for assassination. Knights can't attack royalty without consulting our order, as per our code. I missed my chance. But brand him, and you'll see. And then my duty shall be fulfilled as well."

How interesting. Perhaps there was more to the creature mage's touchiness than he'd thought. *This* changed things. Of course, Daes had worried some of them might have gifts or even be practicing the forbidden magic. But Seulka's pressures and his own doubts had left him feeling those were paranoid fears, long shots.

Apparently, not so paranoid after all. Only air mages could work the forbidden magic. They were much closer to what he feared than he'd dared to believe.

"If he is a mage, you shall have a full bounty," Daes replied. The Fat Master pursed his lips, but nodded. It was only fair. "This mage can't earn a bounty, so it goes to you."

"Thank you, sir. You are indeed fair and just. Farewell, Aven," the knight said, little emotion in her voice. If the creature mage cared for the prince, this knight had nothing but stone in her heart. She turned and left them, dress trailing gracefully in her wake.

"Well, then," Seulka said. "That is unexpected. But beside the point to these weary travelers. You have indeed completed your mission, Miara. Go and seek a healer, you are grievously injured. Get whatever you require to recover from your efforts. You may have three days without work as a reward."

The creature mage nodded, bowing. "Yes, Mistress."

"You, too, Sorin. Now be gone. Your work is done here. Guards—take this man to the dungeons."

But even as she said that, the Tall Master stood up. Everyone quieted, waiting. The Tall Master did not speak often.

"Don't you think… I should have him first?" he said in his soft, gravelly voice.

Seulka let out a bark of laughter. "Aren't you an eager one? And not even finish your lunch? I clearly need a new menu. Fine, let's see if this knight's claim is true. To the smithy with him, then!"

The Tall Master immediately abandoned his food and headed straight for the prince, taking his arm from the creature mage. The guards surrounded them and pushed the mages aside. There was nothing the Tall Master enjoyed as much as making a new slave—food, wine, and women were nothing in comparison. Daes might have been dark, but the Tall Master gave him a run for his money with his very specific sadistic streak. No one relished the pain in their eyes quite like he did. For Daes, it was more a necessary evil to achieve a necessary goal, ensuring their power and preventing mages from destroying everything their nation had ever built.

That said, this was important. Daes stood up. "I'll join you this time."

The mages watched from the doorway as the Tall Master strode out the side door with the prince in tow. Daes crossed behind the others to meet him as the guards opened the door.

The pain on the face of the rebellious one was blatant. Indeed, too much emotion. Perhaps he shouldn't complain. She *had* achieved his goal and the mission. He could decide if her attachment would prove problematic later. Perhaps it would even prove useful, although not to the part of him that had grown fond of that brutal wildness about her.

Later. For now, it was time to make a new slave.

Guards hauled Aven outside again and toward a low, dark building. He carefully studied his jailers. They were lightly armed but did not carry themselves with much of a soldierly air. He doubted they knew much more than how to slash with the pathetic blades they carried.

The two leaders—presumably the ones in charge of this whole place—were not armed at all, although he suspected the one dressed in black probably had something concealed. Overall, it was five average men versus him. Not terrible odds, but not great if even a few of them had any serious combat experience. No, if he was going to make a break for it, this didn't seem like a very opportune time. But if they hoped to make a slave of him, too, would he really get another chance?

He gritted his teeth. Certainly, he had guessed this day would come. He'd known it was almost inevitable. But now that it was here, he still wanted to find a way out. The air picked up around him, whipping angrily with his frustration.

Had Miara been right? If he had actually been able to free her, maybe it would all have been worth it. But he hadn't. He'd failed. As it was, he was giving up everything. And she was still a slave. And now he would be, too. He had let down everyone—Miara, his parents, even his people.

They rounded the corner of the smithy, nearly to the door. With as little warning as he could manage, Aven spun away from the tall one in the direction of the fewest guards. He tried to direct the air in the tall one's direction, but he wasn't sure his magic achieved anything. It was not an ingrained instinct yet. His ability to punch someone in the face, however, was. He collided with the chest of one guard and made use of this skill. The guard was still too surprised to react, and he doubled over as Aven sprinted blindly forward.

Someone tackled him from behind, and they went down. He heaved to his left, seeking to roll over them and away. He did manage to roll onto his back, crushing someone, but the dark one was right behind him and seized him, two guards joining him quickly.

While two guards gripped either side of him more securely, the man in black robes studied him for a moment.

"I admire your spirited attempt," he said, "but it's really a waste. There's no escape from here. Every mage is at my disposal to stop you, hundreds on all sides. Not to mention the guards, and that you're in the center of Kavanar, where an Akarian such as yourself is not welcome."

Aven narrowed his eyes. "I thought Akaria and Kavanar were at peace," he said, snorting.

"Well, I suppose you're about to find out firsthand the truth of that," said the man, smiling darkly. "Bring him."

The dark one motioned, and the two guards jostled him along, the tall one following. Apparently it was the tall one who had tackled him. Aven was not surprised. These guards seemed close to useless. They guarded sheep who couldn't even choose to escape if they wanted to, so that was really no surprise. Didn't mean he was getting away, though.

A hot, stale blast of air hit him as they entered the smithy. The ceiling was low, and ironically, the tall one had to bend to stand anywhere inside the place. Aven could see nearly a dozen blacksmiths working nearby, quite a large number for a smithy. One hearth stood empty but smoldered fiercely. It was there they seemed to be headed.

Instead of an anvil in this area, there was a table with leather bindings at the top and bottom. Clearly it was meant for a person rather than a sword.

One guard shoved him toward the table, and another grabbed his arm from the opposite side and sent him down with a thud. He kicked and tried to twist away from them, but he didn't waste much energy in the attempt. The dark one was right. If there were an opportunity to escape, this was not it.

Leather tightened around his wrists and ankles, holding him fast to the table. Straps wrapped his neck and his chest, coming up through slits in the table and fastened underneath. One guard took a knife to his sleeve, quickly slicing it and ripping it away at the shoulder.

The tall one removed something long, thin, and metallic from his robes and put it into the fire. The dark one stood nearby, crossed his arms, and waited, frowning.

The part of the smithy they occupied was pitch black, not letting in even a ray of light from outside or a glimpse of an overcast cloud. The stars that were supposed to be his guide were a whole world away, as hard to imagine now as the Great Stone in Estun.

In spite of that, he closed his eyes. He saw Miara on her horse, the star over her shoulder that should have been her savior, if he had been good enough. If he had known more. He whispered a prayer to Casel, emitting no sound but moving his lips until suddenly the pain cut through the words. His teeth clenched, and he could only think the prayer in his mind.

Casel, my guide, my star, keep me free.

He felt the searing, hot pain on his own left shoulder. The twisting heat, the energy like sulfurous maggots boring into his skin. He ignored it and repeated his words again. *Casel, my guide, my star, keep me free. Casel, my guide, my star, keep me free. Casel, my guide, my star, keep me free.* He reached out with his mind toward the sky, away from his body, blocking out the leather cutting into his wrists, pulling him, holding him to the hard earth. He reached up, flailing blindly, his only way to fight the white-hot metal against his skin.

Did he feel that icy white energy on his forehead? Was it just his imagination? Desperate insanity? There was no space for logical thought, no energy to wonder at what the truth was in that moment.

Finally, the hot metal against his shoulder was gone. The dark one's voice. "It is done."

"A few more words," said another voice.

He could still feel the throbbing, the agonizing burn vibrating through his chest and up into his skull. Some kind of incantation was in the air—the tall one reciting something to finish the job.

He gasped for breath, realizing only now that he'd held it while the white-hot poker was touching him. Or maybe it was just the pain, or the shock.

He opened his eyes to see the dark one looking over him, studying him.

It was over. Aven was a slave now. And he always would be.

14 SCARS

Sorin led Miara toward the healers in the east ward. A daze had settled over her. Perhaps those slashes on her back were deeper than she'd thought. Or perhaps it was everything else.

Aven was theirs now. And worse, they'd found out that he was a mage. Even after she'd tried so hard to keep it a secret, even from Sorin. Perhaps it would delay his death or even keep him alive. Was that a good thing or a bad thing? And how had that knight found her way *here*? By the ancients, how could anyone build a life around exterminating others? How could anyone convince themselves such a thing was right and holy?

And the one piece of the puzzle she had wondered about—had the Knight been in line to be his wife? Had they been betrothed or only in negotiations? How could he have even considered such a woman? It was ridiculous to feel jealous at a moment like this, when she'd rejected

Aven at every turn and likely just delivered him to his execution—but she couldn't help herself. Could there actually have been something between them? What if they had been in love? Aven had seemed so sweet, a bit naïve and innocent, but definitely an easy flirt—could it have all been a show? Could she have underestimated his charm? Perhaps he had only sought his freedom, and it had all meant nothing. Maybe he felt nothing for her, and she was a fool for falling for it, just as the Knight had been.

No. No, it certainly had meant something. He'd had his chance to run. He hadn't taken it. But that didn't mean that someone couldn't have come before her.

She tried to calm her thoughts as two healers came to work on her; she knew too much turmoil in their presence would drain their energy unnecessarily and made her body not want to heal. They looked her over in a mix of surprise and excitement.

"My goodness, Miara! You're in just terrible shape," the blond one named Fesian cooed. "We hardly ever see anything like this." She was just barely veiling the pleasure in her words. "You are bleeding *profusely*. I can't believe you're still standing. This is wonderful."

"Sorin is really eating this up," the other added. He was a redheaded man named Tameun. "But not you. Not that I'm surprised. Lie down now." Miara complied and lay down on the cot.

"Isn't that always how it is," Fesian muttered. "The real warriors don't puff up their chests and prance around. Now this will just hurt a little."

Miara stared up at the wood beams and tried to keep her mind blank and calm. She didn't know if she should be happy or concerned that the healer considered her a real warrior. But bloody as she was, perhaps anything else would be ridiculous. She was indeed fresh from a battle—both physically, and in her soul. At least the physical fight was over.

Fesian circled around, moved her hand over the scratch on Miara's face, and began to focus on it.

Miara held up her hand. "Leave that," she said.

"But why? We're not short on energy. We've got more than we know what to do with, I promise you. You needn't skimp."

"I'm sorry," she replied. "I can't explain. I just... I have to keep it, at least for a little while. I don't want to completely erase it all. Maybe I'll change my mind and be back tomorrow."

This seemed to assuage them. The talon punctures required several stops and starts and rests in between as they healed them back and forth in waves. The world was fuzzy and seemed to buzz around her. She lay mostly still, eyes shut, dazed, stuck like an insect cocooned in amber.

Each healing spell itself was agony. But they only barely registered in her mind. She had forced herself to stop thinking about the stupid knight. All that was left was... nothing.

There was nothing to think of, nothing to work toward, nothing to care about. Nothing but the tendril of a thought of him, the feeling that someone who had just been in the room was now gone, the cold feeling after a warm hand leaves your side. She sighed. It wasn't that there was nothing left. Something was left: the glaring absence of *him*.

How could she care in a world that would let Aven die? How could she build anything in a world like this? Why would she bring herself to even move? How could she do anything at all, really?

She didn't.

Fesian paused for a moment, frowning at the eternal wound on Miara's shoulder. "Hmph. Odd."

"What is it?" Miara managed.

"Oh, nothing." The healer returned to fussing over the talon punctures on her back. "Just a few more, hold on."

Finally, Tameun roused her with a pat on her forearm. Had she fallen asleep? When had she closed her eyes? "That's enough for now, Miara. Let's see if it finishes the last little healing on its own. There should be few scars."

"On the outside, anyway," she muttered.

Tameun gave a friendly snort, and Fesian wrapped her arms around Miara in a hug. "All things heal with time," she whispered.

Death doesn't, Miara thought. Slavery doesn't. But she didn't voice her thoughts.

The healers left her. She trudged back to the dorm. Her father wasn't there, nor Luha. Of course, it was the middle of the day, and they were working. She sat down on her bed, then threw herself carelessly down, burying her face in the blankets.

There she lay, thinking very little, hardly moving, just staring, as the day marched on.

At one point, she thought she heard a scream in the distance. Was that Aven? She leapt up, running to the window and throwing the shutters open, listening. Nothing.

No, no, it made no sense. It was probably long done. Before she'd even left the healers. The branding didn't take long. It could not be him. It was probably just children playing.

But in her heart, it might as well have been. She may not have heard it, but at some point during the day, there had been at least one such scream. And her heart broke at the thought that they had broken him, that they'd made him into a slave. Just like her.

Now instead of just sitting and staring, the tears finally came. She forgot the open window and collapsed back onto her bed, slowly crying herself into an exhausted sleep.

Exhausted as he was, Aven gave the guards his fair share of trouble getting him up off the table in the smithy and vertical again. One slung Aven's branded arm over his shoulder to hold him upright, and he groaned at the shockwave of pain that resulted. He wasn't aware of anything in the next few moments beyond that pain.

Then they were dragging him somewhere. Where had the woman said? The dungeon? Yes. They entered the main building from the back this time and hauled him down several excruciating flights of stairs. Blackness replaced the midday light, and only a sporadic torch made further progress possible.

Finally, a small, dank room opened up before them. Wet, rugged stone surrounded them on all sides. In the center of the room, red-hot coals in an open hearth left the room almost as sweltering as the smithy. The air reeked of sweat and worse. Cells lined the walls.

Into one of these he was dragged. A guard shackled his hands to the wall and left. He saw the two masters studying him from the base of the staircase before they, too, were gone.

Hell. There was no starlight here. Nor light from the sun or the moon. Nothing to sustain him or revive him as Miara had taught him. His heart started to race in mild panic, that same feeling of being trapped returning so suddenly.

He shivered, finally recovering enough to notice the deep, icy feeling in his chest. At least he had expended *some* magic. Whether it had accomplished anything, he was glad he now knew enough to try.

The dark, heavy walls pressed in on him, bringing back his very worst memories of Estun. How much had changed in just a few days. His worries had been for hiding his magic, finding a wife, getting out of yet another boring social event. Now he couldn't imagine hiding his magic, or finding anyone to marry other than Miara, or wasting a minute in an event he didn't want to take part in. In retrospect, though, brandy and conversation didn't seem quite so bad or so boring.

He studied his surroundings. Why bother with iron bars if he was to be shackled to the wall anyway? The restraints around his wrists were anchored at about shoulder height and left him in an awkward sitting position. His feet and legs were free. His chest still felt hollow with a frigid cold.

He examined the hearth. There was light coming from it, wasn't there? And wasn't fire the domain of the air mage, even if he didn't understand it yet? Perhaps he could draw some energy from that to recharge. He didn't mind the cold with the heat in the room, but who knew when he might need that energy for something?

He closed his eyes and tried to feel the energy instead of looking for it. For a while, all he could sense was his own frigid core. But gradually, he caught another whisper of a strange, dancing, vibrating, twitching energy. The fire.

He pulled from it cautiously, slowly. Would going too fast make it go out? He didn't want anything to be noticed. And he didn't know how much he needed or how this strange, twitchy energy might make him feel.

In the end, though, it felt no different than sunlight or starlight—like glorious sustenance, like pure joy coursing through is veins.

A squeak broke his concentration. A rat was sniffing his boot. He twitched his foot in its direction, and it scurried away. Well. What a pleasant addition to these lovely accommodations.

He took a deep breath. The cold was mostly gone; that was probably enough for now. His shoulder ached, of course. His mind felt unchanged. Did the enslavement spell take time? Could one even notice it at any given moment? What a torture it would be to only remember you were a slave some of the time, when you couldn't do what you really wanted. He thought of Miara and felt sure that must be the way it worked.

He tried to bring his thoughts back to assessing his situation and preparing himself for any future battle that might come his way. He'd rejuvenated his magic. Now the best thing he could do was rest as well as he could in this awful position. He tried to lean his temple against the shackle that held his right hand in the air, and after a few wild head jerks as he nodded off, he finally settled into a tense sleep.

"What the hell just happened?" Daes demanded as soon as they were alone.

The Tall Master shrugged. "I don't think it worked."

A chill ran through Daes's veins. "What do you mean it didn't work?" He spoke numbly. He didn't really mean it. He knew exactly what it meant. He had seen the same thing the Tall Master had. At the end of the process, there was always a strange flash and cracking sound, like the briefest flash of thunder, as the enchantment took hold. But this time, nothing.

But he didn't want to believe it.

"Perhaps your fears were more founded than some of us were willing to believe."

He met the Tall Master's gaze, his expression grim. But Daes said nothing.

"His lips were moving," the other man said. "Did you see it? He was saying something. Maybe saying something to stop the process."

"This is one time I'm not pleased to be right. I hope it is not the case. We must be sure."

The Tall Master nodded.

"I think we should brand him again," Daes said.

"But then he will know that something isn't right." The older man frowned and rubbed his chin.

"If he already has the star magic, then he may already know that he is not a slave. Then again, he might not realize it's anything out of the ordinary. He doesn't know our ways. Perhaps it is the usual second step in the process. Also, check his wound, see if any healing has begun." Daes needed to know more. What did this prince think he knew, where had he learned how to resist them? He had to die—but Daes had to figure out how the prince had gained his knowledge first.

"It's only been a few hours. The wound will not have had time to heal. But I'll check." The Tall Master nodded, eyes dark, and turned to go. But just in the doorway, he stopped for a moment. "Daes," he said, voice deadly serious. "What if he *has* discovered the forbidden magic?"

"Then we will kill him as quickly as possible, and his brothers next. Perhaps try to find out how he learned of it first. But we can't let this knowledge resurface. It was foolish to underestimate it for so long, to assume it was forgotten. We will end it now. We must."

The Tall Master nodded crisply and headed out.

Miara awoke to soft fingers stroking her hair. She blinked her eyes open to her father sitting beside her on the bed. The window was still open. The light of early evening fell on his soft smile.

She sat up quickly and threw her arms around him. He squeezed her hard in return. The way he did it made her suspect he hadn't been sure she'd come home this time.

She had. Although she might have wished differently.

"You're back," he murmured.

She let go of him and smiled. "I made it."

"And your mission?"

"Complete." His face said that he understood the bitter tone in her voice. He understood her like no one else.

"What happened to your face?" He gently brushed his fingers over the scratches on her cheek.

"A wolf."

He frowned. "You ran into a wolf you couldn't charm? Didn't think I'd live to see the day."

"Not a wild one. A human one."

"Ah, I see. They came after him, eh?"

She nodded.

"I would do the same, of course, if I could. Are you all right?" he said.

"No," she said, not wanting to lie. Not to him.

He said nothing, only waited.

"Aven—the prince—is a good man. He doesn't deserve this hell."

He nodded grimly and pulled her back into his arms.

"He fell in love with me," she whispered, feeling her eyes growing blurry, muffling her voice into the wool of his tunic and vest. "It was horrible. He could have run away, but he didn't, because of *me*. He didn't want to leave me; he wanted to help. I couldn't explain any of it. I couldn't warn him. I tried to convince him I didn't—" She stopped short, choked with emotion.

"That was his choice, not yours. A noble and brave choice, too."

"I was still the cause. I've never been in love before, Father. Love should be about being happy, making a family—not luring a man to his death."

He gave a little snort of laughter. "Love is often far more complicated than we like to think, isn't it?" he replied. "We know that all too well. There's what they tell you in children's books and parables. Then there's real life. You and I are not the first ones to be burned by love, my dear."

She said nothing, just holding onto him, letting the tears slow to a hollow stop.

"Of course, one can hardly blame him," he continued. "You have all of your mother's beauty, and much more heart than she ever did."

"I wish I didn't. If only I'd been ugly, or cruel, or had no good spells to stop him. If I'd been worse. The world would be better without—"

He pulled away, put a finger rapidly to her lips, and didn't let her say it. "Don't *ever* say that, Miara. It's not true. Not true at all."

"It *is* true," she whispered. She was too full of emotion to stay her words or think them through. "Don't try to tell me it isn't, Father. What about you and mother? It would *all* have been better without me. What good have I brought to you?" She shook her head.

"No," he spat, his fingers digging into her arms. "You have brought me so much joy, it's indescribable. You can't possibly understand. I know it might seem hard to believe, but it's true. Someday when you are a mother, you will see. Your mother and I would not have lasted. I was living a lie. And so was she. You helped me see that magic—and my daughter's magic—was more important than that lie, whatever the cost. You have the best things about her in you, and then more. I cannot comprehend a world without you. And what the Masters have made you do is *not your fault*. That sin is on *their* souls, not yours. Let me send for Brother Sefim."

"I already know what he would say," she whispered bitterly. "He has told me a thousand times. But it is *still* my hands that have done these things. They are still my memories. I can't forget giving him over to them, seeing them take him away because I was able to do their bidding. Sefim says the Balance will even out all things in the end—but where is the Balance now? Where is the Balance in my life? There is no balance here. No matter how much good I put in, only pain and strife come back in the end."

"You're young, Miara—"

"What does that matter?"

"You have many years of life ahead of you for things to even out. You have lived but a fraction of your time here. Justice is slow, and the Way is long. The Balance will reach you, it just takes time."

"Has it reached *you*, Father?" she whispered.

His jaw clenched at that, and there was a look in his eyes she couldn't decode. "It gave me you," he whispered. "And Luha. Just one of you is more than I could dare to ask for."

"Maybe the Balance is just a lie to keep us going. To keep us from giving up. Something to give us hope, but it's not real. Maybe the world is *not* fair, and there's absolutely nothing we can do about it."

He stared at her. He said nothing for a long while. He didn't seem to be wondering if what she'd said was true, and she was a little glad because she wasn't sure she believed it was. Instead his face seemed to say that he wondered what she could have gone through that could possibly make her feel this way.

"Oh, Miara," he whispered finally. "This has been even harder on you than I thought."

They said nothing for a while, sitting in silence. Outside, a few birds chirped the songs of evening, readying for quiet.

"I will let you be," he said. "I can see you need time to think and be alone. There are no easy answers, and even if I had any, I'm not sure you could hear them right now. But if I could say one more thing... I would say whatever you do, whatever they break in you, whatever they take from you, don't let them take your faith. Don't let them in that far. They don't deserve it."

He ran a hand over her hair, brushed the backs of his fingers along the scar on her cheek, and then stood. He kissed her on the forehead. Then he went to the window and closed the shutters.

"Shall I bring you back a flame for the fire?"

She nodded numbly.

He, too, nodded, bowed a little, and headed from her room. As soon as he was gone, she felt a strange longing. Fathers were supposed to have the answers. He always had before. But if he had the answer this time, he wasn't saying. He was waiting for her to find it herself, or not at all. This time when he left her, the question was still hanging in the air.

She shouldn't have pushed him so hard. She shouldn't have mentioned Mother. Miara was hurt, and she was lashing out by hurting him. The Masters had hurt her and Aven, and she was just passing it onto her father as well. She had to stop the cycle.

But she didn't have the strength just yet. She was still aching. Maybe tomorrow. Or perhaps her father yet had the strength to stop the cycle with him.

Later, he returned and stoked the fire for her, smiling sweetly at her, kissing her forehead, saying nothing. She smiled back weakly. She lay on the bed for the longest time, just listening to him move about his daily tasks in the adjoining rooms. He hummed to himself, a small salve to the emptiness. Her brain wouldn't move, wouldn't think. Every time it did, she hurt too much. Every thought was of Aven.

Eventually, Luha crept in and snuggled to her side, sleepy eyed and sweet. Miara had no idea what time it was, but it had to be very late.

"Can I sleep with you tonight, Miara?" Luha whispered. "It's getting cold, and I had a nightmare."

Miara smiled a little and nodded, and Luha climbed in next to her. Miara wrapped an arm around the little girl, pulling her close. There was probably no nightmare; Luha just wanted to be close. That was okay with her. The air had indeed grown cold, and besides, she had missed her sister.

For a moment, she could see Luha less as a little sister and more like her own little girl. Her father's words rang in her head. *Someday when you're a mother.* Would such a day ever come? What if she had her own little girl to cradle to sleep just like this? Could she bring a life into such a sad and unjust world? And even if she wanted to... who would ever be good enough to lie in her arms, after him?

For a moment, a vision flashed before her eyes—an older Aven with graying hair and a delicate silver crown, cradling a laughing little boy in the crook of his arm. What if... what if things had been completely different? What if she'd been born in Akaria? What if she'd been free? What if neither of them had had any of this stupid magic? What kind of family could they have created?

She blinked away tears, but a few escaped, dripping silently and stealthily from her eyes toward the pillow. She squeezed her eyes shut and hugged Luha tighter, pressing her face into her brown tresses and breathing deep.

The crash of the dungeon doors jolted Aven awake. "Oh, good," he muttered. "I was just starting to get comfortable."

Two soldiers entered, apparently unamused as they unshackled him. They hauled him out again, up stair after stair, past torch after torch after lantern.

When the night air hit him, he gasped for breath, filling his lungs with the fresh, cold air. He may have been imagining it—was he increasingly delirious?—but he felt as though he could feel the starlight tingling on his skin.

They headed back toward the smithy. Inside, the tall one waited, wearing the driest and cruelest expression Aven had ever seen. There was the brand in the coals.

Again?

What could this mean?

"We must complete the process," he muttered to Aven, but the comment was awkward. Forced. A lie? Why did he trouble to address Aven at all when he hadn't the first time?

They lashed him down again. He swallowed and gritted his teeth. It had been one thing to reach out to

Casel before, but he was fast losing energy. Could he do it again? Had it even helped anything? Shackled all the time, he had no way of testing his enslavement.

He gasped as he suddenly realized—all these mages, and he had yet to see another pair of visible shackles. If he *were* a slave, they'd have no reason to keep him chained.

Perhaps it required two treatments, or perhaps there was a phase before the binding really set in. Perhaps there was a whole series of tortures before the process would be complete.

Or perhaps he had done it.

Had he stopped the process? Was that why he was here on this table again? And if he *had* kept them from enslaving him… was it possible he could free Miara, too?

Before he could think it completely through or allow hope to take root, the brand slid rapidly from the coals and into his unwounded shoulder. The pain sliced through his consciousness so quickly, he couldn't breathe for a moment. This time he hadn't had a chance to reach out to the star first. The hungry maggots of energy bored into his skin faster and harder, wriggling wildly, like a thousand screams straight into his veins, and he could hardly keep his thoughts.

Against his own will, he let out a scream.

The physical pain was nothing compared to the magic of the brand. That agony was overwhelming—but it also pushed him forward. He did not need to think, he did not need to try—his instincts reached on their own, groping for salvation. Something in him knew what to do now, found the star, and held tight. He pulled the icy energy with all his might, no prayers, no wishes—just hungry desperation.

Like a sudden river of ice in his veins, he felt her energy spread through him, flying, racing, rooting out the dark magic, turning his body frigid.

At his shoulder, the fire met the ice. The brand was still there, the heat still seared his skin in agonizing intensity. But there it stopped, like two winds blowing directly against each other, each one holding the other back. It was as if the energy of the star wanted to flow beyond him into the brand itself. It didn't want to stop with Aven. Something about the heat wouldn't let it continue.

Finally, the man ceased. He said the same words again, but his voice was strained.

It's not working. They can't enslave me even if they *know* I am a mage. It mustn't be working!

The surge of energy and triumph he felt at that idea quickly dissipated as the soldiers untied him and brought him upright. Yellow splotches whirled before his eyes. He lurched against one of the nearest ones and wished he could say it was part of some clever ruse toward an escape.

They dragged him back past the torches and lanterns, past the over-hot furnace, back into the dungeon cell. As exhausted as he was, his hope hung on what they would do when they entered.

Again, a guard shackled him to the wall. They locked the door behind them.

Aven had never felt so happy to be chained to something. Well, except perhaps to be chained to Miara's bed. Exhausted as he was, he found himself grinning in the darkness.

Was it possible? Was it true? Did he dare believe? And if he'd protected himself... was there a chance Miara was really free, too? Or that there might be some way to free her if he got a chance to try again?

He sat, thinking, eyes alive and watching the coals in the furnace dance. Perhaps he was not such a failure after all. He had to figure out a way to know for sure.

15   BOUNDARIES

Miara jolted awake. Nothing had startled her, as much as she'd suddenly realized how much light filled the room. The sun was well risen. She hadn't woken up this late since she was a child.

She automatically reached for Luha beside her, but she was gone and the bed cold. It was well beyond the morning bell.

How could she have slept so late? The compulsion had greeted her each morning for over two decades now, and the Mistress's release from work had never changed anything before. Perhaps it had been only habit all along. Or perhaps she was just so exhausted. She'd probably woken ever so slightly and fallen asleep again without remembering it.

She stood and cracked open the window farther to get a look at the day. It was even later than she'd thought because the sky was dreary and overcast, nearly as dim as the dawn hours, but too many people were out and about. Judging by that, it must be midday at least.

She stood at the window a long time. Where was there to go? What needed to be done? Nothing. She watched the people walking about and felt the air freeze her skin at each whip of the wind, which only made her think of him and bathing in the river not so long ago.

A bath. And not an icy one. Perhaps that was something worth doing. Aven would urge her to if he were here. Or even join her. She gathered her things and headed for the bathhouse.

Of all the journeys she'd gone on, she never ceased to be grateful to return to these ivory marble halls. The squat building was not far, but the cold, whipping wind chilled her even more deeply in the few moments she was outside. The darkest winter days would be on them soon. But what did it matter? What did any season matter?

What were they doing to Aven?

The thought nagged at the base of her skull. There was no way to know. She shook her head at herself as she reached the baths. Inside, she headed to the right—the women's side—where fresh bathing robes and drying robes hung from hooks near the entryway, places to leave your clothing for laundering, places to wash in small sinks. But the main attraction was through the last set of doors.

She stripped off her clothes and into one of the bathing robes, a loose, light slip that hid little. If a man had been there, she'd have considered herself naked. But in the baths, there were only other women. All was separated. The robes didn't hide much, but they hid enough to not feel the need to stare.

At midday, it was probably empty anyway. She stopped at the end of the dressing room near the shower and dropped the robe long enough to pull the chain. Icy cold water gave her a familiar, exciting jolt as it splashed down upon her. She tried to shake most of the worst grime off, shivering now.

She wandered through the next set of doors, and a wall of lovely, warm steam hit her face. The tile under her feet even felt warm on this cold autumn day. Before her stretched a lovely expanse of soft, blue, steaming water.

She took a deep breath and then moved down the small stairs and into the water. The baths were lined with many places to recline; they were mostly for soaking, not washing. On the far end of the room were more showers for the real cleaning. She would do that last.

For now, she would just allow herself to sit still and be.

Sefim had taught her the importance of meditation, of silence, of simply being—important parts of the Way. From the moment she'd heard Aven's name, she'd been stirred, though, deep in her soul. Simply being had grown harder and harder. Shouldn't it be easier now? Now that it was over? It didn't *feel* over, of course. It would likely just take her a while to accept that.

She found a spot to rest that didn't even require her to hold her neck up, and then she settled in and tried to clear her thoughts. Each time Aven crept in, she tried to still herself, but a few seconds later, he would return. What was happening to Aven? Why had Sorin done what he had done? Would they find out the Akarians knew a mage had been involved? How exactly had Dekana died? What were they doing to Aven? What did the Dark Master really want with him? What would he do?

Would they send her after Aven's brothers? Her blood ran cold. By the gods, she couldn't stand the thought. Where was the Balance in all this? There was certainly little balance within her mind at the moment.

Stilling her mind was not working. She tried to focus on listening instead. She listened to the trickle of the water flowing into the baths, the hum of the cooler water of the showers, waterfalls of all sizes around her. Finally, that beauty was able to calm her for a little while.

Some time passed in peace, but gradually she began to feel that someone was staring at her.

When the feeling would not go away, she opened her eyes and tried to look around casually. No one was close by, but sure enough, off to the right she felt someone abruptly look away.

That old battle ax Menaha. But why? She knew Miara well and had always believed her a capable spy. Menaha shouldn't be surprised to discover that Miara had returned or have any other reason to stare. And Menaha was not the type to stare. Could it be because of Dekana's loss?

Miara closed her eyes and tried to put it out of her mind again, but the brief peace she'd achieved had vanished.

She had soaked enough. She should just shower and be done with it. She raised her hands from the water. Sure enough, raisins.

She rose and headed back toward the stairs out of the water, passing Menaha on the way, nodding respectfully.

"Good day, Miara," she said. She had a voice that was lovely and dark, colored with age and experience. Her white hair was stark against bronzed skin; she still trained outside as much as ever. "Back from your mission? Are you feeling all right?"

Was her dark mood that obvious? She hated being so transparent. "Yes, I'm back. Feeling as well as I could be," she replied. "Why do you ask?"

"Well, it's just that—hmm, forgive me for saying, but…" Menaha started but seemed to hesitate. It was not at all like her.

"What is it? It's all right."

"Well, I don't know quite how to put it, but… your scar. It looks—strange. Different. I could swear it looks *smaller*."

Miara lifted her arm and craned her neck to get a look at it, and sure enough—she had never seen it in such a state. It *did* look particularly scabby, although the water had not been good for that.

"Am I finally losing my wits?"

"Huh," she said. "No, you're right. It *does* look odd."

"It almost looks like it's… healing," Menaha whispered. "I've seen a few wounds in my day, and that's what it looks like." Her eyes studied Miara's shoulder with the same intensity that filled her voice.

Miara frowned. "Strange, indeed."

"You should keep it out of the water for it to heal best, but how…" Menaha trailed off.

"But it can't heal."

They both studied it for a moment.

"Just another new form of torture, I'm sure."

"Indeed." Menaha smiled bitterly and nodded. She leaned back to relax again, her enchantment with the scar broken.

"Have a good bath, Mena," Miara said and headed for the showers.

She returned from the baths and went straight back to her bed. She wasn't sure how much time passed, especially with the grayness of the sky and the seemingly unchanging cold of the autumn air. She stoked the fire occasionally, pulled the blankets up to her chin, and thought of Aven.

She knew it was evening not because of the sun setting or even her stomach aching, but because her father and Luha returned home. Evening prayer was coming, and suddenly, she hated more than ever to have to haul herself out of bed and kneel down for them.

She listened for a while, mind blank, to her father and Luha moving around in the rooms. It was a kind of bliss—or at least serenity—to just hear them nearby, going through the motions of life. The mundaneness of it made her feel at peace. At least she'd made it home. In the past, that peace had always been more than enough.

Not this time, of course.

The bells started to ring their warning off in the distance, and she hauled herself out of bed and made for the fire, trading one warmth as quickly as possible for another. Her father and Luha settled before the fire, too—the prayer could take quite a long time, and the floor was cold. Her room had both a fire and a rug that fit them all.

Her father glanced at her with the usual sadness in his eyes. Prayer had always been something he loved, and she hated making him dread it. Perhaps today she would just kneel down with them, not call the torture down on herself, the inevitable pain. What point did it serve? It hurt her and her father, not the Masters. It accomplished nothing. What good had her rebellion ever done her?

And if there was no such thing as the Balance any-way—what did it matter if her supplication was willing or not, sincere or not?

She stared into the crackling flames, turning the idea around in her mind, letting it settle in, feeling with each bell clang the impending pressure to make a decision. What did it matter? How could she make a choice when no choice of hers would make anything better in the end? Disgusting. Her resistance didn't matter anymore.

She bent to kneel on her own. But before she'd moved more than an inch, she stopped, frozen by a sudden memory against her will—the look on his face when she'd attacked him on that balcony back in Estun. Soon, other images flooded her thoughts—gray-green eyes, his eyes frowning at the first discovery of his shackles. Young girls dancing in the snow. Rosebushes. A healed little boy running in the forest. Sunlight on the river and glistening drops of water on skin.

For a moment, she could see him standing at the edge of the nomad encampment, looking at her with that look in his eyes, dim firelight playing across his features.

She clenched her fists, nails digging into her palms. She straightened.

No. It mattered. Now more than ever.

She was still a woman with an opinion, who had been *born* free, even if she hadn't lived free for very long. And if this was the only way she could show that that woman was still alive under her curse, then so be it. It would be worth a small amount of discomfort on her father's part.

The deep, heavy bells ceased. There was the brief tense silence, the calm before the storm, as she waited for the lighter, higher bells of the prayer service to begin.

Then they came, one after another, deceptively gentle, crystalline with beauty. They built into a delicate and wandering chord, full of glory and the joy of worship.

Miara realized suddenly that her eyes were squeezed shut. The only pain she felt came from her own nails digging into her palms. She opened one eye, then the other.

Luha and her father were both kneeling before the fire, craning their necks as much as possible to stare. She stood beside them, no pain, no pressure, no fear.

No compulsion.

She staggered a step back, then another, and fell partway sitting onto her bed. She clutched at her shoulder, nothing there but a strange lump. No pain. She yanked the neck of her tunic wide to expose her shoulder, and she lurched toward the mirror.

Indeed, it was even smaller than at the baths. Menaha had been right.

It was going away.

"How— What..." she whispered. Her father and Luha could not answer; they only stared. But there was a brilliant glitter in her father's eyes—of hope, of joy, of something even more.

Could it be that something had changed? That something had... broken? How could it be? Was this just part of the days of rest they'd given her?

It had never been part of the days of rest before. They had never forgotten to tell her that she had them, or how many. For the first time in years, she hadn't woken up in the morning.

Was it possible? Could she really be— She couldn't even let the word into her mind, it was so frightening.

She had to know for sure.

She flung the door open and ran down to the hall and stairs, heading for the forest. The freezing air hit her and knocked some sense into her. What did she think she was doing? Every mage was bound to be in prayer— what would she say if someone saw her? Streaking toward the border wall at top speed in the middle of the evening's prayer was highly suspicious to say the least.

She couldn't wait, though. She had to know.

She slipped into the form of a small gray cat and blended into the dying grass and late fall darkness, slinking into the shadows. She took a roundabout path, darting from tree to tree in the pastures, avoiding any shepherds who might still be heading in from the pastures, but her feet raced at top speed. There was no pain, only the elation of the wind moving past and the good kind of burning in her muscles.

She quickly reached the spot she'd reached so many times before. She'd thrown herself against this invisible wall again and again—as herself, as a cat, as an insect, a bird, a bear, *anything*—but always nausea and pain had thrown her back.

She slid back into her own form. She wanted to be herself for this, if it worked. She had passed no one on the way here. She took a step forward, then another.

Nothing happened. Her heart pounded.

Three more steps. Five. Seven. She broke into a run. Soon, she was under the cover of the woods, of night, racing through them with blind, unbridled elation, guided only by the light of an early moon. A few hundred yards into the forest, she felt a wolf who sensed her elation. He, too, raced with her over and under branch and stream, intoxicated with motion unchecked, laughter in their thoughts.

It was true. She was—somehow—free.

Free.

She could hardly believe it, hardly think; instead, the only expression of the explosion of emotions in her mind came through her body, burning out in sheer speed and movement through the trees. The wolf came nearer and raced by her side for a while before heading back into the forest depths. Time disappeared again, and she had no idea how long it was till she tired enough for thoughts to be thinkable again. They crept back in slowly in the form of questions, like... how could this happen? And when?

And then a thought stopped her cold in the darkness. If it was true—as it seemed to be—was there something she could do to help Aven?

She turned on a dime and headed straight back to consult with her father and form a plan.

She was on her *own* damn mission this time.

As she ran back toward the border, she reached out to find her father. She needed to know if the prayer was over yet and if he was still in their rooms or if he'd gone somewhere else to look for her. She found him just outside the dormitory rooms.

I'm on my way back now.

Okay—it's over. What the hell is going on?

I'm not sure. I'll be there shortly. Meet me at home.

She took even more care going back. Some of her excitement had burned off, and there were likely more people about now that prayer was over. In her cat form, she slinked under as much ground cover and as many bushes as she could, darting as though she chased some unseen, tiny rodent. When she felt certain no one was in sight, she transformed back into herself in an alley between buildings and walked with as much calm as she could muster back to the dormitories. Of course, it was suspicious to not have been at home during evening prayer, and quite out of her normal routine, but it wasn't suspicious if no one was paying attention. And why should they be? There was no way for slaves to get free. So there was nothing really to be on the lookout for.

When she arrived back at home, her father and Luha threw their arms around her as soon as the door was closed.

"How did you do that!" Luha demanded.

Father shushed her. "Whisper, dear. What's going on, meesha? Have you looked at your scar?"

She pulled the neck of her tunic aside again, pushing her shoulder up through it and showing them. Her father studied it with wonder, grazing his fingers across the surface; Luha stared, perplexed.

"I don't know any better than you do. Nothing out of the ordinary has happened to it."

They all exchanged glances, unsure of what to do or how to even begin to understand what was happening.

"Except your last mission," her father whispered.

"Yes," she whispered. "I went out. *Outside.* That's where I ran—outside the border. Into the woods. Nothing stopped me. It seems to be… gone."

Again her father and Luha exchanged wondering glances. They were shocked into silence for a moment, until her father burst into action, darting to the closet where she kept her traveling gear.

"Then you have to go. While you can. You have to get out of here, meesha, while you have the chance—"

"No, Father, I can't—"

"You must."

"There's something I have to do first."

He turned to stare at her with sad, worried eyes. "You're not thinking revenge, M—"

"Of course not," she said quickly. "It's Aven—the prince I brought to them. I have to undo the harm I've done him."

Her father came back near them so he could speak more quietly. "Come, let us move away from the door, toward the fire. Could that prince have something to do with this? He *is* Akarian. Perhaps they have some weapon against the Masters?"

"No. He *is* a mage, to my surprise, but he knows nothing. He's had no training. He said they didn't train him, because they hoped his magic would fade away. Can you imagine? Just brushing it under the rug?" She was shaking her fist when she suddenly realized—the map he'd given her! "Wait! There *was* one thing. I didn't know he had it until the very end, but—" She pulled the map from her pocket, unfolded it, and handed it to her father. "Have you ever seen anything like this?"

Her father's eyes searched frantically, scanning the map back and forth. "It's a map—of the stars. This is an ancient mage language. I only know a few of the words, but here, look—*freedom*." He glanced up, fire in his eyes. "This is deeply forbidden magic, Miara. If they find this, they will destroy it. This is star magic—the very magic used to enslave the king."

She took the map from him again and scanned the symbols. None of them made sense, although now she could see some of the star patterns of the sky. "If this records how to enslave, could it also tell us how to free someone?"

She glanced from her father to Luha and back again.

"A good hypothesis," her father said, "and a good reason for them to ban such magic. Of course, without knowing these symbols, we can't be sure. But you can't try to interpret them here. If you really are... free, meesha, then you must get away from here and discover what this map means. That would be the best way to help *all* of us."

She stared at the symbols, finally ending her eyes on the one her father had indicated—*freedom*.

"Aven," she whispered, mostly to herself. "You bastard, you never told me. Why?"

Immediately, she knew, though. He couldn't have known much more about this piece of paper than she did, or her father did, probably less. Even if he had been up to something with it, with his training he couldn't have been very sure it would work. And you couldn't go giving people hope about things like *this* if it was unfounded. Especially if chances were you would fail.

And yet—somehow—perhaps he had *not* failed. If she ever had him alone in the woods again, she was *at least* going to kiss him.

"First, I have to try to help him. He's the one who brought us this map, after all, and maybe he even used it to free me. I *have* to try."

Luha and Father nodded in unison. She had almost expected them to try to force her on her way. She should have known better.

"What can we do to help?" her father said.

It wasn't until nightfall the next day that Daes and the Tall Master were able to discuss the situation again, alone. Seulka had had her eyes on them all day, but he couldn't risk her tendency to employ flawed logic slowing them down or throwing them off track. It had thrown them too much already, since she had insisted it was impossible that the Akarians had kept the star magic or any magic at all.

And yet, here they were.

"Same, again," the Tall Master whispered.

"Did he speak while you branded him again? Could you catch the words?"

"Not this time."

"And the old wound?"

"Still too fresh, can't quite tell."

Daes shook his head, trying to think. What could the prince have discovered? *How* could he have discovered it? How could he have been a mage his whole life, and the Masters were only learning of this now?

"He was visibly exhausted afterwards. I think he's expending energy each time. It's possible if we tried several times in a row, he might run out of energy. Perhaps not be able to defend himself. We could wear him down. But aren't we going to kill him anyway?"

Daes shrugged. "The king ordered his death, *after* his arrival."

"It could be useful to taunt Akaria with their beloved prince on puppet strings."

"It *could* be if we could actually do it," Daes said. The Tall Master scowled at him. "Let's see. The king did not know that the young prince would be a mage."

"Indeed, none of us did."

"So he will not expect him to be enslaved."

He nodded. "So we will not *necessarily* need to tell him that the brand is not working. If we can keep that knight out of the way."

"Perhaps the best strategy," Daes agreed, relieved he didn't have to spell out every little detail. Just then there was the faintest knock on the door. "Hmmm?"

The door cracked open slightly. "Sir, the king has arrived. His carriage has just reached the stable. He will not accept visitors tonight but will be ready to see the prince in the morning."

Daes nodded, and the door shut again. He turned back to the Tall Master. "Well, at least he didn't dally this time."

"Yes. The one time it would have been useful. So, in the morning, we'll do our best to praise the king's brilliant political plan to murder him?"

"We'll do our best."

"See you in the morning, then." And out the Tall Master went with a bit more bounce in his step. That man cared more for human suffering than Daes was sure he was comfortable with. Fine when it was turned on others, but... someday it could be turned on him. Fortunately, he always made sure to have one or two weapons in his bag of tricks against people like the Tall Master.

For a moment, Daes sat alone, doing nothing. He often found that if he listened quietly to himself in such moments, he realized what he truly needed or wanted. He could feel the path that would lead him to rule over these fools and keep them from losing everything they'd built out of reckless hubris.

But as he sat, he only felt afraid.

He knew too little. He had so many questions. What would the king do? What would he want? Would he figure out the prince was a mage? Would it matter? Should he kill the prince right away and prevent the potential embarrassment? How could the brand not be working? How was he doing it? Where had he learned this magic?

And then it hit him. He had questions. The prince was a dead man with the rising of the sun. His time to *ask* those questions was rapidly dwindling.

He jumped to his feet and headed for the dungeons.

The clanking of the iron bars sliding against each other shook Aven awake. No guards greeted him this time, though. It was their leader, the one who dressed in black.

He entered the cell and then stopped, studying Aven.

"If you're trying to figure out if your enchantment worked or not, the fastest way would be to just unchain me and see for yourself."

The man grinned as a guard brought him a stool, which Daes positioned in the corner of the cell. "I don't believe we've been properly introduced. My name is Daes. I am one of the Masters of this hold."

"You know who I am." Aven shifted, but there was no such thing as a comfortable position in this setup.

"Indeed. It was I who sent the slave after you."

"Her *name* is Miara."

"Is it, now? Did you get to know her well on your travels?"

Aven said nothing.

"Quite well, it seemed to me. Well, she was ordered to use any means necessary. She is quite… skilled."

The barb did sting a little. But he wasn't stupid. He wasn't falling for that old ploy. He remained silent.

"She does have quite the air about her, doesn't she? Not many in Kavanar would appreciate it. But I'm an old warrior myself. I must say I admire that certain wild strength. Doesn't it make you wonder what she could *do* with it?" He eyed Aven intently as his smile slowly broadened, his eyes growing amused.

Aven again said nothing. Could this Daes tell that Aven was gritting his teeth? He hoped not.

"Do you know *why* I sent her after you?"

"Because you've got a death wish?"

Daes just continued to smile at him, unmoving, which was more than a little disturbing. "Which one of us is closer to death at this point, my friend?"

"You tell me."

Daes grinned but said nothing.

Aven tried a different approach. "Because Kavanar is populated with scum who require *spies* to do their dirty work, cloak and dagger style?"

It worked. Daes bristled, shoulders stiffening even as he tried to hide his reaction by looking off at the central hearth. Ah, excellent—a sore spot.

"I would prefer a less covert strategy," Daes said, turning his eyes back to Aven. "And there will indeed be time for that. But it will likely be after your death."

Was Daes suggesting what he thought he was suggesting? Aven took a deep breath and waited. Perhaps he would reveal more if he remained quiet.

"There are things you practice in Akaria that threaten the safety of all I hold dear. Dangerous things. That is why I sent the slave after you."

Daes seemed to think that this would make sense to Aven. What the hell could he be referring to—sword fighting? Battle? Akaria was not known for much else. He also seemed to think Aven would know why Daes was concerned about him in particular. What gave him that idea?

Unless... Unless he somehow knew.

"In fact, it's why they are all slaves in the first place." Daes stood from his stool and crouched down in front of him. "Let's not waste any more of each other's precious time, shall we?"

He waited. Gods, what did the man want?

After a long moment, Aven could only raise his eyebrows. "I'm not sure what you're looking for."

"Must we really play these games? I should have known. I detest the type of man who hides behind lies and manipulations."

"I'm not playing any games," Aven said flatly. At this, Daes cocked his head to one side, the slightest crease in his brow. Perhaps he was realizing that Aven might in fact have no idea why they had come after him. Daes had laid cards on the table without realizing it.

"The star magic. Tell me what you know."

Aven wanted to groan. He knew. He knew! How the hell could this bastard, so far away from Akaria, know about star magic? It was *all* Aven could do to discover the tiniest shred of it! No one in Akaria knew, it seemed, except perhaps the Takarans. Of all people! And yet Daes knew? This was a royal mess indeed.

"I don't know what you're talking about."

"*Hmph.* You're a bad liar." Daes gave a nod to a guard who shuffled back toward the central hearth.

"Miara said the same thing," Aven replied.

Daes pressed his lips together, frowning, and signaled a summons to the guard without turning away from Aven. "I've tried to treat you as a gentleman, from one noble to another. Tell me what I want to know. Did you think it was your little Akarian secret? I don't believe you." As he spoke, the guard shambled back with a hot iron poker in one hand.

Aven didn't know what to say to that. He hadn't understood the magic long enough to even wonder who else might know. But assuming it was his little secret was basically exactly what he'd done.

Aven eyed the poker—another enchantment or an ordinary torture device? He tried to sense any magic, groping at awkwardly, but he felt nothing.

"How many of you practice the forbidden magic? Tell me," Daes ordered.

Aven said nothing. What could he say? Daes would hardly believe the truth, and what good would a lie do? Should he tell him everyone in all of Akaria knew, perhaps?

In response, Daes leaned forward and pressed the poker to the inside of Aven's left thigh, face emotionless and cold as a slab of marble.

Aven yelped before twisting away, out of reach. "What forbidden magic?" he panted against the wave of pain.

"How many of you practice the forbidden magic?" Daes repeated, calm and cold as ice. He pressed the poker to Aven's right thigh now, briefly making contact before Aven twisted away again.

"You *will* tell me." Daes came down to one knee. Good idea—this might take a while.

"Not used to people not following your orders, huh?"

Rage flickered in the dark man's eyes for the briefest moment. But then it was gone—contained, bottled up. Aven had found another soft spot. But by the ancients, he did not want to be there the moment that dam burst.

"How many?" Daes said again instead, moving toward his ankle with the poker.

Aven kicked at Daes's temple, sending his tormentor scuttling back and saving his ankle for the moment.

"Must we really persist in this?" Daes sat back down on the stool for a moment. "You may not know me, but I do not quit. I will not stop until I know every bit of the forbidden magic is gone. Eradicated. I will not risk everything I have worked to build here. Tell me what I need to know."

Aven met his gaze levelly. He said nothing because there was no point. No matter what he said, Daes would not believe him. Truth or falsehood, he would have no way to verify.

"I'm only out to protect my country. Just like you are," Daes said. Then he waited. Aven could wait just as long. With a sigh, Daes again rose and coldly, brutally applied the poker at his shoulder. The heat made contact between his neck and collarbone, and a bellow escaped Aven, something between a groan and a war cry. After Daes withdrew it, Aven sat panting, trying to recover for several moments.

"There's only me," he said, trying to let the pain taint his voice as much as he could stand.

"That's not possible—someone must have taught it to you."

"I swear it to you. I discovered it in the library by myself only last week."

Daes's eyes flickered with confusion. "But, only last week—" Aven knew his words would ring true—since they *were* true—and he could see Daes stumble. Because he was buying the truth of it. But his story was also what seemed like the best lie. *Of course* he would claim Akaria was helpless. Daes had to be suspicious of such a claim.

Unfortunately, that was also the truth. Akaria *was* helpless.

Even more unfortunately for Aven at this point, there was almost no way to convince Daes of the truth.

Daes moved forward again, but before he could apply the poker, Aven cut him off.

"Listen, you want to talk noble to noble?"

"No, as a matter of fact, I don't—"

"Soldier to soldier, then?"

Daes stopped, then grunted. "Fine."

"We don't practice magic," Aven spat. "Do your nobles? I should think not. Do your soldiers? Anyone? I couldn't share my powers with anyone. For *obvious* reasons. All magic may not be forbidden, but it is certainly taboo. The knight was the first to discover my powers in over a decade." Well, that was mostly true. If Fayton and the others had known, Aven had had no idea.

Daes paused, seeming to consider this. There was too much of a feeling of truth in Aven's words, most likely. "You said you discovered it in the library. Discovered what, exactly?"

Damn him and his tongue. He had acknowledged too much already. He should have continued to play dumb as to any knowledge of anything. But would Daes have ever believed that? He highly doubted it.

But he could *not* tell him about the map. He could tell the truth about some things but absolutely not that. Nothing was worth revealing it. It seemed to be the only way Aven had defended himself, and for the moment, it was still out there. For the moment, someone could still find it, read it, and do what Aven had done, resisting the enslavement.

And then—finally—Aven understood.

Of course. Daes did not know the specifics, but he knew there was a way to break his power. Aven had proved that much. And Daes was after it. Understandably. Any way to destroy his power must be his primary objective.

Before he could decide how to respond, Daes gave him a little added motivation with another prod near his right hip. The pain was starting to addle him, which was of course the idea. Oh, to be a creature mage and be able to heal himself.

"How did you discover the star magic?" Daes pressed. Ah, so he knew it was of the stars? Daes did know some of the details, then.

"A book. The library. I told you." He was panting with the effort and the pain, without much breath to speak clearly at this point.

"You're lying," the dark man said. "I don't believe any of it."

"No. It's true. I was reading the book on the balcony where Miara found me. Send her back, it might still be there." This was the problem with torture, he thought. Beyond the obvious cruelty, it was almost useless. He was telling the man the *damned truth*, and his torturer still couldn't believe him. The easiest thing for Aven to do right now would be to make up a plausible lie, some-thing that would make more sense than the truth did. It's been handed down in my family for generations and generations and we've all been secretly training to… what exactly? He had no idea.

But he didn't want to lie. He was too foggy with pain to think through the possible ramifications before choosing a story at this point. Damn it all, perhaps he could go down with that one thing to lord over this fool—that he'd told him the truth all along.

"Where did you really learn? Who taught you? There *must* be others." He jabbed the poker into Aven's side. Aven finally let out a short scream before biting it back—there was no dodging or relieving the pain of this one.

Daes withdrew the poker and waited for Aven to recover for a moment.

"You *will* tell me everything you know about the star magic."

"I already have," Aven grunted through clenched teeth.

"We'll see what you say when the pain has driven you mad. Or perhaps I should bring the mage slave in here and apply this poker to *her* and see what you say then?" Daes looked delighted with himself at that idea.

"Do it, and I swear I'll find a way to crush your skull like an egg while you sleep," Aven whispered.

At this, Daes just smiled. "Tell me what I want to know, and perhaps it won't come to that."

"*I* am not your slave."

"Aren't you?"

16 BALANCE

If she could kidnap a man once, she could kidnap him again, right?

At the crack of dawn, she trotted to the library, quickly checking for any drawings of the layout of the rooms in the Master's Hall. Anything that could help her locate Aven. She had no luck, but it didn't matter.

She had worked through the details with her father late into the night, examining a layout they had drawn together from memory, trying to recall the guard's patrol times, what had been said when she'd given Aven to the Masters, what she would need to collect and gather once the sun had risen. Then in the dark of night, she'd stolen out to the woods again, and she'd hidden the map Aven had given her with some supplies about an hour's flight toward Akaria. If she failed, the map could not fall into the Masters' hands.

The sun now completely up, she strode from the library and began gathering her ingredients—web from a spider, hair from a rat and a cat, the antennae of a beetle.

As she ran her hand over one of the wandering gray cats, snatching a hunk of excess fur the cat was shedding, she remembered the wolves who'd attacked them in the temple. *With the Balance, there is always another way*, the wild wolf had said. She hoped it was right.

She felt the quietest touch of hope creep into her heart. Perhaps there *was* a Balance, perhaps this was what her father had meant all along. If this feeling of freedom wasn't somehow a cruel practical joke, if she could actually find him, if they could somehow get away...

That world was too bright to think of, lest her heart be shattered when it didn't come true.

It was not time to think, it was time to act.

Her steps seemed no different from any other day, but on this day, she headed into the Master's Hall of her own accord. The day would not end the way it had begun, that she was sure of.

Inside, she found a quiet corridor, waited until she was sure she was alone, and then slipped into the form of a cat. Then she darted from corner to corridor, again under the guise of hunting rodents.

She began systematically exploring the areas of the Hall that she'd never seen before, one by one, peeking in as a cat, looking under doorframes, sniffing others, even slipping in as a beetle sometimes just to be sure. Several doors concealed only sleeping chambers on the other side; some were empty or held crates in storage. Many nearest to the main hall seemed largely unused. One by one she went, fast as she could, eliminating each in its turn.

Beyond another series of storage chambers with dusty barrels inside, she found a doorway made of iron rather than wood, with bars and a large sturdy lock on the left side. She could barely make out stairs leading down into the darkness.

This had to be it.

The hallway was empty and silent. She could hear no one nearby. She wound herself down, coiled into a spider form, and began climbing, heading for the safety of the highest parts of the wall. Then she crawled past a bar and was plunged into darkness.

A spider was not quite the smallest thing Miara knew how to transform herself into, but it was the smallest one that would be at home in a dungeon. There might also be flies, but they might also be more annoying targets for guards or prisoners to squash. All tiny forms carried many risks—easily crushed, stepped on, brushed aside, or blown away by the wind. Tiny legs went a great deal slower than bigger ones or even feline ones. Eight spider eyes did not work the same as two human ones. Still, she had to hide herself somehow. She had no idea what to expect from this dungeon. However, she *did* know that a spider on a dark wall was probably a fairly normal occurrence no one would pay any attention to.

It was slow going. Her sight as a spider was much blurrier than as a human, but brighter in the dark. She could see more in the low light, though with duller lines. She could tell enough to know that she was going forward and down. Very, very slowly.

Behind her, a loud clanking and smashing sound made her freeze in her tracks. Voices rang out. Guards.

She moved a few inches higher up on the wall, then held very still.

A group of them passed her, headed down. She counted eight, if her eyes were to be trusted. With her strange, new eyes, she couldn't quite make them out perfectly. Where could they be going?

The sound of the soldiers faded. Had they just quit talking, or could she no longer hear them? How far *was* it to the bottom of this dungeon?

Didn't matter. Keep going.

Time blurred and became nothing but the slow, steady progress across the wall: a strange crevice in the rock, a hill here, a valley there. She scaled higher as she neared a torch, unsure how hot it would be, not wanting to end up cooked.

With time came more footsteps. The guards were leaving, but there were no voices this time.

She was about as high on the wall as she could be, but she nestled into a crevice just in case. She waited.

They came around the bend quickly, marching in better form this time, in rows. Two, then two, then three, then two...

Nine? Wasn't that more than had gone down there? She struggled to look harder in the dim light. Was the new figure slumped against them? Was there even a ninth figure?

Yes. They were escorting someone—someone they'd gone down into the dungeons to fetch.

Gods. It was Aven.

She felt every muscle in her tiny body tense as if she could pounce to free him. Her mind raced, trying to figure out what to do. They were taking him somewhere. Her plan couldn't possibly work *now* if there were nine guards surrounding him wherever he ended up.

The guards lumbered with Aven up the stairs, almost out of sight. Think, she commanded herself. *Think, damn it!* They rounded the corner, gone now. She still stared, numb.

Then action returned to her in a rush. She leapt from the wall and let herself drop down toward the floor, and as she fell she twisted her form into a large rat. She hit the floor with a tumble and a roll, and her head spun, but she righted herself and took off after them.

If she wanted to save Aven, she had to know where he was. And right now she was at least close. When she *got* to him, she had no idea what she would do.

One step at a time.

She scampered on at full rat speed, leaping when the uneven stairs were farther than the normal distance apart, throwing all her energy after the sound of the footsteps. After him.

"Put this on," the guard said, tossing a shirt in Aven's face.

Guards had again arrived in his cell, but these didn't seem like the others that had taken him to the smithy. They had a different air about them.

Was it morning? What were they planning?

He could only move slowly, gritting his teeth against new shocks of pain from the night before. He couldn't remember Daes leaving or even passing out, but it must have happened at some point. Even now, he felt himself teetering on the edge of consciousness, whether it was from the pain, the lack of sleep, the mental exhaustion.

One more quick jerk, and perhaps he could have the shirt on—

He felt himself fall to the ground and into darkness.

"He has his father's eyes."

A man's voice. Cold stone pressed against Aven's cheek. His body lay uncomfortably sprawled on its side. He kept his eyes closed, hoping to hide that he'd awoken.

"You have done well for once, Daes, Seulka," the voice continued. "Perhaps I should be asking you more often to attempt things I don't think you can do."

The slightest pause at the awkward comment.

"Thank you, Your Majesty." Daes's voice. Aven longed to clench his fist as a knot tightened in his stomach. It was best not to focus on the night before. At most, he could cling to the fact that he'd stuck to his story throughout.

And now he knew something, at least—the voice was King Demikin of Kavanar.

"The crown prince of Akaria. And I thought the feat impossible. Fine work, indeed. Especially for a bastard."

Again the slightest pause. A bastard, eh? What was that all about?

"Several of our mages are very skilled," said Daes, ignoring the comment with grace. "And only yesterday, I added six dozen to start additional similar training." Aven didn't like the sound of that.

"Excellent."

"Also, these mages may have gotten quite lucky," Seulka added. "We don't know how repeatable it will be."

"Well, we shall have time to find out, eh? And somehow we have yet to receive a declaration of war." From the movement of the king's voice, he seemed to be pacing in front of Aven. War, huh? Was this the intent all along? If they wanted war, why not just attack? Perhaps this was the direct method Daes was referring to. And perhaps they were truly concerned with getting at the star magic first, which made sense. Such a mission would have been significantly harder with a full-blown war underway.

"He's not exactly what I pictured. Can you believe they let themselves get so bulky? Fighting is for foot soldiers. Far too much muscle." The king paused, and Daes cleared his throat. Heh, didn't agree, did he? "Like a damned farmer," the king continued, circling Aven. His steps were soft, his voice like crunching gravel. "Commoners do menial labor, like wielding swords. Not royalty. And no painting can quite capture that stubborn glint around the eyes. But I digress. What shall we do with him, do you think? Daes, your thoughts?"

"We are fully prepared to kill him, sir, as you ordered. The real question is by what means and how quickly."

"Indeed," said the king.

"I recall it was your desire to kill him promptly this morning, after you were able to verify his identity. All preparations have been made, and it would be a worthy revenge for the Akarian wrongs against your family."

"No revenge is worthy enough," the king said, as though he would be the judge of that. What was he even referring to? The mages in the Dark Days had been Akarian, true enough... But they couldn't still be holding on to such nonsense, could they? Oh, by the ancients. "But it will be a start. Especially when we strike fear into the hearts of every Akarian by returning his head on a pole."

For the first time, Aven felt his body tense with the instinct to fight and survive. It had all been so politely diplomatic—even contemplative—up till that point that it hadn't really seemed real. But now... well, he might not hear the details, but he was sure they were carefully calculating the most terrible outcome, at least for Akaria.

Perhaps he needed to think more seriously about how he was going to get out of this before he lost the chance.

Aven risked opening one eye the smallest amount he could. Red velvet robes draped across the black marble floor not far from him—the king. They were in the large receiving room where he'd last seen Miara. He could see servants entering from a side door, carrying steaming bowls. A small, gray cat ran in, dodging their heels as they headed for the dais. He couldn't see it, but he knew the four leaders of this disgraceful place sat there on the other side of the king.

"If you are open to other timelines, however, we could potentially keep him alive for a bit. Find out what we can from him." Daes paused for a second. Letting it sink in, or regretting he hadn't gotten more—that he believed—out of Aven? "There could be much to glean about Akaria's defenses, force preparation, plans for war, diplomatic relations."

"A thoughtful approach. You are quite the brains of this war effort, Daes. But we also have your spies. Is it worth the effort to try to get it out of him? Will he really tell us anything the spies can't find out anyway?"

Another slight pause. "Perhaps you are right, Your Majesty."

Aven wanted to laugh out loud. By that tone of voice, he was fairly sure Daes did not at all agree with the king's assessment. But for his own reasons, he chose not to say anything. Aven risked another slight peek, as the king was focused on Daes.

The gray cat had settled nearby, beside a guard. The king still stood before him.

"We could demand a tribute from Akaria. Returning him would be less rewarding for you, I'm sure, but it would bring much needed resources to the nation, such as their iron from the mountains." So they needed iron? Good to know.

"Well, we could simply not return him after the tribute has been received."

"Brilliant thinking, Cousin," the woman chimed in.

Another slight pause. "Indeed," said Daes. How could the king be missing how much the dark one clearly disapproved? "A tribute could also present opportunities for ambush and a chance at reducing Akarian forces before a war has fully begun. Which would be invaluable, in my opinion. Worth more than this prince, with certainty."

Strange. Amid all this talk of options, Daes had framed the discussion around his death—where, when, and how. Not if. They had yet to mention that he was a mage or any chance of enslavement. Were they hiding it from him? Aven stifled a grin. They didn't want him to know they had failed. That there was someone who could resist them.

That was it, wasn't it?

"What do you think, Your Majesty?" asked the woman.

There was a long moment of silence, in which Aven began to wonder if he was missing something he could not hear and if he should open his eyes. But then the king finally spoke.

"These are all worthy options. But I must say, I lean toward the original plan. His immediate death."

"Of course, my lord," Daes said quickly.

"Are you certain, Cousin?" said the woman. "What is the rush to kill him? Let us make some use of him and *then* kill him."

"I have decided. What is the rush? I want our people to know that our justice is swift, our memory is long, and our wrath is unending. He will serve as an example of the age that is to come."

"Huzzah," she said, a touch of awe in her voice. Well, perhaps this fool did have his kingly moments, even if it was only via hellfire and brimstone.

Daes spoke into the silence. "I have one more course of action that has just occurred to me, Your Majesty." What could this be?

"Let's have it."

"The mage who captured him has proven herself very talented. She's observed him for nearly a week on their journey here. She knows him well now. What if we kill him and then send her back in his place, disguised as his likeness?"

Aven gasped. He could not think of a worse hell for Miara—to pretend to *be* him in front of all those who missed him, all those whom she'd betrayed by bringing him here. Pure torture.

"What was that?" said the woman's voice.

Aven felt a boot nudge his shoulder, seeking to roll him onto his back. He winced in spite of himself—there was more than one wound there at this point.

"He's awake," the king said.

Aven opened his eyes. Indeed, it was Demikin, fool king of Kavanar. They had never met in person, but he bore a resemblance to his etchings and paintings, if much more sour looking. He was middle-aged, with a stout midsection. Probably shorter than Aven, with a balding head and blond beard. His hands bore many rings, among them a large, peculiar ruby on his left hand. He smelled of garlic and fish, and Aven frowned up at him. The king glared back.

The air around Aven had begun to move. He didn't fight it. Not his usual swirling, idle wind, but violent, unpredictable darts. It nipped at the king's robes, the guards' hair and tunics. The tapestries on the nearby wall began to sway. The king eyed the wall and the now sporadically flickering torches.

"Is this how you always greet foreign dignitaries?" Aven grunted.

"If I have the option," the king replied with a dark smile.

"Get him on his feet," Daes ordered the guards, clearly annoyed. A conscious Aven could reveal his secret, adding even more urgency to their current plan.

The king turned to Daes. "I didn't call you the brains of this effort for nothing. It shall be done—we have our plan. Let's have this calf slaughtered and be done with it."

Excruciating shots of pain ran through him as the same guards hauled him to his feet unceremoniously. The air darted more viciously at that, reaching farther from him. It whipped at the fire and the candlesticks on their feasting table.

What could he do if he didn't hold back? Casel help me, he thought. He focused on the feasting table, the king, the fireplace.

"Should I call for the…" The woman trailed off when she noticed the candles in front of her had just gone out. The king's cape whipped over his shoulder awkwardly and sent him stumbling to the right. The nearest tapestry clanged against the wall.

"What the—" the king started.

Daes stood and recklessly kicked his chair out of the way, rounding the table and coming straight for him.

Aven knew the look on his face—a mixture of determination and bloodlust. He had no intention of having his secret revealed.

"Make him kneel," the Dark Master ordered.

"Daes—by Nefrana—not in here!" the woman snapped.

"Shut up," the Dark Master said coldly. Daes strode to the wall where a sword and battle ax hung beside a torch. He took the claymore and unsheathed it, tossing the sheath aside.

Didn't he know an ax would be far better for an execution? Of course, this superior knowledge of human butchery wasn't getting Aven anywhere at the moment.

The guards had hesitated, but at Daes's approach, they finally pushed Aven to his knees. The king swept himself to a position by the fire, probably afraid of getting his robes sullied with foreign blood.

"You said you'd prepared the court—" the woman started again.

The air in the room had almost risen to a wind. The fire wavered mightily, smoke now billowing in the king's direction. He strode away toward the fresh air coming in from the hall, coughing in annoyance.

Daes met Aven's eyes and laid the flat edge of the blade on his shoulder, the edge of the cold steel barely grazing the skin of his neck.

Aven tore his eyes from Daes, focusing them on the dark marble below. He sucked in the deepest breath he could and held it, frantically trying to gather any energy he could from the light and air around him. He felt the heat in him rise hotter, hotter still.

He would only have one shot at this. He could not fail.

"Your Majesty," the Dark Master demanded, "I am sworn to uphold your will. Is it your wish that I should kill this man?"

The king did not hesitate. "Yes. Be done with it, and let our war begin."

The guards released Aven's arms and backed away hastily in either direction as Daes drew back the sword.

Time seemed to slow. Aven felt as though he could watch the sword rise for as long as he might have liked, that if he wished, he could have taken days for it to return along its path back toward Aven and the earth. Aven had all the time in the world. All the time he could possibly need.

He released his breath, and with it, he hurled every bit of the heat in him in one powerful burst out in all directions, but chiefly straight at Daes's chest.

And for once—for once, finally—it worked.

Air rushed past Aven and hit Daes with an audible *thud*. Daes's grip on the sword faltered as he was lifted off the ground, thrown back by the force of the wind. Aven lunged forward, seeking the sword's handle. His fingers found the hilt, seizing it and holding on with every bit of strength he could muster.

Time sped up again. Aven felt the air pushing him in the same direction now—something he hadn't planned—except that someone tackled him, knocking him away from the dark man and nearly to the door. He heard a gasp, a shout, the tapestries clattering violently, the ax crashing to the ground. Everyone who'd been standing nearby was on the floor. Who had grabbed him? One of the guards, a quick thinker of the lot?

No. The sight of red hair dangling in his eyes made him freeze—could it be? The form on top of him rolled off him quickly, jumping to her feet and reaching down to help Aven up.

The sun from the grand windows shone down on the lovely face of Miara.

He took her hand, and even as she pulled him, he also tried to soak in as much energy from the sunlight as he could. Many of them had risen to their feet. Daes, though, was still on the floor and staring, utterly stunned—but now at Miara.

"Guards—at them! Akarian infiltrators!" the king barked.

Miara was dragging Aven toward the archway they'd arrived through, but she stole a lightning-quick glance at the king as he labeled her an Akarian. Aven caught a glimpse of her smirk. Fool didn't even know where his own power—and weaknesses—lay. Even in this moment, he didn't seem to recognize that magic was afoot.

Three disheveled guards staggered to block the exit. Aven batted one into the wall with the energy gained from the sunlight. And the other two he launched himself at, headlong.

He might look like a farmer, but he would have no trouble dispatching two poorly trained, frightened men. He swung the sword round and into position as the men's eyes widened, and he lunged. One blocked Aven's first swing but staggered back at the force of the blow. His next swing sent the second man reeling, and Aven knocked him to the ground with a butt of the sword hilt to the face. The third guard had scampered back and tried to jump him from behind, but he, too, went down with a well-timed elbow to the stomach before Aven spun and buried the blade in his side. Jerking it free, the man staggered away.

They were far from incapacitated or dead, but it would have to do.

This way, she whispered into his mind. *Come on!*

He turned to see her already leaving the hall, several steps ahead of him. Running. Away.

Almost like she was—

Free.

He raced after her, the Masters shouting orders on his heels.

One guard clipped him, then leapt on him from behind, his knee colliding with Aven's sword hand and knocking the blade free. Aven fell, the guard on top of him, and they wrestled, spinning and writhing against the cold stone. Aven twisted free, kicking to get himself some maneuvering room, but the man would not relent. He lunged back at Aven, his full body crashing down on top of him. Aven spun, sending the other man to the floor beside him, and savagely pounded the man's skull against the rock. He went limp.

Aven muttered a prayer to Anara as he stumbled to his feet. Waste of life. A shame. As he turned to race down the stairs after Miara, he saw vines closing themselves around the door to the hall even as swords made progress hacking through them.

At the bottom of the stairs, he was alone. He glanced around frantically.

This way, she whispered again. *The bush. Don't look back.*

From her voice, he caught her direction. He saw the last bit of her dart behind some bushes far to his right, and she was crouched down behind them. Aven sprinted after her and dove blindly into the brush. Unable to steady his landing, he fell awkwardly against her.

The sudden feel and smell of her nearly drove him mad.

She sat with her eyes closed for a moment, not reacting to him at all. He could hear shouting from the main hall, bells starting to ring.

"All right," she whispered. "Let's get these shackles off. Ready?" He felt his hands change suddenly with a sickening twist, and then the metal fell to the ground. His hands and his wrists were finally his own again. Seemed like it had been forever.

"Oh, by the ancients, you're injured!"

"What were those?" he whispered, ignoring it.

"Mandibles. Don't ask."

"Thank you," he said. He rubbed his wrists, his hands in front of him. It hadn't even been a month, but it felt like a lifetime had passed. So much had changed.

"You would do the same for me." She grinned. "*Wouldn't you*, Aven?" He opened his mouth, but she held up a finger. "Don't answer that. There's no time. We're not going to make it out of here looking like this. Think you can take being a mouse one more time?"

"You can turn me into a mushroom if it gets us out of here."

She snorted. "Here it comes."

The twisting feeling grew until the nausea was upon him, the sliding of the world away at so many crazy angles—and suddenly there were dry leaves in front of his nose. And they were much, much larger than they'd been a second ago.

He looked down. Indeed, mouse hands. He turned his gaze up. Beside him, a large black bird was eying their surroundings, looking about to burst into flight. A raven, a crow? Beautiful and keenly intelligent, this close up. It was Miara transformed—he hoped.

One leg reached out, and talons circled around him. Into the sky, they flew.

Here we go, Aven. Pray to all your gods and ancestors and ancients that we make it through the air alive.

She spotted the rock where she'd stashed their few supplies and the star map from a good distance away. The nervous energy of battle had long worn off, and exhaustion had set in. She was fading with every wing beat, but it wasn't much farther. Just a little more, and they could rest... Just a little farther, and she could talk to him, thank him, tell him—everything.

As she flew, she pondered what she should say. How could she possibly thank him? Could she even capture what it meant to have her freedom? And there was so much more beyond that.

Should she tell him how she felt? Should she tell him how much it had hurt to push him away? Since then, she'd turned him over to certain death—even if she couldn't help it. What if he'd changed his mind? What if he no longer cared?

What if now that they were back to reality, he realized that a slave and a prince didn't belong together? Even if she was no longer a slave... she was nothing like him.

There would be time, she decided. She didn't have to tell him anything right away. She could see how he acted, see where things went. She could gauge what Akaria was like, assuming they made it there safely. Assuming they would have her. There was so much unknown, so much to discover.

For the first time in all her years, her life was her own to do anything. *Anything.* Anything at all.

It made her breathless.

Finally, the rock neared. She landed with a skip and a plop, feeling more relieved that she'd made it than she'd like to admit. She carefully released Aven from her talons and then quickly let go of the transformation, setting them totally free, once and for all.

The dizziness twisted her only for a second until she found herself simply sprawled out on the ground, staring up at the autumn leaves and clouds above her, utterly drained. She lay only for a moment, but then excitement forced her to sit up straight.

He lay beside her on the ground, gray-green eyes also staring up at the sky.

"How did you do it!" she demanded. "You freed me."

He smiled at her, sitting up slowly. He, too, seemed tired. There was blood, she realized, on the right side of his shirt. She hadn't been paying much attention, had she?

"You're more hurt than I realized."

"It's nothing." He waved it off.

"Shut up. Take off your shirt."

He smiled and obliged her. As the shirt came off, she gasped at the sight of the burn marks, as well as one huge burn on his shoulder, the size of the brand. It was fresh, seeping, and clearly painful.

"By the gods, did they—" she started, then stopped, unsure of what to say.

He looked down at it. "They branded me," he said. "Twice." He turned and revealed that both his shoulders held the mark. Other burn marks were scattered across him.

"Twice. It didn't work," she whispered breathlessly.

He nodded.

"It didn't work!" she cried.

He grinned at her excitement, gazing up at an angle with those handsome eyes. He turned back to his wounds. "My, that's ugly. I hadn't really seen them before," he said. "The dungeon was dark. Do you think it will frighten women and children?"

She stifled a snicker. "It's not ugly," she chided. "You are the first mage to face them and defy them. Don't you understand? You've beaten them at their own game. I think they are the very most beautiful things I've ever seen."

He muffled his own small laugh but didn't turn his eyes away from the intensity of her gaze. "Well, they're not the most beautiful thing *I've* ever seen," he said after a moment, grinning.

She blushed and snatched the shirt from his hands. "Give me that. We might need to bandage that for now; I'm not sure I have the strength to heal you without some sleep. Damn thing is filthy, anyway."

"Well, you know dungeons aren't known for being the cleanest places."

"Well, I *told* you it was a dark place," she grumbled as she worked. "I *told* you not to follow me."

"And I told you we'd find a way out," he replied, smirking.

She burst into giddy laughter in spite of herself. She kept up her examination of his many wounds.

"It was the star map," he said. "To answer your first question."

"But how did you use it? How did you know what to do? My father and I could barely decode it. I would have no idea how to apply it, even after years of study. That's forbidden magic, you know." She found a relatively clean bit of shirt and began ripping a few strips from it.

"I didn't know it was forbidden," he said, looking thoughtful. "But I guess now we know why, don't we?" He grinned.

"We sure do."

"Do you still have it?"

"Yes, it's here. I hid it under this rock before I came after you so it wouldn't end up in their hands."

"That was very wise."

"Well, you weren't exactly my first mission, Aven. Or should I call you my lord? Your Majesty? Something fancy, certainly. What is your proper title, now that you are my ruler and not my captive?"

"What!" he snorted.

"Well, I can't exactly stay in Kavanar. I thought I would at least come to Akaria and try to live the life of an upstanding citizen. Of course, kidnapping a king—"

"A prince!"

"—is not exactly a minor offense, so it will likely be the gallows for me anyway."

"Don't be ridiculous. Rescuing a prince is not exactly a minor heroic feat, either, so the two certainly cancel themselves out. Don't worry about it, Miara. I don't want you to call me anything."

"I want to be like a normal Akarian. I have to know what they call you."

"No one calls me anything."

"You're lying."

"You'll never be a normal Akarian to me."

She stopped abruptly and glared at him, feeling hugely disappointed. She'd always be a mage slave to him somewhere in his mind, most likely. "I want to be a normal Akarian. What is it, or I'll tie this bandage so tight your arm falls asleep."

He sighed. "My lord, usually. Or liege. But *don't* call me that."

"Yes, my liege."

He winced.

"I just wanted to try it out. I like the sound of that."

"I'm glad *you* do."

"I'm glad that you're glad, my lord."

He winced again. "What if I order you not to call me that?"

She grinned. "You haven't told me how you used the map."

Then he recounted his efforts to interpret the star map and make sense of its ancient language and strange magic. "But I never really got much more from the star map than which star to look for, which I guess I already knew."

"Which one?"

"Casel—the freedom star. But what really gave me the idea was when you healed that boy."

"Galen? First of all, *we* healed that boy, and second of all, how did *that* help anything?"

"You said anything that was against the Way of Things could heal itself with the addition of enough energy of the right type. And I was sure that their slavery was against the Way. So I suspected that maybe, just maybe, the same thing might work on you."

"It *is* healing—look." She twisted her shoulder up through the neck opening of the shirt again to show it to him. It was about half healed now, and the other half was all a crusty scab. "I'm sure it will always leave a scar, but I can deal with a scar."

He bent forward to look closer at it, shaking his head. "I can't believe it. I just can't believe it worked. It was a lucky guess."

"Not lucky! You reasoned it out through the principles of magic as I explained them. Lucky that you were able to actually execute the spell, I suppose, but we had started training you on that, too. But—when did you try?"

"On the ride, on the last night. After the fight with Sorin. He didn't really knock me out."

"I should have known. Weak, foolish—"

"I took it as an excuse so neither of you would notice if I lost so much energy and passed out, like we did with the boy. It was toward the middle of the night. The moon was up. The stars were right there to guide me."

She remembered suddenly the temperature fluctuations, how she'd felt so cold, then so warm, and the feeling in her wound that last night. "I think I remember. I brushed it off, but I did feel something. That's amazing, Aven. But that means—" She stopped suddenly.

"What? What is it?"

"That means I was free when I gave you over to them." Her face fell.

"You didn't know that. Even I didn't know that. I thought I had failed."

"But I didn't even try, I didn't even attempt to resist. Maybe it all could have been avoided—"

"Don't think like that. You got me out of there in the end, so what does it matter?" She scowled, unconvinced. "Besides, if you hadn't done that, then I wouldn't know that it's possible to resist the branding. Now that we know, I can teach others."

She looked up at him quickly, eyes wide. "You're serious."

"Well, yes. Why?"

"But I thought... I thought you needed to hide your magic. To be king."

"There's been a change of plans."

"Aven, it's not worth giving up everything for—"

"Isn't it?" he said. She only stared into his eyes. "Besides, those bastards were not just keeping you around as pets. They've been building an army, a very powerful one, and they're waiting for the right time. And I think *they* think this is it. You're the scouting party. The rest will come. And how are we going to battle them? With swords and spears? With cannon fire?"

She swallowed, probably even more aware than he was of the futility of such weapons against fifty mages, let alone five hundred or even more.

"If Akaria is going to survive, we're going to have to change. Learn new ways to fight. If the enemy changes, so must we. And that's going to require magic. I'm going to make sure my father and his advisors see it."

She just listened to him for a moment in awe. She had often sensed the kingliness about him but had never really seen him in action. She could see the smallest glimpse of it now.

"Well, you're going to need my help," she said, trying to shake off her awkward stare. "I'm going to need some sort of gainful occupation in Akaria. I know all their tricks and how Kavanar will approach combat. I know about fighting as a mage, what is taught, even who teaches it—"

He laughed. "I would be honored to have you at my side. Indeed, I think I may need you to prove a point or two to convince skeptics that mages are a real threat. Perhaps more than a point or two. It was already my plan. I hadn't even considered tackling this problem without you."

"I am beyond indebted to you for my freedom. It is something I will never be able to repay you for in all of my days. I will gladly serve you in any way I can."

"Is that so? Because I had a bit of a different role in mind for you than servant."

"What?" she asked. "Healer? I have the most experience at that, but—"

"Not a healer," he said, laughing.

"An instructor for the mages? You will need a lot of them to make up for lost—"

"Not that, either."

"Well, what then?"

"Queen."

She gasped, involuntarily jumping back a bit. He didn't let that stop him. He leaned forward, grabbed the back of her neck with one hand, and kissed her.

For a moment again, she was stunned motionless. Fear stirred—did he really know what he was getting into? Would he tire of her or find her inconvenient later? Because she couldn't really be a good match for someone like him.

Could she?

All the more reason she should kiss him while she could!

And with that, she felt truly free. She reached for him as well, ran her fingers through his hair, down his back, suddenly starving. In the back of her mind, she heard a snippet of gypsy music on the wind and far-off laughter, as she leaned closer into his arms.

It was a long while before their lips parted long enough to speak. Their arms still circled round each other, his hands gently caressing her back, but now she looked into his eyes, hiding a little less of herself as she did. How much truth could she bare before she died of fright?

"I always loved you, you know. Not from first sight or anything, and I don't know when it started. But once I knew you… And you made *sure* I knew you, because you just wouldn't shut up, would you?"

"Silence has never been my strong suit. But if that's true, you are a very convincing actress. You sure had me fooled."

"Then why did you just kiss me?"

"Well, why did you save me from certain death, putting your brand-new freedom in peril?"

The words stuck in her throat. "I—it was—the right thing to do."

He smiled, looking dubious. "That was all?"

"Oh, don't make me confess what you already know." She scowled and playfully punched his shoulder. "It killed me to say no to you. I acted like I didn't want you, because I wanted you so much. You saw what it was like there, at least a taste of it. You felt the brand, the way it worms into you?"

He nodded more solemnly now.

"If you love someone, you've got to do everything in your power to keep them away from that. To be the vehicle of your enslavement—that stung worse than a thousand brands in my skin."

He ran his hand over her hair, looking deep into her eyes. "You were also the vehicle of my freedom."

"And you were, for me."

"Miara, if you had failed, I wouldn't know how much danger Akaria is in. I wouldn't be able to do anything, and a few months or years from now, we'd be fighting fire with cornstalks. And then all of Akaria would end up enslaved to the Masters, instead of just me."

She felt a stirring inside her, the feeling of pieces fitting together suddenly. If only her father were here. When would she ever see him again? But beneath that fresh new pain kindled a brand-new hope. Perhaps there *was* a Balance after all. That was the feeling that swelled now in her chest, and it was like no other feeling she had ever experienced. All of that pain—there was a chance it really *had* been in service of a greater good. There was a chance at justice. A chance was good enough for her.

"Instead," he whispered, "we know how they work. We know how to fight them. And we will. We'll set things right and end their slavery of mages. The Balance is on our side. Are you with me?"

In answer, she kissed him again.

Afterword

Thank you so much for reading this book!

If you enjoyed it, please consider leaving a review at your favorite retailer. Reviews help others like you discover books they may love for themselves.

Visit my website at rkthorne.com for upcoming book news, free bonuses, updates. You can also join my mailing list at rkthorne.com/get-updates for updates on Miara and Aven's latest adventures.

About the Author

R. K. Thorne is an independent fantasy author whose addiction to notebooks, role-playing games, coffee, and red wine have resulted in this book.

She has read speculative fiction since before she was probably much too young to be doing so and encourages you to do the same.

She lives in the green hills of Pennsylvania with her family and two gray cats that may or may not pull her chariot in their spare time. If you hadn't noticed, fall is her favorite season.

For more information:
Web: rkthorne.com
Facebook: facebook.com/ThorneBooks
Pinterest: pinterest.com/rk_thorne
Twitter: @rk_thorne

10093607R00272

Made in the USA
Lexington, KY
18 September 2018